Year OF LIVING Blonde

Andrea Simonne

Sweet Life in Seattle - Book 1

To John—My favorite geek

Chapter One

> Diet Plan: Extra butter. Extra sugar. Hold the veggies.
>
> Exercise Plan: Work twelve hours a day and then get your zombie on in front of the television.

"I WANT A divorce."

"One second," Natalie calls out. The smell of citrus and sugar wafts around her as she pulls out two dozen lemon ricotta muffins from the oven and places them on a rack to cool. The convection fan buzzes loudly before she closes the oven door.

"Did you hear what I said?"

Natalie sets the timer for three minutes so she won't forget to remove the cooling muffins from their pans before they turn rubbery. "Would you like one of these before you go? There are some cinnamon scones as well, though I haven't frosted them yet."

"No, I don't want a muffin or a scone! Are you even listening to me?"

Natalie turns toward Peter. "What are you doing up so early?" She grabs the powdered sugar. It's five in the morning, her usual baking time, but normally he wouldn't see his first dental patient until eight.

"That's what I'm trying to tell you." He takes a deep breath. "I'm leaving you, Natalie. I want a divorce."

The words stop her. She puts the powdered sugar down. "Is that a joke?" And then she laughs. "Oh, I get it, because it's our wedding anniversary. Very funny."

Peter shakes his head. "I'm not joking."

"What are you saying?"

"I'm saying it's no good between us anymore. You're never around." He turns his head to the side, avoiding her eyes. His skin flushes the way it does when he's nervous. "The truth is I've met someone. I figure there's no point hiding it anymore. Maybe you even suspected?"

Natalie blinks, staring at him as all the blood rushes from her head. "My God, did you just say you're cheating on me?" The oven timer starts beeping, but she doesn't move.

Peter shifts uncomfortably. "Aren't you going to turn that off?"

"Answer me."

"It's not like that. I'm in love with her."

Natalie reaches out to steady herself. There's a metallic taste in her mouth, as if she's eaten the baking powder sitting on her counter. "I can't believe this. You bastard!" The oven timer beeps in the background with the pulse of an alarm.

Peter seems surprised by her fury. "I was hoping we could be civil," he mumbles.

"Civil? You announce that you're cheating on me on our fourteenth wedding anniversary and you want me to be civil?"

"Come on, Natalie, the fact that you're surprised by any of this just shows how dead our marriage really is. It sounds like you had no idea I was even unhappy."

"You never told me you were unhappy! I know things aren't perfect, but—"

"Well, I am unhappy!" he snaps. "I have been for a long time."

Natalie goes quiet, the awful taste still in her mouth. "What about Chloe? She'll be devastated. Don't you care about her?"

"Chloe isn't a baby anymore. She's eleven years old now and besides, I'm not leaving her. I'm leaving *you.*"

Natalie studies Peter. She realizes it's been a while since she's really looked at him—his tall, lanky frame, his pale-blue eyes, all of it so endearing and familiar. He's still a handsome man. She used to worry that she wasn't attractive enough for him, that he'd settled when he married her. But he'd always told her she was a diamond in the rough.

She swallows and asks softly, "Don't you love me anymore?" It's a hard question to have to put to her own husband.

Peter hesitates. "I don't want to hurt you, but I think you deserve the truth. I've fallen in love with another woman. She makes me feel alive."

"And I make you feel what—dead?" Natalie tries to catch her breath. "Who is she?"

"She's someone I met. You don't know her."

"What does she look like?"

Peter shakes his head. "Let's not go through this."

"How *old* is she?" Natalie asks, a hard edge to her voice. She tries to imagine this other woman and it comes to her in a clear vision. Some hot young thing with a great body who figures she's made a nice catch for herself, snagging a successful dentist, and doesn't feel any guilt about breaking up a family. "Peter, you're just having a midlife crisis, can't you see that?"

"You've got it all wrong. It isn't like that. It's not about age."

"Of course it is."

"She's not younger than me. She's forty-eight."

"*What?*" Natalie almost chokes. "You're leaving me for a woman who's," she stumbles over the math, "thirteen years older than I am?"

"I keep telling you it's not about age. It's about the kind of life I want to live. Lena excites me."

Lena. Natalie tries to absorb this, tries to absorb that her husband is in love with a forty-eight-year-old woman named Lena.

The oven alarm is still beeping and Natalie finally reaches over to shut it off. She glances down at the muffins. Ruined. She won't be able to bring them into the bakery. After sitting in the pan so long, they'll be too rubbery to sell.

Peter comes over, stands beside her and leans in close. For a surprising moment Natalie thinks he's going to give her a hug. She softens—is he having second thoughts? But then he's reaching past her. He isn't trying to hug her. He's helping himself to a muffin.

Natalie watches in amazement as Peter stands beside her, takes a large bite, and begins to chew. "These are fantastic. Is this a new flavor?"

"Just what do you think you're doing?" Natalie sputters.

Peter stops chewing for a second. "Eating breakfast?"

"You can't just come in here and announce that you're leaving me for another woman and expect me to let you eat my muffins!"

"I can't?"

"No!"

Peter steps away from her, clutching his muffin protectively. "I'm going to go then." He looks away, but then glances back longingly at the rest of the ones in the pan.

Natalie grits her teeth with rage. "Do you want some more of these?"

"Sure, I—"

"Here you go then!" She reaches down, and in a moment of fury, grabs one of the muffins and throws it at Peter as hard she can. It bounces off his eyebrow with a satisfying *thump.*

Definitely too rubbery to sell.

"Ow!" Peter looks astonished as he puts his hand up to rub his eyebrow. With his pale Scandinavian skin, it's already turning pink. "What are you doing?"

Still riding the wave of fury, she reaches down and grabs another muffin. This one hits him right in the middle of his forehead before crumbling into bits. *Bullseye!*

"Hey, that hurts—stop it!" Peter backs away from her.

Natalie's next muffin gets him in the chin.

"Cut it out!"

Just in time, he manages to swat away the one aimed for his nose. In alarm, Peter turns and runs out of the kitchen while Natalie pelts him with muffins.

"You're crazy!" he yells.

With some satisfaction, she sees that the back of his blue polo shirt is now covered with butter stains.

"That's right, you cheating asshole! You better run!"

The front door slams and Natalie is left panting in the aftermath of silence. She tries to catch her breath, but then dashes to the sink, barely making it in time before she throws up.

NATALIE SCRUBS HER face and brushes her teeth before loading the rest of the pastries and sweet breads she baked that morning into the back of her white van. Despite what just happened, she still has to work. She starts up the van and pulls out.

A memory of her mom comes to her. *It's natural for men to want more than one woman. It's who they come home to that matters.*

Natalie takes a deep breath. She always thought Peter was her home. To her surprise, she feels the sting of tears and quickly touches her eyes, but they're dry as always.

Even now I can't cry.

She swallows and looks out at the road. How did this happen? After all this time, she thought Peter was a sure bet—though as a gambler's daughter, she should have known better.

There's no such thing as a sure bet.

Natalie thinks about the past year, and it's true what Peter said. Work has taken center stage and she hasn't been home much. She and her business partner, Blair, opened their bakery, La Dolce Vita, a little over a year ago and it's taken a lot of time and energy. Though it's been a labor of love, they've worked like slaves. Chloe often came to the bakery after school, but Peter was another matter. They've been apart more often than together. But didn't Peter tell her that he understood? It was the same way in the early days of his dental practice, yet somehow they'd weathered that.

She pulls her van into the alley behind the bakery. It's a typical overcast day in Seattle, and since they're in the U-District, a number of college students with backpacks are walking toward campus for summer school.

It was a stroke of luck when she and Blair found this spot. They'd wanted to open their own bakery for a while and had been searching for the perfect location. When the realtor told them about this coffee shop with a bakery attached near the University of Washington, they jumped on it even though it was smaller than what they were hoping to find. An Italian family had owned the place for years, and they'd decided to keep the name. La Dolce Vita—The Sweet Life. It seemed an appropriate moniker.

Unfortunately, the kitchen isn't big enough, with only two commercial ovens and as their business has picked up, Natalie has been forced to use her own ovens at home. They need to expand, and in a happy twist of fate, the space next door is available, but for some reason their cantankerous landlord is resistant. Actually, resistant is too polite a word. They can only reach him through his lawyer, who has stopped returning their letters and phone calls.

Natalie parks the van right behind the bakery's back door and gets out. The morning air is scented with diesel and damp cement. She props open the bakery's back door, and when she sees Carlos, one of their baristas, asks him if he'll help bring in the baking racks.

It takes the two of them about ten minutes to unload everything. With the last of it, Natalie follows him inside, carrying the final large rack. The familiar scent of butter and fresh espresso from the kitchen surrounds her.

"Thank goodness, you're here." Blair rushes over. "It's been a crazy morning. Two people had birthday cake orders we couldn't find, and I've been scrambling to get them done."

"What happened?"

Blair, a redhead with porcelain skin and a classic preppy style, sighs in annoyance. "The usual. Zoe took a phone order and didn't write it down. When she comes in I'm going to drag her around by that nose ring until she screams."

They'd recently hired two part-time bakers and one of them, Zoe, was a real space cadet. Twice now, Natalie had caught her taking a phone order without writing down a single thing.

Blair shakes out her apron and reties it. "I'm seriously tempted to fire her."

"Let's talk to her about it again. Maybe we could have Carlos take the cake orders when neither of us is available."

"She should be able to handle it. Carlos isn't going to be able to manage both drink orders and the phones."

"I know, but you have to admit she's doing a good job otherwise. She's fantastic with cupcakes." What she doesn't say is Zoe has a young son and Natalie doesn't have the heart to fire her when jobs are so scarce.

Blair smiles knowingly. "You're too soft-hearted."

Natalie shrugs. "I suppose."

"Okay, Zoe stays, but," Blair holds up her finger, "if she keeps screwing up, she's out on her forgetful ass."

"Agreed." Natalie means to grab her white apron and start work, but instead, she sits down.

"Are you okay?" Blair studies her with concern. "You look pale."

"No, I'm not okay." She and Blair started out purely as business partners, but have become good friends over the last year. Natalie sighs. "Peter told me this morning he wants a divorce."

Blair's mouth opens with surprise. "That's crazy. Why?"

"He's been seeing another woman. They're 'in love.'" Natalie uses her fingers to make air quotes.

"I can't believe it." Blair shakes her head in sympathy, then pauses. "You're keeping the house though, right?"

Natalie isn't surprised at Blair's practicality. If Peter takes the house, Natalie won't have access to her kitchen's large double ovens anymore.

"Peter is moving in with his *girlfriend*." Natalie struggles to get the word out. She swallows, still feeling sick to her stomach. "Chloe and I are definitely staying in the house."

"Is there anything I can do? Just name it. You know I'm here for you."

"I know. Thank you for asking. I'm mostly in shock."

"That's understandable. I mean, it just happened and at least he's telling you face-to-face. It could be worse."

Blair's husband, Road, had left a goodbye note on her pillow one morning four years ago and she hasn't seen or spoken to him since.

"I heard Road was in India and saw the Dalai Lama." There's a hard expression on Blair's face. "Can you believe that?"

"Who told you?"

Blair brushes some dried frosting from her white apron. "Tori. She's still my sister-in-law."

Natalie has always wondered if Blair was still in love with her husband. Why not file for divorce? Surely after four years, she could get one on the grounds of abandonment.

Blair waves her hand dismissively. "It's all in the past. Who cares, right? At least I don't have to see his jerk face every day. Plus, I got full custody of Isadora."

Isadora is Blair's classic green 1965 Convertible Ford Mustang. "At least we never had to fight over her."

Natalie imagines Blair and her husband fighting over the car as if it were a child. She hopes she and Peter won't start fighting over Chloe or the house. At the thought, Natalie's eyes narrow. *There is no way on Earth anyone is taking away my daughter or my home.* But she doubts Peter will cause that kind of trouble.

Though, he was furious earlier. He'd come back right away and marched upstairs, reappearing with one of their suitcases. It was so quick that he must have already had it packed and hidden somewhere. He was covered in butter stains.

Natalie tried to apologize for throwing muffins at him, but Peter never gave her the chance.

"I'm moving in with Lena," he informed her in a nasty tone. "Don't bother trying to contact me unless it's an emergency. I'm really disappointed in the way you acted about all this. I can't believe you resorted to violence!"

Natalie rolled her eyes.

Watching him leave, her hand twitched at her side like a gunslinger's, wishing she had one more muffin she could bounce off his head.

"HE'S HERE!" CARLOS pokes his head through the swinging door into the kitchen. "Espresso Breve, table two!"

Natalie takes a sip from her double latte. Espresso Breve is a hot guy who comes in regularly and orders an Espresso Breve, so that's what they all started calling him.

Since all the bakers are women, Espresso Breve is the high point of their day and usually causes a commotion. He's tall, lean muscled, broad-shouldered, and more handsome than God. He's also more charming than the Devil, according to everyone who's waited on him.

Too handsome, too charming, too much of everything. In other words, Espresso Breve is exactly the kind of man Natalie dislikes. In fact, she does her best to avoid him. Unfortunately, she got a good look at him that first time and, as much as she hates to admit it—he's something.

Espresso Breve is breathtaking. The most beautiful man she's ever seen.

"He's wearing that navy-blue sweater today," Zoe says, coming into the back area with an empty bussing tray. "That's my favorite on him. It really goes with his dark hair and eyes." Bakers don't typically buss tables, but everyone makes excuses to go out front when he's here. "He's eating one of your chocolate chunk cookies again, Natalie. This is the third time in a row. He really likes those!"

Still on break, Natalie tries to smile as she takes another sip from her latte.

She started putting those chocolate cookies out a month ago and they've been selling well. They already had a few special orders. The trick is to bake the cookies at a low temperature so they stay soft, and use the finest chocolate she can get her hands on. The real secret is using espresso powder in the dough. It doesn't make them taste like coffee, but brings out the flavor of the chocolate. She ate more than she should have while she was perfecting the recipe, but it was worth it.

"He's gorgeous." Blair stares out the swinging door's round window, admiring the view. "I'd let that man eat my cookies anytime he wants. He's welcome to the whole menu, if you know what I mean."

All three of the women in back laugh.

Carlos gets a look of mock horror on his face. "Ladies, that is TMI and HMJ all rolled into one!"

"I know TMI, but what's HMJ?" Natalie asks him.

"Help Me, Jesus!"

There's more laughter and then Blair comes over to Natalie. "How are you doing? You should go home. You don't have to stay and work if you're not up to it. We'll cover for you."

Natalie considers it as she takes a deep breath. "I'll be okay. All I'd do is sit at home and go crazy, so I might as well keep busy here."

"Have you heard anything?"

"No, nothing." Natalie has been trying to call Peter all day. "I don't know where he is. He's not at work. When I call his phone, all I get is voicemail."

Natalie went by Peter's dental office during her lunch hour, but that turned out to be a mistake. Not only was he not there, but the pitying looks from all the young women who fronted his reception area were more than she could take. Clearly she was the last one to find out there was monkey business going on. It was humiliating.

"You're going to have to talk to a lawyer."

Natalie is taken aback. "So soon? No, I don't think it's time for that yet."

"Maybe not, but eventually you will. At least to protect yourself."

"I don't know." Though Natalie is embarrassed to admit it, she's hoping Peter will just come home. *We've been married fourteen years, so how serious can this thing really be? This woman is a decade older than he is.*

"When you're ready, I can give you the number of the divorce lawyer I've spoken to. She has a small practice, but she's really good. Don't wait too long. It sounds like Peter's been planning this, and probably already has one lined up."

"I doubt that."

Blair shakes her head knowingly. "Just don't underestimate him. You might be surprised at what he's capable of."

Chapter Two

Diet Plan: Pastries, chocolate, and wine. Chew, swallow, and repeat.

Exercise Plan: Work twelve hours a day. Leave angry voice messages for your cheating husband. Sleep like you're dead.

"*I* HAVE AN axe and I'm not afraid to use it!"

Natalie puts her plate down and hits mute on the television where she's watching *Fellowship of the Ring*—one of her favorite comfort movies. *Is there someone yelling outside?* Just as she decides to ignore it, there's more yelling and then—

THWACK!

Natalie jumps, crumbs falling beneath her feet as she rushes over to the window. Outside, she sees her younger sister, Lindsay, tugging on what appears to be a large metal axe now hanging from her front door.

"I don't believe this." She runs over and yanks it open to Lindsay's furious face on the other side.

"What the hell is wrong with you?" Lindsay yells. "I've been calling you for two days with no answer. I finally went by the bakery, and Blair tells me you and Peter are splitting up! Why didn't you call me?"

Natalie stares at Lindsay and then turns her gaze to the red axe firmly embedded in the thick maple of her door.

"Where did this axe come from?" she asks, ignoring her sister's tirade.

"The trunk of my car." Lindsay walks inside, waving her hand dismissively as if everyone carries a fireman's axe in their trunk. "I want you to tell me what's going on."

Natalie closes the door and follows her into the living room, figuring she'll deal with the axe later. She cringes at the mess everywhere, relieved it's only her sister witnessing the empty ice cream container and half-eaten apple pie.

Lindsay shoves a bag of cookies aside as she plops down on the couch. Her gaze goes to the television and then back to the bag of cookies. "Wow, Oreos and *Lord of the Rings*. Things must be desperate." She reaches in and takes one out. "Talk to me."

Natalie sits on the couch near Lindsay and tucks her feet beneath herself. She's silent for a moment as she watches her sister take apart her Oreo and bite into the creamy side. "Peter left me for another woman. She's forty-eight."

Lindsay starts coughing and nearly chokes on her cookie. "My God!"

Natalie almost smiles. Lindsay isn't an easy person to shock.

"When did all this happen?"

Natalie tells her about Peter's announcement a few days ago and how she hasn't heard a word from him since. "He seems serious."

"Christ, what a doofus." Lindsay shakes her head in disbelief. "Leave it to Peter to get something as simple as adultery wrong. Doesn't he know he's supposed to have an affair with someone *younger?*"

Natalie leans her head back. "I guess no one told him."

"So, who is she?"

"I don't know. He said it's just someone he met. Apparently they're 'in love.'"

"Oh, please." Lindsay takes another bite from her Oreo. "You should find out who she is and kick her ass. Kick both of their asses. I'll be glad to help."

Natalie laughs. "What is this, high school? I appreciate the support, but I don't think that would do any good. It never worked for Mom, after all."

"You should have called me." Lindsay grabs Natalie's hand.

"I know. I just couldn't deal with talking about it." Natalie doesn't want to admit to Lindsay how she was hoping Peter would have come home by now.

"Don't worry. I'll help you through it. Having been divorced twice now, you'll have to agree I'm an expert."

Natalie doesn't say anything. While it's true Lindsay has been divorced twice, it was hard to take her marriages seriously, since neither of them lasted longer than a minute. The guys she married were both artists. Both covered in tattoos. Natalie thought all the men Lindsay dated looked like ex-convicts.

"Hopefully it won't come to that. Can I make you something to eat?" Natalie gets up from the couch and heads into the kitchen. Lindsay grabs the bag of cookies and follows.

The kitchen is by far Natalie's favorite room in the house. She took great care picking out the dark-wood cabinets and the sage-green counters. The island has a marble counter top perfect for rolling out any type of dough. The appliances are all restaurant-quality stainless steel and since she's currently using her large double ovens every morning, she's glad they didn't skimp on any of it.

"What's that yummy smell?" Lindsay asks, wandering over to the stove and peering into the large cast-iron skillet. "Bologna hash!"

Natalie cringes. "I don't know what possessed me to make it. Actually, it's been years since I've made that stuff."

"Me, too, but it's perfect comfort food."

The sisters look at each other and a world of understanding passes between them. Bologna hash was a dish Natalie invented when they were kids and there wasn't much money for groceries.

"So, how about you warm some up for me? I sure love your bologna hash. Remember? I even used to request it on my birthday."

"I'd forgotten about that." Natalie opens a cabinet to get out a plate. Bologna hash was nothing but chopped potatoes and bologna fried together with butter. Cheap and simple. "I used to make it for Chloe when she was smaller."

"Where is Chloe, anyway?" Lindsay sits down on one of the tall chairs next to the island. "Is she still up in Bellingham at horse camp?"

Natalie nods, turning the heat up on the iron skillet. "Yes, though today is the last day and then she's going to stay with Peter's parents for a few days. She'll be back before school starts next week."

"She doesn't know, does she?"

"No, of course not. I spoke to her this morning, but I haven't told her anything."

"What about his parents?"

"It doesn't seem like they know anything, though it's hard to tell with them." Natalie's in-laws aren't exactly the warmest people. Peter grew up without much, just like she did, and his parents have always been standoffish about him doing so well. Not that they're unkind. Chloe seems to like them and enjoys visiting every summer after her time at camp.

When the food is ready, Natalie brings two plates over to the island and sits in the chair next to her sister.

Lindsay takes a bite. "You know what this bologna hash needs? A nice bottle of vino. I think we need to pop open one of those precious bottles Peter collects."

Natalie considers this. "Sure, go pick one out."

Lindsay gets up and walks over to their large temperature and humidity controlled wine cabinet. "I'm going to find the most expensive bottle Peter owns and drink that one first." After looking though the cabinet, she finally pulls out a bottle of Romanée-Conti.

Natalie's heart stutters. The bottle was a gift, and they'd been saving it for their fifteenth wedding anniversary. "No . . . I . . . not that one."

Lindsay opens her mouth to make a joke, but when she sees the look on

Natalie's face, stops. "Okay." She puts the bottle back and pulls out a different one, a Pinot Noir from California. "How about this one?"

Natalie studies the bottle. She remembers Peter buying it on a trip they took to Napa a few years ago for his birthday. He spent most of the time complaining because their room didn't have a view of the vineyards, and acted like it was her fault. She could still hear the petulant tone he used. That bottle of Pinot Noir cost fifty bucks.

"Looks perfect."

Lindsay opens the wine. After pouring two glasses, she comes back over to Natalie and places one in front of her.

"Ah." Lindsay takes a sip and smacks her lips ceremoniously. "I believe this wine is the perfect accompaniment to bologna hash."

Natalie finds herself grinning. Lindsay has always been able to make her laugh at the weirdest times. She tastes the wine. It's a great Pinot Noir with a nice, earthy flavor and silky texture. Peter would have loved it. "I believe you're right. It really sets off the saltiness of the bologna."

"Is this Oscar Mayer bologna?"

"Of course."

"I thought so. Nothing but the best for us and these spuds are fried to perfection, I might add."

"Why, thank you," Natalie says graciously. She takes another sip of wine. Who knew a fifty-dollar bottle of wine would go so well with bologna hash? Then again, a fifty-dollar bottle of wine usually goes well with everything.

By the time they're done eating and have started on their second bottle—a nice Cabernet Peter bought at a wine auction—Natalie finally relaxes. She's glad to have her sister here and realizes she should have called her sooner.

"You know what this party needs?" Lindsay stands up. "Music. Let's rock out."

"Oh, I don't think I'm in the mood for that." They used to put on loud music and dance around together when they were teenagers. Natalie feels a mild sense of horror as she imagines what she'd look like doing it now. "It's not really my thing anymore."

Lindsay ignores her, goes over to their CD cabinet and starts skimming her fingers along the titles. Her dark hair falls in soft waves, framing her pretty face. Lindsay has always been the pretty one. In fact, she looks just like the actress, Natalie Wood. They used to laugh at the irony of it. Lindsay's always been tall, slender, and stylish.

While I've always been an overweight Plain Jane.

Even though Lindsay is younger, she's three inches taller. And while Lindsay's legs go on forever, Natalie's most certainly don't.

When they were kids it sometimes bothered her that she wasn't as pretty as Lindsay, but since there wasn't much she could do about it, she figured she'd just be happy for her little sister. Even now, Lindsay looks gorgeous in her casual low-rise jeans and white T-shirt, a thin beaded necklace adding to her air of bohemian chic.

Natalie glances down at her own baggy black pants and butter-stained dark shirt. It's her baking uniform, or that's what she considers it, though she seldom wears anything else. She spots the bright purple clogs she wears every day in the corner by the back door. They're encrusted with flour. All her clothes are butter-stained and encrusted with flour.

Natalie picks up her glass of wine and takes another sip. She closes her eyes, slightly dizzy. When she hears the opening guitar riff for Guns N' Roses' "Welcome to the Jungle" she opens them in disbelief. "Are you serious?"

Lindsay just laughs and starts dancing, throwing her hips into it. "Come on." She wiggles over to Natalie and puts her hand out.

At first, Natalie resists, but then she lets Lindsay pull her up. Standing there awkwardly she tries swaying her hips a little.

Lindsay is already in full rock-out mode, hair flying. Natalie tries to imitate her, but it feels strange. She hasn't heard this song in years. She can feel the music pulling her in, though, and somehow her body begins to move and she finds herself dancing.

Apparently, she's drunk enough not to care what she looks like because pretty soon she's singing with Lindsay, both of them laughing and pointing at each other, trying to imitate Axl's swagger.

"Do you remember this concert?" Lindsay shouts over the music. "God, that was so much fun!"

Natalie remembers it. Lindsay was only twelve, but had begged to go and even back then, when Lindsay wanted something, she was so relentless she usually got it. Natalie took her because if she didn't, Lindsay would have found some other way to go and who knows what kind of trouble she'd have gotten into.

"We should go out dancing together sometime. What do you think?" Lindsay asks. "It could be fun. I know some great places downtown."

Lindsay is one of those ultra-cool people—a sculptress—who's into the Seattle arts scene. She also fills in as cashier at the bakery occasionally. Though Natalie has helped her sister out financially over the years, she's never minded. She's used to being the responsible one. Natalie got her first job in a bread bakery when she was only fifteen and when she got pregnant at twenty-four, she was married and apprenticing as a pastry chef. Peter had been in dental school, and she'd loved him because he seemed so reliable, so different from her father—a man who'd been too handsome and charming for his own good—that she was convinced they'd be happy together. She was right, too. For a long time they were happy.

"Hey, Nat, are you okay?" Lindsay turns the music down and comes over to where Natalie is now sitting on the floor.

"I can't believe he left me. I thought we'd grow old together. I really did."

"I know."

Natalie stares down at her hands. They're covered with various burn scars from years of working around hot ovens. Her forearms have them, too. "I guess he'll grow old with *her* now, though it sounds like she already *is* old!" She looks up at Lindsay. "What did I do wrong?"

"Nothing."

"But why did he leave?"

"Because Peter's an ass clown."

Natalie laughs despite herself. "What the heck is that? Where do you even get this stuff?"

"It's someone whose idiocy goes beyond being merely an ass or a clown. He's both."

"You just don't like Peter. You never have."

"True, but why do you think that is? You're too good for him. He treats you like you're his mother. He's not enough man for you."

"What is that supposed to mean? And besides, if it wasn't for Peter, I wouldn't have Chloe."

Lindsay's face softens. She loves Chloe as much as Natalie, if that's possible. "Yeah, I sure miss that girl. I understand why she's at camp, since she loves horses so much, but why does she have to visit those people?"

"*Those people* are her grandparents and I think it's great how she has a relationship with them."

Lindsay leans back against the sofa and closes her eyes, already bored with this conversation. "Whatever."

"It's good for her."

"I'm sure it is." She suddenly opens her brown eyes and studies Natalie with interest.

Natalie looks at her. "What?"

"You know what. Have you?"

Lindsay knows her so well. She shakes her head. "No."

"Nothing? Not even a single drop?"

"Not one tear."

Lindsay raises an eyebrow.

"You know it doesn't mean anything. I haven't cried since I was a kid, so it's no great shock that I'm not crying now."

"Yeah, right." Lindsay gets up and saunters toward the kitchen. "Hmm, now where's that wine? This second bottle isn't half-bad and I believe it's time for a refill. What do you say?"

Natalie thinks of Peter's face and feels a dark satisfaction at how angry he'll be when he finds out she and Lindsay have been drinking his precious wine. "I'd love another glass."

Chapter Three

Diet Plan: Espresso and Tylenol. Fresh bread slathered with exhaustion. A generous scoop of humiliation for dessert.

Exercise Plan: Work like a dog. Restrain yourself from killing someone.

AFTER BAKING THE next morning, Natalie loads everything into the back of her van. She woke up with a hangover and feeling as if she'd been hit in the head with a bottle of wine instead of drinking one. The axe was still hanging from her front door. Lindsay wanted to call 911 last night and get some "hot firefighter guys" to come help, but luckily, Natalie managed to wrestle the phone out of her hands.

As the day drags on, Natalie alternates between water and coffee until three thirty. Thankfully, the bakery closes to customers at four. She pulls the last of the rosemary loaves out of the oven and finally sits down. Her headache from that morning is back. The aroma of fresh bread smells delicious, though—hot and yeasty, and after slathering a piece with butter, tastes divine.

Between the wine hangover and the emotional hangover, she's never been this tired in her life. As she closes her eyes and chews, she suddenly hears Carlos come into the kitchen.

"Thank God, you're still here! Espresso Breve just came in and wants to order a cake. He asked to speak with a baker."

Natalie swallows and looks at him. "Espresso Breve?"

Carlos nods.

"Can you just ask Blair to help him?"

"Blair isn't here. You're the only one left."

Natalie frowns and looks around. She'd been so deep in thought she hadn't even noticed everyone had left for the day. It's Monday, though, and she typically closed on Mondays.

She puts the piece of bread she's eating back down and wipes her hands on her white apron. "I'll go out there. Just give me a second."

"Sure," Carlos says. And just as he's about to turn away, he surprises her by putting his hand on her shoulder. "Listen, I don't mean to intrude in your business, but I couldn't help overhearing you talk. If you need my help for anything, all you have to do is ask, okay?"

Natalie is touched. "Thank you, Carlos. I really appreciate that."

He smiles. "I'm going to go buss the tables in front and then start shutting down the espresso machine."

"Sounds good. Also, the guy from Santosa's Bistro should be here soon to pick up the bread."

After he leaves, Natalie takes a deep breath and tries to gather herself. She really doesn't want to deal with this, but there's nothing else to do. There's a small mirror by the back door and Natalie walks over to it.

Yikes. She looks frightening. Those dark circles haven't gotten any better and her eyes are still bloodshot. *I look like the Queen of the Undead. Maybe I should have worn concealer.* She never wears makeup though, especially at work, since it melts right off.

Reaching up, Natalie straightens the red bandanna she's tied on her head to keep stray hairs back. Unfortunately, she only makes things worse as some of the gray ones start popping out in front like wiry antennae. She sighs and drops her hands. *I'm an exhausted, sweaty mess and there isn't much I can do about it.*

When she gets to the door leading into the front area of the bakery, she stops and peeks through the window.

Espresso Breve is out there, all right. She can see his dark head bent down as he studies their pastry case. He's wearing a black motorcycle jacket with a white stripe running down each arm and across the zipper. It looks fantastic on him. He's carrying a black helmet at his side. Natalie can also see the strap for his leather satchel running crossways over his muscular chest where the jacket is open. They've all theorized about the type of work Espresso Breve does, but none of them can figure it out. He's too handsome. The only jobs, which seem to fit are model and movie star.

Natalie braces herself, pushes through the door, and marches to the counter, preparing to do her duty.

"Can I help you?" she asks as she plasters a fake smile on her face.

But then Espresso Breve looks up and Natalie's smile falters. Her road map flies out the window. She's lost.

Very lost.

First of all, his eyes aren't at all what she expects. They're a sensual brown and remind her of dark chocolate—her favorite kind. *Callebaut? No, more like Valrhona.* Rich, but with a complexity that doesn't reveal itself right away.

And when he speaks his voice is low and smooth, *like caramel made with the heaviest cream.*

As she tries to think of a good food description for his mouth, she suddenly realizes his mouth is moving.

"Uh . . . what was that?" Natalie asks.

"I asked if you had a book I could look through."

"A book?" With unease, she realizes that she's been tuned out of this conversation way too long.

"Yes, a book of your cake designs." He's eyeing her strangely.

"Oh, sure, you want . . . the book."

Espresso Breve peers behind her toward the swinging door leading to the back. "Listen, is there someone else I could talk to? A baker, or one of the owners, maybe?"

"Sure. No! I mean—"

"It's okay. You're new here, aren't you?" Espresso Breve speaks in a patient voice. And she sees that his eyes aren't just sensual, they're kind. It's something she wouldn't have guessed about him. "Go ahead and find your manager. I'll wait."

Natalie's face burns with embarrassment. She can't remember the last time a man got her this flustered. In fact, she's sure it's never happened.

In desperation, her eyes search for Carlos as if he were a life raft. Natalie knows she needs to take control of this situation and explain to Espresso Breve that she is, in fact, one of the owners.

"On second thought, why don't I just come back tomorrow?" He's studying his phone. "I think I'll have time in the afternoon." Then before she knows it, he's gone. The front door jingles as it closes behind him.

Natalie stands very still, staring at the spot he inhabited. Her body feels strange, as if she isn't inside it anymore.

Her embarrassment has taken her to a Zen place.

Groaning, she rips the bandanna off her head and pushes her way back into the kitchen. *How could I let some hot guy get to me like that?*

She tries to put it out of her mind as she begins closing. He's probably used to it, women making fools of themselves. Though the thought makes her feel even worse.

Checking the ovens are off, she can't shake her embarrassment. *Get a grip.* She opens the fridge and sees the croissant dough is ready for tomorrow. She runs down the list of things they're getting low on and adds a few more items.

When Carlos tells her he's headed out, she manages a weak smile. "Take a loaf of rosemary bread with you."

Finally, she leaves and gets into her van. The incident with Espresso Breve replays itself on the ride home, along with a fresh wave of embarrassment.

Pulling up to the house, she sees Lindsay's red MINI Cooper is still parked in her driveway. Then just as she wonders if this day could get any worse, she realizes it's about to get a whole lot worse. The MINI isn't the only car parked there.

Peter's black Lexus is sitting right behind it.

IT'S A SHOCK to see Peter standing in the entryway. Then she notices that standing beside him and still carrying a backpack is Chloe.

"Hi, sweetheart!" Natalie hugs her daughter. Immediately, she's surrounded by Chloe's familiar citrus shampoo smell.

"Hi, Mom." Chloe grins when they pull apart.

"I didn't know you were coming back today. I thought you were staying with Grandma and Grandpa."

"Daddy picked me up early. I guess it's not a good time right now."

"Oh? Is everything okay?" She looks up at Peter.

"It's fine," he says in a tight voice.

Natalie's eyes stay on Peter. Part of her is glad he's here, but the other part is overwhelmed by a sense of betrayal. It's only been a week, but it feels longer. In fact, he even looks different to her.

Peter meets Natalie's gaze, but quickly looks away.

Is he still with her? Glancing at Chloe, she wonders what he's told her. Chloe doesn't seem upset, so he probably hasn't said anything.

Does that mean there's still hope?

Lindsay makes an appearance, walking into the living room wearing the same jeans from last night. She's borrowed one of Natalie's shirts and, even though it's too large, Lindsay makes it look stylish. Her hair is wet and it's obvious she's just taken a shower.

Natalie quickly scans the house and unfortunately, the place is still a mess. There are half-eaten plates of food and empty bottles of wine. It doesn't look like her sister had a chance to clean up anything. In fact, she probably just woke up, not that Natalie can blame her, if she'd been able to sleep in today, she certainly would have.

"Aunt Lindsay!" Chloe squeals and drops her backpack, as she runs over.

"Hey, Girlie-Whirly!" Lindsay says as the two of them hug and jump up and down with excitement at seeing each other.

They head over to the couch, where Chloe searches for something inside her backpack to show Lindsay.

"I found some more horses I wanted to show you," Chloe tells her. "I think they're in my bedroom. I'll be right back!" Chloe desperately wanted a horse of her own, but it was such a big responsibility that Natalie and Peter both agreed to wait until she was a teenager before getting her one. In the meantime, she was learning everything she could.

As Chloe leaves the room, Natalie feels awkward standing next to Peter. She wishes she'd had some warning so she could have at least pulled herself together. The two of them have a lot to talk about. She's about to ask him if he'll stay while she goes and takes a shower, but then sees him surveying the living room with distaste.

"What the hell happened here? Did you have some kind of party?"

"What do you mean?"

"And maybe you can explain this." Peter pulls out his cell phone. A few seconds later, he puts it on speaker and holds the phone up.

At first, all Natalie can hear is a bunch of loud rock music. But then she recognizes Guns N' Roses, "Welcome to the Jungle."

Oh, no.

Dread rises as she hears a slurred voice talking over the music. It takes her a second to realize that it's her own drunk self who's come on the line.

"And if you think you're going to take away my HOME or my DAUGHTER, then I will fight you to the DEATH. Do you hear me? Do you?" There's more music and she can hear Axl singing, though it's garbled, and then "To the DEATH!"

The message ends abruptly and Peter puts the phone down.

"Damn, how many times did we play that song?" Lindsay asks with amusement.

"Apparently more than once." Natalie tries to hide her own smile.

"I don't think this is funny at all." Peter scowls at the two of them. "Do you know how disturbing it was to receive a message like that?"

"Disturbing?" Natalie looks at him with amazement. "You're going to talk to me about disturbing? You completely disappeared. Where have you been?"

Peter shifts uncomfortably. "I told you I was leaving. Don't act like you didn't know." He walks over to a chair in the living room and then stops abruptly. Leaning over, he picks up an empty wine bottle. His mouth drops when he sees the label, and when he sees the second one on the coffee table, he reaches down to grab it, as well.

"I can't believe you'd do this to me!" He shoves the second bottle up accusingly. "Do you know how expensive this wine is that you and your sister so carelessly drank? I bought this Cabernet at an auction!"

He tips it upside down and not a single drop comes out.

Natalie watches. "I have to admit, it was pretty good."

There's a moment of silence and she can hear Peter's angry breathing. His nostrils flare. "*Pretty good?* That's a hundred dollar bottle of wine!"

"Wow, is that right?" Natalie turns her head toward Lindsay. "Did you hear that? I guess that wine cost a lot of money."

Lindsay, who is thumbing through a magazine, doesn't even bother to look up. "Well, it was, you know . . . *pretty good.*"

A strangled noise comes from Peter's throat while his face turns a shade of red seldom seen outside Cartoon Network. "I can't believe this! What is wrong with you, Natalie? They serve this same vintage at the White House, and you and your crazy sister are knocking it back like its Boone's Farm!"

Natalie rolls her eyes. "So what?"

"'So what?' That's all you have to say for yourself? And just look at this place." Peter waves his arms around. "I'm gone for a week and when I come back, I find that you've completely trashed our house!"

"Don't exaggerate. It's just a little messy."

"There's an *axe* hanging from our front door, for God's sake!"

"Oh . . . well, that's true. But I can explain that."

"I think the axe is cool!" Chloe pipes up as she comes back into the living room.

Lindsay chuckles. "Thanks."

Peter glares at Lindsay. "I knew you were behind that. I hope you have enough money to pay for a new door."

"No problem." She meets his glare with cool detachment. "Though, why do you even care? From what I understand, you don't live here anymore. In fact, where exactly are you living? Why don't you enlighten—"

"Stop it, you two," Natalie cuts her off. "Lindsay, why don't you and Chloe go get some ice cream?"

"Ice cream?" Chloe asks. "But if I leave, I might miss something. You and Daddy never fight. I want to know what's happening."

Natalie looks at Lindsay for help.

"Actually, a new gelato place opened near my apartment," Lindsay tells Chloe. "Do you want to go check it out?"

Natalie can see Chloe wavering. She knows if Lindsay suggests it, it must be cool. In her eyes, everything Lindsay does is cool.

"All right," she agrees.

$$ \ast \; \text{✳} \; \ast $$

AFTER CHLOE AND Lindsay leave, Peter takes a seat in a living room chair and shakes his head. "How could you, Natalie? How could you drink that Cabernet? Or even the Pinot Noir we bought in Napa?"

Natalie sits on the couch. Peter has such a hurt expression she almost regrets drinking the wine. But as she studies him, she realizes he looks different. And it's not just because she hasn't seen him for a while.

"Why do you have a tan?" His hair is lighter as well, as if it's been bleached by the sun. Natalie gets a sick feeling in her stomach. "Where have you been?"

21

Peter has the decency to at least look embarrassed when he answers her. "Mexico." He clears his throat. "We went to Cabo San Lucas for a few days."

Natalie is stunned. While she's been trying to cope with his abandonment, Peter has been on vacation. He traveled somewhere warm and sunny with *her*. She pictures him sitting on the beach with a drink in his hand, the blurry image of another woman by his side. She's so furious it nearly eclipses the pain.

"You know what? I'm glad Lindsay and I drank that wine! I wish I'd poured every single bottle you own down the drain!" Natalie pushes herself up from the couch and goes into the kitchen to get away from him.

She stands next to the sink, trying to calm herself. *Why would he do this to me? Why? After everything we've shared over the years.* She squeezes her eyes shut as hard as she can and wishes she could cry.

"Natalie?"

She turns and Peter is peering around the corner. His face sorrowful. His *tan* face.

"What did I ever do to you that would make you treat me like this? Tell me," she demands.

He walks slowly into the kitchen and stands near the island. "That's not an easy question to answer."

"Yes, it is. You must have some reason!"

Peter seems to be searching for the words. "I don't know. It's just everything. I don't feel a real connection with you anymore."

"Have you even tried? Don't you think I'd like to go to Mexico and sit in the warm sun? Why not ask *me*?"

"I did."

"No, you didn't."

"Last year, I tried to get you to fly down there for vacation with me, but you refused."

Natalie tries to remember what he's talking about and it does sound familiar. Then suddenly it comes to her. It was just after she and Blair had signed the lease on La Dolce Vita. He wanted to fly down to Cabo San Lucas, but she couldn't leave because they were opening their bakery.

"That's not fair. You knew I couldn't go anywhere then. I was starting a new business!"

Peter shakes his head. "It's always something, Natalie. Face it—you have no sense of adventure. All you want to do is work. Day after day, without end. But I don't want to spend my whole life working. I want to live, too."

"I enjoy my work, but that doesn't mean I don't want a break sometimes. We could take a vacation together, if that's what you really want." She walks toward him and tries to take his hand, but he pulls away from her.

"It's too late for that. It's just no good between us anymore, and it hasn't been for a long time."

Natalie swallows. She knows he's talking about their sex life, or the lack of it. To be honest, she's not even sure when they did it last. A quickie in the dark before she had to get up and go to work? "We can fix that, too," she says quietly.

"Lena told me you'd say that."

"What?" A shock runs through her body as she hears that woman's name. "You've talked about this with *Lena?*"

"I talk about everything with Lena. We love each other. She actually listens and cares about what I have to say."

Natalie grits her teeth. *That bitch! Who does this woman think she is, discussing our marriage?* "She's stealing you! Don't you see that? What kind of terrible person breaks up a family? And you're so deluded you think you're in love with her!"

"Lena isn't like that. And she didn't have to steal me, Natalie. The fact is, I was already gone when I met her."

"Because I didn't want to go to Mexico? After all these years, that's enough for you to leave?"

"Look, I don't want to hurt your feelings, but I need more. I want a woman."

"I am a woman!"

"Barely."

"Excuse me?"

"You heard me. I want a woman who cares. Who makes an effort to look, you know . . . sexy."

And even though he says he doesn't want to hurt her, Natalie is hurt. Deeply. It's like a knife through her heart. She knows she isn't sexy or a great beauty, but Peter knew that when he married her. "So you finally decided I'm not good enough for you, is that it?"

"We've simply outgrown each other."

Natalie is silent as the pain sinks in. Her family is going to pieces and there isn't anything she can do to stop it. "What have you told Chloe about all this?"

"Nothing."

"Why not?"

"Actually," Peter looks sheepish, "since you're so much better at these things, I was kind of hoping you would explain it to Chloe. But in a way that's fair," he adds.

Natalie is incredulous and then realizes nothing has changed. Peter might be leaving her, but he still wants her to handle the messy details of his life. She thinks of Chloe and figures at least this way she'll have control over how Chloe learns about their family falling apart.

"Fine. I'll handle it. I always take care of everything, so why should this be any different?"

Peter looks like he's going to argue, but then stops. "Call me after you talk to her." He pushes away from the counter. "Also you should know that I hired a divorce lawyer. In fact, after seeing the state of this house, I'm glad I did. I don't know what you were thinking, throwing a wild party like that. I'm glad Chloe wasn't here."

"Stop exaggerating. There was no wild party. It was just Lindsay and me." She crosses her arms. "And you're not touching my house."

"It's half mine."

A flicker of worry passes through her. *Could he really force me out?* "When did you hire a lawyer?"

"Recently." He takes a step closer to her and she recognizes his 'dentist voice,' the reasonable one he uses when he's trying to convince a patient to follow his advice. "There's no reason things have to get ugly between us, Natalie. Lena thought it was a good idea after that voicemail you left me, and I agree with her. It turns out if we keep things amicable we can be divorced in as little as ninety days."

Ninety days!

Natalie tries to catch her breath. *So Blair was right.* She wants to make sense of everything, but it's all happening so fast. She feels as if she's been thrown into the deep end of the pool without any idea how to swim. One thing's for sure, though. No one is stealing her husband without answering for it.

It's time to pay Lena a visit.

Chapter Four

Diet Plan: Coffee, banana, and two buttery pastries instead of four.

Exercise Plan: Bitch-slap your husband's mistress. Do it again.

URNS OUT DECIDING to confront Lena and actually doing it are two different things. Natalie doesn't know anything about her. She doesn't even know Lena's last name.

"We can follow Peter after he leaves work." Lindsay snaps her fingers. "I bet he leads us right to her."

"How? I think he'll notice if we're following him."

Her sister considers this. "We'll borrow Oliver's van. He's out of town on a photo shoot and he'll get a kick out of us using it." Oliver is Lindsay's current boyfriend whom she lives with.

Natalie tries to picture them following Peter without being seen. "Do you really think it'll work?"

"Trust me." Lindsay grins. "It's Operation Ass Clown."

And so that's how the two of them wind up sitting in a beat-up van outside of Peter's dental practice like a couple of undercover cops on a stakeout. They get there a half hour before Peter's last patient, just in case he's done early.

"I feel silly," Natalie says, glancing around the near empty parking lot. In the interest of staying incognito, she's wearing sunglasses and a straw hat with a big red flower on the side that Lindsay loaned her.

Lindsay is dressed in a similar get-up, though on her it looks glamorous.

"I look like a hillbilly," Natalie complains.

"You look fine." Lindsay studies her, then reaches behind and pulls out the black band holding Natalie's ponytail in place. Her hair falls down around her shoulders. "I don't know why you always wear it pulled back."

"Because it's mousy brown and ugly. Not to mention the grays."

"So color it. I color mine."

"I tried that once, remember? It turned orange."

"That henna you did back in high school? You just need to go to a salon and have it done. "

Natalie shifts in her seat. "It doesn't matter, anyway. I need to keep my hair out of the way when I'm baking."

"Yeah, but you're not baking every second. You should dress up more. Show off your assets."

"What assets?" Natalie mumbles.

"You got to work it, sister."

"Yeah, well, not all of us are lucky enough to be born beautiful."

Lindsay sighs and reaches for her latte. Natalie brought coffee and pastries for them to eat on their stakeout. "I don't know why you're always so down on yourself."

"I'm not. I'm just realistic."

"That's a bunch of crap. You decided to give up, but I don't understand why. There's so much you could do."

"Let's not get into all this right now. I've got enough on my mind." In truth, Natalie is kind of queasy. The thought of seeing Lena is causing her stomach to do flip flops.

"I can't believe my axe is still hanging from your front door. What's it been, over a week now?"

"No one can pull it out. Peter tried again when he came over to get Chloe, but it won't budge."

"Guess I know how to throw an axe, huh? It usually impresses the high school set when I show them how to sculpt with it."

"You use it for that class?" Lindsay participates in a program that teaches school kids about art.

"Yeah, I do an instant sculpture demo with it." Lindsay smiles apologetically. "There may have been some resin glue still on the axe. I thought I cleaned it off, but maybe I didn't get it all. Do you want me to find someone who can help? Oliver might be able to remove it when he gets back."

"Don't worry, at least Chloe's enjoying it." In truth, the axe has grown on Natalie too. There is something about it she likes. Probably the fact that it's annoying Peter so much. "She even decorated it with flowers."

"There he is!" Lindsay suddenly points across the street, where they can see Peter talking on his cell phone as he walks to his car. "The eagle has landed at six o'clock!"

Natalie smiles. This whole thing seems kind of pathetic, but leave it to Lindsay to make it fun.

"I don't think he noticed us," Lindsay says, still watching him, which is something of an understatement since Peter isn't even facing them as he blabs away on his phone.

Natalie watches him and her heart sinks. It's hard to believe he isn't her husband anymore, not in any real way. He's like a familiar stranger.

After he gets into his car, Lindsay starts up the van. It's louder than Natalie's van, but despite its beat-up exterior, seems to run just fine. The back isn't empty and has rolls of canvas material along with a couple of large tripods that Oliver must use for work. The materials shift around as Lindsay pulls out of the parking lot.

Natalie has to admit, she does a good job keeping pace with Peter. She's staying a couple of cars back, but they can still see him easily.

"I wonder where he's going?" Natalie murmurs.

"We're about to find out. Hopefully, it's to meet Lena."

Natalie sighs. "Yeah, hopefully."

Lindsay looks at Natalie with sympathy and then reaches out to squeeze her hand. "It's okay, don't worry." Her expression changes into something determined. "We're going to nail that bitch to the wall."

Natalie isn't sure how to respond to this, but squeezes Lindsay's hand in return.

They follow Peter as he gets onto I-5 heading south. He takes the exit for the U-District, which surprises Natalie, since it looks like he's driving to La Dolce Vita. But instead of going east, he goes west and drives to the Wallingford area. It's an artsy part of town with hippies and granola types.

At one point they wind up directly behind Peter at a stop light, and Natalie slouches in her seat, worried that he'll notice the two of them. Apparently, their disguise is solid, because he doesn't notice a thing.

"He's so oblivious. I wonder if he'd notice if I rammed him with this van and dented that Lexus," Lindsay says, clearly relishing the thought.

It isn't long before Peter slows down and turns into a small parking lot.

"I think he's going to that yoga studio." Natalie points across the street.

"I see it."

Lindsay circles back around the block and manages to maneuver the van into a spot that gives them a clear view.

"Peter's not into yoga," Natalie says, watching the studio, wondering what he could be doing in there. "Do you think he's picking up Lena?"

"Could be."

Natalie's stomach is doing flip flops again. She shifts around uncomfortably as they wait for any sign of them. Obviously, she wants to confront Lena, but she's not sure if she's up to the task.

And then she sees them. Her heart nearly stops. Peter walks out with a woman next to him. She has long blonde hair and a trim, athletic body. Natalie can't take her eyes off them. Even from this distance, she can see how Peter has his hand on her lower back, can see the goofy grin on his face as they're talking to each other.

"Oh, my God." Natalie's whole body breaks out in a cold sweat and for the first time in her life she thinks she's going to faint.

"Are you all right?" Lindsay looks at her with concern. "Put your head between your knees."

Natalie closes her eyes and puts her head down, trying to regain her equilibrium.

"Do you want to go?"

"Yes. *Please.*"

Lindsay shoves the van in gear and tears out from their parking space.

Natalie keeps her head down for a while, taking deep steady breaths. Finally, she sits up and leans back against the seat.

Lindsay is calling someone on her phone, but Natalie doesn't pay attention until she hears her ask for Lena.

"All right, thank you," Lindsay says. She looks at Natalie. "Bingo! Lena works there. It sounds like she's the owner. They told me she just left for the day."

Natalie nods. "Okay. We learned something, at least." She swallows, still feeling ill. "I can't believe I fell apart like that."

Lindsay is incredulous. "Jeez, cut yourself some slack. That was intense. It's not every day you see your husband with his mistress."

"I suppose you're right." Natalie thinks about Lena. She's not at all what she imagined her to be. In her mind she was just this hazy figure. As odd as it sounds, she always figured Lena looked a bit more ordinary, more like herself. Not a sexy athletic blonde, that's for sure. *How can I compete with that?*

THE NEXT MORNING, Chloe is sitting at the kitchen table, peeling a banana for breakfast, when Natalie joins her. It's been over a week since Natalie explained things. She expected the tears, but didn't expect Chloe to blame herself for Peter leaving. All Natalie can do is reassure her that none of this is her fault. After Natalie told Chloe that Peter had moved out, Chloe insisted on calling him and asking him to come home.

Natalie couldn't hear his response, but Chloe was quiet the rest of the night, so she assumed he told her no. Peter and Chloe had always been close, and it's difficult for a child to find out their family is breaking up.

"I've been thinking about it. I'll be just like everyone else now. Most of my friends' parents are divorced." Chloe slowly chews a bite of banana.

"I hadn't thought of that, but I guess that's one way of looking at it."

"Daddy says I'm going to like his girlfriend, Lena, but I don't want to meet her. I don't have to, do I?"

Natalie had asked Peter not to mention anything to Chloe about Lena yet, that they should wait and tell Chloe together, but he'd gone ahead and told her anyway. It infuriated Natalie.

"You don't have to meet her if you don't want to. I'll talk to him."

Chloe picks at her banana and sighs. "I wish Daddy would come home."

Natalie doesn't say anything. The image of Peter and Lena yesterday is still fresh in her mind—burned there forever. While the shock of it is still strong, a deep anger is taking hold. Natalie was awake all night.

Her daughter's pale-blue eyes meet her own and Natalie can see all the hurt in them. She reaches out and takes Chloe's hand. "I know how hard this is, sweetheart. Everything is going to be okay and you still have two parents who love you."

Chloe nods. "Aunt Lindsay told me your dad left when you were little, too. Is that true?"

"When did she tell you that?"

"She called last night, but you were already asleep."

Natalie lets out a deep breath. "My dad left Grandma when Lindsay and I were kids." What she doesn't tell Chloe is that her dad left and came back over and over.

"Aunt Lindsay said that he wasn't reliable and that's why you guys are so close."

Natalie lifts the cake dome on the counter and reaches for a chocolate croissant, but then stops herself. An image of Lena's trim body suddenly comes to mind. She puts the lid back down. Instead, she pulls off a banana like Chloe.

"It's true. He wasn't the best father, and Grandma had her problems, too." Natalie thinks back to her childhood and it's like another lifetime ago. Her mother was flighty with artistic aspirations that never panned out, and her father was only around when he was winning poker tournaments. It was up to her to be the responsible one, the one to make sure there were clean clothes to wear and hot meals to eat.

Chloe sighs. "I wish I had a sister."

Natalie gazes at her beautiful daughter. Chloe looks just like Peter. She has his same willowy build and his blue eyes, but her personality is all her own. Peter used to say that she and Chloe were the center of his life, that he couldn't live without them. When did all that change? She tries to picture a time when this heartbreak will end and she'll feel normal again. It's hard to imagine. "What else did Lindsay say?"

"She called Daddy an ass clown."

"That wasn't very nice. You have to understand that Lindsay and your dad have never gotten along with each other."

"I know."

Natalie peels her banana. "You may hear some things while this is happening. Just remember that despite everything, your dad and I both love you."

Chloe is quiet. "I don't know why he wants to go live with someone else. How could anyone be better than you?"

She's touched by her daughter's words. "I wish I had an answer that made sense. We're going to figure this all out though—okay?"

"Okay."

Natalie finishes up her banana. It was sweet and surprisingly delicious. She gets up to make herself some coffee as Chloe leaves the kitchen to go take her shower before school.

She thinks about everything that's happened, all the hell she's been going through, and decides today is definitely the day she's paying Lena a visit. Lena needs to be told face-to-face about the damage she's done.

"I'M GOING WITH you," Blair says, untying her apron. "I'll work late tonight if I have to."

"Oh, that's not necessary," Natalie says. "I can handle it."

Lindsay, who has just arrived at the bakery, is standing next to Blair. The two of them are a united front.

"There is no way we're going to let you confront Lena without us. You know that," Blair continues.

Lindsay nods in approval. "That's right. We got your back."

Natalie shakes her head and smiles at them. "All right. I guess you guys can come." Even though she was planning to confront Lena alone, it'll be good to have the support. The truth is, she's nervous.

Of course, Blair insists they take Isadora. Natalie rides shotgun while Lindsay goes for the back seat.

"Wow, this is a sweet ride," Lindsay says, settling herself in. "I didn't know this was your car. And you call her Isadora? That's so cool."

"Thanks." Blair smiles. She then turns to Natalie. "I didn't want to take her just because it's sunny, though. Riding in style to confront Lena will help get you in the right frame of mind. It's like wearing new clothes. You feel different about yourself. You'll see."

Natalie looks around. "Hey, I'm not arguing. I feel different already."

Blair motions at both of them. "All right, ladies, sunglasses please."

The three of them immediately put on their sunglasses. Natalie feels like she's being initiated into some sort of club.

Blair turns and inspects everyone. "Hmm, luckily there's some red lipstick in my purse." She directs Lindsay to the purse on the floor behind the driver's seat. "Why don't you get some out for Natalie? In fact, we could all use some."

"But I don't wear lipstick," Natalie complains.

"You do today. And don't argue. Lipstick and Isadora go together like cupcakes and butter cream frosting. Good lipstick is armor, and from what I've heard, you're going to need all the armor you can get."

Lindsay finds the tube in Blair's bag and puts some on. She passes it up to Natalie.

"You don't need a mirror?" Natalie asks her.

"Nope."

Natalie turns to look at her and, of course, her sister's lipstick is perfect.

Lindsay kisses the air and then grins. "Years of training. My specialty is putting on makeup in a moving car while getting dressed."

Blair laughs while Natalie rolls her eyes. "I'm not sure if I want to know how you acquired that specialty."

"In a completely innocent way, I assure you."

"Yeah, right."

Natalie opens the tube grudgingly and pulls the sun visor down. "Well, I definitely need a mirror," she mutters.

It feels strange putting on red lipstick, but Natalie has to admit the color is right. It's not a clown red, but more like the color of ripe sweet cherries. She puts her sunglasses back on and turns toward the two of them. "How do I look?"

"Not bad," Blair says. "Not bad at all. There's something missing, though."

Lindsay reaches behind Natalie and pulls the ponytail band out of her hair, so it flows freely.

Blair grins. "Perfect! You should wear your hair down more often."

"That's what I'm always telling her, but she won't listen."

Natalie checks herself out in the sun visor again. She's surprised by her appearance. Between the lipstick, sunglasses, and her hair flowing loosely, she looks okay.

She leans back in the seat and rests her arm on the door, feeling glamorous. It's a foreign sensation, but she has to admit she sort of likes it. Maybe Blair is on to something with this whole traveling in style business.

"So do you know what you're going to say to Lena?" Blair glances over at her as she drives.

Natalie has been thinking about it all morning. "I'm going to ask her how she can do it, you know? How she can be with a married man. I want her to know there are consequences from her actions and that she's hurting people."

Blair nods. "That's not a bad approach."

"Well, if you ask me, I think you should go in there swinging." Lindsay leans forward. "Forget talking to her. That bitch deserves a world of hurt."

Natalie laughs. "I'm not exactly the violent type. Besides, did you see her yesterday? She looks more muscular than Peter."

"So what? If you need help, we can take her. What do you say, Blair?"

Blair shrugs. "I am pretty strong."

"Plus I just started a boxing class last month, so I've got moves," Lindsay says.

"Oh, I was just reading about boxing for women recently," Blair exclaims. "How is it?"

"It's totally awesome. Way more fun than I thought it would be. Plus it's great for self-defense."

As the two of them talk about the boxing gym Lindsay goes to, Natalie thinks more about what she plans to say to Lena. *She needs to hear how she's destroying my family.*

THEY PARK ACROSS from the yoga studio and case the joint. Like a lot of the buildings on the street, it's in a small house that was once someone's home. The outside is painted lavender with light blue trim and there is gold trim around the door. Herbs are growing neatly in the front yard and an elaborate wind chime hangs near the entrance. The sign is written in what looks like both English and Sanskrit. The studio is called "Lotus Flower Yoga."

"I can't believe Lena works in a yoga studio," Blair says. "I've done yoga off and on for years to help me stay focused. It's hard to believe someone into yoga would be a home wrecker."

"Oh, she's focused, all right. The problem is *where* she's focused." Natalie leans back in her seat, trying to stay calm.

She continues to study the small house and notices a green flower hand painted on the front door. It looks like it was done with care. She thinks about how ironic it is that both she and Lena are small business owners. The thought helps calm Natalie. *Maybe I can reach her somehow. Get her to go away and leave Peter alone. Then somehow we can put the pieces of our family back together.*

"All right." Natalie lets out a deep breath. "It's now or never."

The three of them get out of the car and make their way up the sidewalk to the studio. Natalie is in the middle with Blair and Lindsay on each side. She suddenly imagines them walking in slow motion together like an old western movie—the gunslinger and her posse.

Natalie opens the door to the studio and is immediately assaulted by the smell of incense. It's overwhelming. She thinks of how La Dolce Vita always smells like delicious things—fresh cakes, butter, and espresso. There's no comparison.

A young woman in tight yoga clothes is standing near a wooden counter. The front room looks like it was once a living room, but has been converted to a small shop. There are clothes for sale along one wall, along with books, candles, and more incense.

"Can I help you?" the woman asks.

"Yes." Natalie clears her throat. "I'm looking for Lena?"

"Oh, are you guys signing up for her new class? Because it's starting in just a few minutes." She motions to the next room and Natalie can see a sheer curtain separating the two rooms. There are a number of people sitting on mats.

"No. I just need to speak with her. It won't take long."

"I think she's upstairs in the office. I'll get her."

The young woman leaves and Natalie starts to feel nervous again. She can't believe this is what her life has come to. Standing in some hippie den, gagging on incense as she waits to confront the hussy who's cheating with her husband.

Blair gives her a supportive smile. "You're doing the right thing. We're with you all the way."

Lindsay waves her hand in front of her face. "Jeez, I can't believe how much it stinks in here. Are they trying to hide the smell of B.O. or something?"

Natalie laughs nervously. "I know. It's hard to even breathe."

She hears footsteps and when she looks up an attractive blonde woman walks toward her with a sexy sway to her hips. She's wearing the same kind of tight yoga clothes the younger woman at the desk was wearing.

It's Lena.

And for Natalie, it's as if time has stopped. She feels sweat break out on her forehead. *Dear God, please don't let me faint or make a fool of myself.*

Lena stops in front of the three of them expectantly. "Can I help you?"

Up close, Natalie can see that Lena has an air of command. Her toned body looks like she's in permanent boot camp. She's definitely in her forties, too. She looks older than she did from a distance. *That hair is something else, though.* Natalie has to admit that Lena's long blonde hair is striking and glamorous. She's as blonde as Britney Spears, but while her hair might look like Britney's, her face sure doesn't. It gives Natalie a sense of satisfaction to see all the lines at the corners of Lena's eyes and on her forehead.

She's also deeply tan. Tan just like Peter. That image she had of him on the beach in Mexico lounging next to some hazy figure is now replaced with the sexy clarity of Lena. A wave of outrage comes over Natalie.

"What kind of person are you?" she says, trying to keep her voice from shaking. "Have you no shame?"

"Excuse me?"

"I'm Natalie. Peter's *wife.*"

Lena's blue eyes widen, but she recovers quickly. "I see and what exactly can I do for you?"

"I want you to stop sleeping with my husband!"

Lena frowns and looks around to see who overheard. The class in the next room seems oblivious. She erases the frown and starts speaking in a compassionate voice. "I'm sorry that you're having a hard time with all this. I really am, but Peter and I love each other. You finding that hard to accept, Natalie, doesn't change anything."

"How can you be with a married man? What's wrong with you?"

Lena sighs patiently. "He's not married to you anymore. Not really. In his heart your marriage is over."

"Is that what you tell yourself? Peter and I have been married for fourteen years. We have a daughter together. You're breaking up our family!"

"Yes, I know about Chloe. In fact, I'm looking forward to meeting her."

When she hears her daughter's name coming from this woman's lips, Natalie's anger becomes a black and ugly thing. "Stay away from Chloe. She doesn't want anything to do with you."

"I'm sure we're going to get along great," Lena goes on. "Peter and I were thinking about taking a trip together with her. It would be a nice way to get to know each other. Possibly Europe next summer? I understand she's never been."

Natalie grits her teeth, crazed at this woman making plans to travel with Chloe.

Lindsay suddenly speaks out. "Look, you can forget that. You're not taking Chloe anywhere!"

"Yes, what's wrong with you?" Blair chimes in. "Don't you have a conscience?"

Lena looks at her. "Who are you?"

"I'm Natalie's friend and business partner."

"I see." Lena turns to Lindsay. "And you must be the wacko sister—I've heard all about you." She gives them a hard smile. "I suggest you both mind your own business though, because this has nothing to do with you."

In response, Lindsay and Blair glare at Lena and take a step closer to Natalie.

"Don't talk to them like that," Natalie says. "And my sister is not a wacko!"

There's movement from behind the sheer curtain that leads into the next room. People waiting for the yoga class are starting to notice their conversation.

"Natalie, I'm not just a yoga instructor. I'm also a life coach. So I understand why you came here today to confront me. But as a life coach, let me tell you it's time for you to move on." Lena is trying to sound patient and guru-like, though Natalie can tell her façade is slipping. "I truly hope this meeting between us has given you a sense of closure. Now, if you'll excuse me, I have a class to teach."

She's dismissing me. After wrecking my life, now I'm being dismissed!
"How dare you!" Rage clouds her vision.

Lena opens her mouth to say something more, but Natalie doesn't give her a chance. Without a thought, she raises her hand and then . . .
SLAP!

Natalie's hand stings as she stares at Lena in shock. *My God, what have I done?*

Lena appears shocked, too. Her fingers go to her cheek, which is turning bright pink. She seems momentarily confused. But then her eyes narrow and all semblance of the peace-loving yoga guru is gone.

"You fat bitch!" she snarls. "You're dead!"

She shoves Natalie so hard that she loses balance and lands on the floor. Pain shoots through her right shoulder. She tries to get up, but Lena is suddenly on top of her.

Natalie panics as Lena tries to punch her in the face. She nearly succeeds. Lena is fit and toned, but it turns out Natalie is just plain strong. Hauling around big bags of flour and sugar all these years has its rewards.

"Get off me!" Natalie demands, grabbing Lena's wrists. "That's enough!"

"You're going to pay," Lena growls, struggling to free herself. "No one slaps me and gets away with it."

In desperation, Natalie releases one wrist and slaps Lena again.

"Stop that!"

"Then get off me!"

Infuriated, Lena tries once more to punch Natalie, but Natalie blocks her and gets in another loud slap.

"Bitch!" Lena sobs with frustration.

Lena pushes downward and manages to grab hold of Natalie's hair, jerking her head back. There's a roar in Natalie's ears. It hurts like hell and, as she tries to loosen Lena's grip, the pain brings back memories. She and Lindsay used to fight when they were kids, and when they did, Lindsay fought dirty. Eye poking and nipple twisting weren't beneath her.

Natalie reaches up and shoves her fingers into Lena's eyes. Immediately her hair is released as Lena starts howling. Hands are grabbing Natalie. Somebody is pulling them apart.

That's when she realizes people are yelling. There's a bunch of strangers standing around them.

"Stop it! Someone help! Do something!"

Finally, they're separated. Natalie tries to catch her breath. Her hair hurts and her shoulder and butt ache from when she hit the floor, but as far as she can tell there's no other damage.

"Are you all right?" Blair asks. She and Lindsay are kneeling down beside her. "I can't believe she jumped you like that!"

"Although I'll bet she regrets it now," Lindsay says with a smirk, glaring over at Lena.

"I'm fine." Natalie tells them.

Lena's hair is a tangled mess and there are red slap marks on both of her cheeks. She's rubbing her eyes. "Hey, are you okay?" Natalie asks her.

A crowd of people has gathered around, though most of them seem bewildered. This isn't exactly the kind of scene you expect to find in a yoga studio.

Lena gives Natalie a nasty look. "Just go away. I never want to see you again!"

"That works for me." Natalie pushes herself up and straightens her clothes. Lindsay and Blair join her. After a quick search, she finds the sunglasses that were knocked off her head and puts them back on again. Just before she leaves, she goes over to where Lena is leaning against the wall, still breathing hard. "You know what? You were right about what you said earlier. I think I do feel a sense of closure."

And then Natalie turns and heads toward the door.

Taking her posse with her.

Chapter Five

Diet Plan: Trade whole milk lattes for low-fat. Beef burgers for veggie. A small helping of grim determination on the side.

Exercise Plan: Try out that strange device in that strange room called the gym.

THE RIDE BACK over to La Dolce Vita is a quiet one. Natalie doesn't feel like talking, and sensing this, Lindsay and Blair keep their thoughts to themselves.

When they get to the bakery it's nearly closing time, though the place is still busy, filled with students and people chatting over coffee and working on their laptops. Luckily, a corner table opens up and Natalie immediately heads for it. It has a small red love seat on one side and she collapses onto it.

Lindsay and Blair take a seat, too. No one says a word.

The familiar sounds and smells of the bakery settle around Natalie like a comforting blanket. Finally, she breaks the silence.

"I guess it was a mistake confronting Lena."

Lindsay scowls. "That woman is a lunatic and here she was calling *me* a wacko!"

"I agree," Blair says. "She's nuts. I still can't believe the way she jumped you. I've never seen anything like that."

Natalie just shakes her head. "It's my fault, though. I started it."

"How?" Lindsay asks.

"By slapping her."

"Well, I think you're wrong," Blair says. "It sounds to me like Lena started it. She started it months ago by sleeping with Peter."

"And now she's talking about taking Chloe to Europe?" Lindsay scoffs. "That's going to happen over my dead body, I can tell you that."

"I hated even hearing her say Chloe's name. My God, what did I ever do to this woman? She stole my husband and now she wants to steal my

37

daughter, too?"

Lindsay shakes her head. "Not going to happen. Not in a million years. Chloe would never go with her anywhere."

"Lena has Peter, though."

They're all silent again and the mood is somber.

Finally, Blair speaks up. "Okay, it's probably inappropriate, but I have to ask. What did it feel like to let her have it?"

Natalie thinks about how satisfying it was giving Lena a taste of pain. She bites her lip. "It felt good, but it was still wrong."

"You took her by surprise, that's for sure. She definitely didn't see it coming."

Lindsay looks at Natalie admiringly. "I'm sure she never dreamed you were going to give her an ass-kicking. We would have jumped in to help, but you didn't look like you needed it at all."

Blair nods in agreement. "You definitely had it under control."

Natalie considers this. "Do you guys really think I kicked her ass?"

"Are you kidding?" Lindsay says. "You slapped the slut right out of her!"

Natalie and Blair's eyes meet and they both burst out laughing.

"Hey, it's true!" Lindsay says, laughing with them.

While they're still laughing, Carlos comes up to the table. "I don't mean to interrupt your pow-wow, ladies, but would you like anything?"

Natalie tries to get herself under control. She nods at Carlos. "Would you mind getting me a latte?"

"No problem, anyone else?"

Blair and Lindsay say they'll take one, too, along with a piece of caramel cake for Lindsay.

As Carlos turns to walk away, Natalie stops him. "Can you make my latte with two percent instead of whole milk?"

Carlos eyes her. "Are you sure?" Natalie is notoriously picky about her coffee.

"Yeah, I'm sure."

"Okay."

Natalie sighs and lets her eyes wander around the bakery. The place is still buzzing even though it's almost closing.

"I wonder if we should consider staying open late again," she muses. It's something she and Blair have discussed a few times.

"I'd love to, but I think we need to wait until we can get the space next door," Blair says.

"You're right. It all hinges on that, doesn't it?"

Both Natalie and Blair turn and stare with frustration at the brick wall that connects them to the empty shop that sits on the other side.

Lindsay looks confused. "This place is always hopping. Why can't you guys stay open later?"

"Because it's more expensive," Blair explains. "We'll have to hire more people and we need more space to pay for that."

"Plus, we're still in a bind with our ovens, so it'll be impossible to make enough food to sell," Natalie continues.

Carlos comes over and brings them their lattes, along with the caramel cake.

Blair glances down at Lindsay's caramel cake. "That reminds me! I'll be right back." She gets up and runs into the kitchen.

"What's up with her?" Lindsay asks, stuffing cake in her mouth.

Natalie shrugs. She takes a sip from her two percent latte. It's surprisingly good. Not as good as whole milk, but she thinks she can live with it.

When Blair comes back, she has a mischievous grin on her face. "I forgot to tell you who came in the other day to order a cake. Espresso Breve!"

"Is that right?" Natalie keeps her voice neutral, pretending to be surprised.

"Yes, and I found out his real name."

"Wait a minute," says Lindsay. "Who's Espresso Breve?"

"He's this totally hot guy who comes in a few times a week. Natalie's never told you about him?"

"No."

"Well, he came in the other day and ordered a birthday cake for someone named Serena."

"Probably his girlfriend," Natalie muses. They'd already decided Espresso Breve wasn't married, since he didn't wear a wedding ring.

"Probably," Blair agrees. "Lucky woman, that's for sure."

Natalie tries to imagine the kind of woman Espresso Breve would be with. She pictures some hot blonde with a great body. Yuck. With disgust, she suddenly realizes she's imagining Lena.

"So, what's his name?" Natalie can't resist asking.

Blair smiles. "Anthony Novello. It suits him, don't you think?"

"Novello? That name sounds familiar."

"He must be Italian." Lindsay finishes her cake, licking the back of her fork. "There's a lot of really hot Italian guys."

Natalie is still thinking about the name, when it suddenly comes to her. "Wait a minute, Novello—that's the name of our jerk landlord."

"Really?" Blair says. "Well, it must be a coincidence."

Natalie thinks about it. "Yeah, it must be. He does look kind of young to own this building. I pictured someone older and more stern. "

"I'm sure it isn't him. That would be too weird. He comes in here all the time. Why wouldn't he want us to expand?"

After Lindsay leaves and Blair goes back into the kitchen, Natalie sits by herself for a moment, finishing her latte. She wiggles her shoulder around. It's still sore.

What a crazy day.

She can't believe any of it. Most of all, she can't believe she acted just like her mom, something she never thought she'd do in a million years. *Though at least I'm not making excuses for Peter's infidelity.* Her mom slapped more than a few of her father's floozies, but she always placed the blame solely on them. Her father was a womanizer, but in her eyes he was a prince. Even after he died, predictably, in bed with someone, she wouldn't let either her or Lindsay say a word against him. *She loved him too much.* That's the conclusion Natalie always came to as a child. It frightened her. She never wanted to love a man like that.

I'm nothing like her, Natalie reminds herself. *Peter is not a womanizer and I don't only blame Lena. I blame them both. In fact, Peter is the betrayer here.* She sucks in her breath as the familiar hurt and anger wash over her.

Trying to push it out of her mind, she gets up and grabs her mug along with the plate that Lindsay left behind. She sees another empty table that has a few dirty dishes on it and busses those, too.

Juggling an armful, she turns toward the kitchen and nearly bumps into someone.

"Excuse me," she says to some guy, but her pulse jumps when she looks up and sees it's Espresso Breve. Anthony, she corrects herself.

He glances at her, and then stops in recognition. "Hey, how's it going?"

Natalie looks down at the cake box he's holding and he follows her gaze. "Yeah, I came back and spoke to the owner. She helped me order the cake."

"That's . . . great." It occurs to Natalie that this would be the perfect time to fix the false impression she gave him the other day and explain that she's one of the owners herself. "Listen, I wanted to tell—"

To her surprise the cell phone in his hand starts blasting the *Star Wars* theme music. "Hang on." He transfers the cake box to his left side and answers it. "Yeah, I've got it right here. No worries, *bambina.* I'll be there soon. Okay, I love you, too."

Anthony fumbles a little with the cell as he turns it off and Natalie is mesmerized by his hands. His fingers are tan and masculine. His nails clean and short. She feels a peculiar breathlessness staring at his hands, as if she wants something from them.

"Good luck," he tells her, with a quick boyish grin that does something funny to her insides. "You'll get the hang of things around here before you know it."

"I . . . uh."

In frustration, she watches him leave with the wrong idea. Again.

NATALIE HEADS HOME with plans to put the whole ugly mess with Lena behind her.

"Oh, no," Natalie groans as she heads down the street toward her house.

Peter's Lexus is sitting in the driveway—big, black, and foreboding as a hearse.

"Just what I need." She knows why he's here. Of course, Lena went running to him after what happened. She should have predicted this. *And I'll bet she blamed the whole thing on me.*

After parking, she opens the back of her van and pulls out the covered racks she uses to carry the baking she does every morning. She waits for Peter to come running up to her in a fury, but he doesn't.

He must be inside the house. The thought irritates her. Peter shouldn't be allowed to come and go as he pleases anymore. *He moved out. It's my house now.*

She considers changing the locks, but then wonders if that's a bad idea. It's time to find a lawyer, someone who can help guide her through this morass.

Walking up to the house, she discovers Peter isn't inside after all, but standing by the front door, hands on hips, studying the axe. She watches as he grips the handle and tries to pull it out. He still doesn't seem to be having any luck.

"What are you doing?" she asks, mostly to annoy him.

"This damn thing won't budge at all!" He puts one foot on the door to brace himself and starts twisting his body around while he continues to pull. "How did your sister manage to get it stuck like this?"

Natalie shrugs, secretly glad he can't remove it, and enjoying how silly he looks as he tries.

"And I can't believe you let Chloe decorate it," he says, referring to the flower wreath Chloe made and hung on it the first week of school.

"She likes it."

"We have to get this thing out!" Once again, he grabs hold of it with both hands and pulls, his face turning a mottled shade of red. Suddenly, there's a loud *CRACK* and Peter stumbles backward holding a large piece of the axe handle.

"Jesus!" He straightens himself and stares down at the broken handle.

"Are you okay?" Natalie asks, though it's obvious he's fine.

Peter is staring at the axe head, which is still stuck in the door. Though now instead of a handle, there's only a short stump attached. "Did you see what just happened? I could have been killed!"

She rolls her eyes.

"This thing is a menace! I'd sue that sister of yours, if she had any money!"

Natalie shifts, as the baking racks are getting heavy. "Just leave the axe for now. Who cares?"

"What's gotten into you, Natalie? Since when do you not care whether our house goes to ruin? Besides, I think we need to discuss putting it on the market, and we certainly can't sell it with an axe sticking out from the front door."

Natalie reels for a few seconds at his words. "We are *not* putting this house on the market," she informs him. "You can forget that."

"It's the next logical step."

"It's my home and it's Chloe's home. Just because you don't want to live here anymore doesn't mean we should be forced to move."

"Fine. Whatever. We still need to have it appraised for its current value."

Natalie sighs. "Peter, I'm tired. It's been a long day. Is this why you came here?"

Her turns to her with a hard expression. "You know why I'm here."

She doesn't say anything as he steps back, wiping his hands on his pants. "Let's go inside. I'd rather not discuss this in front of the entire neighborhood."

He opens the door and Natalie trudges in behind him. She heads for the kitchen and lays the racks out on the table. Peter is standing on the other side, glaring at her. It's the angriest she's seen him since the morning he left.

"How could you, Natalie? How could you assault Lena?"

Natalie is incredulous. "I did no such thing! That's quite an exaggeration."

"Well, that's what she said. She told me you came into her place of work and assaulted her. In fact, she wants to file both assault charges and a restraining order against you."

"*What?*" Natalie looks up at the ceiling and closes her eyes. She doesn't know whether to laugh or cry, and since she can't cry, she decides to laugh.

"I hardly find this amusing!"

Natalie laughs some more anyway. Shakes her head. "You're right, it's not funny, but it's absurd."

"I don't know what's gotten into you. You've always been so sensible. I've never seen this side of you before. First you attack me, and now Lena. Honestly, I'm wondering whether I should be worried about Chloe living here."

Natalie's body tenses and her expression turns to steel. "Don't you *dare* threaten me with Chloe. Because if you want a war, you'll get one!"

Peter holds her stare for a few seconds and then looks down at his hands.

She takes a deep breath and lets it out. "Look, I went over to talk to Lena today and I admit I lost my temper and slapped her. Nothing more. I know that was wrong. After that, she attacked *me,* okay? She jumped me. All I did was defend myself. In fact, my shoulder is sore from her knocking me to the ground."

Peter studies her. "Why should I believe anything you say?"

"Come on, Peter, don't you know me better? Is she even injured? That woman is built like a Marine."

"I have to admit I was surprised by her story." He appears to mull things over. "She's pretty upset, though, and I don't blame her. I wouldn't go near her again, do you understand?"

"I have no desire to see her again. Believe me. I just felt she should realize that her actions have consequences. She's hurting people."

Peter gets agitated. "Listen, you need to get past this. I'm not coming back, okay? Our marriage is over."

Natalie swallows. "I understand that." She wants to say something spiteful, but stops herself.

"How did you even know where she works?"

"I, uh. . . ." Natalie tries to think of a plausible explanation. Obviously, she can't admit that she and Lindsay followed him. It wasn't hard to imagine Peter taking that too well. The way things were going, he'd probably take out a restraining order and accuse her of stalking. "I looked her up on the Internet."

Peter frowns, but seems to accept this. "I want it to end here. I don't want you frightening her like that again. "

Natalie tries not to scoff as she imagines Lena playing up this whole thing and acting as if she were frightened. *I'll bet she's only upset that she didn't take a piece out of me.*

Lena was like a pit bull with lipstick and tight yoga pants.

By the time Peter is done adding recriminations about lawyers and legal actions, Natalie is so fed up she wants to scream. It's a huge relief when he leaves.

She heads upstairs to the guest bedroom, having moved all her things in there after Peter moved out. It was too depressing sleeping in their old bedroom alone. During the day, she's busy at the bakery, but at night things are different. It's hard to sleep alone. The bed in the guest bedroom is only a queen, and not as large as the king she and Peter shared, but she still doesn't know where to sleep on it. Oftentimes she wakes up at night confused and adrift, wondering where she is. Though they seldom had sex anymore, Natalie discovered she misses Peter the most at night. She misses his presence. She misses having someone she can talk with about the minutia of her day, to share her ideas with or even just the comfort of sitting in bed together, each of them reading something. In truth, it has been a while since they'd been close, but now she realizes how much of it she took for granted.

Of course, she still has Chloe, and Lindsay has basically moved in. In fact, she wonders what Oliver thinks about all this and if he minds that his girl-friend has abandoned him. She's only met him briefly, but most men wouldn't be too pleased. Lindsay claims he travels a lot and doesn't care, but it's hard to tell whether that's the truth or not, since she's so terrible with commitment.

Natalie opens the guest bedroom closet to get out some clean clothes. As always, her decision on what to wear is based solely on comfort and practi-cality. All her pants are dark and baggy with a drawstring waist, all her shirts more of the same.

Quickly she grabs a pair of gray sweats and a loose T-shirt with the words "I Eat Therefore I Bake" on the front—a Mother's Day gift from Chloe last year.

She pulls her ponytail out and refashions it, so it feels tight again.

Leaving the guest bedroom, she walks down the hall past Chloe's room, which has horse pictures plastered all over the door, and then past what she and Peter have designated as their home gym. For some reason she stops. The door is open and inside she sees the elliptical machine, along with a treadmill, a workout bench, and a row of shiny weights. Peter spent a lot of money on this room, only to join a gym in the end, claiming he felt more driven to exer-cise with other people around.

For Natalie, their home gym may as well have been attached to an orbit-ing space station, as often as she visited it.

Timing was always the problem. Should she exercise in the morning or at night? Her mornings were so early that adding an hour meant getting up at 2:30 am, something she wasn't about to do. Exercising at night meant finding the motivation when she was exhausted from working all day.

She's exhausted just thinking about it.

Yet she doesn't leave.

Instead, she thinks of Lena and her toned, muscular body. Then she thinks of how good it felt to slap her. Not a nice thing to acknowledge about herself, but letting her frustrations out in a physical way had felt good.

With that thought in mind, she wanders over to the elliptical machine. Natalie stands next to it awkwardly, as if getting up the courage to ask it to dance. Finally, she makes a decision and climbs aboard.

Immediately she fumbles as her legs swing around and she grapples with the handlebars.

Whoa. Is that how this thing works?

Within a few minutes, she gets the hang of it. Before long, Lindsay and Chloe are home and find her upstairs. Lindsay's been picking up Chloe after school lately, since it's so close to her art studio.

"How was . . . school . . . today, sweetheart?" Natalie asks, sweating from the exertion.

"When did you start exercising?" Lindsay asks.

"About . . . ten . . . minutes . . . ago." Natalie is huffing and puffing, but doesn't stop. Oddly, it feels good. Like her stress is flowing out along with her sweat.

"School was fine." Chloe looks a little worried. "Would you like a glass of water, Mom?"

"That . . . would . . . be . . . great!"

Natalie keeps pushing herself. She thinks about everything that's happened, every dark emotion that's gripped her since Peter announced he wanted a divorce. It only drives her harder.

Lindsay continues to watch, but doesn't say anything.

Finally, Chloe comes back with the water and Natalie stops, panting for breath. "Thank . . . you." She takes the glass and gulps it down. "I think I'll make veggie burgers tonight, do you guys want one?"

"Sure," Lindsay says.

"I love veggie burgers!" Chloe's eyes light up.

Natalie doesn't usually eat vegetarian burgers, but Chloe decided to stop eating meat last year, so she's been making them more often. Oddly, she finds herself thinking that maybe it wouldn't hurt to lay off meat a little herself, start eating lighter.

After taking a quick shower, Natalie heads downstairs where she checks on Chloe, who is in the family room watching *Flicka* for what must be the hundredth time. Lindsay is in the kitchen, sitting at the island filling out some kind of paperwork. In some ways it feels like old times, having her sister around so much, and Natalie appreciates the support.

"You know, I've been thinking," Natalie says to Lindsay, as she grabs the burgers from the freezer. "If you're going to stay over so much, why don't you sleep in the master bedroom instead of on the couch? Obviously, I'm not using it."

"I don't mind the couch. Besides, it'd feel weird sleeping in your *marital bed.*" Lindsay gives a small shiver.

"Don't be so quick to dismiss it. That bedroom has its own bathroom with a sunken tub. Plus, it will drive Peter crazy if he finds out you're sleeping in there."

Lindsay grins. "I can't believe I didn't think of that myself! I'll move my things in there tonight."

"I'll put clean sheets on right after dinner."

"And next month I'm going to decorate his nightstand with a big bowl of Halloween candy." Lindsay smiles deviously. "I can't wait. I only wish I could see his face when you tell him."

"Don't worry, he'll hate it."

"That's what I'm counting on. Pissing off the ass clown."

Being a dentist, Peter is a stickler about sugar, something that was occasionally a point of contention, seeing that Natalie bakes sweets for a living. They'd learned to compromise, and even Peter agreed some sweets in moderation are okay. In truth, Natalie thought he secretly loved desserts, but just didn't want to admit it. He hated Halloween candy with a passion, though.

"Are you starting a diet?" Lindsay watches as Natalie puts a large frying pan on the stove.

"No, I don't think so. Why do you ask?"

"Because you were exercising, and now you're eating vegetarian food."

"I'm making veggie burgers for Chloe." Natalie thinks about Lindsay's question though as she cooks. *Maybe I am starting a diet.* Natalie feels a small sense of panic even thinking those words. She's started so many diets over the years. It seemed like every Monday of her life she started a diet, until she finally gave up.

When the food is ready, Natalie goes to get Chloe and discovers her talking on her phone in the family room. Against Natalie's wishes, Peter recently bought Chloe a smartphone, even though they'd agreed to wait until she was older. Peter kept insisting it was in Chloe's best interest to have a phone now, just in case she needed to reach him. Chloe was, of course, thrilled. Natalie didn't like it, but there wasn't much she could do.

"Who were you talking to?" Natalie asks.

"Daddy."

"I see."

Chloe is quiet as she follows her to the table and the three of them sit down for dinner.

Natalie decides to eat her veggie burger without mayonnaise, and is surprised to find that it doesn't taste too bad. Piling on the lettuce and tomato seems to help.

The three of them are eating silently until Chloe suddenly speaks up. "Daddy told me that you hit Lena today. Is that true?"

"*What?*" Natalie nearly chokes on her burger.

"He said you got into a fight with her." Chloe's voice quivers.

Natalie is ready to call Peter and scream at him, when she suddenly feels Lindsay's hand on her arm.

"Your mom was amazing today," Lindsay says to Chloe.

"She was?"

"You should have seen the way she handled Lena."

"Lindsay!" Natalie shoots her sister a dark look. "This is not something we should be talking about!"

"Hey, Peter's obviously already told her. We might as well set the record straight."

"What do you mean?" Chloe asks, her gaze roaming between the two of them.

Lindsay wipes her hands with a napkin. "There's no point denying the truth. She's old enough to handle it, aren't you?" Lindsay turns to Chloe.

"Of course!" Chloe says eagerly.

Natalie puts her burger down. She feels like she's standing in the path of a hurricane and there's nothing she can do about it. Peter is determined to cause trouble. And her sister is like a force of nature when she puts her mind to it. Peter should never have said anything to Chloe to begin with, though.

"Your mom paid Lena a visit today," Lindsay tells Chloe with a smile, "and she gave her the business." She then proceeds to tell the whole story. Natalie has to hand it to her, too. Lindsay makes her sound like a superhero, though that isn't exactly accurate.

"It was wrong of me to slap her," Natalie says quickly. "Don't let Lindsay glamorize it. I never should have done that."

"Daddy never told me that Lena tried to hurt you."

"Exactly why I wanted to set the record straight," Lindsay says, turning to Natalie. "See, she gets it. I knew she would."

Chloe nods and seems to accept the explanation. Still uncomfortable, Natalie wants nothing but to end this whole conversation. She's going to call Peter as soon as she can and give him a piece of her mind. How dare he drag Chloe into all this!

After dinner, they settle in the living room with a bowl of popcorn to watch a movie on Netflix. To Natalie's relief, Chloe doesn't seem upset at all anymore. She reflects on the way her mom used to handle all her dad's infidelities. Maybe she'd judged her too harshly all those years. In truth, it wasn't all bad growing up. They had some good times, too, especially after her dad won the World Series of Poker. It wasn't as big a deal then as it is today, but it was still something special. There was money, prestige, and both her parents were the happiest she'd ever seen them. Her dad was home all the time, and she and Lindsay honestly believed their lives had changed for the better. It didn't last long, but it was still one of Natalie's fondest childhood memories.

When the movie is over, and after she helps tuck Chloe into bed, Natalie finds Lindsay and thanks her for turning things around during dinner. "I swear, I could almost kill Peter! I don't know what he was thinking, telling Chloe about the fight with Lena."

Her sister's eyes narrow. "Oh, I know what he was doing. He was trying to work the whole thing to his advantage."

Natalie is quiet as she considers Lindsay's words. "I don't want things to get ugly between us, but he's making that hard."

"Face it, divorce is ugly."

"I know." Natalie gets up to leave and then lingers in the doorway. "Do you remember back when Dad won the World Series?"

"Of course."

"That was the best time, wasn't it?"

Lindsay's face softens. "Yeah, that was pretty great."

Later, when Natalie is lying in the guest bedroom staring at the ceiling, she reflects on her own life. *Are my best times over?* She considers Lindsay's diet question. Part of her wants to start a diet, but part of her is afraid of all those past failures.

After that veggie burger, she didn't give in to her usual late night snacking and even ate her popcorn without butter. She still feels kind of hungry, but remembers reading somewhere once that it's good to go to bed slightly hungry.

Can I do this? She thinks of Peter and Lena together. Lena with her sexy body and her long blonde hair. The way she sneered at Natalie, as if she were nothing.

A grim determination comes over Natalie.

I'm hungry, but it's for a lot more than food this time.

THE NEXT MORNING Natalie sets up an appointment with a divorce lawyer. It's time for her to get her act together and be smart about things.

Leaning back in her chair, she feels surprisingly clearheaded. She's sitting in La Dolce Vita's small back office. There's a desk with a notebook computer on it they use to keep track of expenses and payroll. Her eyes stop on the binder where they keep all the letters and other correspondence having to do with their lease. She thinks about Espresso Breve's real name. Anthony Novello.

It really is an odd coincidence.

Curiously, she reaches over and grabs the binder. They've been sending their landlord and his lawyer letters and financial statements, showing them how well they're doing. Every response has been curt. He said he didn't believe La Dolce Vita could afford both the price of remodeling the space next door along with the accompanying increase in rent. It doesn't make sense, as if he's trying to hold them back on purpose. Meanwhile the space next to them has been empty for months, so surely he's losing money?

Natalie finds the letters and immediately opens one, scanning down to the signature. It says 'A. Novello.' She checks each one and they're all signed the same.

Is it possible that A. Novello is Espresso Breve?

When she finds Blair, she's in the kitchen piping a three-tiered wedding cake with brown fondant and delicate white petal dots.

"That looks fantastic," Natalie says.

Blair shrugs.

Natalie sighs. Even though Blair is younger, Natalie has found her to be a level-headed and solid business partner. She's never regretted teaming up with her. Unfortunately, Blair is also an obsessive perfectionist who is way too hard on herself.

"What happened with that young couple who came in earlier? I noticed they didn't look happy."

Blair wipes her forehead with the back of her arm. "I know. I had to send them to Markoff's." Markoff's was a bakery in Seattle specializing in wedding cakes. Blair used to work there before she and Natalie opened La Dolce Vita. "I hate to turn business away, but we're bulging at the seams. The fridge is full. I have no place to stuff another large cake."

"Speaking of which, why don't you take a look at these?" Natalie holds up the letters.

Blair puts her pastry bag down and takes her gloves off. "What is it?"

"Just look at the signatures."

Flipping through the letters from their landlord and his attorney, Blair's brows go up and stay that way until she's seen them all. "I can't believe it. Do you think it's really the same guy? It makes no sense."

"I know one way to find out."

"What's that?"

Natalie takes the letters back from Blair. "Confront him. Next time he comes in, we need to ask him if he's our landlord."

"I suppose you're right." Blair picks up her plastic gloves and flips them back and forth absentmindedly. "I don't want it to be him. I hate the thought he's in here all the time and yet won't let us have the space next door. He must be a jerk."

"It's a distinct possibility."

"So, are you going to ask him?"

"*Me?*" Natalie is startled. "I thought maybe you could ask him, since you already sold him that cake."

"I know, let's both ask. It'll be harder for him to squirm out of it."

Natalie agrees. "Good idea. Plus, if we go down in flames, it will be together."

Chapter Six

Diet Plan: Non-fat lattes. Go to bed
hungry.

Exercise Plan: Elliptical every weekday.
Weekends? Let's not get crazy. You sure
hope humiliation burns calories.

*T*HINGS ARE BUSY at work, but she and Blair remember to keep an eye out for Anthony. A few weeks pass and there's no sign of him. Luckily, they have Carlos manning the front and he's as good as any early warning system.

Meanwhile, Natalie meets with a divorce lawyer who tells her she and Peter need to draw up a formal separation agreement. That way there are no misunderstandings about the house or Chloe. Peter balks after he reviews the paperwork she faxed to his lawyer's office.

"I'm not going to knock before I enter my own house," he tells her over the phone. "Why should I do that?"

"You moved out. Or maybe you'd like to give me a key to where you're living now, so I can come and go as I please."

"Don't be absurd. Besides, it's not my place, it's Lena's."

Natalie tries to rein in her temper. "Look, do you want to move forward with this divorce or not? You can't have it both ways."

Peter sighs as if he's being put upon in the worst manner. "Fine. I'll knock, but don't change the locks. There's no point in that."

He agrees to have Chloe one night a week and every other weekend. The agreement feels surreal to Natalie, but she's glad it's in writing. What's also becoming clear to her is she's going to have to buy out Peter's half of the house. Now, more than ever, she could use the income boost that expanding the bakery would provide. She makes a decent living, but not nearly as much as Peter's dental practice.

She's in the back kitchen putting the finishing touches on a chocolate truffle cake when Blair comes up to her. The cake smells delicious, but Natalie ignores it, still holding strong with her diet. It's been over a month now. The longest she's ever stuck with it. She's been using the elliptical every night, too, and has even started eyeing the row of shiny weights, wondering if she should give them a try.

"He's here finally," Blair tells her. "Looking as hot as ever, I might add."

Natalie finishes the last rosette and puts down her piping bag. She doesn't need to ask who "he" is. There's a bowl of chocolate shavings beside her that she starts to sprinkle on top of the cake.

Blair watches her. "There's someone with him, though. I'm guessing it's his girlfriend. Do you think we should still confront him?"

"Definitely."

Blair nods. "Good, I agree. And if it turns out he's our landlord, I'm going to offer him my body in sacrifice. Actually, even if he's not our landlord I'll offer him my body in celebration."

"That's big of you," Natalie's tone is dry, "but what about the girlfriend?"

"She's pretty, but how could he resist this?" Blair sweeps a regal hand in front of herself. With her long auburn waves and hazel eyes, she looks like she should be married to an English prince.

"You're right. I think you should offer yourself to him lounging on a fancy cake platter with a side of whipped cream."

Blair laughs. "I can work with that." She walks over to the mirror by the back door and fluffs her hair out. "I'd better get some lipstick. Do you want some?"

"No, that's all right." Natalie picks up the truffle cake and takes it into the back fridge. On the way out, she sees a bowl of whipped cream that Carlos made to use for coffee drinks. She remembers Anthony's tan hands and imagines him dipping a masculine finger into the whipped cream, painting it on her, then bending over to lick it off her skin. Her breath catches. *Wow.*

AS THEY APPROACH Anthony's table, Natalie can see Blair is right. There is an attractive young woman sitting across from him. And judging by the way she's smiling and making eyes, they're definitely involved.

It's Blair who speaks to him first. "Excuse me—I'm sorry to interrupt."

Both Anthony and the woman look up, though he's the one who speaks. "Yes?"

"Your name is Anthony Novello, right?" Blair continues.

He nods. "I know you, don't I?"

Natalie steps forward and blurts out, "Are you the landlord of this building?"

She watches the surprise register on his handsome face. "Yes, I am." His eyes linger on her with a glimmer of confusion, but then go back to Blair.

"Anthony!" The young woman sitting across from him giggles. "You own this building? What other secrets are you hiding?"

He shrugs. "It's not exactly a secret."

"But, like, wow—you're a landlord?"

Natalie examines his girlfriend, curious about the kind of a woman who attracts a man like this. She's probably in her mid-twenties, with large brown eyes and a mouth that's glossed up in a flattering shade of pink. Her blonde hair is pulled back into a stylishly messy ponytail. There are flashes of gold everywhere—ears, neck, wrists, and hands. She's wearing more jewelry than a gypsy fortune teller, though Natalie has to admit it doesn't look bad. She manages to pull it off. Despite the strong aroma of coffee and baked goods in the air, Natalie can still make out her perfume, which is something floral with a kick of patchouli.

Anthony glances across at the giggling girlfriend, but then his eyes go back to Blair and Natalie, who in contrast are not smiling.

"What's your problem with us taking over the space next door?" Natalie asks pointedly.

"You want the space next door?"

"Yes, of course. We've sent you a bunch of letters laying out our financial situation, but your response is always the same. You tell us we can't have it, but you never tell us why."

Anthony takes in her words and then nods slowly. "I do remember what you're talking about. Your financial information didn't work out, though. My attorney sent you a letter explaining it all." His voice has a note of finality.

The giggler starts moaning. "O.M.G.! This red velvet cake is amaaazing! Have you tried this, Anthony?"

"No, I haven't."

"I'm going to give you a bite. You've got to try this!"

"That's all right, Justine. I'm good." He waves her away.

"Oh, come on, just one bite." She leans forward and holds the fork up to his mouth so he's forced to eat it.

"Isn't it heaven?"

Anthony chews and swallows. "It's too sweet."

Natalie's eyes widen in disbelief. Did he just describe her red velvet cake as too sweet?

Justine turns to Natalie and Blair. "Anthony only likes Italian pastries. Isn't that crazy? You guys are amaaazing bakers. Seriously!"

"Thank you," Natalie says, glaring at Anthony. *Too sweet. I'll show him too sweet. My red velvet is perfection.*

"That cake is one of our biggest sellers," Blair informs him.

He looks mildly surprised. "It might become your biggest seller if you cut back on the sugar."

Blair looks at Natalie and rolls her eyes as if to say—can you believe this guy?

"What do you mean, our financial information doesn't work out?" Natalie asks him.

"It means, I took all your data into consideration and the numbers were not in your favor. I'm sorry," he adds as an afterthought.

It's clear he's done talking about this, but Natalie and Blair don't move. "Look, no offense, but we need more than that," Natalie tells him. "A lot more."

"Definitely," Blair agrees. "This is our livelihood. You can't just say the numbers don't work and expect us to accept that."

Anthony takes a sip from his espresso breve as he considers the two of them. "Tell you what," he puts down his cup, "how about we set up a meeting and I can show you exactly what I'm talking about?"

Blair looks at Natalie, who nods. "That would work."

They set up a time to meet the following morning at seven, before La Dolce Vita opens.

When she and Blair are back in the kitchen, Natalie pours herself a glass of water. "That was interesting," she says, leaning against the counter. "I'm not sure what to make of him."

"Gosh, I think it's amaaazing that he's our landlord. Don't you think that's amaaazing?"

Natalie laughs. "You sound just like her."

"Why do guys who look like that always go for women who are nitwits?"

"Uh, maybe because she's gorgeous?"

"Skinny with big boobs. I guess that's every guy's type."

"I suppose so." Natalie frowns. "Do you think it's possible my red velvet is too sweet?"

Blair gets an incredulous expression on her face. "Please, your red velvet is *perfection*."

"That's what I always thought."

"Don't listen to Mr. Your-Numbers-Don't-Add-Up. He may be hot, but clearly, he's no genius. I can't wait to hear how he explains this to us tomorrow."

THE NEXT MORNING as Natalie rolls out dough for tangerine currant scones, surrounded by the scent of cinnamon from the apple turnovers fresh from the oven, she keeps going over the meeting planned with their recently unveiled landlord. Despite his criticism of her red velvet cake, he clearly likes La Dolce Vita, since he's a regular customer. She's genuinely curious as to what his reasons are for not letting them expand.

Before she's ready to load everything into her van, she heads upstairs to the bathroom and dabs moisturizer on her face and puts a little concealer under her eyes. Even though she knows it doesn't make much difference, she still decides to take extra care with her appearance. When she pulls her hair back, she uses a small mirror to make sure her ponytail looks a little disheveled, trying to imitate the messy style she sees so many women wearing.

She slips into a clean pair of black work pants and notices they don't seem as tight. *Is it possible that I've already lost weight?*

The idea startles her. She's been snacking a lot less and trying to go to bed hungry every night. Plus, she uses the elliptical every day when she comes home.

When she looks at herself in the closet's full-length mirror though, she still sees the same plain overweight Natalie. For a moment, she feels let down by the lack of change, but then she pushes the thought aside. *If that bitch Lena can do it, so can I. I'm every bit as disciplined as she is.* She even thinks of Justine, the ditzy blonde with Anthony. *Granted, I'm ten years older than her, but so what? Lena is at least that much older than me.*

She rubs lip balm on her mouth from the small container she keeps on her nightstand. Her lips are on the full side and have a tendency to get dry.

When she's finally dressed and ready to leave, she takes one last look at herself. It's ridiculous that she cares what Anthony thinks. From everything she can tell about him, he's just like her father—a too handsome for his own good womanizer. She suddenly remembers the birthday cake for Serena he'd picked up recently. Yet, he wasn't with her yesterday. Yesterday it was Justine. He probably has a half-dozen women at his beck and call. The thought annoys her so much that she purposely rips out her messy ponytail and brushes it back into her usual tightly controlled style.

I don't care what that Lothario thinks of me. All I care about is that he lets us expand our bakery.

By the time seven o'clock rolls around, Natalie and Blair have set up a table in front with an assortment of pastries. At two minutes after seven, a guy wearing a light gray suit is knocking on their front door, but it's not Anthony.

"Sorry, we're not open yet," Natalie tells him through the glass.

"I'm Anthony's lawyer." He holds up his briefcase as if that explains everything.

Blair comes over to investigate as Natalie unlocks the door.

"Hi, I'm Graham Spence," he says, holding out his hand to shake each of theirs. "I'm the attorney who manages Anthony's property."

Natalie recognizes his name immediately from the paperwork on their lease and lets him inside. "Thank you for coming."

"How did you know we were meeting this morning?" Blair asks.

"Anthony called me yesterday afternoon and asked if I could stop by. He said you had a problem with your lease and wanted to discuss it."

"It was nice of you to come on such short notice," she says, smiling, and Natalie thinks she detects a note of flirtation in Blair's voice.

He pushes his glasses up his long nose and grins enthusiastically. Between the grin and the blue bow tie, he reminds Natalie of a preppy college student, though he's obviously in his thirties.

"Would you like some coffee or tea?" Blair asks him sweetly.

"No, thanks, I don't drink coffee."

"How about some freshly baked pastries? We just pulled them out of the oven." And now Natalie is certain she's flirting, since Blair is rarely this accommodating with anyone.

"That sounds great. It smells fantastic in here."

Blair guides him over to the table while Natalie goes in back to grab her nonfat latte. The back kitchen is busy, with everyone scrambling before they open. Natalie stops to look at the list of cake orders that need to be filled today. Most of them are the usual restaurant orders. She sees a local catering company hired them to supply the cakes for a dinner party they're putting together tonight.

"Zoe, did you see the list here? We need to have these cakes done by two o'clock."

"I'm on it. I've got two hazelnuts in the oven and I'm almost done with the Mexican chocolate. The white ones are cooling."

Natalie nods and sips her coffee. "Okay, I'll take care of the rest when I'm done with my meeting."

Natalie inspects a few of the items on the cooling racks. There are some golden cherry tarts that look delicious. Natalie can feel her stomach rumbling. She and Chloe had fruit salad and non-fat yogurt for breakfast, but a cherry tart would really hit the spot.

She takes a deep breath and lets it out.

I'm hungry for more than food.

Pushing her tart craving aside, she goes back out to where Blair and Graham are chatting cozily. There's still no sign of Anthony.

She looks at the clock and sees it's almost quarter after seven.

Apparently, his time is more important than ours. So typical of men like that.

She sits down at the table with Blair and Graham, listening with half an ear to their conversation about Santosa Bistro up the street. Her fingers drum on her mug as she gets angrier by the second over Anthony's tardiness.

"Isn't that the bistro you bake rosemary bread for, Natalie?" Blair asks.

"Yes, it is. I know the chef from when we used to work together at a hotel downtown."

Santosa Bistro is in a lovely old brick building. The owner and head chef, Austin Santosa, is temperamental, but overall a good guy. They worked together long before he was a chef, back when he was a line cook and she was a pastry apprentice. *He really got lucky with that space.* It has a large kitchen with every upgrade imaginable. She imagines what she and Blair could do with a space like that. They'd add a few savory items to their menu, plus a small assortment of artisan breads. Not to mention the increase in cakes and other pastries they could sell. No more turning away customers.

She glances at the clock. It's nearly twenty after seven now, and there's still no sign of Anthony.

"Is he always this late?" Natalie asks Graham.

He gives her a lawyerly smile. "I'm sure he'll be here shortly."

"I hope so, because I have work to do."

"I understand." He looks over her shoulder and his face registers relief. "Actually, here's the man right now."

Natalie hears the front door jingle and, when she turns, sure enough Anthony is coming through, wearing navy jeans and a green sweater that contrasts nicely with his dark hair. The sight of him makes her pulse jump.

I'm not attracted to him. I don't like gorgeous men who can't bother to show up on time.

Anthony pulls the strap of his crossbody satchel over his head, removing it as he walks to their table and sits down across from her. Natalie gets a whiff of sandalwood and something else—something purely male that's all his own. He smells so good she wonders what it would be like to bury her face in his neck and breathe him in.

I don't care how good he smells.

"Hope I didn't miss anything," Anthony says. He flashes that boyish grin and Natalie is momentarily disarmed. She imagines him as a child, winning everybody over with that smile.

She's nervous, but concentrates on how annoyed she is instead.

"We were just talking about how late you are," Natalie tells him.

"Oh?" Anthony's grin falters as he looks around the table at the others to see if she's joking.

"We've been waiting for twenty minutes," she continues in a stern voice. "I really don't appreciate that. Maybe you don't run on an actual schedule, but I do."

His boyish grin is completely gone now, and Natalie feels a pang of regret for having been the one to remove it.

"I didn't realize I was that late," he says stiffly. "I had a short meeting before this one."

Yeah, right, I wonder what her name is? "Well, maybe if you looked at a clock—"

"Would you like some coffee, Anthony?" Blair asks, interrupting her.

"That would be great. An espresso breve, if you don't mind."

"I'll be right back," Blair says, and as she stands up, her eyes drill into Natalie. *Shut up!* she mouths.

Natalie knows Blair is right. She needs to be nice. No matter how much she may dislike Anthony, they still need to convince him to lease them that space.

She puts a fake smile on and watches the two men across from her.

Blair comes back with Anthony's espresso breve. "Thanks." He sees the plate of pastries and using a napkin takes one of the chocolate chunk cookies.

My cookies, Natalie notices. Apparently, *those* aren't too sweet for him. "Shall we finally get started now?" she says, leaning forward impatiently. Blair kicks her under the table, but she ignores it.

Anthony glances up. "Sure, although I'm a little confused. I think maybe we need to go over introductions again. Obviously, I'm Anthony and you both met Graham here." He looks at Blair. "I know you're the owner, it's Blair, right?"

"Yes," Blair nods. "And this—"

"But why are *you* here?" Anthony cuts her off, looking directly at Natalie.

"Me? I'm one of the owners, too. Blair and I are business partners."

Anthony raises his eyebrows in surprise. "What's your name?"

"Natalie Anderson."

"You're one of the owners?"

"Yes, I said that already, didn't I?"

"But, I thought . . . are you a baker?"

Natalie tries not to let her irritation show. "Of course I'm a baker."

"That doesn't make any sense."

"I baked that cookie you're eating," she snaps. "In fact, it's my recipe."

He still has a perplexed expression. "But you didn't even know how to fill out a cake order that time I came in."

Oh, no.

A tidal wave of embarrassment washes over her, and if she could drown herself in it she would. *Why did he have to remember that?* Even Blair is eyeing her curiously.

"You caught me on a bad day. That's all," she says tightly.

For a long moment Anthony doesn't reply, but she can feel his eyes on her. When he speaks, his voice has a bemused quality. "Is that right?"

Natalie's head is down, but she glances up at his tone. When she meets his gaze she can see the perceptiveness in his brown eyes. She lets out her breath. There's a sinking feeling in the pit of her stomach that she recognizes as humiliation.

Chapter Seven

Diet Plan: Grit your teeth. Pastries can't get in your mouth that way.

Exercise Plan: Elliptical until you're dripping sweat. Discover there are layers to humiliation. Just when you think you've touched bottom there is always one more.

"SO YOU'RE THE one who makes these cookies?" Anthony takes a bite. "They're good."

He watches Natalie swallow as her face grows a brighter shade of red. Even her ears are red. He'd chuckle if her embarrassment didn't look so painful.

The truth is, she was busting his balls about running a few minutes late today, and so maybe he's enjoying her embarrassment.

Just a little.

"We're scratch bakers and Natalie creates most of our master recipes," Blair tells him. "She's one of the few bakers I consider talented enough to work with."

Blair grins over at Natalie, who still looks like she'd commit hara-kiri if he so much as handed her a butter knife.

He suspects Natalie isn't the kind of woman used to feeling embarrassment about anything. Ball-busters seldom are.

Anthony takes another bite of his cookie and chews thoughtfully. Decides to cut her some slack. "I have to agree with your partner here, Natalie. These are the best chocolate chip cookies I've ever tasted."

"Chocolate chunk—" she starts to correct him, but then stops herself. "Thank you," she replies, not quite meeting his eyes. "It took me a while to get them just right." She picks up her coffee and takes a sip and he can see she's on more comfortable ground now.

Anthony leans back in his chair and studies her. Women usually like him. Although it's clear Natalie doesn't. She's attracted to him though, and her attraction is pissing her off. He's tempted to get a rise out of her again, but decides not to bother.

Plain, plump, and persnickety.

Anthony knows the type and they're typically humorless. Best to just get on with the meeting.

"I know you sent me all your financial information," he says, speaking to both women. "Let me show you what I did with it." He reaches for his bag and pulls out his laptop, moving his coffee aside so he can place the computer on the table in front of him. "Basically, I have financial software I use for all my tenants. It's a program I wrote myself called *A Conti Fatti*." His laptop is in sleep mode, so it only takes a few seconds to bring up his business software and find their file. "Graham is already familiar with it, but let me show you two how it works."

After opening the file for La Dolce Vita, Anthony brings up the page that shows the financial overview of the bakery. He then turns the laptop toward Natalie and Blair.

They both lean forward in their chairs, focusing on his computer.

"What I've done is create this software that takes in all the financial variables involved in running a small business," Anthony explains. "It tells me whether or not you can afford your lease."

He brings up some pie charts to show them what he's talking about. "I created this to help screen my tenants, and then I let Graham here handle the paperwork and all the rest of it."

Natalie looks perplexed. "But I still don't understand why you won't lease us the space next door."

Anthony turns the computer around and brings up their profit and loss page. "According to this, you can't afford it. In order to inhabit that space you'd need to first remodel, plus your monthly lease would double."

"We've already gotten bank approval for the remodeling loan, though," Blair puts in. "And we have savings, too."

"I know," says Anthony. "But it would still be a bad investment on my part."

Natalie frowns. "That space next door is empty and has been for months. Aren't you losing money?"

"Yes, but all that information is accounted for. My software tells me it's safer to find a new tenant than allow you to rent that space and have to abandon it. Believe me, I've included every variable, and it isn't a good idea."

He watches the women as they study the computer screen. Blair, the redhead, is leaning on one elbow as she reads. The ball-buster is facing forward with a scowl on her face. She licks her lips in what appears to be frustration and picks up her coffee mug.

The movement catches his eye and when she puts the mug down, he's still watching.

Anthony's eyes widen as he focuses on her mouth. It's shockingly sensual. Even with the scowl. What's a mouth like that doing on a stern woman like this? Full lips with a natural pout and a pink flush that clearly isn't makeup. From what he can tell, she isn't wearing any makeup at all. Her skin is pretty and he decides she doesn't really need it. Her hair is light brown and pulled back in a severe ponytail.

He scans her body quickly, but there isn't much to see. She's sitting, but even standing he suspects he couldn't see much. Her clothes are black and baggy and he figures she's trying to hide that she's overweight.

Natalie suddenly looks at him, sensing his perusal.

He grins and surprisingly her scowl goes away. That erotic mouth looks even better. Such perfect cherry lips. He wonders what she looks like when she smiles. A real smile, not the fake ones she's been giving.

"So if I begged a little, do you think you'd give me your cookie recipe?" he asks.

He continues to smile, but she doesn't smile back. In fact, the scowl has returned and is deeper than ever.

Dude, she probably never smiles.

NATALIE FROWNS. *DID he really just ask me for my cookie recipe? Like I'd hand it out?*

She knew he was looking her over, too. *He's probably comparing me to his harem of women who all look like variations of Justine—a cake pop with breasts and gold earrings.*

If that's the measure he's using then she knows she falls short. Very short. *Not that I care anyway.*

Her eyes go back to his computer and the pie charts and graphs he's showing them. It all seems like a bunch of nonsense. And to think, this nonsense is the reason they can't expand La Dolce Vita.

"What about all the business we turn away? How is that factored into your program?" Natalie asks.

Anthony meets her eyes. *Was he just looking at my mouth?* She licks her lips, hoping she doesn't have food on her face.

It takes him a moment to process her question. "I didn't know you turned business away. How often does that happen?"

Natalie looks over at Blair, who shrugs. "Every day. I have a waiting list for my wedding cakes," Blair explains.

"We've been approached by various caterers and restaurants to supply desserts, but I've had to turn many of them down, since we don't have the baking capacity." Natalie sighs. "It's frustrating."

Anthony's brows knit together as he chews on this. "Very interesting. Did you know about this, Graham?"

"No, this is the first I've heard of it."

Anthony reaches down into his satchel and pulls out a black case. When he opens it, Natalie sees it contains glasses. Thick black ones, like Clark Kent. He turns the computer back toward himself, squinting a little before putting on the glasses.

She finishes the last of her latte, trying not to stare at Anthony as he clicks on his keyboard and then starts typing rapidly.

Graham is asking them if they've kept track of any of the business they've had to turn down. "Do you have numbers we can look at?"

"I can show you the waiting list for my wedding cakes, if that helps. I'm not sure if Natalie has written anything down, have you?" Blair turns to Natalie.

"No, though I could probably come up with an estimate." She's still watching Anthony.

The glasses slip down from his nose and he pushes them up a few times. He looks like a geek. The only thing missing from those oversize black glasses is a piece of duct tape holding them together.

As she watches him squinting at his computer, she has a revelation.

My God. He *is* a geek.

Granted, an absurdly handsome one.

"What do you do for a living, Anthony?" Natalie finds herself asking curiously.

"I'm an astronomer," he says, still typing, not bothering to look up.

Natalie opens her mouth. It wasn't at all what she expected him to say. Although, now that she sees him with his geek paraphernalia, it doesn't seem that far-fetched.

Blair is still talking to Graham about some of the business she's had to turn away, but when she hears Anthony's comment, her attention is caught. "You're really an astronomer?"

"That's right," Anthony murmurs, focused on his computer.

"You sure don't look like one."

"What do I look like?" he asks, still concentrating.

Graham grins. "Professor Heartthrob, or at least that's what I think she's trying to say."

"You're a *professor?*" Natalie asks. For some reason the notion is alarming. Even though she knew he wasn't really a model or a movie star, she never expected this.

"Meet Professor Novello," Graham tells them with a flourish. "Anthony teaches astrophysics at the University of Washington."

"Wow," Blair says. "I never would have guessed that. You look so young."

"I'm not tenured yet," Anthony tells her.

Blair is still studying him. "I'll bet your classes are jam-packed."

Graham laughs. "I'd say every pretty girl on campus is suddenly interested in astronomy."

Natalie expects Anthony to make some flippant remark about 'fighting them off with a stick,' or 'more than he can handle,' but he doesn't say anything.

Instead, he clears his throat. "Would you mind getting me your cake waiting list, Blair? I'd like to see it, if you don't mind."

"Uh, sure."

While she's in back getting the list, Natalie wonders if she's misjudged Anthony. Maybe he's not really a hound dog. As she's thinking this, she hears *Star Wars* music blasting from his cell phone. In context, that music is kind of cute.

"Hi, Nicole," Anthony answers. He listens, nodding for a moment and then chuckles. "Sure, that's no problem. Seven is fine. Okay, I'll see you tonight."

Graham meets Natalie's gaze and smiles. Neither of them says anything. Natalie somehow refrains from rolling her eyes.

Nicole? Justine? Serena? How does he keep track of them all? Professor or not, he's obviously exactly what she thought.

When Blair comes back, she hands Anthony the blue three-ring binder she keeps track of all her wedding cake orders with. When he opens it, she shows him the waiting list.

Anthony makes a note on his computer and then turns to both of them. "I thought I'd accounted for every variable, but you two pointed out something I hadn't considered. I'm going to enter this in and we'll see where we're at." He looks at Blair. "Would you mind adding the approximate price of each wedding cake on that list?"

Blair takes a seat across from Graham. "I can do that."

"And Natalie, would you start keeping track of any jobs you have to refuse as well? I'll need those numbers."

Natalie leans back in her chair and lets out a heavy sigh. "I suppose I could do that."

Anthony starts shutting down his computer. "Is there a problem?"

"The problem is I don't like it. The software, the pie charts—any of it."

He stiffens. "This is how I conduct my business."

"You come in here all the time, so you've seen with your own eyes how busy we are. Doesn't that count for anything?"

"No, it doesn't. I need hard numbers, not speculation."

She thinks about how as a single parent now she'll need more money to keep her house. "You're just wasting our time. We've already told you we're bursting at the seams and we turn away business every day. Who cares what the exact numbers are? We make more than enough in profits to pay for the lease on the space next door."

"I care." Anthony speaks in a cold voice. "You can think whatever you like. The fact remains that I own this building, so I'll be the one to decide whether I lease that space to you."

Natalie's eyes lock on to Anthony's. He's still wearing the nerd glasses and it gives him an owlish appearance. His eyes are intelligent and she can see she's made him angry.

"Come on, Natalie," Blair says. "I think we should at least give his method a try. And besides, it's not like we have a choice."

"I'd listen to her if I were you," Anthony says.

Natalie throws her hands in the air. "But this whole thing is ridiculous!"

"You want to hear ridiculous?" Anthony shoves his laptop back into his satchel. "I'll tell you ridiculous. You own a bakery called *La Dolce Vita* and you don't sell a single Italian pastry!"

When he pronounces La Dolce Vita he slides the words together, rounding the syllables in a way that makes her suspect he speaks fluent Italian.

"Then why do you bother to come here at all?" Natalie counters. "Especially if you dislike it so much! It can't be just because you own the building."

Anthony stops what he's doing and pushes his glasses on top of his head. He glances out the front window and then back to her. "Your espresso is excellent, I'll give you that."

Natalie can't help her nod of approval. She's very picky about coffee herself. "It's Lavazza. I have to special order it."

"I know, I recognize it." Which surprises Natalie. "And as I mentioned, those cookies of yours aren't half bad, either."

His compliment is a peace offering and she knows it. But she doesn't want a peace offering. She doesn't want his charm or humor. All she wants is his signature on a piece of paper that says they can expand, but he won't give it to her.

Anthony stands up and slips his satchel over his head, so the bag settles against his left hip. A lock of dark wavy hair has fallen across his forehead and Natalie tries not to notice he's the hottest college professor she's ever seen in her life.

He turns to Graham. "I think we're done here, aren't we?"

"Yes." Graham looks at Blair. "I'll call you later?"

She gives him a flirtatious smile. "Sounds good. We could check out Santosa's, if you like."

Natalie watches the two of them in amazement. Clearly, Blair and

Graham are making a love connection.

She glances over at Anthony and their eyes meet. Quickly they both look away from each other.

Don't worry, I don't want you either.

After the men leave, Natalie finds herself face-to-face with a furious Blair. "What the heck is wrong with you?" she yells. "Were you trying to piss Anthony off? Because that's exactly what you were doing!"

"He's being a jerk."

Blair gives her a level stare. "He's not the one being a jerk, Natalie."

"What are you saying?"

"I think you know."

"He was twenty minutes late and then all he has to show us is some dumb computer program. I'm sorry, but my life is not dictated by a computer algorithm." She crosses her arms.

Blair sighs. "Look, I'm not crazy about it either, but Graham says Anthony's not going to back down on this. Besides, I think he is trying to help us."

"I doubt it. All he cares about is cold facts. Didn't you hear him? He's Mr. Logic. And what's up with you and Graham, anyway?"

"Just dinner."

Natalie raises an eyebrow.

"Okay, so I kind of like him." She smiles a little. "He's cute, don't you think?"

"He's cute, but he's the enemy's lawyer."

Blair tilts her head. "You need to chill. Can you believe Anthony is a professor? Guess I was wrong about him."

"What do you mean?"

"When I said he was no genius. He teaches astrophysics, so he's obviously smart."

Natalie stands up. "I don't like him. And I don't care how smart he is. Some people are smart, but dumb as donuts." She looks at the clock and realizes she needs to get busy with those white chocolate truffle cakes. "Although," Natalie bites the corner of her lip, "I'm embarrassed to admit it, but he's right about one thing. With a name like La Dolce Vita, we should have some Italian pastries on our menu."

"HAVE YOU BEEN dieting?"

It's been a week since their meeting with Anthony, and Natalie is sitting at one of the counters in the back kitchen studying the notebook where she keeps all her master recipes, trying to find a good Italian dessert. She puts her book down and looks up at Carlos. Over the years people have sometimes asked her if she's losing weight, but it's always polite small talk she wishes they wouldn't bother with.

"I think I might have lost a little," she admits.

Carlos assesses her with a quick sweep from head to toe. "I can really see it, especially in your face. Plus your clothes look baggy."

"Really?" Natalie sits up a little straighter and smiles shyly. "I've been sort of dieting for a while now, though I didn't think it was noticeable to anyone."

"Oh, it's totally noticeable." He puts the empty cake plate he was carrying down near the large sink and walks back over to her. "Well, I guess this explains all those non-fat lattes."

"You're the first person to say anything. This is the longest I've ever stuck with a diet." She leans toward him confidingly. "It's been really tough. I'm worried I'm going to slip up, especially at work."

He lets out a sigh. "Tell me about it. Working in a bakery with all these carbs is complete torture."

Natalie is surprised. "But obviously you're not dieting. You're already thin."

"I'm not dieting per se, not to 'lose weight,'" he makes quotation marks in the air with his fingers, "but I've been trying to eat better. Ryan is a personal trainer and he's got me watching my carb intake. And let me tell you, he's a slave driver."

"Your boyfriend is a personal trainer?"

Carlos nods. "You didn't know that? I brought him to that picnic a few months ago."

Natalie vaguely remembers Ryan. A short, handsome young guy, who, as she recalls, did look remarkably fit.

"Of course, we'd just started dating then. He hadn't started putting me through my paces yet." Carlos laughs. "Now he's got me eating healthy and working out every day. I barely recognize myself!"

"I've been exercising, but all I've managed so far is the elliptical. I'm just not sure what else to do."

"You should give Ryan a call. I'm sure he can help you figure it out. He works at Lou's Gym downtown, but goes to clients' homes as well."

"Really?" Natalie had never imagined herself with a personal trainer before. It sounded like something reserved for celebrities or fitness fanatics. "Would I have to go to a gym?"

"Not if you don't want to. Hang on a second, I'm going to get you one of his cards." Carlos leaves for a moment and comes back with a business card. "He's really good and has all sorts of different clients."

"You said he's a slave driver, though?" Natalie takes the card and stares at it as if it might start ordering her to do push-ups this instant.

"Honey, he's tough, but he'll whip you into shape, too."

"I don't know."

Carlos shrugs. "No pressure. It's just something to consider. Especially if you get bored with the elliptical."

She nods. The truth is she's very bored with the elliptical and wants to learn how to use the other equipment in that fancy home gym. "Let me think about it. There's been a lot of stuff to deal with lately."

"That reminds me. How did that meeting go with Espresso Breve last week? Everyone's buzzing over it. We can't believe he owns this building and he's a professor."

"Believe me, Blair and I were just as surprised."

"Is it true he won't let you guys expand? He always seemed pretty nice."

Natalie scoffs. "Don't let his appearance fool you. He's totally full of himself."

"Really?"

The kitchen door swishes open behind them and Carlos looks up in surprise.

"He's got this stupid computer program that defies all common sense. It's unbelievable."

"Uh." There's an odd expression on Carlos's face. He starts to shake his head at Natalie then motions with his eyes above her.

"I hate to say it, but he's basically an asshole."

Carlos is shaking his head vigorously now and Natalie turns to see who's behind her.

Adrenaline spikes through her.

Anthony is standing there, and he doesn't look happy. His brown eyes meet hers. "Who's an asshole?"

"It's nobody," Carlos says quickly. "Just one of the delivery drivers."

Natalie sees that Anthony isn't listening to Carlos, though, and is staring directly at her. She knows she should take the lifeline Carlos has thrown her and tell him it's the delivery driver.

"It's you," she says, unable to stop herself. "You're the asshole."

The kitchen grows quiet behind them as Natalie's words carry.

Anthony's jaw tightens. "Is that so?"

She knows she's being wildly unprofessional. There's a strange recklessness coursing through her. It's as if an obnoxious alien has taken over her body.

"Why mince words?" she says. "You know where I stand."

His eyes remain locked on hers, and she's surprised to discover that he's difficult to read. Unlike their last meeting where he was obviously angry, today he's keeping it close to the vest. It fleetingly occurs to her that he'd be a good card player.

"Is this how you talk to all your customers?" he asks mildly. "I can't believe you have any left."

Her cheeks grow warm. "You're not a customer."

"Aren't I? I've spent plenty of money here, and as I recall, I bought a cake recently."

"Our customers don't want to put us out of business."

"That's not what I'm doing. I'm saving you from making a huge financial mistake."

Natalie shakes her head. "No, you're standing in the way of our success. Don't kid yourself about that."

"I never kid myself. And I'm never wrong."

Natalie rolls her eyes at his arrogance. Though she's surprised at the steel she senses from him. She glances over at Carlos, who is watching quietly. The whole kitchen appears to be listening in stunned silence, and Natalie gets an uneasy glimmer of the mortification she's going to feel when she reflects on this conversation later.

"What are you doing here?" she finally asks Anthony.

"I came by to get the numbers from you regarding the jobs you've turned down this week."

"You don't need to come into the kitchen for that."

"I was looking for you. This seemed like a reasonable place to check."

Embarrassed, Natalie realizes he's right and stands up. "I started a notebook. It's by the cash register."

"YOU KNOW, IT doesn't have to be this way between us," Anthony says when they're standing out front. He watches as Natalie searches for her notebook. He still can't believe she called him an asshole right to his face. Could she be any more unpleasant? He's dealt with tantrums from students and obnoxious colleagues, but few of them have ever insulted him so directly.

For a moment her eyes meet his and he sees a flicker of uncertainty, but then she looks down again.

"Here's the notebook," she says, holding it out.

He takes it from her and flips to the page with the list. It appears they've turned down two small catering jobs, though it doesn't look like much money was lost. If these are the kind of numbers she plans to convince him with, she's in for an unpleasant surprise.

"And there's no way you could have completed these jobs?" he asks.

Natalie gives him another one of her scathing looks. "Of course not. Do you think we turn down business on purpose?" She seems to think of something else for a second, but then continues to make her case, going on about their lack of ovens.

Anthony studies her as she talks. Her hair is pulled back into another severe ponytail with only a few gray hairs managing to spring free. It suits her stubborn personality.

He sneaks a peek at her body when she looks away. Like last time, she's wearing dark shapeless clothes, except today she has on a white apron dusted with flour and chocolate. It's hard to tell for sure, but he suspects she's curvaceous.

"Do you have everything you need?" Natalie asks, pursing her lips.

His attention returns to her face. And then there's that mouth. It still amazes him that an overbearing woman could have such a sensual mouth. He wonders what it would take to make it say nice things instead of calling him names. For a crazy instant, he imagines kissing Natalie. That would certainly put her mouth to good use. What would she do if he tried? Slap him or call him an asshole again. She'd acted so nervous around him last time that he'd figured she was attracted to him, but now he isn't so sure.

"So, have you decided to add any Italian pastries to the menu?" he asks.

Natalie doesn't reply, and he senses she might be embarrassed.

"Because I thought it was a good suggestion," he continues. "You guys should at least sell *Tiramisu*. It's one of my favorite desserts."

Her blue eyes widen, but she still doesn't say anything.

"My family is Italian, so I'd be happy to offer ideas. My biggest advice is to lay off all the sugar. Italian desserts aren't as overly sweet as your American ones." He adds that last part mostly to irritate her, and he can see it worked. She looks pissed again. *Good.* That's what she gets for calling him an asshole.

"You know, you're the only one who's ever complained about my cake being too sweet."

He shrugs. "Doesn't mean I'm wrong."

"And since Americans like sweet desserts, those are the kind I bake. I have to create recipes that sell, though if you continue to box us in it won't matter."

He opens his mouth to start lecturing again on how his program works, but then notices the dark circles under her eyes and worry lines on her forehead, and decides to back off. She looks tired and stressed. He recognizes all the signs of someone who's overworked, having seen plenty of it in his own family growing up.

"What do you for fun, Natalie?" he asks, suddenly curious about her.

"What?"

He repeats the question.

She blinks. "Fun?"

"Yeah."

She looks confused. The question appears to have stumped her.

"I bake," she finally says. "I like to create new recipes."

"That's still work. How do you relax?"

She bites her bottom lip and it catches his attention. He's always had a weakness for a pretty mouth. "I don't know. I watch movies. Especially *Star Wars* and *Lord of the Rings.*"

Anthony raises his eyebrows. "You're into *Star Wars?*"

"And *Lord of the Rings.*"

He takes this in, surprised. "Look, I really do have *La Dolce Vita's* best interest in mind. I know you don't believe me, but working with complex equations and analyzing data is what I do best."

Natalie's expression hardens. "I need to get back to work now, if you don't mind."

"I'll leave you to it, then." He turns to leave.

"Wait a minute. Don't you want to write this stuff down?" She holds up her notebook.

"Don't need to. I've already got it memorized."

Natalie appears skeptical, a reaction he's gotten a lot over the years. "You seriously memorized everything I just showed you?"

"I did."

She studies him for a moment. "Prove it." She holds the notebook close to her chest, as if he had x-ray vision and could somehow see through the front cover.

Anthony brings up the data in his mind. "The first job wanted four cakes and two dozen cupcakes and the second job wanted six cakes." He rattles off all the figures she gave him down to the last penny. "Obviously, that's not the whole story though. I'll be able to tell you the net profit after I put these figures into my program."

She opens her book and checks his figures. "That's quite a party trick. Do you have a photographic memory?"

"Sort of. I'm good with numbers."

"That's impressive, but . . . I don't know. I think you should still write everything down to be on the safe side."

"I just showed you why I don't need to do that."

"You might forget after you leave here and then what?"

"I'm not going to forget." *It's just the cost of a bunch of cakes.* He'd be embarrassed if he couldn't remember something that simple. "Trust me, if I can remember pages of differential equations, I can easily remember the cost of a few cupcakes."

"It's two dozen cupcakes. You're already forgetting."

Face it, she's impossible.

Anthony lets out his breath. "You know what? I'm done. You can deal with Graham from now on."

"Fine! I'm done, too."

Their eyes meet and Anthony watches as she slams the notebook down and marches back into the kitchen.

Chapter Eight

Diet Plan: Fruits and veggies. Salads.
Small square of dark chocolate. A large
scoop of self-discipline.

Exercise Plan: Elliptical twice a day,
every day, including Saturday.
Yeah, baby!

"YOU WANT ME to do *what?*" Natalie has just arrived home and is unpacking some tangerine currant scones she'd set aside for Chloe and Lindsay, though she can't stop thinking about how horrible she acted toward Anthony.

"I think you should come to my boxing class tonight," Lindsay says.

Natalie listens as Lindsay starts talking about a new class she wants her to try and how Blair has already agreed to come as well. "But you already know how to box and I've never done it in my life."

"This class is for all levels. There are a couple different teachers and I hear they really kick ass. It should be great!"

Natalie tries to imagine herself in a room full of women with as much verve and energy as her sister. She'd be the big slow moose in a group of sprightly antelopes. "It doesn't sound like something I'd enjoy."

"Come on. It's Blair's first time, too, plus you need to get out more. All you ever do is work."

"Look, I don't want to go, okay? Stop asking."

Lindsay raises an eyebrow. "What's eating you?"

"I had a horrible day. I just want to sit home tonight with a glass of wine and put it behind me."

"Is Lena still hassling you? Because I would be happy to go over there and talk to her."

After the fight at the yoga studio, Lena started sending Natalie nasty text messages. She's not even sure how Lena got her cell number. She must have stolen it off Peter's phone. Natalie was tempted to show the texts to

71

Peter, but figured there was no point, since he'd just take Lena's side anyway. She's been trying to ignore them. Initially the texts were threatening her with assault charges and a restraining order, which seemed ironic to Natalie. Why bother with texting at all? But recently, they've changed and are now dumb platitudes about "moving on" and "finding peace," as if she wanted to hear any of that crap from Lena.

"I called my landlord an asshole to his face today."

"Wow, really?" Lindsay grabs a scone from the pile and puts it on a napkin. "The super-hot one?"

"What's wrong with me?" Natalie sits down on the stool next to Lindsay. She reaches for one of the scones, but then stops herself. She eyes the bowl of fruit she's started leaving on the counter, but decides to get a pickle from the fridge instead. Low calorie and zero fat—dill pickles have become her new best friend. "First that awful fight with Lena last month, and now this? I don't feel like myself at all. I was so rude to him. Not to mention, the whole kitchen heard me."

"What did he do?"

"He kept his cool." Natalie describes how well Anthony handled it and that his body language gave nothing away. "It was kind of impressive, really."

"Wow, most guys would have been furious."

"I know, I had to admire his self-control." Natalie takes a bite of pickle and thinks about his reaction. "It occurred to me he'd make a good card player. Plus, it turns out he's some kind of math whiz."

"Really?"

"I can't believe I acted so horrible, though. And now I'm going to have to apologize."

Lindsay smiles. "Why don't you invite him over for a hand of strip poker? Then you can apologize the right way—with a few extra sprinkles on top."

Natalie lets out a laugh. "Trust me, I'm the last person in the world he'd want to play strip poker with!"

"You never know." Lindsay shrugs. "How many cute guys do you have in your life right now? Besides, I don't think you should be so hard on yourself. You've been going through a lot."

"That's no excuse for bad behavior, and I need this guy on our side. Blair is going to kill me when she finds out what happened today."

"This may sound like a dumb question, but have you two considered moving to another location entirely? I mean, what if the hot landlord never leases you that space?"

Natalie sighs. "We have. We even hired a real estate agent to keep an eye out for us, but nothing good has come up. At least, nothing as good as where we are now."

The problem is La Dolce Vita is in the perfect location. It's close enough to campus to get the university crowd, yet far enough that they also get plenty of business from the neighborhoods nearby. Santosa's, the bistro down the street, was the only spot Natalie could picture that was better than theirs, but of course they weren't going anywhere.

"Well," Lindsay says. "It sounds to me like you've had the sort of day where throwing a few punches might feel pretty good."

"Maybe."

"And you've been exercising regularly, too. Don't think I haven't noticed. Everyone's noticed you've lost weight. In fact, I think it's time to go shopping and get some new clothes. Those are practically falling off you."

Natalie's mouth opens in surprise. "Do you really think so?" She's noticed that she has to tighten her belt on everything, but has been too afraid to weigh herself, worried she'll only be disappointed.

"It's true. So come to that class with us tonight. Besides more weight, what have you got to lose?"

My pride, my dignity, my self-respect. Natalie thinks of all the stress she's going through now that Peter is gone and realizes she's already lost those things.

"All right," she sighs. "What time is this class?"

"Seven tonight, and bring a water bottle." Lindsay gets up to leave. "I'm going to go work in my studio for a while, but I'll text you the class location."

After she's gone, Natalie fishes in the jar for another pickle. An image of Anthony's face comes to mind, the way it looked right after she called him an asshole. For an instant, she did sense a flicker of something from him. Probably anger, but she wasn't entirely sure. Was it possible she hurt his feelings? *I hope not. Even he doesn't deserve that.*

Her cell phone chirps and Natalie reaches for it, figuring it's Lindsay texting her with the location of the boxing class. She frowns when she sees it's from Lena.

Be the butterfly emerging from its cocoon for the first time. See the world as new!

Natalie rolls her eyes. Before she can stop herself, she texts back.

Save your platitudes for a fortune cookie.

Her phone chirps again.

Those who judge will one day be judged themselves. Accept your life. Live love!

Natalie stares at her phone. Seriously?

STOP SENDING ME THESE STUPID MESSAGES.

Hopefully that will put an end to it.

I feel sorry for you, Natalie. Peter told me your heart is closed and it's true. Open your heart! See the beauty in the world!

Aaargh. What on earth does Peter see in this woman? Besides being thin and gorgeous, it's clear she's insane. This whole thing is infuriating. Natalie thinks about the boxing class and finds herself looking forward to it.

"ALL RIGHT LADIES, give me fifty!"

Natalie groans. She's on the floor with the rest of the class, doing a second set of push-ups. They've done three sets of jumping jacks, lunges, and squats. She's already half-dead and they haven't even finished the warm up yet.

The class is in a small gym only a couple of miles north of La Dolce Vita. Natalie got there early, but waited in her car, wondering why she ever let Lindsay talk her into doing something this crazy. She's never been good at exercise classes, or even gym class in high school. She's basically a klutz.

Watching the people come and go, she was surprised to see they looked pretty normal. Maybe it wouldn't be so bad. And Lindsay was right about at least getting out of the house. Sitting at home every night watching *Lord of the Rings* or *Star Wars* is probably a little pathetic. Ironically, it's the one good thing about Peter leaving. He never liked watching any kind of fantasy or sci-fi, and now she can watch whatever she wants.

When she saw Blair heading toward the entrance, she figured it was time to get out. All hope that Blair hadn't heard about what happened with Anthony earlier was dashed when she saw the stormy expression on her face.

"I take it you heard?" Natalie asked, biting her lip. "I didn't mean—"

"Don't talk to me about it." Blair held up her hand to cut her off. "Seriously. Just fix it."

"I will. I promise!"

"You better."

The two of them walked into the gym together. They found Lindsay off to the side, flirting with some guy who had a thick tribal tattoo on one arm and a kaleidoscope of ink that ran down the other.

"Call me," she heard Lindsay say before she sashayed over to join them. "Hey, I'm glad you guys made it."

"Who's that?" asked Natalie.

"Just a friend. A *new* friend." She gave them both a mischievous smile.

"What about Oliver?"

Lindsay shrugged. "What about him? We're still together. I figure it's a good idea to have a guy or two in the wings, you know, just in case."

Natalie doesn't say anything. Lindsay was just like their father, though she'd never admit it.

Blair was looking around the gym in admiration. "Check out some of the guns in this place. It's like I've died and gone to heaven."

Lindsay laughed. "Didn't I mention that? It's one of the side benefits of going to a boxing gym."

Natalie was confused at first. Guns? Then she realized they were talking about guys' arms. She suddenly felt like a dork. This wasn't her scene. It was some kind of singles gym and she wasn't single. With a jolt, it struck her.

I am single.

Being discreet, she glanced around the gym, curious to see some of these 'guns' for herself. There were definitely some nice-looking men here, and to her surprise, some of them were looking her way.

Adrenaline shot through her. *Are they checking me out?* But then one of the guys' eyes met hers and looked away with disinterest.

It's not me, it's Blair and Lindsay who are drawing attention.

She cringed. Pretended not to care. A flood of familiar emotions she hadn't experienced in years came over her. The memory of what it was like being the invisible sister next to Lindsay's vivacious beauty. The surprise on people's faces when they met her. She'd learned to ignore it when she was younger, and after she got married it hadn't mattered anymore.

Now she was the invisible sister once again.

"Come on, you two," Lindsay said. "Let's go. I think they're starting class."

FORTY MINUTES LATER, Natalie is struggling to do another push-up. With relief, she notices that a couple of other people are struggling, too, so at least she isn't the only one suffering.

Finally, their instructor, Jessica, tells everyone to take a break and grab some water.

Since the three of them brought their own bottles, they sit off to the side and cool down.

"Wow," Blair says, "this class is already kicking my butt and we haven't even started boxing yet."

"I know, isn't it great?" Lindsay puts the cap back on her water bottle.

Natalie leans against the wall and tries to catch her breath. "I hope at least one of you knows CPR. I may need it before the night is over."

"Don't worry, just take it at your own pace," Lindsay tells her. "Like I said before, this is for all levels."

"Speaking of which," Blair looks over at the wall clock. "What time does it finish? I have a late dinner date with Graham tonight."

"You're still seeing Graham?" Natalie looks at her in surprise. "You never mentioned that."

"I am, though I'll probably have to warn him about you now."

"Look, I'm sorry, okay? I said I was going to fix this business with

Anthony and I will."

"You better, because I don't know what you were thinking. I know these past few months have been rough, and I feel for you, but you have to hold it together. And yes, I'm still seeing Graham. We're both so busy this is only our second date. It's too early for me to even give him the Bandito Test."

"What's that?" Natalie asks.

Blair closes her bottle. "Haven't I told you guys about that? It's this test I give the men I date, sort of like a litmus test."

Lindsay smirks. "Is it written or oral? Please tell me it's oral because that's my favorite kind."

"Lindsay!" Natalie laughs, hoping no one around them is overhearing their conversation.

She shrugs. "I'm just telling it like it is."

"That's my favorite kind too," Blair says with a smile, her eyes wandering the gym. "In fact, there are a few guys here I wouldn't mind helping with their studies. Though by the time men are our age, you think they'd know their way around the enchanted forest." She glances down pointedly.

Lindsay laughs. "You would think so."

Natalie thinks about her own enchanted forest. It's been a long time since she's had any visitors. "So what's the Bandito Test?"

Blair eyes them both. "It's based on this western movie I saw years ago. It's about a woman who's kidnapped by a group of banditos. Her fiancé refuses to rescue her because he thinks it's too dangerous. He doesn't want to risk his life, so he plans to leave her with the banditos."

"What an ass." Lindsay frowns.

"Yeah, but there was this other guy, a second man. The second man also wants to marry the kidnapped woman, but she turned him down. Despite her rejection, this guy says he's going to rescue her no matter what. She's worth it. The fiancé tries to talk him out of it, but he won't listen."

"What happens?" Natalie asks.

"The second man rescues her and she marries him instead."

"So what's this Bandito test?" Lindsay wants to know.

"Well, when I'm dating someone I ask myself—what kind of man is he? Is he a first man or a second man? In other words, is he the kind of man who would leave me behind or would he forget his own safety and rescue me?" Blair flashes them an embarrassed grin. "I know it all sounds silly, but I don't know if I would have married Road if I'd given him the Bandito Test."

"Road wouldn't have passed?" Natalie asks.

Blair shakes her head slowly. "I doubt it. Not for me, anyway."

Lindsay is thoughtful. "I think Oliver would pass the Bandito Test."

"Maybe you should marry him," Blair says.

"No—not that he's asked or anything—but two failed marriages are enough."

"What about you, Natalie? Would Peter pass the Bandito Test?" Blair asks.

Natalie thinks about it. "I'm not sure."

"It's hard to be objective when you're going through a divorce. Think back years ago, would he have passed it then?"

Lindsay rolls her eyes. "I can answer that for her. Peter is a selfish coward. There's no way he'd pass that test. It's like I've always said—you're way too good for him. Speaking of which, maybe it's time we got you out there again."

"What do you mean?" Natalie asks.

"I mean dating. Take a look around."

"That's crazy. I'm not ready for something like that." Natalie is lightheaded with panic just thinking about it. Being with another man sounds as foreign to her as moving to China and speaking Chinese for the rest of her life.

"Maybe not yet," Blair says. "But you will be at some point. It's going to feel strange at first, but eventually you'll want to meet someone new."

Luckily, Natalie is saved from the rest of this conversation by Jessica, their instructor, coming over and telling everyone that class is starting again.

Everyone follows Jessica to an area near the front of the gym, where Natalie is surprised to see boxing gloves that come in a rainbow of colors. They even have girl colors like pink and fuchsia.

"What color do you want your wrap?" Jessica asks Natalie, pointing to another student who's already wrapping her hand with boxing tape.

"Purple," Natalie says without hesitation, since it's her favorite color. Jessica helps her and Blair and the other new students wrap their hands before putting on boxing gloves. Blair chooses green, while Lindsay does her own wrap in red.

For someone who works with her hands all day, it feels strange to have them encased. The gloves seem huge. Excitement drums through her when they're led over to rows of punching bags in the center of the room.

Natalie spends the next half hour doing various drills. She learns punches, hovers, and jabs. Her hands and arms feel sore at first, not to mention her shoulders, but after a while, they become numb. She keeps thinking of everything she's been going through the last few months. Lena and Peter. The end of her marriage. All the stress it's put on Chloe. She thinks about Anthony and her embarrassment.

By the time the class is over, Natalie is exhausted and dripping with sweat.

"So what did you think?" Lindsay asks.

Natalie smiles. "That was awesome."

Chapter Nine

Diet Plan: Oatmeal for breakfast. Veggie burger for lunch. Large green salad for dinner. Sliver of chocolate cake (frosting scraped off) for dessert.

Exercise Plan: Elliptical every day. Boxing every week. Start using free weights. Eyes on the prize.

*F*OR THE FIRST time in her life, Natalie finds herself in a situation she couldn't have imagined. Not only does she sign up for boxing classes twice a week, but she also calls Carlos's boyfriend, Ryan, and hires him as her personal trainer.

He comes to the house for the first time after work to show her how to use the equipment in her home gym.

"I'm still kind of sore from the boxing classes I started a couple of weeks ago," Natalie explains.

"Are you stiff?"

"Yes, though it's getting better. Thank God, I had the day off after that first lesson, because I could barely get out of bed."

Ryan chuckles. "If you're still sore, you should take it easy. You don't want to cause an injury. Let's at least look over your equipment though and talk a little about your expectations."

An hour later, after he's gone, Natalie takes a shower and decides to do something she hasn't done in a long time.

She walks over to her bedroom closet and opens the door. There's a full-length mirror on the wall. For a moment, she gathers her courage and then lets her bathrobe slip from her shoulders to the floor, so she's completely naked and looks at herself.

"Aaaah!"

The urge to grab her robe and scurry away is overpowering, but Natalie holds her ground.

I can do this.

She forces herself to check out her naked body. At first, she's horrified, but then decides to try approaching it from a different mindset.

What if I only focus on the things I like about my body? Surely, there's something.

She also decides not to compare herself to Lindsay. She's been comparing herself to her sister her whole life, and maybe it is time to stop. After all, they don't look anything alike. For starters, she's three inches shorter than Lindsay and far more curvaceous.

And that's where she decides to begin.

Okay, I've got curves. Lots of them. There's enough here to open my own boobs and butts store.

But as she studies herself, she realizes something else. "I've got a waist!"

And it's true. Her dieting has made a difference because it's clear she has a waist again. She puts her hands on hips and sucks in her breath.

Now we're talking. She turns this way and that. Her stomach looks almost flat. If only she could walk around like this all the time. Still sucking in her stomach, she walks into the closet where she keeps her scale. It's in the back, buried behind some shoes, so she has to wrangle it out.

Finally, the moment of truth. She gets on it and looks down.

At first she's confused by the number she sees, but then it dawns on her. *I've lost weight.* Natalie does some quick calculations in her head and discovers she's lost somewhere in the neighborhood of thirty pounds.

Thirty pounds! Can it be?

She gets off and on the scale about five more times and the number doesn't change. She puts her robe back on and sits down on the bed, letting reality sink in. All the comments people have made about her losing weight are true. Natalie is amazed. Yes, she's been dieting and exercising like crazy, and yes, she's even started spitting out the pastries she's had to taste test instead of swallowing them, because—let's be honest—she used to eat the discards, but somehow she never expected this.

Wow.

When she finds Lindsay and Chloe downstairs, she makes an announcement.

"I want to go clothes shopping."

"OH, MY GOD!" Lindsay shrieks. "I've been waiting for this moment my whole life!"

Natalie rolls her eyes.

Lindsay and Chloe are in the living room, dancing and rocking out to the new Muse album. They used to ask Natalie to join them, but she always said no, so they don't bother anymore.

Lindsay turns down the music. "Can I burn your old clothes? Please, pretty please?" She puts her hands together in prayer and closes her eyes. "It would give me such awesome pleasure."

"Burning my clothes? I don't know about that." Natalie frowns.

"We'll start with those hideous mom jeans. And then I'll burn those big white sneakers, too." Lindsay is nodding.

"I'm sorry, Mom," Chloe chimes in. "But Aunt Lindsay is right. Those sneakers are really ugly."

"That horrible brown *Lord of the Rings* hoodie will be next!" Lindsay says, clapping her hands.

"Hey, no one is burning my *Lord of the Rings* hoodie! And I don't know about getting rid of my white sneakers, either. Those are very comfortable."

"Don't worry, Mom, we can get you a super cute *Lord of the Rings* T-shirt with Legolas on the front," Chloe assures her.

"Yes, a *woman's* T-shirt," Lindsay agrees. "Not that huge over-sized hoodie which is obviously meant for a man twice your size."

"I prefer Aragorn," Natalie says, trying to salvage some of her dignity. "Legolas is cute, but I'm an Aragorn girl all the way."

"Definitely." Lindsay nods. "Whatever you want. When can we take you shopping—this weekend?"

"I thought you had to work this weekend?" Lindsay recently won a bid to create a sculpture for the public library in Tacoma.

"I'll work at night. I also want you to go see my hairdresser."

"I don't know." Natalie puts her hand up to touch her ponytail.

"Trust me, you need a decent haircut and some color to fix those grays." Lindsay gets up. "Damn, where's my phone? I have to call Blair. I know she's going to want to be in on this."

While Lindsay is looking for her cell, Natalie wonders what she's getting herself into. She hasn't gone clothes shopping in years. Paying attention to styles has never been her thing.

She heads into the kitchen to make herself a salad for dinner. Despite all the insults being slung around about her current wardrobe, there's a bounce in her step. She keeps thinking about that bathroom scale.

Thirty pounds!

Lindsay has finally found her phone and Natalie can hear her talking to Blair.

"Yes, she's agreed to a makeover!" There's a tiny shriek projected through the phone, which Natalie can hear all the way over by the fridge.

Natalie listens to them as they decide on clothing stores and which salon spa is best. They sound like two generals planning a military campaign.

Except, I'm the battlefield.

THE REST OF the week is a blur as Natalie pretends she isn't nervous about the coming weekend. She's not quite sure how going clothes shopping has suddenly turned into a makeover, but it has. Lindsay made a salon appointment for her that's alarmingly called "The Works."

Peter phones to discuss the holidays. He wants Chloe to spend Christmas with him and Lena.

"I doubt she'll go for that," Natalie points out. Their parenting plan said Chloe was to spend part of Christmas day with Peter, but Chloe didn't want to go if Lena was there. She wouldn't even go over for Thanksgiving.

"Help me out, then. My parents are coming down to meet Lena for the first time and I'm hoping it will help Chloe warm up to her."

"Let me get this straight. You want me to help Chloe warm up to Lena?"

"Yes, as a favor to me."

"Why would I do that?"

"Because it will make all our lives easier."

"You mean *your* life, don't you?"

Peter lets out a frustrated sigh. "Just forget it. Lena is right about you. You are totally closed off."

Natalie pushes down her anger. *How did I become the bad guy in all this?* "Lena doesn't even know me."

"She's been trying to reach out to you, but you keep shutting her down. You know she's a life coach, right?"

"Are you talking about those awful texts I keep getting?"

"There's no reason for any of us to have bad feelings toward each other. I'm hoping we'll all be friends someday."

Natalie scoffs. "What happened to her wanting to take out a restraining order against me?"

"We talked about it and realized you lashed out because you're hurting, but she wants to help you move past that."

"Lena wants to help me?"

"Yes, Natalie," he starts in with his phony dentist's voice, "she helps people all the time. If you give her half a chance, you'll understand she's a great person."

"What planet are you on?" *And what kind of drugs are you smoking there?*

"Very funny. The truth is, I feel like a new man."

"How nice for you."

"Don't be like that. You could benefit from her advice, too. Lena's got me doing yoga and eating healthy. None of those rich pastries you're always making. We eat everything raw."

"Raw?"

"That's right. Just raw fruits and vegetables. Lena doesn't cook anything."

"Is that safe?"

"Of course it's safe. It's a very healthy way to eat."

"You seriously don't cook anything at all?"

"No. Nothing." Peter's voice takes on an annoyed tone. "We also don't eat meat, dairy, sugar, or wheat. I feel incredible. You should try it."

Natalie decides she'd rather fall on a sharp stick than give up chocolate or butter, but decides to keep that to herself. Even with all her dieting, she still has the occasional treat. Life's too short for anything less.

"Will you talk to Chloe about coming here for Christmas or not?" he asks.

Natalie thinks of all the ways Peter has hurt her. "Sorry, but I'm done fixing your messes. Ask Chloe yourself."

After hanging up she has a pang of regret. *Maybe I should be nicer about all this.* But then she thinks about the last time she saw Peter and how he'd threatened to sell the house. He'd created this situation and now he could deal with it.

They have a short bakery meeting that afternoon. The kitchen staff gathers in their tiny backroom where the television is playing *As the Clock Ticks,* a favorite soap opera. It occurs to Natalie that her life has become like a soap opera. She decides to apologize to everyone for the way she behaved with Anthony recently.

"I'm sorry you guys had to see that. It was very unprofessional of me to insult our landlord." *Even if he is being a pain in the ass.*

"Don't worry," Ginger, one of their part-time bakers, says. "That was nothing. I've seen plenty worse in some of the kitchens I've worked."

"Oh, yeah." Zoe tells a story about how she worked with a sous chef once who used a knife to threaten anyone who disagreed with him.

Natalie nods. "In truth, I've seen some crazy stuff over the years, too, but it's not the way we want things to run here." She and Blair agreed from the start that their bakery's kitchen was going to be a calm workplace.

"Besides, we know you've been under a lot of pressure lately," Zoe says. "Nobody thinks less of you. You've never been anything but generous with us."

There are murmurs of agreement around the room and Natalie is touched.

Unfortunately, she's still waiting for Anthony to come in so she can finally apologize to him. She even rehearsed in front of the bathroom mirror at home. The problem is, he hasn't shown up.

"Are you sure you haven't seen him?" she asks Carlos the next day. "Doesn't he come in every week?"

"Usually, but I haven't seen him for a while."

"Let me know when you do."

She heads back into the kitchen to finish the piping on a chocolate dome cake and wonders if Anthony is avoiding her. *Was I really that awful to him?* Unfortunately, the answer she keeps coming up with is yes.

By the time Friday rolls around and he still hasn't shown, she decides to take action.

Natalie goes out to find Blair, who's building a three-tiered cake with lace fondant. Ginger is helping her.

"Are you still seeing Graham?" Natalie asks.

Blair attaches candied white pearls to the side of the cake where the corners of the lace meet. "Still going strong."

"Do you think you could ask him for Anthony's cell phone number?"

Blair glances at her. "I suppose. Why do you want it? I'll need to give him a reason."

"I want to apologize. He hasn't been in for a while and now I think he's avoiding me."

"I see." Blair nods, considering things. "That's probably a good idea. Let me finish this up and I'll give him a call and see what he says."

LATER THAT AFTERNOON Natalie is in the back office working on payroll when Carlos tells her there's someone here to see her.

"Is it Anthony?"

"No, it's some woman. I asked her if she wanted to order a cake, but she said she needed to talk to you."

Natalie follows Carlos out front and is disturbed to see Lena standing near the pastry case. Her long, blonde hair falls in a cascade over her shoulders. She's wearing a short beige raincoat that's tied at the waist and high-heeled black boots.

Lena is examining the display, but looks up when Natalie approaches.

"It's that lady over there," Carlos motions toward Lena and heads back behind the counter.

Natalie can't take her eyes from Lena. It's like discovering there's a shark swimming in your pool.

"What are you doing here?"

Lena gives her a phony smile. "You came to my place of business, so I thought it only fitting that I come to yours."

"I know you're not here to buy a cake, so what do you want?"

"There's no reason for that tone." Lena rearranges her features into what Natalie imagines is her life coach-yoga teacher face. "Peter told me about your phone call a couple days ago. I really want to help you move past all this anger."

"I don't want your help and I like my anger just the way it is."

Lena shifts uncomfortably. "Do you mind if we have a seat and talk? My feet are killing me in these boots."

"I'm actually kind of busy at the moment. Why don't you come back another time? Like—never."

"This will only take a minute."

"Fine." Natalie leads Lena over to a table in the corner, so no one overhears their conversation.

After they sit down, Carlos comes over and asks them if they'd like anything.

"I'd love some herbal tea," says Lena. "Mint, if you have it."

"Nothing for me, thanks." She turns back to Lena after he leaves. "I thought this was only going to take a minute."

Lena smiles and considers her. "You look different. Have you lost weight?"

Natalie shrugs. "A bit."

"You should try yoga. It's amazing for your health. Come by the studio sometime if you're ever interested."

"Is that why you came here? To get me to join your yoga studio?"

"No, I'm hoping we can talk woman to woman, Natalie."

"About what?"

"The man we both love."

Natalie blinks. Tries to hide the effect those words have on her. "I see."

"Peter is really unhappy that you're struggling so much with all these changes. And when he's unhappy, I'm unhappy, too. What can we do to make it right?" Lena looks at her earnestly.

Carlos brings her the tea and Lena thanks him.

Natalie studies her as she pours the hot water into her cup and adds the tea ball. Lena's fingernails are long and glossy, painted with a French tip. They're very stylish. Her gold hoop earrings catch the light when she moves her head. Natalie has to admit she's glamorous, and even though Lena is more than a decade older than her, she could probably have any guy she wanted.

"Why Peter?" Natalie finds herself asking. "Of all the men out there, why have you decided on being with Peter?"

Lena's eyes widen with surprise, but then she smiles. "Many reasons. He's fun and I enjoy spending time with him. He's a good listener."

"But why choose a married man who has a family?"

"I didn't choose him," she says, still smiling. "The universe chose him for me."

"So the universe chose my husband to be your lover?"

Lena's purses her lips and Natalie is happy to see that it ages her about ten years. "I see you only want to judge." She takes a breath and closes her eyes. When she opens them again, the yoga teacher face is back. "But why not leave that behind? Look to your future and all the beautiful things that are waiting for you."

My God, she actually talks in these silly platitudes. Natalie knows it's an act though and if she rattles her cage she'll see the real Lena, the Lena who jumped her and tried to punch her in the face.

"What's the reason you're here?" Natalie asks.

"It's just as I said earlier. I want to help you. I know you think I'm a bad person, but I'm not. I'm sure if we got to know each other better we might be friends. We even have things in common," she motions around, "since we're both small business owners."

"I don't want to be friends with you. You stole my husband."

Lena smirks and slowly shakes her head. "Don't be so naïve. Do you honestly think a man like Peter was going to stay faithful to someone like *you* forever? If it wasn't me, it would have been someone else. At least I'm a decent person."

"Someone like me?"

Lena looks at her from head to toe. "Let's be frank. Peter is a handsome and successful man, and you're, well . . . I wouldn't say you're ugly, but you're kind of plain. Not that there's anything wrong with that. We all have to be ourselves in this life."

Natalie's head snaps back as if she's taken a blow. *So Lena is getting her punch in, after all.*

"I'm just trying to be honest," Lena continues. "Don't worry, you'll meet another man someday, someone who's more . . . on your level."

"On my . . . level?"

"Yes." Lena nods.

"I'd like you to leave now," Natalie says through gritted teeth. "This conversation is over."

Lena leans forward, her thick blonde hair framing her face like a lion's mane. "You'll be happy again someday. Believe it or not, Peter and I want the best for you."

Natalie is shaking. "Get out."

✦ � ✦

NATALIE IS STILL upset when the weekend arrives and it's time for her hair appointment. Blair picks her and Lindsay up in Isadora. It's just the three of them, since Chloe is going to Peter's this weekend. Natalie doesn't tell anyone about her conversation with Lena. It's too humiliating. And the worst part is, what Lena said was true—Peter has always been better looking than her. She knew he was out of her league when she married him.

"I thought I was just getting my hair trimmed. Why is my salon appointment three hours long?" Natalie adjusts her *Lord of the Rings* hoodie. Lindsay didn't want her to wear it today, but Natalie insisted on being comfortable. "And what exactly is 'The Works'?"

"A little of this and a little of that," Lindsay says enigmatically.

"That's not much of an answer."

Blair looks over at Natalie. "Don't worry. They won't do anything without your permission."

"Is that supposed to comfort me?"

They park the car in a garage and walk a block through the crowded shopping area in downtown Seattle. It's early December, so the streets are busy with people getting ready for the holidays.

"I wish you hadn't worn that hideous sweatshirt," Lindsay gripes. "And thank God we're going shopping. Those pants are practically falling off you. You look like an ass-less wonder."

Natalie lets out a laugh. "In my dreams I look like an ass-less wonder."

"Then your dreams have come true."

They enter the salon and the front desk hands Natalie a robe and directs her to a dressing room. She hasn't been to a salon in years. Nervous energy spirals through her.

Lindsay and Blair wait with her for the stylist, chatting about some of the stores they plan to go to while she's having her hair done.

"We'll put clothes on hold and you can come and try them on when you're done here," Lindsay tells her.

Finally, Natalie finds herself sitting in a chair in front of Marcus, Lindsay's hairdresser. A group of people are gathered around her, examining her hair and consulting each other like scientists discussing a new lab specimen.

She can't get that horrible conversation with Lena out of her mind. The way she arrogantly swung that blonde mane around, calling Natalie plain. *Plain.* She hates that word. It's plagued her all her life.

"I want my hair blonde," she suddenly announces to everyone. "Very blonde."

They all stare at her.

"Really?" Lindsay asks. "Are you sure? That's a drastic change."

Natalie nods. "Yes, and I don't want to cut it short. I want to keep it long."

No one is going to call me plain ever again.

Marcus seems to be thinking it over. He studies her, pulling her hair back from her face and then letting it fall forward again. He smiles and nods. "I think I can work with that."

In a clipped voice, Marcus starts ordering people around. Natalie bites her lip. *I hope I haven't made a huge mistake.*

Someone brings her a cup of tea and a stack of magazines. She thumbs though them and pretends everything is normal as she watches Marcus paint strands of her hair with colored goop and wrap them in foil.

"What is that stuff?"

"Mostly bleach."

Bleach! Natalie tries not to show her panic. She's never lightened her hair before. Her only experience with color was the orange henna incident in high school. And this is clearly more radical than that.

While she's under the dryer, a manicurist comes over and does her nails. Then another person plucks and smears more goop onto her eyebrows. When Natalie asks what's happening, Marcus explains they're shaping and lightening them to go with her hair.

"Don't worry. When I'm finished, you'll barely recognize yourself."

Natalie squeaks.

At one point, Lindsay and Blair come back to check on her.

"We're finding a lot of great sales. Is there anything in particular you want us to put aside for you?" Lindsay asks.

"I don't know. Nothing too wild."

"Okay, no leather bustier."

"Wait." Natalie grabs her arms before she leaves. "I want colors."

"What do you mean?"

"I want to wear more colors. I'm sick of all the black."

Lindsay raises an eyebrow. "Finally out of mourning, are we?"

Later, while her hair is being blown dry, Lindsay and Blair return from shopping. Marcus has Natalie facing away from the mirror and even though she wants to turn and look, she's too nervous. Instead, she hopes she'll be able to gauge the results from the reaction of the two of them.

"Oh, my God!" Lindsay shrieks when she sees her.

"Wow!" Blair's mouth falls open as she stares at her in shock.

"What?" Natalie's adrenaline skyrockets. "Do I look that *bad?*" She turns in a panic, straining to see herself in the mirror.

"Be still," Marcus commands. "I'm almost done. You can wait a few more minutes."

"No, it's okay." Lindsay smiles now. "It doesn't look bad at all. You look amazing."

"I do?"

Blair nods. "Totally gorgeous! I barely recognize you."

"Gee, thanks."

"You know what I mean. It's a big change."

Finally, Natalie decides she can't stand it anymore and forces the chair around. For a moment, she's disoriented. Her eyes widen as she takes in her own reflection.

I'm blonde.

Very blonde.

And it's . . . stunning. It's true what Blair said.

"My God," Natalie murmurs. "I can't believe it. I really do look like a different person."

She swings her hair down. It's long and shiny, falling over her shoulder in a shimmery cascade just like Lena's. *Holy shit.* Leaning closer to the mirror, she sees her eyebrows are lighter and have been nicely shaped. The makeup artist did a wonderful job. Natalie told her how she seldom wore makeup and the amount is subtle, but effective. They also told her about some makeup that could withstand the heat of the kitchen.

"Face it," Marcus says with a smile. "You're a hottie now. Sizzle!"

"Thank you," she tells him, dumbfounded. "It's fantastic. Truly."

After paying, she follows Lindsay and Blair outside. They walk down the street toward some of the department stores, but Natalie keeps stopping to stare at her reflection in every passing window. There's a sense of freedom pulsing through her. Though she's worried, too, worried she's going to go into shock later. She doesn't do well with big changes.

"You look really pretty," Blair tells her, coming up to stand beside her. "I don't think I've ever seen you with makeup on. It brings out your features."

Lindsay grabs her arm. "Come on, my beautiful sister, now we need to get you into some decent clothes. No more black and no more pants so baggy and ugly that they look like garbage bags."

Natalie knows she should be insulted, but she's in too much of a daze about her hair and makeup. "My clothes do not look like garbage bags," she finally says.

Once in the dressing room, she realizes Lindsay is telling the truth. Her new hair is shining a light on everything. Between her huge *Lord of the Rings* hoodie and her baggy pants, she's drowning in her own clothes.

How could I not have noticed this?

"Here you go." Lindsay knocks on the dressing room door. She hands Natalie a few more items to add to the pile she already has in front of her.

When she sees the sizes Lindsay has brought, she balks and tries to hand them back. "Size ten? That's way too small. I'll never fit into those jeans."

"Just try them on, okay?"

"Fine." She takes them, thinking this is a waste of time. To her astonishment, she zips them right up.

Natalie stares down in disbelief. They fit perfectly. Turning to the side, she's amazed when she sees her own rear view.

I remember that ass.

It's been a long time since she's seen it, and she's certainly never seen it encased in a pair of modern-cut jeans before.

She tries on the rest of the clothes Lindsay and Blair have picked out. Some of them don't work at all. *Tight leather pants? Pencil skirts? I don't think so.* But most of them do. There are skirts, sweaters, and more jeans. And the colors are like a rainbow—emerald greens and vibrant purples.

In the end, she decides to buy everything—even the black leather pants and pencil skirts—and puts it all on credit, figuring *what the heck.* She hasn't gone clothes shopping in years.

"I can't wait to see you in these clothes," Lindsay says. "You are going to look so hot. You'll be turning heads left and right."

"Oh, speaking of hot, that reminds me, Graham gave me Anthony's cell number." Blair pulls her phone out and brings up the number, handing it over to Natalie.

"Did you tell him why I wanted it?" She copies the number into her own phone.

"Yes, and I've never seen Graham laugh so hard."

"He thought it was funny I called Anthony an asshole?"

"He thought it was funny *any* woman would call Anthony an asshole. Apparently, that's not the kind of endearment Anthony's used to."

Chapter Ten

Diet Plan: Chinese takeout. A little food for thought on the side.

Exercise Plan: Gawk at yourself in the mirror with disbelief. Harass a hot guy.

ATALIE STARES AT Anthony's number on her phone. *Why on earth did I think calling him would be a good idea?*

She's sitting on the bed after putting away all her new clothes. Lindsay is downstairs starting dinner. At Lindsay's urging, she's wearing new jeans with a low-cut cornflower blue sweater. Every time she passes a mirror, she has to stop and stare at herself. Having never been a vain person, Natalie can't remember the last time she felt good about her appearance, and is hovering between elation and panic.

She runs a hand over her long blonde hair and resists the urge to pull it back into her usual ponytail.

It's Saturday night, she thinks, staring at her phone. Anthony is probably out somewhere with a beautiful woman at his side.

Oh, grow a pair already.

She hits call and starts rehearsing her apology speech. His phone is ringing.

"Hello?"

It's *him.* Yikes! Shit! Her mind goes blank. She can't even remember why she's calling. All she can focus on is his sexy sounding hello. It's just right. Deep enough to be manly, but not deep enough to be creepy.

"Hello?" he repeats.

There's silence when he hangs up.

The Professor isn't very patient, is he? How does he know there isn't a pathetic overworked baker on other the end, trying to get her nerve up to speak?

Natalie takes a few calming breathes. *I can do this.*

And this time when his phone rings and he answers with that super-hot "Hello," she's ready.

"Hi, this is Natalie from La Dolce Vita."

There's a long moment of silence.

"I feel really bad about what happened between us," she goes on. "I wanted to call and apologize."

"Natalie?"

He sounds distracted, as if he doesn't want talk to her. Which isn't that hard to imagine, considering she called him an asshole right to his face.

"Yes, it's Natalie."

"How did you get this number?"

Natalie hesitates. "Graham gave it to me."

The phone is silent and Natalie decides to keep talking. "I just wanted you to know how terrible I feel about what happened. I never should have said what I did to you."

"Listen, I'm kind of busy right now."

"Oh, okay."

The phone is silent in her hand and it takes her a moment to realize he isn't on the line anymore.

He hung up again!

Natalie puts her phone down on the nightstand and stares at it, frowning. And then she picks it up. Hits redial.

"What now?" he growls.

"Look, I'm trying to apologize. Or maybe you don't get it."

"Yeah, I get it."

"The only reason I've been forced to call and interrupt whatever important thing it is you're doing on a Saturday night is that you've been avoiding me."

"What are you talking about?"

"You haven't come into the bakery, and it's obvious why. I wouldn't want to go someplace where someone called me an asshole, either. At the same time though, it's very annoying because you aren't giving me a chance to apologize!"

The phone is silent.

"You're crazy," he finally says.

"I know it seems that way, but I'm not normally like this. I have a daughter. I'm a successful business owner. There are extenuating circumstances in my life right now." Natalie knows she's babbling.

"Look, I haven't been avoiding you or your bakery. I'm in Hawaii."

"What?"

"I've been here for ten days."

"So . . . you're on vacation?" Natalie groans inwardly.

"No, I'm at the Keck Observatory on Mauna Kea."

"What's that?"

"It's a telescope observatory. That's what I do. I'm an astronomer."

"So you're looking through a telescope right now?"

"No. Right now I'm in bed sleeping." He sighs with irritation. "Or trying to."

"I see, so you're in bed sleeping and that's why you're busy?" She tries to give a light-hearted laugh, though it sounds more like she's coughing. Her stomach is filled with a swarm of butterflies.

"Yeah, I'm going to be awake again all night and could use some shut-eye."

Natalie wonders if it's possible to still salvage this. "I'm sitting in bed right now, too, though obviously I'm not sleeping, but I do keep baker's hours."

Anthony doesn't reply.

Natalie glances down at her new clothes and an odd boldness comes over her. "So, what are you wearing?" Instantly, she's mortified at her dumb attempt at flirtation. *The bleach must have gone to my brain!* "Oh, my God! I can't believe I said that. Erase it from your mind." She sucks in her breath. "Though you probably can't because you have a photographic memory!"

"Damn, you really do sound crazy." Though she senses humor behind his words.

She sighs. "I know. You probably want me to let you go, huh?"

"Yeah, I do."

"Can you at least tell me where we are on the bakery expansion? Have you considered the numbers I gave you yet?"

"It's only—"

"I mean, I hope you were able to memorize them like you—"

"Stop, just stop talking," Anthony tells her. "Jesus, are you always like this?"

"Always like what?"

"Pushy."

"No, of course not." She pauses. "Well, maybe."

"That figures."

"I'm actually a very boring person. All I do is work. Though I did start a boxing class recently."

"*Boxing?*" Anthony starts to laugh. "Seriously?"

"Is that funny?"

"Yeah, kind of. Actually, boxing sounds right up your alley."

"It does?"

"I'll bet you're good at throwing a punch."

She wonders whether she should correct him. Obviously, she hasn't been boxing very long and has no idea what's she's doing. In the end, Natalie decides she likes his impression of her as a tough girl. "Hey, that's the way I roll. I'm a badass."

Anthony laughs some more. "Good to know." He pauses for a second. "Were you serious when you said you were into *Star Wars?*"

Natalie sighs. "I know that sounds pathetic. I'm not *that* into it or anything. I do have a life."

"That's all right. I'm into *Star Wars,* too."

"You are?" And then Natalie remembers his phone's ringtone.

"Yeah, what's your favorite *Star Wars* movie?"

"*Empire Strikes Back.*"

"Good choice."

She opens her mouth to ask him what his favorite movie is, but doesn't get a chance.

"All right," Anthony says. "It's probably the sleep deprivation talking, but I'm going to consider accepting your apology."

"Really?"

"Yeah, I could tell it was heartfelt."

Natalie laughs. "You're just saying that. I was actually angry when I called you again."

"I know, that's why I'm only *considering* whether to accept it."

"Maybe we could have a truce where I promise not to call you any more names?"

"I'll think about it."

"Okay."

"And it's a white T-shirt and black boxer briefs," Anthony says.

"What is?"

"What I'm wearing right now."

"Oh."

He chuckles. "Goodnight, Natalie."

A WHITE T-SHIRT and black boxer briefs. Anthony's voice is still echoing in her head. Is that what he always sleeps in? It's such an intimate detail.

I'll bet he looks fantastic. Of course, he'd look fantastic in anything.

Was Anthony flirting? No, he was just making a joke. She doesn't want to start having delusions. Men like Anthony never look twice at women like her.

She decides the phone call with Anthony went pretty well. They ended the conversation on a good note and it sounds like he mostly accepted her apology. Blair will be pleased. Maybe he'll be nicer about leasing them that space now.

Natalie heads downstairs. She finds Lindsay hasn't started dinner yet and is sitting cross-legged on the couch with her laptop. There's a glass of wine at her side.

"Why haven't you started cooking yet? Chloe will be home soon."

"There you are." Lindsay looks up and is taken aback. "Wow, this is going to take some getting used to. You look so different it's startling."

"I know, I'm in shock every time I pass a mirror."

Lindsay studies her. "All right, I need you to go put on some lip gloss. Actually, there's some in my purse if you want to grab it."

"Why?" Natalie picks up Lindsay's glass of wine.

"I need it for the photo."

"What photo?"

"The photo we're going to use for all these online dating sites I've just signed you up for."

Natalie nearly chokes on her sip of wine. "Please tell me you're kidding!"

"Of course I'm not kidding. In fact, you've already got some responses, though these guys must be total losers. Who would want to date someone without even seeing what they look like first?"

Natalie doesn't move. "I am *not* going out on a date with anyone."

"Why not? Just think how much it will bug the ass clown when he hears about it."

"He'll be happy. He wants me to find someone new." She puts the wine glass back down.

Lindsay smirks. "Trust me. It'll get under his skin. He's a man and all men are territorial over their women. Peter only said that because he doesn't think you'll ever meet someone."

Natalie wonders if that's true. She doubts it. *He has Lena now, so what would he care?*

Lindsay places her computer aside and picks up her camera from the coffee table. It's a big heavy thing with a monster lens. She angles it and peers through the viewfinder at Natalie. "Oliver is back in town, so I invited him over for dinner tonight."

"I didn't even know you two were still together. I mean, you've basically moved in here."

"Oliver's down with it. He knows why I'm staying here."

"You don't have to stay if it's causing you any problems."

Lindsay shakes her head. "It's not, and I want to stay. You need me."

Natalie goes into the kitchen to get a glass of water with lemon when she hears the doorbell ring. Lindsay answers it and there are shrieks and exclamations from the other room and then a man's voice, which Natalie assumes must be Oliver.

A few moments later, a tall muscular guy with spiky bleached hair walks in smiling, presumably because Lindsay has wrapped herself around him like a vine. Her longs legs are around his waist and he's carrying her while juggling a large brown paper bag of what looks like takeout food.

Eventually the two separate. "Here he is," Lindsay says, still holding on to his arm, her cheeks flushed.

"Hi, Oliver, we've met once before. It's nice to see you again."

Oliver nods, his eyes roaming over Natalie's hair, face, and body. "You look really different. And let me just say—wow."

Natalie's face grows warm. "Thank you."

"I know, she's hot, isn't she?" Lindsay winks at Natalie. She turns back to Oliver. "And you brought the food like I told you—awesome. What kind is it?"

"Vegan Chinese."

Lindsay makes a face, but Oliver just smiles. "You'll like it, trust me."

Natalie is amazed that her sister invited Oliver for dinner and then asked him to bring the dinner, too, but Lindsay is always getting away with stuff like this and the men she dated never complained. If anything, they loved it. As far back as she can remember, Lindsay has always been the dumper and never the dumpee.

Natalie takes the bag of food from Oliver, who seems happy to relinquish it. She pulls the containers out and places them on the table along with plates and chopsticks. As she's filling a pitcher with ice water, she hears another car and goes to the front door to find Chloe arriving home from riding lessons. She carpooled there with a friend, and Natalie waves to the other mom from the front porch.

They both come into the dining room where Lindsay has taken over with the ice water, filling each glass.

"What are we having for dinner?" Chloe asks. "Is it something I like?"

"Oliver brought vegan Chinese," Lindsay tells her.

"Cool!" Chloe tries to sit down at the table, but Natalie tells her to go wash her hands first. Luckily Chloe has already changed out of her riding clothes.

"I noticed Lindsay's axe is still stuck in your front door," Oliver says to Natalie as he pours soy sauce on his rice. "I tried to pull it out, but it's really stuck. I could try prying it out with a tool, but I think it would damage the door too much."

"You really don't think you can get it out?" Lindsay asks.

"You can't pry out Excalibur with a tool!" Chloe says, coming back to the table. "It has to be pulled out by hand. Only someone worthy can do it."

Oliver looks confused. "Am I missing something?"

"Chloe's named the axe," Natalie explains.

"I'm going to hang a wreath on it," Chloe continues. "It'll be our Christmas axe. We'll have to get some of those twinkly lights for it, too."

Natalie takes a sip of water. "Your dad won't be happy about that."

"Yeah, the ass clown is going to have a heart attack if he sees that," Lindsay says.

"That's enough, Lindsay." Natalie shoots her a look. "I don't want you calling him ass clown in front of Chloe."

"Why not?"

"Because Peter is her dad and she loves him."

Chloe picks up some broccoli with her chopsticks. "I just wish Daddy would come home."

Natalie and Lindsay's eyes meet across the table.

Oliver dishes out some more food from one of the takeout boxes. "I suspect you're going to have to get a new front door."

Lindsay gives Natalie an apologetic smile. "Sorry about this."

In truth, Natalie's not that surprised about the door, since Peter had already come to the same conclusion. It wasn't long ago he left an angry voicemail telling her to order a new front door and "give Lindsay the goddamn bill!" It's the only way they communicate anymore—by phone. It's clear he's avoiding her. He'd started picking up Chloe with a call from the driveway, and she hasn't seen him face-to-face in months.

Natalie sighs as she considers her ornate-styled front door. It's silly maybe, but she's fond of it. Their house was built back in the nineteen-forties, and that thick door was the original one put on the house.

After dinner, Chloe leaves the table to go do homework in her bedroom and Natalie goes to help her with a few things. When she comes back downstairs, she discovers Lindsay and Oliver are still sitting at the table. She tells them goodnight, but Lindsay stops her. "Let's have Oliver take a quick photo of you before you go to bed."

Natalie frowns. "I already told you I'm not going on a date with anyone. I'm not ready for something like that."

"Come on, don't be a coward and besides, Oliver will take a fantastic photo."

"I'm not a coward! You have no idea how hard it's been for me since Peter left. Everything is on my shoulders."

Lindsay picks up her water glass. "Do I need to remind you that I've been divorced twice?"

"It's not the same thing."

"Oh, and why is that? Mine don't count?" Lindsay rolls her eyes. "You're such a martyr."

"I'm not a martyr. You were barely even married to your husbands. The first one was less than a year. The second one was like fifteen minutes! It's different when you've been together as long as Peter and I have, and you never had a child to think about." Natalie stops, wishing she could take that last part back. Lindsay had desperately wanted a baby, but for some reason was unable to get pregnant.

Lindsay gives Natalie a level stare, then looks away.

"I'm sorry about the child part," Natalie says. "But not the rest."

Oliver glances between the two sisters and then leans forward, putting his muscular tattooed arms on the table. "Listen, it's obvious you two care about each other. You guys need to stick together." He turns to Lindsay. "Maybe you should back off and let her decide when she wants to start meeting new guys."

"Maybe," Lindsay mutters. "But what is she waiting for?"

"Don't be like that," he says. "Give her the time she needs."

He then turns to Natalie. "And you're lucky to have a sister who cares about you so much. I know for a fact Lindsay would lie down in traffic for you."

Natalie takes a deep breath. "I know."

Lindsay turns to her. "I know you always feel like you have to take care of everyone, and that you practically raised me, but the only person you have left to mother is Chloe."

Later, after Natalie is upstairs in her room, Lindsay comes to find her to let her know she's going home with Oliver. "It's just for tonight. We haven't seen each other in weeks and I'm horny as hell."

Natalie smiles. "I really like him, and I can see why you said he'd pass the Bandito Test."

"Yeah, he's all right. Plus, he's a hunk."

Oliver is unconventional in his looks, but Natalie has to agree he's sexy. Especially in that bad boy way Lindsay likes.

"Try not to break his heart, okay? He doesn't deserve that."

Lindsay tosses her hair. "Hey, I'm not breaking anybody's heart here. Trust me, he's getting lucky tonight."

"I'm sorry about what I said earlier. I know your divorces weren't easy for you."

Lindsay waves her off. "Don't worry. Water under the bridge."

"I couldn't believe it when Chloe said she still wants Peter to come back." Natalie lets out her breath. She can't stop thinking about it. "I didn't know what to say."

Lindsay studies her. "What would you do if he came crawling back?"

"I wouldn't take him back. How could I ever trust him again? Though, I have to admit I hate to see Chloe hurting."

"I know, me too."

"Besides, he'll never come back. He's happy with Lena and you're right,

I probably should try getting out there. I need to move on. I am being a coward."

Lindsay comes over to give her a hug. "No, Oliver is right. You should wait until you're ready. I'll see you tomorrow."

Natalie listens a few minutes later as Oliver's van starts up outside and they drive away.

The question is—will I ever be ready?

ANTHONY SITS BACK in his chair at the control room in Waimea. It's been a productive night. The cloud cover cleared and for the second night in a row they've been able to open up the telescopes. He's tired, but exhilarated that his team was able to accomplish so much. Glancing toward the control room windows, he sees that it's almost dawn. The first orange and purple rays are peeking over the edge of the sky.

"I'm packing it in," Anthony says, shutting down his computer. "I'll see you guys tomorrow. Thanks for all your help."

A couple of his students are still working and wave good night. His assistant, Maya, has already gone off to bed.

Andrew, his support astronomer at Keck, nods. "See you tomorrow. It's been a great night."

Anthony steps outside into the crisp early morning. He starts walking back to his room, but realizes he's not tired enough to sleep, so sits on one of the benches outside. The mountain air tastes brisk and clean.

He keeps thinking about Natalie's phone call, and the way she called him an asshole the last time he saw her.

She was rude as hell.

He's deserved that from a few women, but ironically, he didn't deserve it from Natalie. Though at least she apologized.

Just before he flew out to Hawaii, he'd found out he was nominated for the Smyth Medal for astrophysics. It's a huge honor and he should be thrilled, but for some reason isn't feeling it.

The ceremony is being held in Seattle this year. Winning that medal is a long shot, but a nomination in itself is highly prestigious. He even called his parents, inviting them to attend, though he doesn't know why he still bothers.

"You should be using your brains and talent to help people," his father told him after he got his Ph.D. in astrophysics. "No offense, but this degree is a joke. I'll never call you Doctor."

Anthony tried not to let the effect those words had on him show. "Do you think Einstein was unimportant?" Anthony had asked. "Or what about Hawking? How else can we learn about our world and our universe?"

"So now you're comparing yourself to Albert Einstein and Stephen

Hawking?"

"Of course not, but Einstein and Hawking didn't get there by themselves. They built their theories on the work of others."

"No wonder you have such a high opinion of yourself. I didn't realize you were putting yourself into a class with two of the greatest minds of the last century." His father glanced at his Rolex impatiently. Some things never change and his father's schedule was one of them.

Anthony knew there was nothing he could say that would make any difference.

He wonders if his parents will bother coming to the ceremony. Even if he won the medal, his dad would act like it was nothing important.

I'm not saving lives, after all.

He gets up and walks back to his room. The accommodations at Keck are austere, but it doesn't matter, since all he does is sleep in them.

Once he's lying in bed, though, he's restless. Can't shut his mind off. He tries reading, then finally grabs his cell phone before realizing there's no one he can call. Who would be awake at this early hour? And then he remembers Natalie and grins.

This should be fun.

He searches back through his call log until he finds her number. She answers on the third ring.

Her voice sounds frantic. "Please don't tell me one of the ovens is down."

"Not as far as I know."

Natalie pauses. "Who is this?"

"It's Anthony, your evil landlord."

"Really?"

"Yes, it's really me. The landlord you love to hate."

Another pause. "I wouldn't say I hate you."

"But I'm not your favorite person, am I?"

The phone is quiet.

"Come on, Natalie, be honest. I can take it."

"No, you're not my favorite person."

Anthony smiles at her bluntness. "You're breaking my heart."

Natalie laughs softly. Her early morning voice sounds a little husky and he kind of likes it. He pictures her sultry mouth close to the phone and feels a stirring of desire.

"So, why are you calling?" she asks.

"I figured I'd get my daily insult."

She laughs some more, though he can tell she's nervous. If he had to guess, he'd say few people made Natalie nervous. "Someone has to do it."

"And you're just the woman for the job."

"Otherwise all you'd hear is how pretty you are."

Anthony blinks with surprise. "That's sweet. Do you really think I'm pretty?"

"Just like Cinderella."

"I'm still looking for the glass slipper that fits, though."

"Can you hang on a second?" He hears beeping in the background and what sounds like her putting the phone down. The beeping stops and he hears scuffling noises. It's quieter than he'd expect a busy bakery to sound at this hour. Eventually she comes back on the line.

"Are you still in Hawaii?"

"Yeah, though tomorrow is our last night of telescope time."

"What's it like there? Is it just a room with a big telescope inside?"

"Not quite." Anthony explains a bit about the Keck's twin telescopes on Mauna Kea. "Each one is eight stories tall and weighs 300 tons."

"Wow."

"Definitely awesome," he agrees.

"So what are you looking for?"

"Quasars. But my main research is with long gamma-ray bursts."

"Gamma rays? Like *The Hulk?*"

"Yeah, except I'm not turning green and tearing the building apart."

"Cinderella would never do that."

"Of course not. I'm just a sweet old-fashioned girl."

Natalie laughs. He really likes the sound of her laugh. She's always so stern it's a surprise to discover she laughs easily on the phone. Even though he's not particularly attracted to her, he kind of wishes he could see what she looks like right now.

"So, what are your extenuating circumstances?" he asks.

"What do you mean?"

"When we spoke the other day, you said you didn't normally go around calling people names, but had extenuating circumstances."

"Oh." She pauses. "I've been going through a divorce."

Anthony nods in understanding. "That's rough. I've been there myself, though it was years ago."

"You're divorced?" She sounds surprised.

"Yeah, I married too young and it was a mistake. It only lasted a couple of years. Though I don't regret . . ." He stops talking because he very nearly told her about Serena. *It probably doesn't matter. I don't plan to get romantically involved with Natalie.* Still, he doesn't say anything further.

"You don't regret what?"

"I don't regret getting divorced. We're both happier as a result."

"It's complicated for me, since I have an eleven-year-old daughter." She hesitates like she's going to say something more, but doesn't. Anthony figures she's holding back a tirade about her husband.

"So how's the boxing?"

"I like it. Though I should admit I haven't been doing it very long, so I'm not really the badass I claimed to be."

"Yeah? Going through a divorce, I imagine it feels pretty good to hit something as hard as you can."

"It does." Her voice grows soft. "I don't usually make any New Year's resolutions, but decided I'm going to make one this time. I'm pushing myself to try some new things."

"That's not a bad idea. I get the impression you work a lot."

"I do." She sighs. "I enjoy it, but I'm starting to see there's more to life. Can you hang on a second again?" Anthony hears that same beeping in the background. There are more scuffling sounds. He wonders why it's so quiet and he doesn't hear anyone else working.

"Where are you?" he asks when she comes back on the line.

"At home."

"Oh, I thought you were at the bakery. I figured you'd be working."

"I am working. I work out of my own kitchen in the mornings, because we don't have enough oven space to accommodate everything."

Anthony is taken aback. "I didn't know that. So you bake at home and then bring it into *La Dolce Vita?*"

"Are you really that surprised?"

"Of course. I never realized things were that tight."

"I guess now you understand why we want that space next door so badly, and why I can't stop insulting you."

"Hey, you never told me any of this. This is a new variable." Anthony's already thinking of how he's going to add it to his calculations.

"A new variable? That's all you have to say?"

"How many mornings a week is this?"

"Five."

"Natalie, you have to tell me these things. How would I know otherwise? Don't blame me because you never mentioned it."

"I shouldn't have to go through all this. Any sane landlord would have leased us that empty space months ago."

Anthony's tightens his grip on the phone. "Look, why don't you two just move your bakery to another location? I've had enough with all the static you're giving me."

Natalie scoffs. "Are you kidding? I'd love to move! You don't think we've tried to find another building? Unfortunately, we're stuck with you."

"Then get over it."

"I'm a single mom now, too, and I need that extra income. I'm trying to keep my home, but I have to buy out my husband."

"I don't mean to be a dick, but that's really not my concern. Maybe it's never occurred to you, but I also have mouths to feed. I can't afford to lease you guys that space next door and then discover you aren't able to pay the rent."

"I thought you were a college professor."

"I don't know what you think college professors make, but we're not wealthy. Besides, I'm not tenured yet. So a large part of my income comes from that property."

"So in the end, all it comes down to is money for you?"

"Basically, yeah."

"What about giving someone a chance?"

"I'm not running a charity."

"A charity?" Natalie pauses. He can hear her sharp intake of breath. "You know what? You *are* a dick!"

The phone goes silent in Anthony's hand and he realizes she's hung up. He tosses his phone onto the nightstand, though he feels like throwing it at the wall.

Donna pazza! Crazy woman!

Chapter Eleven

Diet Plan: Discover the "Too Angry to Eat Diet."

Exercise Plan: Boxing and lifting weights. Does controlling your temper burn calories? You hope so.

NATALIE HAS ALWAYS enjoyed the holidays at work, and it's fun decorating the bakery for Christmas, filling the front window with angel cookies, fruit cake, and other seasonal treats.

On a personal level though, the holidays are depressing. All she can think about are past Christmases with her family, and how she'll never have that again. To make matters worse, Peter somehow convinces Chloe to go over to Lena's house the latter half of Christmas Day, which only depresses Natalie further. A couple hours after Chloe leaves, there's a phone call from her. Natalie worries something is wrong, but Chloe quickly dissuades her of that notion.

"Guess what?" Chloe's voice is high-pitched with excitement. "Daddy says he's buying me a horse!"

"He what?"

"It's my Christmas present! We're going to start looking right away!"

"He's buying you a *horse?*" Natalie repeats, stunned.

"We're going to stable him, of course, but he'll be all mine. Or she will," Chloe amends. "I'm not sure if I want a stallion or a mare."

Natalie is dizzy with shock that Peter would do something like this without consulting her. "A horse is a big responsibility. We talked about you getting one when you were a little older."

"Daddy and Lena both say I'm old enough. You're not saying no, are you?" Chloe's voice takes on a worried quiver.

Lena says she's old enough? "Can you put your dad on the phone?"

Natalie listens as Chloe calls Peter to the phone. There's some scraping sounds and then she hears Peter's testy voice. "I know what you're going to say, Natalie, but I don't see the problem."

"The problem is we agreed Chloe isn't old enough to care for a horse yet." They'd talked about how it would be good for Chloe as a teenager to have the responsibility, that she could even get a part-time job to help pay for the horse's upkeep. Apparently, those plans have all been flushed down the toilet along with her marriage.

"We'll find a good stable for the animal. As Lena pointed out, we can just pay the stable to care for the horse until Chloe is old enough to take over."

Natalie grits her teeth. "This is a parenting decision we already made together. You can't just change things without consulting me!"

"Have a heart, Nat. It's Christmas. Do you really want to tell Chloe no?"

"And look like the bad guy? Of course not! How could you do this to me, Peter?"

He sighs as if she's being unreasonable. "Don't be ridiculous. No one is doing anything to you. Lena said you'd make this all about yourself, and she was right."

Natalie wants to curse, but instead, takes a deep breath, trying to gain control. "This is just like that smartphone you got her. You think you can buy Chloe's love and forgiveness, but you can't. Those things aren't for sale."

"I just want my daughter to be happy. Why is that so hard to understand?"

She almost chokes on the words she wants to say, that if Peter truly wanted Chloe's happiness he wouldn't have left her for Lena in the first place.

NATALIE TRIES NOT to dwell on her resentment against Peter, though it isn't easy. Chloe is over the moon and looking at horses online every day. She's at least glad to see her daughter's enthusiasm, so she doesn't say anything more against the idea.

For some reason, Natalie can't stop thinking about her last phone conversation with Anthony. Fighting with him probably wasn't the smartest way to handle things. There's something about him that makes her reckless. And the worst thing is, *he* called *her* that second time and she suspects it was to show he'd forgiven her for the asshole comment.

"Are you still planning to add some Italian pastries to our menu?" Blair asks after Natalie has finished unloading her morning baking.

"Yeah, now that the holidays are over I plan to add some. I want to update our biscotti offerings, maybe do a weekly special. Also, I'm thinking about adding a panna cotta and a tiramisu. What do you think?"

Blair considers Natalie's suggestions. "Sounds good. I wonder if we should ask Anthony for ideas. It might put us on his good side."

"Let's not bother him," Natalie says quickly. "I'm sure he's busy right now with classes."

"They always say the best way to a man's heart is through his stomach. Of course, if that were true, men would be beating down our door."

Natalie grabs a clean apron, thinking about Blair's words. She remembers how Anthony told her tiramisu is one of his favorite desserts.

Blair is watching as she ties on the apron.

"What is it?" Natalie glances over.

"I'm still getting used to you as a blonde, not to mention the new clothes and makeup."

"I know," Natalie sighs. "Everyone keeps commenting on it. In truth, I feel self-conscious. And then I discovered that Lindsay and Chloe hid my *Lord of the Rings* hoodie!"

Blair laughs. "I can't say I blame them, but you look great."

Natalie has been trying to relax and enjoy her new appearance. She never told anyone, but she went back to the salon for lessons in applying makeup and blow-drying her hair. Some days she feels great and others she feels uncomfortable with the attention. She's noticed that people—especially men—are treating her differently. Where she used to be invisible, now they're holding doors open for her and trying to talk to her. The biggest surprise is how much other blonde women stare at her. Who knew women were checking each other out so much?

"I'm trying to relax, but it's just out of my comfort zone. Lindsay and I went out for dinner the other night and some guys sent drinks to our table."

"*And?*"

"And that's never happened to me in my entire life!"

Blair smiles. "You'll get used to it. It might even be time to go on a date."

"I'd be so nervous that I'd have to carry a barf bag and hold it over my mouth the whole time. That might turn him off."

Blair laughs. "I doubt it would be that bad."

AFTER A BIT of online navigation with her computer and a quick phone call to the university's Astronomy Department, Natalie figures out Anthony's class schedule and office hours. Now she needs to come up with the perfect tiramisu. It can't be too sweet, obviously. And it has to be the real thing. Something you'd find at a cafe in Venice or Rome.

Natalie smiles and leans back in her chair. This is familiar territory.

Angels will sing. He'll be weeping with pleasure after the first bite.

She imagines Anthony's handsome face—his eyes closed with bliss. Warmth spreads through her. *His pleasure will have come from me.* She thinks about how Lindsay and Blair are pushing her to date. *If only a man like Anthony showed interest.*

But then she stops that fantasy. She could never date Anthony. The evil landlord. Not that he'd ever be interested in her, anyway.

Natalie has made tiramisu before, but she's not sure how authentically Italian they were. Reading online, she discovers more than a few "traditional" recipes.

Luckily, she knows someone who can help.

Santosa's Bistro, run by Chef Austin Santosa, is a few blocks up from La Dolce Vita and Natalie decides to walk there. In the past she would have driven, but after taking Ryan's advice, she's been finding ways to incorporate exercise into her daily life.

Having a personal trainer seemed strange at first, but she has to admit that Ryan has been helping her stay on track. In fact, she has more energy than ever. Between that and the boxing, she's probably the fittest she's ever been.

Admittedly, she'd still like to lose more weight. And exercising so much is making her hungry. Ryan has assured her that as she builds muscle she'll lose inches without the scale going down.

Let's face it though, I'll never be skinny.

When she reaches Santosa's, she finds they aren't open yet, so she heads around to the back entrance. There's a bustle of activity going on in the large kitchen, which she can't help comparing to La Dolce Vita's own cramped space.

"Is Austin around?" she asks one of the prep cooks.

"He's out front."

"Okay, thanks."

Natalie heads into the front of the restaurant and immediately sees Austin's bulky frame and his long brown ponytail. He's standing with his back to her, talking to an older woman she recognizes as his sous chef, though she can't remember her name.

"Excuse me, Austin?"

He tosses a look over his shoulder. "I'll be right with you. Take a seat." But then he turns back and his blue eyes widen. "*Natalie?*" He scans her up and down. "You look fucking hot! I didn't even recognize you."

She draws her shoulders in and smiles. "Thanks, I think."

"It's definitely a compliment. Jesus, I thought you were a vendor." He turns to the woman beside him. "What do you think, Tanya, doesn't she look hot?"

Tanya nods. "You look really great. Also, that Herbes de Provence bread you sent over for us to try last week was fantastic."

"Oh? I'm glad to hear it. I was playing around with a new recipe."

Austin nods. "It was real popular. Can you hook us up with a regular order on that?"

Natalie already knows she doesn't have time for it, but figures she'll work late. "Sure, no problem."

"Awesome."

Tanya motions. "I'm heading back into the kitchen now." She nods at Natalie. "Good to see you again."

"Same here," Natalie replies.

Austin leans back against the counter and looks at her expectantly. "So what can I do for you?"

"I came here to flatter you and tap your encyclopedic knowledge of Italian food. I'm looking for a great tiramisu recipe, but it has to be old school. Something traditional that you'd actually find in Italy."

He nods slowly. "Is this for the bakery?"

"Possibly. Mostly I'm trying to apologize to our landlord." Natalie explains what happened.

Austin laughs. "Is the guy really that much of a dick? I don't think I've ever met him. Though I heard you and Blair were trying to expand. You know," he lowers his voice, "I haven't told anybody this yet, and maybe I shouldn't be mentioning it, but we're thinking about moving to that new complex being built on Roosevelt. We've talked to the developer there, although there's nothing solid yet."

Natalie stops breathing. "You might be leaving this space?"

"Yeah, are you guys interested?"

"Are you kidding me? I love this space. Who's your landlord?"

"Some investment group. We mostly deal with their lawyer—this dude named Graham."

"I know him! We deal with him, too."

Austin nods. "Like I say, nothing's definite, but there's talk. I don't want to get your hopes up."

"Okay, understood. Hopefully, we can just expand where we are anyway. Our lease isn't up for a while."

He pauses. "Let's go back into the office and I'll check my files. I think I do have a tiramisu recipe I picked up in Venice."

They head back into the recesses of Austin's office, which is about as much in disarray as she's ever seen a place.

"How's Lindsay doing these days?" he asks, grabbing a black binder with the word Venice scrawled on the side.

Natalie tries not to smile. Lindsay dated Austin a few years back, and she's pretty sure he's never gotten over it. He was one of Lindsay's many dumpees. "She's fine. She just sold a piece to the library in Tacoma."

"Is that right?" Austin flips through his binder. "Tell her I said hello. Ask her if she'd like to go have a drink sometime."

"You know she's seeing someone, right?"

He smirks. "Isn't she always?"

Natalie has to agree that her sister is seldom without a man on her arm. And Austin is just her type. A temperamental artist who looks like an ex-con, but in a sexy, bad boy kind of way.

"I'll mention it to her."

Austin pulls out a sheet of wrinkled paper. "Here, I found it. I got this from a small cafe in Venice. As I recall, it was exceptional."

He makes her a copy and hands it over. "I hope it works out and you can get this guy on your side."

Me, too. "Thanks, I'll let you know."

WHEN NATALIE GETS back to the bakery, she's surprised to see Chloe in the kitchen. Chloe used to come and do homework after school, but hasn't lately.

"Chloe?" she says. Natalie notices there's a cup of hot chocolate and a fresh croissant in front of her, though by the looks of it she hasn't touched either of them. Blair is standing beside her and the rest of the kitchen staff are hovering nearby. 'What's going on?"

Chloe turns and when she sees Natalie, immediately runs into her arms, bursting into tears.

"It's Peter," Blair tells her quietly.

"Has something happened to him?" Natalie hugs her daughter. The thought of Peter being harmed or injured is alarming. Despite everything, Peter is still her husband.

"We just found out he—"

"He's marrying Lena!" Chloe sobs and hugs Natalie tighter.

The kitchen quiets around them.

"What?" Natalie is stunned.

Blair nods. "That's what he told her."

Chloe pulls away and starts to talk between sobs. "I went by Daddy's work and Lena was there. They told me they're getting married!"

"They both told you that?"

Chloe nods. "Lena has a big diamond ring on her finger."

Natalie is frozen in place. A wave of sharp pain washes over her. Apparently somewhere deep down, without realizing it, she was still hanging on to the small hope that things between her and Peter would work out and she'd have her family back. It was like a fresh betrayal all over.

"They're having an engagement party. Lena even asked me to be in their w . . . wah . . . wedding!"

Natalie closes her eyes for a moment and smoothes her hand over Chloe's hair. "It's going to be all right," she tells her. "Listen, I'm going to go talk to your dad—okay? Blair is going to stay here with you."

Blair puts her arm around Chloe. "Drink a little hot chocolate. If you want, you can come and help me decorate one of my wedding cakes. You used to like that—remember?"

Chloe nods and sits back down. She reaches for her mug.

Blair squeezes Natalie's hand and speaks into her ear. "Go tell that selfish bastard he can go to hell."

"I DON'T CARE if Dr. Anderson is with a patient. Tell him his *wife* is on the line and that it's urgent!"

Natalie is put on hold again. Her hands are shaking with fury.

Finally, she hears Peter's voice and he sounds annoyed. "Natalie, I can't talk right now, I'm busy."

"I just want to know one thing. Is Lena more important to you than your own daughter?"

"No, of course not."

"Really? Because Chloe is here right now crying her eyes out."

Peter sighs. "I'm sorry to hear that, but I don't really understand why she's so upset."

"Maybe it's because you just got engaged to another woman while you're still married to her mother!"

"But our marriage is over. We'll be divorced soon and besides, I thought she was warming up to Lena."

"Do you think that's how she sees it? You've wrecked her family."

Peter doesn't say anything.

"When were you even planning to tell me about this?"

"I was going to let you know about it tonight when I dropped Chloe off. I wanted to tell you face-to-face. I realize we haven't seen each other in quite some time."

"You couldn't have at least waited until we're divorced before you asked Lena to marry you?" Natalie grips the phone in frustration. "What's the rush? And I understand you're also having an engagement party?"

"That was Lena's idea," Peter admits. "I told her we should probably wait on that, but she wants to announce to the world that we're committed to each other and I didn't see the harm in it."

"There is harm, though. Chloe is miserable and the whole thing is in poor taste. Has this woman robbed you of your common sense?"

"Of course not!" Peter snaps. "You're just jealous. Lena said you would get like this when you found out."

"I'm just trying to protect Chloe."

"She'll be fine. She's tougher than you think."

Natalie grits her teeth. "You know what? I've had it with your selfishness.

I've tried to be reasonable about things because I didn't want to upset our daughter more with a big drawn-out battle, but I'm calling my lawyer. If you want out of this marriage you're going to pay."

"What's that supposed to mean?"

"I want the house free and clear."

Peter scoffs. "Forget it. I'll never agree to that."

"Then I'll drag this out as long as I can. In fact, I want alimony, too."

"I'm not paying alimony! Why should I pay you alimony? You have the income from the bakery."

Natalie tightens her grip on the phone. "You still make a lot more money than I do. Believe me, Peter, I can make this go on forever."

"Lena is so right about you. You're jealous and closed off, but you're only hurting yourself. I feel sorry for you, Natalie."

"Save the sympathy for yourself—because when I'm done with you, you're going to need it."

Natalie hangs up, shaking. She's glad she decided to finally play hard-ball. Lindsay and Blair had both told her she was being too soft on Peter.

She has her boxing class that night and as she takes out her frustrations with punching drills, she thinks about what Anthony said, and he's right—it does feel good to hit something as hard as she can.

Now I just need to fix the mess with him.

Later that evening as Natalie is getting ready for bed, her cell rings. It's Peter's name on the caller ID.

"What do you want?"

"Is that any way to talk to me? You could at least be polite."

Natalie thinks back to her class earlier. *I may have to install a punching bag in the living room.* "It's late for me and you already know that, so if you have something to say spit it out."

He takes a deep breath and releases it. "I'm giving you the house."

Natalie is stunned. "Could you repeat that?"

"Lena and I talked it over and we've decided to give you the house. She didn't want to at first, but I talked her into it."

"I see." She wants to point out that this isn't any of Lena's business. Lena doesn't own any part of their house, but she decides to keep her mouth shut.

"This is on one condition, though."

"What's that?"

"I'm not paying you alimony."

Natalie pretends to think this over. In truth she doesn't really care about the alimony as long he pays child support. The house is what she wants. "Okay, I accept your terms. I'll take the house free and clear, but I won't ask for alimony."

"Good. I'll tell my attorney to contact yours. Does this mean you're ready to sign divorce papers?"

Divorce papers? Natalie's heart is suddenly in her throat. A judge still has to sign off on their parenting plan, but it will only be a formality. Peter sounds so eager to be rid of her. To start the next chapter of his life. But he and Chloe have been her life for so long. She takes a deep breath and lets it out.

Peter doesn't want me anymore.

"Okay," she hears herself say. "I'll sign the papers."

Chapter Twelve

Diet Plan: Fruits and veggies. Green smoothies. A bite of tiramisu.

Exercise Plan: Elliptical. Boxing. Weight lifting. Ogle a hot guy.

"EXCUSE ME," NATALIE stops some young guy with a backpack. "Can you tell me where the Physics-Astronomy Auditorium is?"

She balances the cold pack holding her tiramisu inside as the kid explains how to get there.

"Okay, thanks." Natalie is only vaguely familiar with the University of Washington's campus, but she printed up a map and thinks she knows what he's talking about.

"Happy to help," he says with a grin, glancing down at her chest. "Are you a new student?"

"No, I'm meeting someone."

The kid's eyes wander to her chest again and stay there. "I could show you around," he says. "Maybe we could grab a latte?"

Natalie studies him. He doesn't seem to be aware that he just asked her breasts out for coffee. "Sorry, we're too busy for that," she tells him.

She's been getting a lot of this lately. Guys staring at her chest and asking her out. *My breasts need to get their own social secretary.* Lindsay told her she's lucky, but Natalie isn't so sure.

"I don't think I'm wearing anything that revealing, am I?" she asked Lindsay after some guy asked her breasts out for drinks while they were waiting in line at the movies.

"No, you look nice. But you're stacked. I wish I had a rack like yours."

"Yeah, right."

"I'm serious. I'd love to have your body. Why didn't I get those genes? You obviously got lucky and take after Mom's side of the family."

Natalie laughed. "You're kidding, right? I've spent my whole life wishing I looked like you. I always felt like a whale."

"Well, you're getting the last laugh now. I look like a boy standing next to you."

"No, you don't." The wind was blowing Lindsay's long brown curls around her heart-shaped face. "You're beautiful, and I'm glad for you. I always have been."

"You really don't get it, do you?" Lindsay was shaking her head. "You're gorgeous. And I'm not kidding when I say I wish I had a body like yours. I'm too skinny. I've learned how to work it, but you have the kind of body men love."

Natalie didn't know what to say to that.

"You need to loosen up and have some fun with it, though," Lindsay continued. "You're finally single again."

"Yeah," Natalie sighs. Her divorce was made final only a week ago. She felt sad, of course, but mostly she felt numb. In some ways, it was still hard to believe any of it was real.

"Thank God, you agreed to go on a date. That's progress."

Natalie had finally let Lindsay talk her into going out with someone from one of the matchmaking websites. "I'm dreading it, though."

"You'll be fine. It's a healthy step." Lindsay smiles. "And, besides, you've got me to help guide you."

NATALIE CONSULTS HER map and heads toward Drumheller Fountain. According to Latte Boy, the Physics-Astronomy Auditorium is the next building after the Chem Library.

She transfers the cold pack with the tiramisu to her left arm and looks at her phone. His astronomy class starts in five minutes, but she figures the building straight ahead has to be the auditorium. A number of students are entering and she heads over to follow them.

She pulls her wool pea coat close against the cold outside. Underneath she's wearing a purple sweater and black pencil skirt. It isn't easy, but she's getting better at putting clothes together. A salesgirl at Nordstrom had introduced her to the miracle of shapewear, and that changed everything. It made her look ten pounds lighter, though she felt wrapped as tight as a mummy.

Walking with heels was also taking some getting used to. Her feet were already sore, but she loved the glamorous black boots she'd bought. She glances down at them with a smug smile.

They look just like Lena's.

Natalie works her way down the auditorium steps and takes a seat, placing the cold pack on the small desk in front of her. She glances around, impressed by the number of students here. The fruity smell of perfume drifts her way from a group of sorority girls sitting directly behind her. Most students are pulling out notebook computers and there's a general hustle and bustle as everyone finds a seat and gets themselves organized.

Searching the front near the whiteboard, she doesn't see Anthony anywhere and hopes she didn't get the wrong class. According to her phone, it's five after the hour. But then she sees him toward the front, talking to a student.

Wow.

Her breath stops at the sight of him. It's possible he's even more handsome than she remembers. He's wearing a chocolate brown sweater and jeans and is carrying his usual leather satchel. She studies his broad shoulders and how they taper down. *Nothing but miles of lean muscle.* His dark wavy hair is longer than when she last saw him and gives him a roguish quality.

She feels a peculiar hunger looking at him. *I want him.* The thought comes to her unbidden and she pushes it aside.

"There he is," she hears one of the girls behind her whispering.

"God, he's hot. I still can't believe he's the prof."

"I know, I'd do him in a second!"

Laughter.

"I'm so glad he's back from his vacation or whatever."

"Me, too. This is so my favorite class!"

The room quiets when Anthony speaks. "Welcome back to Astronomy 101. I trust everyone had a good holiday and that you're all relaxed and ready to get back to work."

Smiles and murmurs run through the auditorium.

Anthony smiles, too. "I thought I'd quickly outline what we'll be going over this quarter." He offers up textbook page numbers and everyone starts typing into their computers.

Natalie, not having a computer—and obviously not even a student—is content to sit back and watch Anthony, and watch him she does. Every move he makes. It's like having her own live Anthony channel.

If only I had a pair of those little binocular glasses people bring with them to the opera.

She almost feels guilty for the way she's ogling him. But she can't pull her eyes away. How he moves, the sound of his voice, even the way he puts on his black geek glasses and goes over to write something on the whiteboard. She studies him from behind. His jeans are loose enough to be stylish, but tight enough to show that he has a first-class ass.

God, I feel like a peeping Tom.

For a moment, Natalie even considers sitting in on his astronomy lecture every week.

It's not as if he'd notice me in the crowd.

She watches Anthony's mannerisms. He uses his hands when he talks and rubs his jaw when he's thinking something over. Everything he does strikes her as impossibly sexy. She can't remember being this strongly attracted to anyone in her entire life.

It just figures it would be him.

As she continues to ogle, she remembers how he told her he slept in a white T-shirt and boxer briefs.

What I'd give to see that.

Anthony isn't the type of lecturer to stand still in front of a podium, but cracks jokes and paces the floor energetically. Natalie wonders how he does it. There's no way she'd feel comfortable speaking in front of so many people.

Occasionally, she even listens to what he's saying. Some of it is fascinating. Most of what she knows about astronomy comes from watching science fiction movies, so hearing Anthony talk about black holes as a real phenomenon is intriguing.

Eventually, the class is over and everyone starts to pack away their computers.

Natalie takes a deep breath and stands up. There are butterflies in her stomach. She grabs her cold pack with the tiramisu inside and pushes against the crowd as she makes her way down the stairs to the front of the room, where Anthony is talking to students.

He's not going to be happy to see me.

Hopefully, her apology with a delicious dessert will be enough.

As she moves closer, she sees that he's surrounded by young women fawning over him like groupies.

I'm surprised he isn't signing autographs.

Clearly, he's enjoying himself as he charms them all with his boyish grin. For a moment, Natalie is sucked in like the rest of them, rendered powerless by his smile. Anthony seems so good-natured. It feels familiar, but then she knows all about self-centered men like him from her father.

As the girls all giggle over some joke Anthony just made, Natalie pushes her way through the crowd.

"Excuse me, Anthony?"

He glances over at her. "Yes?"

"Do you have a minute?"

He glances over again, but then does a double take. His brown eyes grow wide as he stares at her for a long moment. "Natalie?"

She tries to hide her nervousness. "I know this is a surprise. I wonder if I could talk to you?"

Some pretty brunette is asking him why there are craters on the moon, but Anthony ignores her.

Instead, he keeps staring at Natalie, his mouth open, an alarmed expression on his face.

He's probably shocked I have the nerve to show up here.

Natalie holds up her cold pack. "I brought you a peace offering. Do you think I could follow you back to your office?"

Anthony still appears on the verge of panic. "What happened to you? Your hair . . ."

"I know. I had it done blonde."

"And other *things.*" He looks her up and down.

Some of the girls around him are starting to get irritated. "Professor Novello, we were hoping to meet up with you after class today. Maybe get coffee?"

Continuing to ignore them, Anthony scans the crowd behind her. Natalie turns to see what he's looking at, but all she finds are more students. Mostly guys. One of them smiles at her, and she smiles back.

Anthony frowns.

"Professor Novello, will you—"

"I'm done answering questions for today," Anthony says, standing up. "Feel free to email and either my assistant or one of my TAs will get back to you."

He grabs his satchel.

Natalie is still clutching her cold pack, trying to look humble.

"Are you coming?" he asks.

She glances around and then back to him. "Are you talking to me?"

He shifts his satchel impatiently. "Yes, of course."

"Oh." She smiles sheepishly. The women who were fawning over Anthony are now watching Natalie with disappointment instead.

✦ ✸ ✦

THEY LEAVE THE auditorium together. Anthony walks quickly and Natalie struggles to keep up in her high-heeled boots.

"Is your office much further?" she asks.

"It's just over in the Physics-Astronomy building."

His eyes linger on her before he looks away. He's still wearing an expression that's bordering on alarm. *I must be really putting him on the spot.*

"I'm sorry if this is a bad time."

"It's not, I . . ." Anthony suddenly notices her cold pack and stops walking. "Here, I can carry that for you."

"Oh, it's fine. I've got it."

He takes it from her hands. She lets him, since it's his tiramisu anyway.

After what feels like ten miles, they get to his small office. It's on the third floor of a newer building. Anthony's desk is in the corner near the window and is crowded with books, papers, and various academic paraphernalia.

There's a bookshelf next to the desk and a whiteboard pushed to one side that's covered with mathematical equations. She takes a deep breath. It smells like stale coffee and high IQs.

He shoves some papers aside and sets the cold pack down.

Natalie eyes the chair, wishing she could sink into it and take her boots off, her feet hurt so badly. *That's what I get for trying to be as glamorous as Lena.*

"I enjoyed your class," Natalie tells him politely. "I don't know much about astronomy, but it was interesting." Her butterflies are back, but her foot pain is a good distraction. She hopes he doesn't try and quiz her about the lecture, since she spent more time ogling him than actually paying attention.

He turns to her again, his eyes still lingering. She notices the alarmed expression is gone and instead, he's studying her with interest.

"I've never seen you outside the bakery before."

"I suppose not."

"You're not what I thought. You look . . . different."

Their eyes meet and a flicker of something passes between them.

"There was no need to sit in on my entire lecture," Anthony says. "You could have just met me after class."

Her face grows warm. *He probably knows I've been drowning in his sex appeal for an hour.*

Anthony pulls his leather satchel off and hangs it on his office chair. "So, I take it you came here to apologize to me again?"

Natalie tries to appear contrite. "How did you know? I would have come sooner, but things were busy with the holidays."

"So what's in the package?"

She walks closer to his desk until she's standing on the other side. His hands are resting on the cold pack and her eyes linger on them. They're tan and well-shaped with long fingers. She remembers wondering how it would feel if they touched her.

"Open it and see."

He finds the side zipper and then, after peering into the pack, reaches inside and pulls out the container.

"It's a tiramisu," he says in surprise.

"You mentioned once that it's one of your favorite desserts."

"You made this?"

"I did. I hope you like it. I tried to make it as authentic as possible."

Anthony nods slowly. "Thanks."

Natalie shifts awkwardly from one foot to another. "Well, I'd better get going. I don't want to take up too much of your time. I know you're busy." She thinks of all the young women clamoring for his attention.

"Wait a second, I thought you came to apologize."

"I did."

"So where's my apology?"

Natalie gives him a funny look. "It's sitting on your desk right in front of you."

"So it doesn't include the actual words, I'm sorry?"

"Would you like me to say the actual words?"

"Yes." Anthony crosses his arms. "I would. Face-to-face."

Natalie tries not to let her annoyance show. She wants to leave. Her feet are killing her and she'll probably be crippled by the time she makes it back to her car. "Fine," Natalie says. "I'm sorry."

Anthony frowns. "I don't think so. Try again."

"I'm very sorry."

"For what?"

"For being rude to you."

"Is that it? You can do better than that."

"Are you kidding me? I *did* do better than that." She points to her cake. "I baked you the best tiramisu you'll ever eat in your entire life!"

"We'll see if that's true. I'd still like a real apology, though." A smile plays around the edges of his mouth. "Come on, Natalie. You can do it."

She leans into the desk, trying to ease the pressure on her feet. "I'm very sorry I called you a *dick,*" she says enunciating slowly. "That was rude of me."

Anthony chuckles and uncrosses his arms. "Damn, you're stubborn."

Natalie tries not to smile, but can't help herself. "I may have heard that once or twice."

"I'll accept your apology on one condition."

"What's that?"

"You stay and have a piece of tiramisu with me."

"So you can make me grovel some more?"

"Hey, you're the one having difficulty with a simple apology." He motions for her to take a seat. "Grab a chair, I'll be right back. I'm going to get us a couple of forks."

"Fine," she mutters and then hobbles over to sit down. "The truth is you had me at the word chair."

He leaves the office and she reaches down to unzip her boots. Pulling them off, she sighs with nearly orgasmic bliss as she wiggles her toes around. She glares down at the pile of high-heeled leather on the floor. *Devil boots.* It figures something from Lena would cause her so much pain.

While Anthony is gone, Natalie takes in her surroundings.

Anthony's desk is really cluttered. She wouldn't have pictured him being so messy. There are papers and books stacked everywhere. There are a couple of cartoons pinned to the wall and she gets up to take a closer look.

Astronomy humor. After reading them twice, she still doesn't get either joke. She sees a Yoda doll still in its case on the bookshelf and picks it up. "Cool," she murmurs. There's an X-wing fighter, too, though it's not in the box anymore. He really does like *Star Wars.* There are all sorts of small objects sitting on a nearby shelf that on closer inspection she realizes are puzzles. There's a Rubik's Cube—solved, naturally—and some other wooden puzzles.

Natalie notices a couple of coffee mugs. One has the inscription "Astronomers Do It Better in The Dark," which makes her smile. She can think of a few things she wouldn't mind doing with Anthony in the dark.

But then she stops herself. *I wouldn't do anything in the dark with him. Even if he begged me, which, let's face it, would be a miracle.* A fantasy comes to her where Anthony's hands are on her hips. He's pulling her close, whispering in her ear, begging . . .

She takes a deep breath and wonders how any woman can be around him without losing her mind.

There's another coffee mug and she picks it up, surprised to see the words "World's Greatest Dad."

Is Anthony a dad? She stares at the mug, trying to make sense of it. He's never mentioned having a child, but then she barely knows him.

Suddenly, she hears his voice coming down the hall and quickly puts the mug down and takes a seat again. He's talking to a pretty young woman who follows him into the office. She has a flirtatious smile on her face until she sees Natalie.

"I'm actually in the middle of something right now," Anthony explains to the woman. "If you want to send me an email, we could set up a time to go over your final."

"Sure." The young woman glances at Natalie with frustration. "I guess I can do that."

After she's gone, Anthony sets down a couple of paper plates, along with two forks and a knife.

Natalie motions toward the door. "One of your many fans, I see."

"It never ends," he says cheerfully, though there's an edge to his voice.

She watches him pull the cover off the tiramisu and quickly cut a piece for each of them.

"This better be as good you say it is." His brown eyes meet hers. "I don't like to be disappointed."

Natalie feels a nervous tingle run through her. "You won't be."

Anthony picks up his plate and takes a bite. She watches the fork slide from his lips, waiting for his reaction.

He chews slowly and seems to be thinking it over. "Not bad," he finally says.

Natalie's mouth opens. She worked on this recipe for days and knows for a fact it's a masterpiece. "Oh, I think you can do better than that," she mimics him. "Try again."

Anthony laughs. "All right, I'll admit it's delicious."

"Do you really think so?" Despite her confidence, she discovers that she cares what he thinks.

He takes another bite and closes his eyes while he chews.

It's hard not to stare at him. *No one should be this good looking. It isn't natural.*

When he opens them again he nods. "You were right. It's the best tiramisu I've ever tasted."

"It's not too sweet?"

"No, it's perfect."

She smiles. "Thank you. So I don't have to grovel anymore?"

Anthony's eyes flicker from her face to her body, lingering briefly on her breasts. He's wearing an expression she can't quite place and when he speaks his voice is slightly husky. "No more groveling required."

Natalie picks up her own cake, but puts it down again when she hears her phone chirp. She gets it from her purse figuring it's Blair or Chloe. Unfortunately, it's a text from Lena.

We are all children of the universe. Be at peace. Live! Be filled with joy!

"Not again," she groans. "I don't believe this." It's been a few weeks since Lena texted and Natalie had hoped she'd finally grown tired of the whole thing.

Anthony, who is eating his cake with enthusiasm, glances over. "What's wrong?" he asks mid-chew.

"My husband's mistress keeps texting me."

He raises his eyebrows.

"Actually, she's my husband's fiancée."

"Your husband has a *fiancée?*"

The comical expression on Anthony's handsome face forces a laugh out of her. "Actually, he's my ex-husband now."

"I remember you said that you were going through a divorce."

"Yes, it's finally official. Though he got engaged while we were still married. His lunatic fiancée keeps sending me these awful texts."

"What do they say?"

"See for yourself." She hands him her phone.

He puts his cake down and reaches for it. His fingers brush hers briefly as he takes the phone and sits back in his chair.

Anthony chuckles. "Are they all like this?" He thumbs the screen and continues to read. "These are a trip. Wait a minute, she was threatening to charge you with assault and take out a restraining order against you?"

"It's a long story. We sort of got into a fight."

"What happened?"

"I slapped her and she jumped me."

"An actual girl fight," he murmurs. "Wish I could have been there."

Natalie rolls her eyes. "It was awful, believe me."

Anthony hands her phone back. "Who is she? She sounds like a piece of work."

Natalie tells him briefly about Lena, leaving out the part about how gorgeous she is, figuring he doesn't need to know that.

"I just signed the divorce papers last week though, so that's it. In fact, I'm going out on my first date in fourteen years tonight."

He eats more cake. "Is this part of your try-some-new-things plan?"

Natalie's eyes widen. She'd forgotten that she'd told him that. Ironically, he's the only one she's mentioned it to. She decided not to tell Lindsay and Blair since they'd have her jumping out of airplanes and scuba diving before you could say the word "adventure."

"Yes," she admits. "I figured it was time to get out there again. Try to move on."

"Is that why you colored your hair blonde?"

Her hand immediately goes up to touch her hair. "I guess so. It's a change." She'll never admit to anyone she was copying Lena. They'd have to torture it out of her and even then she doubts she'd admit it.

"I like it. Mostly I like your hair down. I've never seen it that way before."

"I usually wear it pulled back for work."

"It looks pretty like this."

Natalie's hand freezes. There's an odd quivery sensation in her stomach. Self-conscious, she quickly reaches for her untouched cake. "Thanks," she murmurs, staring at her plate, trying to catch her breath.

He finishes up the last of his tiramisu. "Have you ever been to a star party?"

She takes a bite of cake, still in a daze over his compliment about her hair. "With actual movie stars?"

Anthony laughs. "It's a party where astronomers get together with their telescopes to stargaze."

"No, I've never been to anything like that."

"Would you like to come with me to one this weekend? A friend of mine is having a star party at his house in Monroe."

Natalie is too stunned to speak. Her pulse skyrockets. *Is Anthony asking me out on a date?* It's like she's entered an alternate universe, where the laws of physics have changed and someone like Anthony is attracted to her.

He grins. "It could be another new thing for you to try."

I should tell him no. It would be a mistake. I can't go out with him, of all people.

"Okay," she hears herself say.

"I'll text you with the details."

Natalie's head is spinning. She feels giddy with excitement, though she's trying not to show it.

Suddenly, there's a woman's voice coming from behind her.

"Knock, Knock! Anybody here?"

Anthony's eyes widen. "Justine?"

Natalie turns in her chair and sees Anthony's girlfriend. The one she completely forgot existed. Justine with the gold jewelry and the endless giggling is standing before them in living color. Natalie feels as if she's been slapped in the face.

I am ten thousand kinds of stupid.

Justine sweeps into the room, her rich perfume overpowering the small space, and Natalie can't help but notice that Justine is gorgeous. And to quote Lindsay, she has quite a rack, though Justine's rack is on a skinny body. *As opposed to mine.*

"What are you doing here?" Anthony asks her.

Justine giggles. "I came to see you, of course!" She suddenly notices Natalie sitting there. At first there's confusion, but then her expression clears and her brown eyes narrow. "It's you again."

Natalie gets up hastily. "I was just leaving. I need to get back to work." Embarrassed, she realizes she's still in her stocking feet and has to put her devil boots back on.

"I came by to see if you'd like to get some dinner," Justine tells Anthony. "I made reservations for us downtown."

Anthony's jaw tightens and he looks annoyed. "I don't know why you did that."

"Because you have to eat, silly!" she giggles.

Natalie finishes with her boots and stands. Her coat is draped over the back of the chair and she grabs it along with her purse. "I should go now and leave you two. I didn't mean to take up so much of your time!"

Justine wears a smug smile, but Anthony looks pissed.

"Don't go—"

"I need to get back to work anyway," Natalie says quickly as she heads for the door. "I'm glad you liked the tiramisu."

"I'll get in touch about this weekend," Anthony calls after her, but she ignores him.

I'm so stupid, is all she can think walking down the hall away from his office. *And I'm throwing these boots in the garbage.*

"WHAT DO YOU want, Justine?" Anthony says, annoyed. "I thought I made it clear that we are not dating. I'm not interested."

Justine moves closer. "I know, but I was in the area and thought I'd drop by and see if we could get a bite to eat."

"Right, and you happened to make dinner reservations?"

She sits down on the corner of his desk near him. Her coat parts and he can see she's wearing a miniskirt beneath it. There's a lot of tan skin showing between the top of her boots and the bottom of her skirt. "Don't be like that." She catches him gazing at her legs and leans closer, pouting. "I think we'd be good together. You should give it a chance."

Anthony looks into her perfectly made-up face. He used to date women like Justine. They know all the right moves, all the right things to say to get a man's attention.

But he's done with that and has been for a while now.

"It's just dinner, Anthony." She tilts her head and smiles with very white teeth. "I really like you." She giggles.

"I understand, and I don't want to hurt your feelings, but like I said, I'm not interested." He already regrets meeting her for coffee at La Dolce Vita. Clearly that was a mistake, because now he can't shake her loose.

"I don't believe that." She gives him a sexy smile.

"Believe it. In fact, I'd like you to leave now. I'm busy."

"Come on, Anthony." She's still smiling, but then something occurs to her and Justine's lips turn down with displeasure. "Is there . . . someone else?"

Anthony is about to tell her no, but then gets a sudden inspiration. "Yeah, there is actually."

"Who?"

"You just met her."

"*Her?*" Justine takes this in and gets a bitchy expression on her face. "That baker? You can't be serious."

"Why not?"

"Because she's . . . fat."

Anthony raises his eyebrows and then chuckles. "I wouldn't describe her that way."

Natalie flashes through his mind. It was a shock seeing her after class. He had no idea that's what she looked like without those baggy black clothes. She's a knockout. It was alarming to discover he'd been so wrong. He's seldom wrong about anything, especially women. She isn't a plain matron type at all, but more like an old fashioned pin-up girl. She seems unaware of it, too. The way those guys were checking her out after class, and how she'd smiled so innocently, she didn't know what they were thinking, but Anthony knew. And he didn't like it.

"She's chunky," Justine says, pouting.

Anthony suddenly has a vision of Natalie sprawled across his sheets. Nothing but lush curves, full breasts, and a plump ass. And that sexy mouth. She'd be a handful in every way.

Damn.

But then he comes to his senses.

I can't get involved with Natalie.

There are too many reasons to name. She's extremely stubborn and he suspects she still thinks he's a dick despite all her endless apologies. Plus she's newly divorced. And finally, she's his unhappy tenant.

I don't want to go there.

He realizes he asked her to that star party without thinking it through.

"Are we still going out to eat?" Justine asks, as if dinner had been his idea. "Because we're going to be late for our reservation."

"No, we're not. And I've still got papers to grade, so it would be good if you left now." He stares pointedly toward the door. He doesn't want to be an asshole, but with some women that's what it takes.

She stands up. "You don't know what you're missing."

"I'll take that chance."

Chapter Thirteen

Diet Plan: Bake a special batch of chocolate chunk cookies. Be strong and resist temptation. Okay, fine, but just one.

Exercise Plan: Squeeze into shapewear. Try on every sweater you own.

"HOW WAS YOUR date last night?" Anthony glances around the bakery's busy back kitchen. The smell of fresh pastries is making him hungry.

Natalie turns to him in surprise. She's standing in front of a mixing bowl that's as big as a bathtub while a huge paddle mixes chocolate batter.

There's flour dusted in her hair and chocolate smeared on her cheek. She's sweaty and disheveled, but Anthony's first thought is that he wouldn't mind seeing her sweaty and disheveled more often. Sweaty and disheveled in his bed would be a good start.

Dude, get a grip. When did you become this attracted to Natalie? Seeing her after class yesterday has been causing all sorts of thoughts to go through his head. And, yeah, most of them involve Natalie sweaty and disheveled.

She pouts.

Anthony feels his groin tighten. *That mouth.*

"It was great!" Natalie says too quickly. "I had a great time!"

He can tell she's lying, but feels a peculiar twinge of jealousy anyway. "Good for you. Another new experience under your belt."

She's watching the mixing bowl, but shoots him a dark look. After a few seconds she reaches over to turn the machine off. It's clear she's annoyed with him about something, but he has no idea what.

He smirks. "Whatever it is, I swear I'm innocent."

"What do you mean?"

Anthony shakes his head, chuckling to himself. "Forget it. I came in to get the numbers from you and to talk to you about that star party. Why don't you come out front when you're ready?" He leaves the kitchen and makes his way out to the front counter to get in line for coffee. Two of the women in line are smiling at him, but he pretends not to notice. Instead, he gets out his phone and studies his email.

He orders his usual espresso breve and takes a seat by the window. As soon as he sits down his phone starts playing the *Star Wars* theme song. A glance tells him it's Graham.

"Hey brah, what's up?"

"Just thought you should know I got some interest in the space next to the bakery."

Anthony glances around. He's not sure if he wants to have this conversation right here.

"They want to come by and see the space," Graham continues. "What should I tell them?"

Anthony quickly runs through possible scenarios in his mind. He knows Blair and Natalie aren't turning enough business away to warrant leasing them that space. At this point he's certain they'd overextend themselves.

"When do they want to see it?"

"Tonight."

He thinks it over. Serena's school tuition is due next month, and he promised Nicole he'd take care of the entire amount. "Okay, tell them that's fine. Don't have them sign anything yet though. Let's make sure their financing is solid. Also, how do they plan to use the space?"

"Clothing boutique."

"Okay. Let me know what happens."

Anthony hangs up. He doesn't want to screw Natalie and Blair over, but at the same time that space has been empty for months and he needs to find a tenant who can afford to pay.

Natalie is still in back so he pulls his computer out. He and a colleague are working on a proposal for time with an orbiting telescope called SWIFT that detects gamma-ray bursts. He talks with his assistant, Maya, to get the information he needs. Anthony is so focused on his computer as he talks that he doesn't even notice Natalie until she takes a seat in the chair right across from him.

"Got to go, Maya," he says into his phone. "I'll see you in a short while though, yeah?"

Natalie is studying him and still seems annoyed for some reason.

"You wanted to see this?" Natalie asks, holding up the notebook where she records the business they've had to turn away.

"Sure."

She finds the relevant page and hands it over. He looks over the new numbers, quickly memorizing everything before handing it back.

"I'm still amazed you can do that."

Anthony shrugs and takes his glasses off. He works with plenty of people like him who can do complex equations in their heads. Memorizing numbers doesn't seem that impressive, though it's true, he can memorize quite a bit more math than most people.

"Have you ever counted cards?"

Anthony looks up at her in surprise. "That's an odd question."

Natalie gives an embarrassed smile. "I don't know why I asked that. Listen, I can't go to that star party with you."

Anthony doesn't say anything for a few seconds. He tries to remember the last time a woman turned down a chance to be with him.

"I know I'm new to this whole dating thing, but I'm not stupid. Justine is obviously your girlfriend, so I'm not sure why you even asked me to go."

He picks up his coffee. It's his turn to be annoyed. "Justine is not my girlfriend."

"She's not?"

"No, I agreed to have coffee with her one time—actually, the day you and Blair came up to me."

Natalie is surprised and then skeptical. "What about when she showed up in your office yesterday?"

"That's exactly right—she showed up, on her own. I had nothing to do with that."

Natalie opens her mouth and then closes it.

"And I asked you to go to the star party because I thought you might enjoy yourself," he continues.

She considers this. "Well, it's still a bad idea."

Anthony puts his coffee down. Is Natalie playing hard to get? It's an intriguing notion.

"And why is that?"

"Because you're our evil landlord. Plus, I'm newly divorced and that complicates everything."

Even though Natalie just gave him the exact reasons he decided to call it off, he finds himself disinclined to let it go. "And did your date last night have something to do with this decision?"

She fiddles with the notebook in her hands and then looks out the window. "Not really."

He studies her face as she takes in the street view outside. She's wearing very little makeup and in the window's natural light he sees dark shadows under her eyes. Her newly blonde hair is swept back away from her face in that stern ponytail she always wears at work. Despite her prickly façade, he senses vulnerability beneath the surface.

Anthony decides he'd like to tear that ponytail down. Tear that apron off, too. He's surprised by his reaction to her because he still finds her stubbornness annoying as hell. She's getting under his skin, though.

"My date didn't exactly happen." She turns back to him. "I only made it to the parking lot."

"What do you mean?"

"Just that. I drove to the parking lot of the restaurant where I was supposed to meet him, and then left." She studies the notebook in her hands.

"You didn't go inside?"

"No."

He chuckles. "You just left that poor guy sitting there waiting for you?" This cheers him up quite a bit.

"I texted him from the parking lot and told him I couldn't make it."

"What did he say?"

"He didn't like it. Said I was rude to cancel at the last minute."

"He sounds like a jerk."

She looks up. "Do you think so?"

"Yeah." Though he really has no idea. He just knows he doesn't want Natalie going out with some loser. "What did you do then? Go home?"

"No, I couldn't go home because my sister Lindsay was there and she would have freaked out, so I went boxing. Luckily, I still had my gym clothes in the car."

Anthony has a vision of Natalie wearing nothing but skimpy boxing shorts and a T-shirt two sizes too small. She's sweaty and her hair's coming loose, bouncing against him. Those magnificent breasts are barely contained.

God. He swallows.

"The boxing was the best part of my evening," she says, and then starts to laugh. It reminds him of their phone conversations. Her laughter is earthy and real and full of promise. He likes it. A lot.

"Sounds like you're a badass after all," he tells her, shifting in his chair to accommodate the erection now plaguing him.

She laughs some more. "Yeah, all I need is a motorcycle. Maybe I could borrow yours!"

Anthony tilts his head back slightly. "How did you know I ride a motorcycle?"

"You sometimes wear a motorcycle jacket and I've seen you carrying a helmet around."

"You're very observant."

Her cheeks flush. "I just happened to notice."

"What else have you noticed about me?"

Natalie's cheeks turn a darker shade of pink. "Nothing. I haven't noticed anything."

She's so embarrassed Anthony wonders exactly how much she has been observing him. His phone vibrates and he glances down at it, freezing when he sees the time. He has a meeting in twenty minutes with a group of post-graduate students to discuss the data from their recent Keck observing run. "Shit. I apologize, but I have to go."

Natalie watches him as he stands up and quickly packs his computer away. "Can I ask you something?"

"Sure."

"Have you ever been on time for anything in your life?"

"No," he admits. "I'm usually late for everything."

"You need to be more organized."

He snorts. "So I've been told."

"I always keep track of when I'm supposed to be somewhere. As a result, I'm never late."

"Good for you." He remembers all too well how she busted his balls for being late to their first meeting. Despite that, when he turns to her and finds those sultry lips are smiling at him, he suddenly wishes he could stay longer. Anthony slings his bag over his shoulder and motions toward the door. "I got to jet. *Ciao,* Natalie," he says with a grin.

"*Ciao.*" She grins back.

For some reason, he's still smiling halfway up the block before he realizes what he has to do. He glances at his watch. He's going to be crazy late for his meeting.

The aroma of espresso and fresh pastries surrounds him when he enters the bakery again. There's a new line of people near the counter, and he murmurs, "Excuse me," to everyone as he pushes his way to the front. Natalie is there behind the pastry case, rearranging things. She looks up in surprise to see him.

"Anthony? Did you forget something?"

He hesitates. For some reason, he's nervous. "I want you to come with me to that star party on Saturday," he says, breathless from running. "No excuses."

"I don't think—"

"You have to. It'll be your next new thing."

Natalie bites her lip and glances to the side. "I just . . . it's not a good idea. I don't want to hurt your feelings, but you're not really my type."

Anthony doesn't move. He's too stunned to speak for a couple seconds. "I'm not your type?"

"You're very handsome, obviously," she says quickly. "But I don't think we're well suited."

He stares at her and realizes she's completely serious. *I'm being rejected.* It's an odd sensation to have a woman reject him and he lingers over it for a moment. Quickly he regroups and decides to handle her the same way he does his family. He tries again.

"Come with me anyway—as friends."

"Friends?"

"Yes, friends. Nothing more."

She appears to mull it over.

"Star parties are a lot of fun. Have you ever seen the rings of Saturn?"

"No, I haven't."

"Or Jupiter's great red spot?"

"I can't say—"

"The weather should be clear, too, so don't miss this opportunity." Anthony groans to himself. *Dude, you sound like you're selling her a refrigerator.*

"Okay," she finally agrees. "I'll go, but only as friends."

IT'S SATURDAY NIGHT and Natalie is running late.

Late.

After telling Anthony how she never runs late.

Come to think of it, I must have sounded like a bitch talking to him like that.

"I thought this wasn't a real date and that you were just going out with the landlord to be friendly?" Lindsay says. She's lying on Natalie's bed propped up on one elbow.

"We are just going out as friends. It's going to be fun and informative. I've never seen the rings of Saturn."

"And that's the fourth time you've mentioned the rings of Saturn. Who gives a crap about Saturn?"

Natalie glances down nervously at the clock on her nightstand. It's ten to nine. Anthony sent her a text yesterday asking for her address. He also told her he'd pick her up at nine and to dress warmly. Unfortunately, it's hard to dress warmly and still look attractive when you have large breasts. The problems start every time she tries on her puffy white coat.

I look like a polar bear. A polar bear stuffed into shapewear and bootcut jeans.

"And why are you putting on so many clothes?"

"It's a star party," Natalie explains to Lindsay as she tries to pull her coat on over her sweater again. "Remember, I told you about it. We're going to be outside all night."

Lindsay watches from the bed. "You can't wear your puffy coat over that sweater. You look like a polar bear."

Natalie groans. "This is impossible."

"Just wear the sweater without the coat."

"But then I'll be freezing all night."

"Who cares? Better to freeze than look ridiculous."

"Maybe I should just cancel." She glances at the clock again. "He'll be here in five minutes!"

But wait, Anthony is always late. It's five to nine, which means he probably won't be here until quarter after. Natalie lets out a little sigh of relief.

Lindsay gets off the bed. "Don't you have another jacket you can wear?"

"I have my black pea coat, but it's shorter and I don't know if it's warm enough."

Lindsay taps her finger against her lip, studying Natalie. "Hold on, I think I have a scarf you could borrow. You could wear that along with the pea coat."

Just as Lindsay leaves the room and Natalie is struggling to pull off her puffy coat, the front door bell rings.

No.

It can't be.

Anthony is always late.

Natalie rushes over to the bedroom window and sees a black SUV parked in her driveway.

He's here and he's on time.

For me.

She stops for a second and smiles.

Lindsay pops her head in the door and throws a couple of scarves at her. "Try these with your pea coat. I'm going to go answer the door."

Natalie picks up one of the blue scarves and attempts to arrange it in the stylish way Lindsay always wears hers. She ties it this way and that. The more she fiddles with it, the more it looks like something someone blew their nose in.

She wonders if she should go downstairs. Isn't it rude to keep him waiting?

Suddenly her bedroom door swings open, with Lindsay on the other side. "Wow," she says, breathless. "He's hot! I know you and Blair told me he was good looking, but damn—he's smokin.'"

She notices the mess Natalie has made with the scarf and hurries over to fix it. "Why the hell didn't you tell me he was this hot? We should have started on you *hours* ago!"

"I had to work today. I left early as it is."

Lindsay just shakes her head. She pulls the scarf off, does something with it and slips it over Natalie's head in a tidy stylish knot. "That's better. You need more makeup now."

"Do I really need more makeup? I mean, I probably shouldn't keep him waiting much longer."

"Don't worry, this will only take a few seconds. Plus, it's good to keep a guy waiting. Don't you know anything?"

Lindsay pulls Natalie into the bathroom and grabs some blush from the counter.

"Don't put too much on," Natalie says.

"You need more makeup at night. Trust me."

Natalie doesn't say anything, but just watches her sister go to work on her face. The truth is, she does trust Lindsay.

After a few minutes, Lindsay steps back and gives her a wink in the mirror. "There you are. Now go get him."

Natalie studies her reflection. "We're just friends. And I've always wanted to see the—"

"—rings of Saturn, I know!" Lindsay laughs. "Only now I understand why!"

WHEN NATALIE GOES downstairs, she finds Anthony leaning against the wall in the front entryway, studying his phone. He looks up, meets her eyes, and her heart nearly stops. He's so blindingly handsome it's like having a movie star in the house.

"Hel-lo," she manages to choke out.

He smiles. "Hi."

"Sorry to keep you waiting."

"That's okay. Are you ready to go?"

"Almost, I just need to get something from the kitchen."

Star Wars music starts playing on Anthony's phone and he glances down at it. "Excuse me, but I have to take this. I'll just wait for you outside, if that's all right?"

"Sure." She watches him walk toward the door and wonders if it's another woman calling. *This isn't a date, so what do I care, right?*

Natalie gets the container of cookies she baked that afternoon and checks on some dough she has rising on the kitchen counter.

Lindsay comes downstairs, carrying her laptop. She glances around. "Where did he go?"

"He's outside on his phone. I'm leaving now. I'm not sure if I'll get cell reception out where we're going, so if there's any problem I told Chloe to call you." It was Peter's weekend so Chloe was staying over there. She seldom called, but Natalie still worried anyway.

"Sure, that's fine."

"And you don't have to bother waiting up for me. I doubt I'll be home until well after midnight."

Her sister puts her laptop down on the coffee table. "Hey, stay out as long as you want. Ride that man like a bronco and don't come home until you've put him in the hospital."

"Lindsay!" Natalie bursts out laughing. "It's not like that!"

"Whatever. Just tell him you want to play with his big *hard* telescope and that you know he has one."

"Oh, my God, I'll talk to you later."

Natalie is still chuckling when she finds Anthony on her front porch. He appears to be finishing up his phone call.

"Yeah, brah, no problem. Thanks, Graham."

"Oh, is that Graham? Please tell me you're finally giving us that space."

Anthony stares at his phone. "Uh, no, not yet."

"How many more weeks do you think we'll have to wait?"

"I'm not sure. What's in the container?" he asks her.

"Chocolate chunk cookies. I put a couple extra dozen aside this afternoon to bring for the star party."

"That was nice of you." He smiles, but she can tell he's distracted by something. "Shall we go?"

They both head over to Anthony's black SUV. He holds the passenger door open for her, which flusters Natalie.

"I thought this wasn't supposed to be a date." She tries to climb inside, but stops because there are books and papers all over the seat.

"Sorry," Anthony says. He reaches past her to grab everything and tosses it into the back. "There you are . . . oh, wait." He brushes the crumbs away.

Natalie climbs inside, kicking aside a few more papers on the floor. She reaches down and adds them to the backseat.

"You need an assistant or something," she tells him as he's getting settled in the driver's seat.

"I have one."

"Really?" She glances at him, but when she tries to look away discovers she can't. His profile draws her back. Anthony's nose is straight, his jaw square. His lips aren't full, but they're even. He's like something out of an Italian Renaissance painting.

She notices his hair is long in back and a strong desire to touch those dark curls takes hold.

It's with real effort that she finally forces herself to turn away.

But then Natalie notices his scent is everywhere in the car. A woodsy smell mixed with something else, something musky and delicious that can only be Anthony himself.

Lust spirals through her.

I could sit in this car smelling him and worshipping his profile all night.

She shifts in her seat. Being this close to Anthony is doing funny things to her insides. There are butterflies dancing in her stomach and her breathing is erratic.

To take her mind off it she asks him where he was raised. "Are you from Seattle?"

"No, I grew up mostly in L.A."

Natalie nods. "Los Angeles. That definitely explains it."

Anthony glances over at her as they pull out onto the main road. "Explains what?"

"The way you talk."

"How do I talk?"

"Well, you're obviously very intelligent. Sometimes you sound refined, almost snobbish. But other times you sound like a surfer dude."

Anthony merges lanes so he can get into the correct lane for the Interstate. "I can't tell for sure, but . . . are you insulting me again?"

Natalie laughs. "I hope not. I'm trying to behave."

He gives her a look from the corner of his eye. "Miss Natalie, what am I going to do with you?"

"I'll be good the rest of the night. I promise."

"And if you're not, do I get to decide your punishment?"

Natalie is tongue-tied at his flirtatious tone. She's not sure what to do. Her flirtation skills are as rusty as an old hippie bus full of Grateful Dead fans. "So, uh, why did you move to Seattle?"

"Mostly work and some other obligations. I was offered tenure track at the UW and decided to take it."

"What's tenure track?"

"It means I'm on track to be a tenured professor, but they haven't offered it to me yet. I have to prove myself first."

"Sounds stressful."

Anthony lets out a breath. "Yeah, it can be."

"So, why else did you move here? You said you had other obligations."

Anthony gives her a smirk. "What is this, an interrogation? I refuse to answer any more questions until you give me one of those cookies."

"But these are for the star party."

He reaches over and tries to take them from her and she squeals. "Hey, hands off!"

"You wouldn't even be going to this star party if it weren't for me."

"Maybe so, but I brought them to share with everyone." Her hands are on top of the container, holding it shut. "You'll have to wait."

"Why are you so cruel to me?"

"I don't know." Natalie knows he's only joking, but she finds herself pondering his words.

"Come on, Natalie, just one cookie."

Anthony surprises her by sliding his hand on top of hers. His touch sends a shock wave through her whole body.

"Did you notice what time I showed up at your house tonight?" he murmurs.

"Yes," she says, trying to hide the breathless quality in her voice. His hand is warm. He slides his fingers between hers to the edges of the lid, trying to get inside. "You were on time."

"And where were you?"

"Late."

"Exactly. So where's my cookie?"

Natalie laughs, surprised at her own sultry tone. "Okay, I'll give you a cookie."

He takes his hand away and Natalie opens the container, releasing the aroma of fresh chocolate and vanilla into the car. She takes one out and hands it to him.

"Thanks," he says. "You're formidable when you're guarding your . . . cookies."

Their eyes meet and Natalie feels herself pulled in.

If I'm not careful I could get in deep trouble here.

She knows about men like him and they typically aren't worth the trouble. But a little voice inside her is saying, so what?

Have some fun. When was the last time a man like this flirted with you?

Uh, never.

So there you go.

But she knows she can't let her guard down. It isn't in her nature to be reckless. Lindsay's maybe, but not hers.

They talk more on the drive, though Natalie notices how cleverly he deflects answering any real questions about himself. For all his friendly charm, she suspects Anthony is a deeply private person.

"So what area of astronomy do you work with again? Gamma radiation?" She'd looked up both "astronomer" and "gamma radiation" when she got home from work that afternoon, figuring it might come in handy. "I remember it was kind of like the Hulk."

"My main area is gamma-ray bursts. Particularly long gamma-ray bursts."

"So what about gamma-ray bombs? Are those real?"

"No," he chuckles, "but I'm impressed. You know your Hulk superhero origin pretty well."

"I'm kind of a closet fantasy sci-fi fan."

"Yeah? I remember you mentioned liking *Star Wars*."

"I'm big on *Lord of the Rings,* too. I have this cool hoodie, but I'm not allowed to wear it anymore. Actually, my daughter and sister hid it from me."

Anthony laughs. "Why would they do that?"

"Apparently, it's ugly."

"You should show it to me sometime."

Natalie imagines modeling her *Lord of the Rings* hoodie for Anthony and the thought makes her chuckle to herself. Lindsay would have a fit. "I don't think I'm allowed."

"I won't tell anyone if you don't." Then he looks over and flashes one of his boyish grins and all Natalie can think is, *deep trouble.*

Chapter Fourteen

> Diet Plan: Big fat slice of humble pie.
> Cool taste of a hot man.
>
> Exercise Plan: Hang out with science
> nerds until your brain hurts.

THEY PULL UP to a ranch-style house that's on some land with a row of evergreens in front. A number of cars are parked in the long driveway, but with the exception of a glowing red porch light, everything else is completely dark.

"Is anybody here?"

"Don't worry. They're all in the backyard."

They both get out of the car, with Natalie holding the cookies and a thermos of coffee Anthony asked her to carry. He walks around to the rear and opens the trunk, fiddling with something in back.

Eventually, he comes around to the front carrying an enormous case.

"What on earth is that?"

"It's my telescope."

"It looks huge."

He glances down. "This is nothing. Just wait until you see some of the other scopes people have. "

"Really? I thought telescopes were slender brass tubes like the one Galileo used."

Anthony chuckles. "Not quite. That was four-hundred years ago."

They make their way around to the back of the house, following a footpath lit by a row of small red lights. It's so dark, she can barely see anything.

Natalie starts to wonder if coming here was a bad idea. It only now occurs to her that she's at an astronomy party with a bunch of super geeks. Everyone there probably has an advanced degree, while she never even finished college.

How long is it going to take them to figure out that I'm a science doofus?

Not long.

She clutches her cookies. *Well, super geek or not, I can bake the pants off anybody here.*

Once they round the corner, she finds herself in a large open field. It's dark but she can see there are people milling about, with more flashes of red light everywhere.

"What's with all the red lights?"

"It helps protect your night vision. Otherwise you'd have to readjust your eyes every time you turned on a flashlight."

Natalie hears voices. She and Anthony head toward them. It's pitch black outside and people are standing around talking to each other.

"Anthony, glad you could make it," an older guy says. "And it looks like you brought Cassie."

"I did. She's ready for some clear skies tonight."

"Yes, we got lucky with the weather for a change."

"Rick, this is my friend, Natalie."

"Hi there, Natalie. Welcome."

Natalie widens her eyes trying to get a better look at Rick. "Thanks, it's nice to meet you." Widening her eyes doesn't make any difference though. She still can't see him.

"I need to talk to you, Anthony," some woman across from them says. "It's about the Smyth Medal. The *Seattle Times* has been trying to get ahold of you."

"Yeah, thanks. I already got the message."

Anthony introduces her to the rest of the group. Natalie smiles and says hello, but it's so dark out she doubts she'd recognize any of them in the light of day.

"And what do you have there?" Rick asks her.

"I brought some chocolate chunk cookies to share."

"Thank you. You can put them on the table if you like."

There's a picnic table a short distance away with a dim red lantern on it. Natalie starts to walk over, but her foot hits something and she stumbles. Suddenly, there's a firm grip on her arm.

"Are you okay?" It's Anthony. She didn't realize he was following her.

She lets out a short laugh. "I can't see anything! There isn't even moonlight."

"I know. It's a new moon. Don't worry, it gets easier once your eyes adjust."

"I'm pretty sure they are adjusted."

Anthony chuckles softly and the sound is intimate. "It takes at least thirty minutes for your eyes to become dark adapted. Hours, actually, if you want to get technical about it."

"Really?"

He nods. Or she thinks he's nodding. She can't tell for sure. Her attraction to him isn't any less intense. Part of it is that she can still smell him, and his scent mixed with the night air is divine.

"Don't worry," he says in a low voice. "You get good at doing all sorts of things in the dark." Anthony stops talking and she can hear him chuckling again. "I don't know what it is about you, Miss Natalie." He lets out a breath. "You make me nervous."

Natalie is stunned. Her first thought is that he's playing her. "I seriously doubt I make you nervous."

"Why would you doubt that?"

"I'd say your beauty would be the first reason."

"My beauty?"

"You're too handsome. Too charming. Too much of everything really."

Anthony is silent. And Natalie is already regretting the harsh way her words came out. "I'm sorry—"

"Don't say it," he cuts her off. "Don't bother saying it anymore."

She bites her lip. Strange to think that telling someone they're too handsome and charming is an insult, but she knows it is. For him, especially.

"I'm going to put these cookies on the table."

He doesn't respond.

Placing her container on the picnic table, she notices there are quite a few sweets laid out. There are even containers of what looks like homemade ice cream.

Anthony waits for her. Despite what she said, he doesn't comment on it again. Instead, he takes her around and politely introduces her to the other astronomers.

To her surprise, everyone at the party is super friendly. Her fears about seeming foolish amidst all these geeks were unfounded. If anything, people are overly eager to be helpful when they discover this is her first star party.

Anthony was right about the other telescopes, too. Some of them are impressive. "What are these called?" She points to one of the giant tubes attached to a square base.

"Dobsonian," Anthony tells her. "It's a Newtonian scope, designed by John Dobson back in the seventies."

"We also call them light buckets," Ronan, the owner of the Dobsonian tells her as he makes some kind of adjustment. "Would you like to take a look?"

Natalie steps forward and peers into the eyepiece. She sucks in her breath. Before her she sees a mass of bright stars surrounded with a pale hazy glow.

"It's beautiful."

"That's M42, or the Orion Nebula," Ronan says. He explains to her that nebulae are the birthplaces of stars.

Anthony informs her that he's going to go set up his own telescope. "You can stay here if you prefer. I'll be over there on the west side of the field." He points to a flat grassy area.

"That's okay. I'll come with you."

She follows him as he lugs his telescope over. It's cold enough to see her breath and she keeps her hands in her coat pockets. Unfortunately, she forgot to wear gloves.

Anthony sets his case on the ground and starts to pull out pieces, setting the tripod up first.

"Is there anything I can do to help?" she asks.

"I've got it covered."

"Why do you call your telescope Cassie?"

"Because it's a Schmidt-Cassegrain."

Natalie waits for him to continue, but he doesn't offer anything more.

She notices a definite chill in the air and it isn't just the weather. He's been polite to her since the comment she made earlier, but not much beyond that.

"Actually, you can hold this," he says, handing her what looks like a mini telescope.

"What is it?"

"Finderscope."

Natalie knows she's lost ground with him and what's worse is she suspects she's hurt his feelings.

How can I fix this if he won't let me apologize?

She takes a deep breath. "I didn't have the greatest childhood."

Anthony doesn't stop what he's doing, but she can tell he's listening.

"My father was very handsome and charming. Everyone loved him. He was also a womanizer who couldn't be faithful to my mother for five minutes."

Anthony was lengthening the tripod legs, but stops now and looks over at her. "So you think I'm like him? Is that it?"

"I don't know. Are you?"

He doesn't respond right away, but continues setting up the telescope. "You barely even know me, so how can you ask that?"

"I know that women are always calling you or following you around. You're always on your phone and every time, it's with a different woman. It's Nicole this or Justine that and last time at the bakery, I heard you talking to someone named Maya. Plus you ordered a birthday cake for another woman named Serena."

Anthony's brows knit together. Natalie can see him more clearly now. He was right, it took some time but her eyes have adapted to the dark.

"Justine isn't anyone to me, as you well know. Nicole is my ex-wife. Maya is my assistant. We are *not* romantically involved."

Anthony adjusts the final leg on the tripod and stands up. He takes the finderscope from her. "And Serena is my daughter."

"Daughter?"

"Yes, I have a daughter."

"You've never mentioned her before."

Natalie remembers the coffee mug she saw in his office. *So Anthony is a dad after all.* She watches him situate and attach the main part of the telescope to the tripod. It's large and awkward, but he manages it easily and it's obvious he's done it many times before.

"And you're right, women do sometimes follow me or they try to give me their phone numbers. Occasionally, they're even aggressive." He pulls out a small keypad and attaches it to the telescope. The numbers on it light up red. "I don't encourage it. I mostly discourage it, but if they're in one of my classes there isn't a whole lot I can do about it."

He punches in some numbers and the telescope makes a whirring noise as it slowly turns. Anthony looks through the finderscope and then fiddles with the eyepiece.

"How old is your daughter?" Natalie asks.

"Serena is ten." Anthony steps away from the telescope. "Do you want to take a look?"

Natalie's eyebrows go up. "Our daughters are almost the same age. Chloe is only a year older."

"I know."

She studies him. For whatever reason, she senses he's not inclined to talk about his daughter.

"What is it?" Natalie asks, stepping close to the telescope and putting her eye to the viewfinder. When she sees the bright-ringed image in front of her, she squeals with delight. "Saturn!" A huge smile spreads across her face. She pulls back, still grinning. "Thank you. This is amazing!"

He grins back. "You're welcome."

She continues to check out Saturn, relieved that the chill between her and Anthony seems to have dissipated. It's surprisingly exciting to see the planet with her own eyes and she finds herself curious about other celestial objects.

"Ready for more?" he asks, as if reading her mind.

"Definitely."

He types in coordinates and the telescope makes a whirring noise as it slowly turns.

Anthony shows her Jupiter, the Pleiades or Seven Sisters star cluster, and the Andromeda galaxy.

"I can't believe I'm looking at a whole galaxy!"

As she's staring through the viewfinder, a couple of people approach them.

"Anthony, you brought more of these addictive cookies!" a woman about her own age is saying to him. She's Hispanic and has short, curly, dark hair.

"I did more than that," Anthony tells her. "I brought the baker who created them."

"Really?" The woman turns and Natalie notices she's carrying her container.

Anthony introduces Maya, explaining that she's his assistant. He also introduces the two guys with her as two of his postgraduate students.

"Are you really the creator of these insane cookies?" Maya asks, chewing on one. "Anthony brought them to Keck and we couldn't get enough of them."

Natalie glances at Anthony in surprise. "You took my cookies to Hawaii?"

"Yeah, not that I got to eat any with these vultures around."

Maya points at Natalie. "*You* are a freaking genius."

Natalie laughs. Coming from a group of people whom she suspects actually are all geniuses, it's an interesting compliment. "Thanks, I'm glad you like them. I'm curious, though. Is it my imagination, or do all astronomers really like desserts?"

They laugh. "We like anything that helps us stay awake at night," Anthony tells her.

"So that's why you like coffee so much."

"Basically."

Maya turns to Anthony. "Have you finished your SWIFT proposal yet?"

"No, we're still pulling it together."

The four of them start talking about various projects. Natalie hears the words grant and proposal a lot. She looks through the telescope again, studying Andromeda as they talk. *This astronomy stuff is pretty cool.* There's something about seeing another galaxy that makes her problems seem awfully small.

"I heard the *Seattle Times* wants to interview you about your nomination for the Smyth Medal," Navez says.

The comment captures Natalie's attention and she tunes back in to the conversation.

"Yeah," Anthony sighs. "They left a message the other day."

Maya motions toward Anthony. "I'll say this much. You're sure to get tenure now."

"Maybe. I'm still a long shot to win."

"What is this Smyth Medal I keep hearing about?" Natalie asks everyone.

"It's a medal given out by the Smyth Institute of Science," Maya explains.

"They give out awards every year for a major contribution in one area. It's really prestigious and Anthony's been nominated for astrophysics."

"Wait a minute, is this the Science Awards Banquet I keep hearing about on the news? That sounds like a really big deal."

They all nod. "It changes location every year," Maya tells her. "This year it's happening in Seattle at the Convention Center. It's not as big as the Nobel, but it's definitely a big deal, especially for scientists."

They talk a little more and eventually Maya, Navez, and Brad decide to wander off and chat with other people, leaving Natalie and Anthony alone again.

"So why do you think you're such a long shot to win that medal?" Natalie asks.

"The competition is really tough. It should help me gain tenure, though. Maya was right about that."

"Well, good luck. I hope you win!"

"Thanks."

Natalie grins. "And what is this I hear about my cookies in Hawaii?"

Anthony rolls his eyes in mock exasperation. "All right, I admit it. I took a dozen with to Mauna Kea."

"I'm honored."

"You should be. It was right after you called me an asshole and I didn't want to go back into the bakery, so I had to ask Maya to buy them for me."

Natalie shifts uncomfortably. "I apologized for that. Should I apologize again?"

"It can't hurt."

"I'm sorry."

He doesn't say anything, just puts new coordinates into his telescope's keypad.

"Can I ask you something?" she asks.

"Sure."

She bites her lip. "Why do you like me?"

Anthony continues what he's doing, a smile playing around the edges of his mouth. "What makes you think I like you?"

"Because you invited me here tonight. What is it you see in me, exactly?"

"I don't know." He attaches the keypad back to the telescope. "In truth, I've wondered about it myself."

"What kind of answer is that?"

Anthony chuckles. "I'm just being honest. You're not exactly easy to get along with."

"I'm not sure why I'm always giving you such a hard time."

"I am."

"Why is that?"

"It's because you're into me."

Natalie's face grows warm. "No, I'm not."

His hand is still on the telescope. He gazes over at her. "Yeah, you are."

"I'm not."

Anthony lets go and moves closer. She can smell him again, his woodsy soap. He's taller than her and she has to look up at him.

"I'm not into you," she insists, though her pulse quickens.

Their eyes meet. He's so near now, she can see the dark fringe of his lashes. The stubble of his beard. She shivers with anticipation.

"Yeah, you are, but it's okay," he says softly, leaning close, "because I'm into you, too."

And then he kisses her. Natalie is dizzy with shock.

Anthony is kissing me!

It's the first time she's been kissed by a man other than Peter in fourteen years and it feels odd. Odd, but good. Very good.

She closes her eyes and gives in to the kiss.

Anthony's tongue licks her lower lip and when she opens her mouth to him, a small groan escapes his throat.

The sound thrills her. He tastes like chocolate and coffee. She slides her arms around his neck, her fingers weaving through his hair where it's longer in back. She can't believe she's actually touching him.

His mouth is firm, and his tongue is decidedly wicked as it tangles with hers. Peter never kissed her like this, not with this kind of playful eroticism.

He really knows what he's doing.

Her heart pounds with the sensual way he's kissing her—it's crazy—but it feels like the first time she's ever been kissed.

Anthony's arms wrap around her. With all the clothing layers between them, they're as well-padded as a couple of astronauts landing on the moon.

Natalie giggles at the image and Anthony pulls back.

"Something humorous I should know about?"

She tells him and he grins. "You'll get no argument from me. There's definitely too much clothing between us."

When he talks, she notices he keeps glancing down at her mouth. She licks her lips with nervousness and he seems riveted.

"Just one more," he whispers.

And then he's kissing her again. Her blood rushes with desire as she pulls him close. A part of her knows this is a mistake, but she can't help herself.

This time when he stops, he turns his head away, his breath coming out in puffs of white smoke from the cold.

"We're not alone," he points out.

Natalie nods and then a big smile breaks out across her face.

"What is it?"

"That was my first kiss in a really long time."

"I see, and how was it?"

"Not bad."

He seems bemused. "Maybe I should kiss you again. I think I can do better than not bad."

"I'm willing if you are."

His expression grows sober and then his mouth is on hers—plundering. Natalie can barely catch her breath. Her hand slides to his jaw, and she isn't sure if she's encouraging him or trying to gain control.

"How is that?" he murmurs, sliding down to her neck. She gasps as he works his magic there. Finally, he pulls away.

Natalie studies his face as she tries to pull herself together. He's so handsome it almost hurts to look at him. "That was interesting." She's determined not to be another one of the groupies who throw themselves at him.

Though who am I kidding? I'm kissing him like the world is going to end tonight.

Anthony puts his hand up to her face. His thumb rubs over her bottom lip and the move is so provocative it sends a pulse of lust straight between her thighs. "You have such a sexy mouth, Miss Natalie."

"I do?"

"I've had . . . thoughts . . . about this mouth of yours."

Natalie is stunned. No one has ever told her that in her entire life, including Peter. "So I've been walking around all this time with a sexy mouth and didn't know it?"

"Guess so."

Anthony has a sexy mouth, too, but she decides not to compliment him on it. *I'll bet compliments on his appearance are all he ever hears from women.* "Well, you have a very sexy," she searches around for something to compliment him on, "telescope!" she says, remembering Lindsay's joke from earlier too late.

His eyebrows rise. "I have a sexy telescope?"

"Don't you?"

He grins. "I like to think so."

✦ ✸ ✦

ANTHONY STARES UP at the night sky still smiling to himself about the telescope joke. *What the hell are you doing?*

He knows he shouldn't have kissed Natalie. She's fresh from a divorce. Plus he's her landlord and they still haven't resolved any of their issues.

It's that mouth—along with her stubborn attitude. For some reason it turns him on.

He knows what kind of man she thinks he is. *And by kissing her, you just*

145

proved her right.

It's not like he wants to lead Natalie on. In fact, he likes her. A lot more than he suspects she likes him. She's the real deal. When she finds out he's agreed to lease the space next door to her bakery, she's not going to be happy.

And you think she's antagonistic now?

When Graham called earlier tonight it was to tell him that the two people who saw the shop space yesterday definitely want to lease it. Graham ran a background check on them and it's all in the clear. Everything's in order.

He's not sure how he's going to tell Natalie.

"What do you like to look at with your telescope?" Natalie asks him. She puts her hands up to her face, rubbing them together and blowing into them. "I'm guessing it's not Saturn and Jupiter."

He watches her. "Didn't you bring any gloves?"

"No, I forgot."

"Here." He takes her icy hands in his and covers them both with his own.

"You're so warm," she says in amazement.

"Yeah, my temperature tends to run a little hot." He holds her hands in his, kneading them, trying to bring some heat to her fingers.

"So what do you look at?" She fidgets and he can tell she's nervous again.

He lets out a breath. "You're right, I don't look at our local neighborhood—our solar system—very often." He thinks about what he enjoys viewing with his telescope at home. He has a large Dobsonian that he built himself. "I like to go deep."

"Deep?"

He's still rubbing her hands. "My area of astronomy deals with the very distant past. We're trying to figure out what happened right after the Big Bang. And that," he pauses. "That fascinates me."

Her hands seem warm, so he lets her take them back.

Anthony gets out his thermos and pours more coffee for both of them. Glancing at his watch he can see that it's almost two.

He's impressed she's lasted this long. Occasionally he's tried to bring girlfriends to star parties but stopped because they all wanted to leave after a half an hour.

"We should probably wrap it up," he tells her. "It's almost two o'clock in the morning."

Natalie is looking through the viewfinder again. She turns to him. "Really? I can't believe it's already that late."

The drive home is a quiet one and he figures she's probably tired. When they get to her house, Anthony parks in the driveway right behind a white van.

"You don't have to walk me to the door," she tells him.

"Of course, I do. I want to."

They both get out of his car.

Natalie is still quiet and he wonders what she's thinking. She's been acting kind of jittery since they kissed. When they get to the porch his instinct is to reach for her hand, but he doesn't get the chance.

"Look, that was fun," she says, turning to him. "But I don't think we should take it any further between us."

"Why?"

"I just think it's a bad idea. I'm not ready for a relationship and when all is said and done, you're still our evil landlord."

"I'm not actually evil, you realize."

Natalie smiles. "I suppose not."

"But?"

"But I'm just not ready for anything more than kisses. This is all very new for me."

"Okay." He shrugs.

"Okay, what?"

"We won't do anything more than kiss. I'm all right with that."

Natalie looks stunned and in truth Anthony is stunned himself.

Did I really just say that? What kind of torture am I setting myself up for?

"Oh." Instead of raising an eyebrow with a healthy dose of skepticism, as she should, Natalie looks a little hurt.

She thinks I don't want her.

"It's not that I don't want more," he tells her. "I like you, but we don't have to make a big thing out of this. Let's hang out and have fun. See where it takes us."

She nods slowly and appears to be thinking it over. Finally, she gives him a small smile. "It would be another first for me."

No sex? This is going to be a first for me, too.

Anthony smiles back. "All right, that settles it."

"I have some trust issues, you know? That's not your fault, though."

He's silent. Now would be the perfect time to clear the air and tell Natalie that he's leasing out that space next door to the bakery.

Yeah, go ahead and tell her. Let's see how much time she'll want to spend with you then.

Anthony pushes away his guilty feelings. He has Serena to think about, after all. He needs that income.

Instead, he asks her, "Have you ever ridden on a motorcycle?"

She shakes her head. "No."

"Then I'm picking you up tomorrow at noon."

Natalie's blue eyes grow wide. "On your motorcycle?"

"Yeah, we'll go for a ride, and then grab some lunch."

"Is it safe?"

Anthony gives a slow grin. "Miss Natalie, would I ask you to do something that wasn't safe?"

She doesn't seem to know how to respond. Oddly, he enjoys her reluctance. He's so used to women chasing him that it's refreshing to be the one doing the chasing for a change.

"What should I wear?"

He groans to himself. *Something tight and low-cut, please.* "Just be comfortable."

They study each other. Standing under the porch light, he notices the strain on her face from being tired. It's so late the sun will be up in only a few hours. "Guess I should go."

"Thanks for inviting me tonight," she says. "I had a nice time."

Anthony steps closer. He can see on her face she knows he's planning to kiss her again. "Give me your hands."

She pulls them out of her pockets and he takes them. They're still cold. He looks down and sees a round scar on the base of her thumb. Turns them over and there are more scars—one on her wrist and another by her index finger.

Anthony runs his thumb over the one on her wrist. "Battle scars?"

"The hazards of working around hot ovens all day."

He warms her hands and then pulls her to him.

Natalie comes easily and he feels a small sense of triumph. Suddenly he hates the fact she's been hurt and is distrustful of men. "I'm going to kiss you now," he whispers.

"Okay," she whispers back.

And then he lowers his mouth. She tastes sweet and luscious. Like a woman who hasn't been well-kissed in a long time and who, frankly, needs it. He knows she was married for years, but there's an innocence about the way she kisses.

Though their kiss is getting hotter by the second. He keeps thinking about her body. Those soft curves pressed into him. Those full breasts. He's already getting hard. By the feel of her, Natalie is built like a playboy bunny circa nineteen-fifty-five and he wants to pull her in tight. Let her know what she's doing to him.

Instead, he lets her go, gratified that Natalie doesn't seem in any hurry to end things either. It's quiet outside and he glances around her neighborhood.

"This night has taken me by surprise," she murmurs.

"In a good way, I hope."

"I think so."

He's still, holding her hands. "And now I have to ask you a question I've been wondering about since I picked you up."

She blinks. "What's that?"

"Why is there a broken fireman's axe sticking out of your front door?" Natalie's face changes to quiet laughter.

"Is there something strange going on here I should know about? A psycho running around loose in your neighborhood?"

"That's Excalibur," she tells him, still laughing.

"King Arthur's sword?"

"It's a long story, but yes. My sister threw it at the door one night months ago and now it's stuck. No one can pull it out."

Anthony considers this. "No one?"

She shakes her head. "Everybody keeps trying. It sounds like I'm going to have to buy a new door, which is a shame."

Anthony walks over to the door and studies the axe. From what he can tell, it went in at a sharp angle and the door's thick maple has been expanding around it with the weather. As he's examining it, considering various ideas, the perfect solution comes to him. "I'll be right back," he tells her.

"Where are you going?" Natalie watches as he walks back down to his car and pops the rear gate on his SUV open. It's a good thing he still has everything with him. He pulls out the Dewar flask, along with an old rag, and a pair of safety gloves and brings it all back to the porch. "What the heck is that?" she asks.

"Liquid nitrogen."

Natalie's eyebrows go up, but she doesn't say anything, just watches as Anthony puts on the safety gloves and readies the Dewar flask. He unwinds the metal coil and switches the lever over to liquid. "Stay back," he tells her. "This stuff is extremely cold and you don't want to get any of it on you."

"Why do you have liquid nitrogen in your car?"

"Some of my students were using it to cool telescope camera optics for a project they've been cobbling together this quarter." He chuckles. "They made ice cream with it, too. It tasted pretty good."

Anthony presses the rag over the axe head and then puts the coil tip right up against it. He opens the valve and immediately there's white smoke as the liquid nitrogen sprays across the rag pressed against the metal. There's a crackling sound as everything freezes.

"That should hopefully do it," he says. Still wearing the safety gloves, he grabs the blunt back of the axe head and gives a hard tug.

POP!

The axe comes out of the door easily.

He hears Natalie's loud gasp. "Oh, my God!" Suddenly, she's on top of him, throwing her arms around his neck as if he's just won the Olympics. "You did it!"

Chapter Fifteen

Diet Plan: A big scoop of lust. Kisses sprinkled on top.

Exercise Plan: Ride around on a motorcycle with a hot guy. Try and remember to breathe.

CRUNCHING NOISE interrupts Natalie's sexy dream about Anthony. She tries to tune it out, to ignore it, but it's only getting louder. What strange monster is making that racket?

Natalie opens her eyes. Lindsay is sitting on the edge of her bed.

"Thank God, you're finally awake." Her sister is eating a bowl of granola and yogurt—her favorite anytime snack.

"What time is it?"

"Nine o'clock." Lindsay smirks. "And now let me ask you a question. What time did you get home last night, you little tramp?"

"Three in the morning."

"Hmm, just as I thought."

Natalie pulls the covers over herself. "Go away. I want to sleep some more."

"Not until I get details." The crunching continues.

"What details? I went to a star party and saw some celestial objects. There's nothing more to tell." Natalie tries to stop herself from smiling, but can't quite manage it.

"I see that tramp grin on your face, so spill it. Did you ride that man western style or side saddle?"

Natalie groans and covers her face with a pillow. "I don't even know what that means."

"It means if there was hanky-panky, I want to hear all about it. Not to mention, how did Excalibur wind up sitting on the dining room table this morning?"

Natalie takes the pillow off her face and tucks it behind her head. "Anthony pulled it out when we got home. He used liquid nitrogen. Isn't that crazy?"

She remembers how pleased he looked, too, standing there with the axe. She couldn't help but throw herself on him. It was momentous.

Lindsay nods. "I figured it was him. Chloe's going to think Anthony walks on water when she finds out."

"Have you talked to Chloe? Is everything okay?"

"She called this morning. Everything is fine. She's going with Peter to check out stables today."

"I see." Peter and Chloe finally decided on a horse recently—a beautiful Quarter Horse that Chloe named Cinnamon because of her reddish brown color—but the next big decision was where to stable her. Natalie hasn't met the horse yet, but has seen pictures.

Lindsay crunches some more and raises an eyebrow. "You're holding out on me."

"All right, he kissed me, but that's all."

"And . . ."

"And it was nice."

"Nice? Having someone make you a sandwich is nice. How was it for real?"

Natalie thinks back to Anthony's kisses. They were unlike anything she'd ever experienced. The way he licked her lips and the corners of her mouth before delving inside. It was as if he was eating a piece of fruit, only it was her. She'd never realized it before, but there was something stiff, almost formal, about the way she and Peter had been kissing each other all those years.

"It was . . . erotic," she finally manages to say.

"Mmm, now we're talking. I'm not surprised, though. I have an instinct about these things."

"An instinct?"

"I can usually tell if a guy is going to be good in bed." Lindsay stirs the contents of her bowl some more. "And Anthony doesn't look like he'd need a road map to find the enchanted forest."

"No, I doubt it." She suspects Anthony could be a tour guide.

"So why didn't you sleep with him? It would be good for you to rope that man."

Natalie sits up and grabs her phone to shut off the alarm. "Could you please stop it with all these dumb rodeo metaphors?"

Lindsay chuckles. "Don't change the subject."

"I told Anthony I wasn't ready to take things further. I mean, I just got divorced. This is all kind of overwhelming."

"What did he say?"

"He said, okay. That he was fine with just kissing."

"And you believe him? That's the oldest line in the book."

"It is?" At the time Natalie worried that maybe Anthony wasn't all that attracted to her and was trying to let himself off the hook. "He seemed sincere. He said we could just hang out—no pressure."

Lindsay sighs and scrapes out the last of the yogurt from her bowl. "When are you seeing him again?"

"At noon. We're going out for—"

"Today?" Lindsay stops scraping.

Natalie tells her they're going out for a ride on his bike this afternoon.

"My God, there's a motorcycle involved!" Lindsay jumps up. "Why didn't you tell me this before? How much time do we do have?" She stomps around the bedroom like a Hollywood director whose leading lady is having her first press conference. "I can't work under these conditions! We need a bowl of ice water immediately!" Lindsay heads for the bedroom door.

"I'm not doing the ice water," Natalie calls after her.

For years, she's watched Lindsay stick her face in a bowl of ice water every morning as part of her beauty regime. Turns out Kate Hudson and Goldie Hawn have been doing it for years, too. *See,* Lindsay said, *Kate and Goldie would know.* Lindsay claims it helps with puffiness and lines but Natalie has never tried it, and never intends to, either.

NATALIE PULLS HER face from the ice water. And howls.

"Don't be such a baby." Lindsay hands her a towel and instructs her to dab gently.

Afterward, Natalie gets a cup of coffee and tries to warm herself. Besides the ice water, she does every other beauty trick Lindsay tells her to—including her famous Pepto-Bismol face mask.

"You'll love this. It makes your pores so tiny your skin looks like glass!"

"I just hope it doesn't constipate me," Natalie says, lying on the sofa, covered in pink minty goo.

"We all have to suffer for beauty." Lindsay is sharpening a pair of tweezers and stops to give Natalie a sadistic grin.

What's more, Lindsay insists that Natalie not wear any of her beloved shapewear. "You don't want him feeling you up and running into all that nylon. That's a turn-off."

"But we're only kissing."

"Please, there's no way he's not going to want to get his hands on *those.*" Lindsay motions toward Natalie's ample chest. "And if he doesn't make a move for those headlights, you got bigger problems because then he's gay. But don't worry, he's not gay."

By the time Anthony arrives at noon—on time again, she notices with a thrill—she's been plucked, blow-dried, and groomed within an inch of her life.

She sees the slow appreciative smile that spreads across his face as he takes in her appearance and decides it was all worth it.

I'd do it again and more.

And she has to hand it to Lindsay, too, because she got it just right. A little cleavage, not too much. Flattering makeup. Tight jeans with pointy-toed black boots. Her long blonde hair is loose and flowing over her shoulders.

She can't remember the last time a man gazed at her with this kind of desire.

Certainly not Peter.

"You look great," Anthony says.

Natalie bites her lip and it immediately draws his attention. She remembers his comments about her mouth last night and feels shy. It's one thing to look the part, but it's another to *be* the part.

She turns and catches Lindsay's eye and her sister gives her a quick wink.

"Hi, Anthony." Lindsay steps forward with good cheer. "What's your secret? I'm dying of curiosity."

"Secret?"

"How did you manage to pull out Excalibur? Many men before you have tried and failed."

Anthony rubs his jaw. "Well, I used liquid nitrogen to bring down the temperature of the axe and contract the metal." He starts monologuing about something called the Leidenfrost effect and how he used the rag to counteract it.

"Wow," Lindsay whispers to Natalie. "He really is a geek."

Natalie nods, though she's getting turned on listening to him.

"In any case, I'm glad it worked and you can keep your door," Anthony finally says with a grin.

Lindsay has her phone. "Would you mind if I take a quick picture of you with the axe. My niece is going to be curious about who pulled it out."

"Uh, sure."

"Oh, and you should come to our potluck dinner on Friday," Lindsay says.

Natalie turns to her in surprise. This is the first she's heard about inviting him for dinner.

"Thanks, but I already have plans on Friday," Anthony tells her.

"Are you sure?" Lindsay tosses her hair. "You'll be missing a great party. We throw a kick-ass potluck."

"Let's invite him another time," Natalie interjects quickly. It's clear that

Anthony doesn't want to come for dinner. She tries not to let herself wonder if it's because he has a date. It's just a small gathering, anyway. Lindsay invited Oliver, Blair is bringing Graham, and Natalie told Chloe she could have a few friends over for a slumber party.

Lindsay goes to grab the axe and Anthony holds it while she snaps a few photos with her phone.

Finally, Natalie and Anthony say their goodbyes and head out to where his motorcycle is parked in her driveway—a glossy red Ducati with a sleek aerodynamic design.

Sex on wheels.

It's exactly the kind of motorcycle she'd expect a hot young guy like Anthony to ride. *How old is Anthony, anyway?* The thought gives Natalie pause. *A little bit younger than me, but how much?*

He hands her one of the black helmets attached to the back and Natalie puts it on, though she isn't quite sure how to deal with the fit.

"Do you need help?" Anthony comes over to her. As he leans close, fiddling with the adjustment, she studies him.

He's blindingly gorgeous. Except for some dark stubble, their late night hasn't affected his appearance at all. His eyes are clear and the whites almost glow. Natalie finds herself fascinated by his beard. Peter with his blond hair and pale skin rarely had stubble and always kept himself closely shaved. She wants to reach out and touch his face, but she's too timid. Unsure if she can claim that kind of familiarity.

"How does that feel?" he asks, after fastening the helmet. "Comfortable?"

"It's good."

Anthony grabs his own helmet and seats himself on the bike with his usual easy grace. He's wearing a *Star Wars* T-shirt with that same motorcycle jacket she's seen on him before—black with a white stripe that runs across the chest and down each arm. It's well-fitted and shows off his broad shoulders to a near devastating effect.

After slipping his helmet on, he takes the motorcycle off its kickstand and motions to her.

"Climb on."

Here goes nothing.

She slides on behind him with more clumsiness than grace. It's awkward and strange and she doesn't know what to do with her arms, which are flapping beside her. Not to mention how her groin has slid tight against his ass. She tries to scoot back, but just keeps sliding forward again.

"Hold on to me," he says, speaking through his helmet. "And lean in with me when I make a turn."

"Okay."

Lindsay, having had numerous boyfriends with motorcycles over the years, gave Natalie some etiquette tips. Her biggest one—don't grab his dick by mistake.

Which is, of course, all Natalie can think about until she slides her arms around Anthony's waist. Then all she can think about is how strong and solid he feels.

Thank God, lust can't kill me.

He starts up the motorcycle with a gritty roar and before she knows it they're riding. She hangs on tight and tries to lean into the turns like he instructed. At first she's self-conscious, but after a short while starts to enjoy herself. Along with the steady hum of the motorcycle, there's a steady hum of excitement building within her.

I could get used to this.

Even though it's winter and the temperature is bracing, it's a clear sunny day. Her body is snug against Anthony's back and as they ride she discovers there's an intimacy with her surroundings that you don't get with a car.

Anthony takes her for a drive around Lake Washington on the Seattle side.

"How are you doing back there?" he says above the roar of the engine.

"Great!"

They ride around the lake for a while, but eventually Anthony heads toward downtown Seattle. They cruise along the water until he finds a place to park near Pier 54.

They both climb off the motorcycle. Anthony pulls off his helmet and then turns to help with hers, too. "Hungry yet?"

"Starving," she admits.

"Me, too. Let's go find some grub."

He attaches their helmets to the bike and locks everything up while she checks out their surroundings. It's been years since she's been down to the Pier.

Rows of street vendors line the sidewalk near where they parked and when one of them comments "nice bike" to Anthony, he asks the guy if he's planning to be around for a while. "Yeah, why?" Anthony offers him twenty bucks to keep an eye on his motorcycle—an offer the guy jumps at.

"Do you usually do that?" Natalie asks when they start walking.

"Sometimes. It depends on the area. A nice motorcycle can be a real target for thieves."

As they walk together, a tingly excitement still hums through her and she suspects it has less to do with the motorcycle ride and more to do with being this close to Anthony. They wander past a few shop windows. It's difficult not to notice how many lingering glances he gets from women. At least he seems to ignore them.

"So, how was your first motorcycle ride, Miss Natalie?"

"I loved it."

"Yeah? I'm glad to hear that. I took it easy with you at first, but you seemed comfortable enough that I started to punch it."

Natalie remembers how he drove fast, but she felt safe the whole time. With some surprise she realizes she trusts Anthony. There's something capable and solid about him.

"Is it hard to ride a motorcycle?" she wonders aloud.

"Not really. Like anything, it takes practice."

"Do you think I could try it?"

They're passing a tourist shop selling T-shirts and Anthony stops and turns to her with a horrified expression. "You want to ride my *Ducati?*"

"Not alone or anything," Natalie says quickly. "But with you in back, sitting behind me."

His horror appears to be turning into panic.

"Just for a short distance," she adds. "Like maybe around a parking lot."

Anthony's handsome face goes blank as he's clearly searching for something to say. He blinks at her, but still doesn't speak.

"Do you need a paper bag to breathe into or something?"

He offers a small grin. "More like one to throw up into, I think."

"You can say no." She laughs.

He puts his hand up. "Just give me a second. I'm waiting for my heart rate to stabilize."

"Think of something peaceful. Like me *not* ever riding your motorcycle. How's that?"

"Yeah, okay—thanks, that's helping a lot."

They start walking again and Natalie can't quite control her amusement. "So you're really attached to your motorcycle, huh?"

"If you knew how much I paid for it, you'd understand. It was a real extravagance on my part."

"All right, well, I'll settle on being a passenger—for now."

Seagulls fly overhead and the air is tangy with the smell of saltwater. When they walk by an outdoor fish and chips place, Anthony motions toward it. "What about eating here?"

Natalie shades her eyes and looks over. "Okay."

"You sure? We can go to a restaurant if you want, but I was thinking it might be nice to sit outside."

"This is good. I like sitting outside. Plus, we'll get some exposure from our nearest star, right?"

"That we will."

They get in line to order food and Natalie decides to ask him why he can't make it to dinner on Friday. "Do you have a date?"

"Sort of."

"Oh." She feels kind of let down. Of course he's still seeing other women. This is just a casual thing, after all.

They get up to the window and after asking her what she wants, Anthony orders food and drinks for both of them. She offers to pay for the meal, but he dismisses the idea with a shake of his head.

"I'll just go find us a place to sit then."

The seating area is packed, but as she scans the crowd, a table suddenly opens up right near the water. Quickly she pushes her way through the throng and gets there right before a punk girl with dreadlocks does. The girl glares at Natalie, but Natalie pretends not to notice.

Suck it up, sister—age before beauty.

As Natalie tries to scrub the grime off the table with a napkin, she decides that it doesn't matter if Anthony has a date on Friday. No matter what happens, she's going to relax and let herself enjoy today.

"Hey, I'm glad you found a spot." Anthony comes over with the food. He's wearing mirrored aviator sunglasses and is so hot that if he stepped near a canister of gasoline she's certain it would explode.

"You look straight out of *Top Gun* with those sunglasses," she teases. "Maybe I should start calling you Moondoggie."

He takes a seat. "Except the character you're thinking of was named Maverick, not Moondoggie."

Natalie takes a sip from her soda. "I don't think so."

"Yeah, it's Maverick. The other guys were Iceman and Goose." He puts a basket of food in front of her and then one in front of himself.

"No, it's definitely Moondoggie. I can't remember the other characters' names."

Anthony tears open a couple of mayonnaise packets and squirts them near his fries. "You're seriously going to argue that Moondoggie was Tom Cruise's character in *Top Gun?*"

"Yes, because I'm pretty sure I'm right."

"And I'm one hundred percent sure you're wrong."

Natalie tries to control her grin. She knows the character's name was Maverick, but it's fun to get a rise out of Anthony.

"Well, I prefer Moondoggie," she tells him. "It's far more poetic, especially for an astronomer."

Anthony opens his mouth, but then closes it. He starts to chuckle. "You're shining me on, aren't you?"

"Yes, I am, Moondoggie."

He shakes his head. "What am I going to do with you?" He looks at her though she can't see his eyes behind the sunglasses. "Keep this up and I might have to bend you over my knee, Miss Natalie."

She nearly chokes on a french fry. The images flooding her mind are overwhelming and she can't decide if she's repelled or titillated.

He smirks. "I can see I've finally left you speechless."

Natalie nibbles her fish and watches as Anthony eats his fries. "Do you always eat french fries with mayo?"

"Yeah, this is how I grew up eating them."

"Is it gross?"

Anthony laughs. "No, it's not gross. In Italy, when you buy french fries, they come wrapped in a paper cone, and you eat them with mayonnaise on the side."

"Really? Can I taste one?"

"Sure."

Natalie takes one of Anthony's fries and dips it into the mayo. She eats it tentatively.

"What do you think?"

"It's good. It sort of reminds me of potato salad." She tries another one and has to admit they're delicious. "So you're Italian for real, huh?"

"Yeah, my parents are both Italian, though my dad grew up in the States."

"And you've spent time in Italy?"

He nods. "As a kid, I spent most summers visiting my grandparents in Rome."

It sounds wildly adventurous to Natalie, who's never even been to Europe. Peter wanted to go years ago but she thought it was too extravagant. She's come to realize that was a mistake on her part.

"What about you?" he asks. "Are you a native Northwesterner?"

"No, but I've lived here for years."

"Where did you grow up?"

She picks up her soda and plays with the straw. "All over, but mostly Nevada."

"Did your parents work for the government or something?"

Natalie snorts. That certainly would have been something. "Not hardly, my father was a professional gambler."

Anthony stops eating. "Really?" Then he laughs and shakes his head. "You're shining me on again."

"It's true. My dad played professional poker. He even won the World Series Main Event."

Anthony takes this in, studying her. "That would explain your odd question—about whether I've ever counted cards."

Natalie is embarrassed she asked him that. Ironically, between his good looks, charm, and facility with numbers, her father would have approved of Anthony. *And I'd do well to remember that.*

"So do you gamble, too?" he asks.

"No, never." People used to assume she gambled, but Natalie never wastes money like that. "I play cards for fun sometimes, but that's it. People always think being around poker players sounds glamorous, but trust me—it wasn't. At least not for my family."

Anthony takes a drink from his Coke and studies her. There's something about the way he's doing it. Almost like he really gets it.

Natalie dabs her mouth with a napkin and sets her finished basket of food aside. "Anyway, traveling to Rome every summer sounds way more interesting." She leans forward. "Maybe I should insist that you speak Italian to me."

"But you wouldn't understand anything."

"It's the language of romance though, isn't it?"

Anthony grins. "*Sì, mia bella signora.*"

Natalie swallows. *Oh. My. God.*

AFTER EATING LUNCH, they walk along the pier and when Anthony sees a sign advertising "Shrunken Heads Inside" at Ye Olde Curiosity Shop, he points at it.

"I think it's our duty to check this out—what do you say?"

"Shrunken heads? They're on the top of my disgusting things I've always wanted to see list."

"Me, too, what a coincidence!" His brows rise with amusement.

They venture into the shop, which is a hodge-podge of postcards, books, and Native American knickknacks. They wander a bit and discover a wall of peculiarities clustered in the back of the store. The whole place smells musty with a tinge of sea air and they're the only people checking the place out. They peruse the selection of oddities. Various petrified and jarred animals are on display, along with other strange items. Including said shrunken heads.

"So, Professor Novello, what's your opinion, are they real?" Natalie turns to him.

"The shrunken heads?"

"Any of it." She waves her hand.

"Sure, it's all real."

"You're kidding."

"Real plastic."

Natalie laughs. He's discovered he loves to make her laugh. She really lets loose when she laughs.

"Do you think it's plastic? Some of it does look real to me."

"I agree the mummies are real. The other stuff is dubious, though."

She nods, leaning forward to inspect a stuffed mermaid. "This is an odd place."

He's inclined to agree with her.

"Oh, wait, look over there." Suddenly Natalie is pulling on his arm and he follows her over to a gypsy fortuneteller machine. "Let's have our fortunes told. Do you have a quarter?"

Anthony digs into his front pocket for some change and holds his palm out to her.

As Natalie delicately sifts for a quarter, his eyes wander down. Underneath her jacket she's wearing a shirt that's tight enough for him to see her curves and yet only shows a small tantalizing peek of cleavage. He can't tear his eyes away from that peek of skin, though. It feels as if he's been staring at it all afternoon, trying to visualize what's below.

"Are you sure you're ready to hear what Madam Estrella has to say?" She looks up at him. Busted for staring at her chest, he quickly meets her eyes.

"Sure, hit me."

"Maybe it'll tell us if you're going to win the Smyth Medal."

"That would be something. I wouldn't hold my breath, though."

"I know! It'll command you to lease us that space next door."

Anthony nods. *You have* got *to tell her the truth.* He tries to ignore his feelings of guilt. *I'll tell her soon.* It's still hard for him to believe his first impression of Natalie was so off the mark, though he has to admit she is a bit of a ballbuster. After hearing a little about her childhood, though, he understands why she's probably had to be that way. In truth, he admires her for it. He doubts she gives anyone her good opinion unless they deserve it.

Natalie puts the quarter into the machine and after some minor theatrics with lights flashing, it spits out a small card. She picks it up and her eyes widen when she reads it.

"What does it say?" he asks curiously.

She hugs it close. "I'm keeping this one to myself."

"Hey, you can't do that. I paid good money for that fortune. Hand it over."

"What makes you think it's for you? I'm the one who put the money in."

"And I'm the one who bankrolled it."

It's in her right hand, and when he playfully tries to grab it, she quickly puts it behind her back. "Too slow, Professor."

"Now I definitely have to see what it says."

Anthony tries to grab it again. She keeps thwarting him and before he knows it he has her pressed against the wall. He slips his arm around her, his hand closing over hers.

Natalie laughs, but there's a breathless quality to it that's going straight to his groin.

"Give it up, Miss Natalie."

"Never!"

She squirms against him. Instead of relenting, he feels her hand tightening around the card even more. *Little minx.* And then he has an idea that might work.

"*Dai*," he murmurs. "*Fammi di averlo.*" Come on, let me have it.

She meets his eyes and her expression changes. Those blue eyes darken and her amusement turns to something else entirely. When her mouth opens, Anthony can't help himself, he leans in and kisses her.

At first she's hesitant, but then gives in with a breathy moan. One of his hands immediately goes to grab her ass and pull her to him.

Damn.

They kiss enthusiastically and when Anthony feels her hand with the card inside loosen, he plucks it from her.

She breaks the kiss. "What are you doing?"

"I'm taking what's mine."

She tries to pull away, but he won't let her and keeps her body firmly pressed into his.

Natalie gives him a saucy smile. "It's not yours yet."

And then to his surprise, she snatches the card right back from his hand. He looks down and sees her fist tighten around it.

"What are you going to do next?" he jokes. "Eat it?"

"If I have to."

He lowers his voice. "Should I speak Italian again? It appears to be your kryptonite."

Natalie laughs. "God help me, please don't."

He considers her and decides if she really wants to keep the fortune to herself this badly, he'll let her.

"All right." Anthony releases her. "Keep the card. But now you owe me."

She puts the card in her coat pocket. "I don't think so."

"Yes, you do. And believe me, I plan to collect."

Once they're outside, they walk side by side along the pier, with Natalie occasionally meandering ahead of him. And being the pig he is, he can't take his eyes off her body, especially her ass. It was dark at the star party last night, but in the light of day Natalie is luscious with an ass every bit as ample as her breasts. He remembers that she was a bit heavier when they first met, and that she's obviously lost weight, but he prays to God she doesn't lose any more. Women in the States always act like they can't be skinny enough, and she's perfect the way she is.

Natalie suddenly sees something in a shop window. "Wait a minute!" She stops walking and pulls on his arm.

"What?"

She doesn't answer and instead leads him back to one of those shops that sell tourist souvenirs.

There are only a few people around and she goes straight for a T-shirt rack near the front window.

"Look! I have to get it for you."

At first, he's not sure what she's talking about, but then he sees she's pointing at a rack of Hulk T-shirts.

"Or do you have a whole closetful already?" Natalie seems to be having misgivings. "People probably give them to you all the time. Forget it. It's a stupid idea."

"No, wait." He grabs her arm. "This is cool. And I swear I don't own a single Hulk T-shirt."

"Really? Because I think it's perfect, being that you're an expert on gamma radiation."

"Long gamma-ray bursts," he corrects her automatically, "but close enough." He grins.

"What size do you wear?" She starts flipping through the shirts.

"Large."

"How's this?" She pulls out a black T-shirt, holds it in front of him.

Anthony looks down at it and nods, deciding he likes being the object of her good intentions for a change. "I approve." The shirt has bold red lettering that says *The Incredible Hulk* and a green angry Hulk on the front.

"I think it should fit. I'm getting it for you. I can't resist!"

"Okay, thanks." Their eyes meet.

In truth, a lot of women have bought him gifts over the years, but Anthony finds he's touched that Natalie wants to buy him something. While she's up by the cashier, he wanders the shop a bit, wishing he could find something for her, too.

And just when he's nearly given up, he sees the perfect thing.

Chapter Sixteen

Diet Plan: Savor the sweetest day you've had in a long time.

Exercise Plan: Forget the elliptical. You've discovered a "new and improved" way to get your heart rate up.

"HOW DO I look?" Anthony asks. He'd slipped into a public restroom and put on the Hulk T-shirt.

Good enough to eat. Natalie lets her eyes linger over his lean muscled torso. Even the shirt looks happy to be worn by him.

Never thought I'd envy a T-shirt.

"The shirt looks fantastic," she says. "It's a pity you're so darn unattractive though."

Anthony smirks, but doesn't say anything.

Natalie reluctantly hands him back his motorcycle jacket. She was holding it for him while he went and changed and has been drowning in its delicious Anthony scent. At one point, she even held it up and stuck her face inside. Luckily, he was still changing and didn't see her.

"How is it a woman who bakes such sweet things for a living never has anything sweet to say?"

Natalie shrugs with a helpless smile. "It's just my way."

He puts his jacket on while she holds the sales bag with his *Star Wars* T-shirt inside.

"Not that you deserve it, but I decided to get you a gift, too. I bought it when you were in the restroom earlier."

Natalie looks up in surprise. "Really? You bought me something?"

"Yes, even though you're cruel to me."

"I . . ." She fumbles around for some kind of response. "What is it?"

"You'll see, but you have to stand still and close your eyes."

She does as he asks. There's a rustling noise and then she senses Anthony standing directly in front of her. His hands gently tuck her hair behind her ears and then something slides in place, resting on her cheeks and nose.

"All right," he says. "You can open them now."

The world is shaded. Her hands reach up to touch the sunglasses on her face.

"Very nice." He nods with approval as he takes her in. "I bought you some aviators. Now we can both look like the famous Moondoggie."

Natalie squeals with delight. "You did? I have to see them!"

They head over to the nearest shop so she can examine her reflection in the glass. After checking herself out for a few seconds, she can't help herself, she squeals again. "I love them!"

"Now you look just like the badass you are, Miss Natalie. Though, you might want to cut back on all that screaming."

"Thank you," she tells him. Suddenly, she feels shy. Natalie can't remember the last time a man bought her a gift when it wasn't her birthday. It feels like years—eons. There's an ache in her chest and a deep longing she doesn't want to examine too closely.

They're both still looking at their reflections in the window when she gets on her tiptoes and kisses him on the cheek.

Anthony turns his face toward hers and slowly shakes his head. "*No,*" he says and points to his lips, "*baciami qui.*"

Her heart flutters as she puts her hands on his cheeks. They feel scratchy under her fingers. Then she draws him toward her and kisses his mouth.

Afterward, he pulls his own aviators out from inside his jacket and puts them on too. "What do you say? Let's both be badasses."

Anthony takes her hand in his and Natalie tries to act casual about it. As usual, his hands are toasty warm. They continue their stroll along the pier and Natalie is as excited as a teenage girl on her first date with the cutest boy in school. She doesn't even mind the way women stare at him anymore.

For once, I'm flying first class.

"Do you want to take a ride on the Ferris wheel?" He points toward the end of the pier where the large wheel is rising out of the water like a giant sea monster.

"Uh, okay."

He glances at her. "We don't have to."

"I want to. It'll be fun," she says with forced enthusiasm. Hopefully, everything will be okay. *Just stay calm,* she tells herself. *You can do it.*

They walk down to the Ferris wheel, and after getting tickets, wait in line behind a group of tourists. She feels like a tourist herself. This whole day has been like an out-of-body experience.

Anthony takes his sunglasses off and puts them on top of his head. "Listen, my daughter's coming over this weekend. That's why I can't go to your house for dinner on Friday."

"Serena?"

He nods. "Just want to clear that up. I didn't mean to give you the wrong impression earlier."

"That's okay. Why don't you bring her along? My daughter, Chloe, will be there and she's invited a few friends over."

Anthony doesn't say anything. He looks out in the distance toward the water. Pensive.

She studies his perfect features, trying to figure out why he would be so hesitant.

"I don't typically introduce Serena to any of the women I date. It's easier that way. No offense."

"Oh, I didn't know that." Natalie reflects on what he's saying. "I'm not offended. You sound like a protective father, that's all."

He lets out a breath and seems relieved. "I'm glad you understand. I've been divorced for a long time. I was a kid when we got married and it only lasted a couple of years. Nicole's been remarried now for a while."

"Was she pregnant when you got married?"

Anthony looks embarrassed. "Yeah, it was an accident. I was in my senior year of college at UCLA."

Natalie quickly does the math in her head and figures Anthony must be around thirty-two or thirty-three years old.

Thank you, God.

She relaxes a little since she was worried he might still be in his twenties or something.

"At least you stuck by your daughter. And you still managed to earn a Ph.D.—that's pretty impressive."

He shrugs. "I suppose."

"You don't think a Ph.D. in astrophysics is impressive?"

"It's not like I'm saving lives or anything."

She gives him a strange look. "Most of us aren't saving lives, Anthony."

He stares at her for long time, but doesn't say anything. Finally, he puts his sunglasses back on and turns toward the front of the line.

Natalie studies his profile. *What was that all about?*

✳ ✸ ✳

THEIR TURN ARRIVES and Natalie steps into the capsule of the Ferris wheel with trepidation. It's encased in glass, except for the section beneath their feet.

She takes a seat on one of the benches and Anthony sits beside her.

"At least we'll have our privacy," he points out.

Natalie smiles a little, trying not to give away her nervousness.

The door is shut and the capsule moves forward a bit and stops as more people are loaded into the next capsule behind them.

"Actually, this isn't bad." Anthony puts his arm on the seat padding behind her and stretches his long legs out at an angle so they fit. "And I'll bet the view from the top is phenomenal."

"I'm sure it is." She turns to look out the window. *The view will be nice. Maybe this won't be so bad.*

They continue to move forward a beat at a time, inching their way higher and higher. Natalie swallows and takes a few deep breaths.

This is fine. Everything is fine.

Anthony is cracking jokes about the family sitting in the capsule behind them and how they're acting like wild monkeys in an ape house.

"You've got to see this," he says, chuckling. "These little kids are hilarious. Two of them are licking the glass. And now they're waving 'hello' to us." Anthony waves his hand in the window.

Natalie would love to see, but the problem is it requires that she look *down,* since those people are below them. And she's pretty sure she wouldn't be able to handle that.

"Why aren't you looking?" he asks.

"I'm just not that interested right now."

"Not interested. What's wrong?"

She shrugs and tries to act casual. "Nothing's wrong. What makes you say that?"

"Because you're acting strange."

"I'm fine," she says too quickly. "Really."

He's silent for a long moment. "Do me a favor and take off your sunglasses."

"I prefer to keep them on. I really like them and they're comfortable." She glances at him. His sunglasses are on top of his head again. His expression is flat and she can't read him at all.

He'd definitely make a good card player.

"Take them off," he says in a voice that doesn't leave much room for argument.

Natalie slips her sunglasses from her face and puts them in her pocket. She stares at the red padded bench across from them and takes a deep breath. Trying to forget all the windows. Forget how high up she is.

Everything is fine.

"Let me see your face."

She turns to him and he studies her. Finally, he frowns. "What's wrong? Tell me."

"Nothing. I just . . . I'm a little bit afraid of heights, is all."

He raises his eyebrows. "You are?"

166

She nods.

"Why didn't you say something earlier? We didn't have to go on this ride."

"We were having such a perfect day," Natalie says in small voice. "I didn't want to ruin it." What she doesn't say is that this whole day has been like a miracle, a mirage in the desert of her life. It's been a long time since she's felt this alive. "And now I've gone and ruined it anyway."

Anthony seems taken aback. "You haven't ruined anything. It's still a perfect day."

She stares into her lap. "I was thinking I could handle it. It's been a while and this isn't like a roller coaster."

"You have a problem with roller coasters?"

"We took Chloe to Disneyland when she was younger and I freaked out." She grimaces. It's embarrassing to admit she couldn't handle something as simple as an amusement park ride, especially when all those little kids seem to do just fine.

"Which rides there freaked you out?"

She shrugs a little. "All of them. Peter insisted I keep trying, but it was a disaster. Pirates of the Caribbean was the last one and then I gave up."

"You were scared of the Pirates of the Caribbean ride?"

Natalie laughs a little. "I know it sounds abs—" she gasps as the Ferris wheel suddenly jerks to a stop. Their capsule starts to swing. Her hands grip the side of the bench as she tries to stay calm, but then she makes a big mistake.

She looks outside. They're at the very top.

"Oh, my God!" Her eyes grow wide. Her stomach drops and adrenaline rockets through her. All she can think is how she's suspended in this tiny capsule high above the ground and it's a long way down.

"Natalie, look at me."

"No, I . . . can't . . ." The panic is setting in. She recognizes it from Disneyland. Her vision swims and she feels like she's going underwater and can't breathe.

"Now—dammit!" He pulls her face toward him. "Look at me!"

And then she sees Anthony. His handsome face is directly before her. His firm and sensual mouth. His chocolate-brown eyes.

"Valrhona," she says.

"What?"

She swallows. The panic is starting to recede somewhat.

"I want you to breathe, Natalie. Take a deep breath and let it out slowly."

She does what he tells her. The outside is fading into the background and the underwater feeling is starting to go away, too.

He nods. "That's good. You're doing just fine."

"I'm scared."

"I know, baby. You're fine though. I'm going to take care of you. Just keep looking at me."

"Okay," she whispers.

Natalie keeps her eyes on him. He tells her to take another deep breath and she complies. His gaze is steady and doesn't waver for an instant. Somewhere in her mind she realizes it's a treat to look at him as much as she wants. "God, you're gorgeous," she murmurs before she can stop herself.

Anthony grins a little. "I thought I was pitifully unattractive."

She sinks into his gaze. It's like coming in from the cold and sitting next to a warm fire. "How do you say 'kiss me' in Italian?" she asks softly.

He doesn't reply right away. Just studies her. "*Baciami*," he says finally.

She puts her hands on his face, his scratchy jaw beneath her fingers. "*Baciami*." And then she leans over and kisses him.

BEFORE ANTHONY CAN decide whether it's a good idea or not, Natalie's mouth is on his. She tastes fresh like a winter's day and he doesn't want to stop kissing her, but gently pushes her away.

"Please," she murmurs and tries to pull him back.

Damn, how can he resist a beautiful woman begging him to kiss her? And she's clearly in need of comfort. He doesn't want to take advantage, though.

It was terrible to see her so scared, especially a woman as self-reliant as Natalie. She seemed on the verge of a full-blown panic attack. He's never heard of someone with a phobia of amusement park rides. She didn't have any problem on his motorcycle, so it must be the height more than anything.

Anthony glances outside. They're still near the top of the Ferris wheel, hanging right on the edge. He wonders how long this ride lasts.

Unfortunately, it doesn't appear to be a short one.

The bench seat is narrow and he repositions himself so the padding isn't digging into his back. His arm is resting behind Natalie and he puts the other hand on her hip.

Her eyes are closed. She opens them, but he's alarmed when he sees them wander toward the window.

"Natalie," he says, his voice a command.

Her blue eyes widen and flash back to him. She looks so unsure of herself that he decides another kiss probably isn't such a bad idea after all.

"Tell me to kiss you again," he says gently. "Can you say it in Italian?"

"*Baciami?*"

And then he draws her close and puts his mouth to hers. She doesn't need any persuasion and slips her arms around his neck easily. He traces Natalie's full lips with his tongue and when she opens her mouth to him, he explores her slowly, taking his time to drink her in, her mouth so velvety and warm.

She moans softly and rakes her hand through his hair, and the sound does something to him. Pulls him in further, his cock already straining against his jeans. Her mouth is wet and willing as he glides his tongue over hers, tasting her. There was a hesitancy when he kissed her last night, but he notices it's gone now.

Instead, she's doing some exploring of her own, sliding her mouth down to his neck. When she bites a tendon, he groans.

Christ.

"You smell so good," she says. "I wish I could eat you."

"Me, too." His balls tingle at her words. And then he kisses her again. His other hand travels up from her hip to feel more of her, but he's frustrated to find her jacket in the way.

"Can you unzip this?"

Natalie looks down at herself and then back to him.

"Let me touch you," he says softly. "Just through your clothes." *Please.*

She blinks and then he watches as she pulls the zipper all the way down. The coat falls open.

And Anthony's mouth goes dry. He can barely think straight.

Even though she's wearing a T-shirt, those voluptuous breasts are right there. Along with that peek of cleavage that's been driving him crazy all afternoon. He can't pull his eyes away.

Sliding his hand up, he cups one breast, weighing and molding her. And even through her clothes, he can tell they're magnificent. Every wet dream he had as a teenage boy seems to be personified in Natalie.

He rolls his thumb over one of her nipples through the fabric and her breath quickens.

"Anthony," she whispers.

Her eyes fall shut as he plays with her, her fingers trailing through his hair. God, how he wishes they were anywhere else but sitting on this Ferris wheel.

He moves his thumb up and runs it over the smooth line of her cleavage. He snakes the tips of his fingers inside her shirt, skimming the top. She's soft everywhere.

I have to taste her. Just a taste. He puts his mouth down to her décolletage, licks her skin. She smells and tastes like vanilla, like all the delicious desserts she creates.

Natalie sucks in her breath. Pulls the back of his head to her. He pushes his thigh between her legs and her body rubs against him. His mouth slides up to nuzzle her neck, and then before he knows it, she grabs his face with both hands, drawing him to her as she kisses him urgently—whimpering into his mouth.

Jesus Christ.

Anthony's balls tighten and he actually worries he's going to lose it.

The Ferris wheel is moving again and an alarm is going off in the back of his mind. Natalie is arching against him, practically in his lap now, and it's difficult to stop. He doesn't want to. His hands are grabbing her hips, sliding down to her ass, and she feels so good. He can't remember the last time he was with a woman who felt this good.

Dude, you need to dial it down. The Ferris wheel has been stopping and starting and it occurs to him that they're letting people off.

"Natalie," he says, pulling away, his voice ragged.

Her eyes are still closed. He glances down and sees they're only a few capsules away from it being their turn to get off.

"It's finished. We have to leave now."

She looks at him, dazed, her mouth open, and he hates to leave her in this state of arousal.

"You're beautiful like this," he tells her and then he kisses her again softly.

Anthony glances down to her breasts. Hell, he hates to leave himself in this state. He shifts on the seat and wonders how he's going to walk out of here with a huge hard-on.

"The ride is over?" she asks, looking around. She glances down with trepidation, but then grows bolder as she leans closer to the front window. "Oh, it is."

"You made it," he tells her. "See, you could do it."

She turns to him with a shy smile. "I can't believe I'm saying this, but I almost wish we could go again."

Later, Anthony and Natalie ride home on his bike—her arms hugging him tight the whole way. He decides he likes the feel of them. Somewhere during that Ferris wheel ride, he and Natalie slipped from casual territory into something else. Something off the map. Uncharted.

"When can I see you again?" he asks.

They're standing on Natalie's front porch. It looks the same as last night, except the axe isn't hanging from her front door anymore. He feels a peculiar sense of ownership for having been the one to pull it out. Like a dog pissing on a tree—except this dog pisses liquid nitrogen.

She considers his request. And he gets the sense Natalie is a woman only starting to understand her feminine power.

"I have a busy workload this week."

"Tell me when I can see you."

She bites her lip.

He wants to reach out for her, but holds back. "Maybe I'll just climb through your bedroom window one of these nights."

Natalie's eyes darken and he can see she isn't opposed to the idea. If he had to guess, she's more than a little excited by it.

"Wednesday might work." There's a slight tremor in her voice. "And you're still welcome to come Friday, if you change your mind. I'm pretty sure Graham will be here, too."

This gets Anthony's attention. "Graham is coming to your pot luck dinner?"

She nods. "Blair invited him."

Shit. A sliver of panic races though him. If Graham tells Blair about him leasing out that space, he's screwed. Natalie will never forgive him.

So tell her yourself right now.

But when he looks at her face, he knows he can't do it. He can't ruin their perfect day.

"Thank you," Natalie says. "For the Ferris wheel."

He watches as she reaches into her coat pocket and pulls something out. Anthony recognizes it as the card from the fortuneteller. "Here." Natalie hands it to him. "You paid good money for that."

Anthony takes the card and reads it.

A secret admirer will soon reveal their heart. Take care of it.

Chapter Seventeen

> Diet Plan: The sweet taste of a
> delicious man is better than chocolate.
>
> Exercise Plan: Take one tiny step on the
> path toward forgiveness.

"SO I UNDERSTAND you're seeing someone," Peter says.

Damn.

Natalie wishes she hadn't answered her phone. If she'd ignored it though, Peter would just keep calling. In truth, she's been walking around in a girlish daze since the weekend. It's probably a mistake, and she'd never admit it, but she's been thinking about Anthony non-stop. *I need to pull it together and stop acting like a naive schoolgirl. This is only supposed to be a casual thing.*

But he took care of me on that Ferris wheel.

In more ways than one. Her pulse races every time she remembers how the two of them were all over each other.

It was a far cry from the way Peter treated her when she'd panicked at Disneyland. His solution was to get angry and tell her she was ruining their vacation. And when that didn't work, he acted helpless. Peter didn't know what to do when she was scared, because he was used to her being the one who took care of him.

But maybe I want someone to take care of me for a change.

"Chloe told me he's some kind of professor at the university," Peter continues.

"Look, I'm busy. I'm in the middle of about a dozen different things right now." She taps her piping bag impatiently against the table where she needs to finish the rosettes on a Sacher Torte.

"And I understand he managed to remove that ugly axe out of our front door."

Natalie bristles. "It's *my* house now, so it's *my* front door."

"There's no reason to be so antagonistic. I keep hoping we can be civil, friendly even—at least for Chloe's sake."

Natalie grits her teeth, but there isn't a lot she can say to that. He's right.

"I understand he's an older gentleman," Peter continues. "And that he used some kind of chemical to pull it out."

Older gentleman?

Natalie wonders where Peter got the impression that Anthony was older, but then remembers Chloe's reaction to the photo Lindsay showed her of Anthony with Excalibur. Lindsay had been saying how a cute guy pulled the axe out, but when Chloe saw the photo, she wrinkled her nose and said, "He's not cute, he's old." Which made Lindsay and Natalie both laugh.

Natalie decides not to correct Peter's impression of Anthony as a senior citizen. *Who cares what he thinks?*

"I know we've had our differences," Peter continues, "and that this whole thing hasn't been easy, but let's try to bury the axe." He laughs. "You know what I mean."

Natalie sighs. It's hard for her to let go of such a deep betrayal, but it's probably time for her to try and move past it. Their marriage wasn't perfect, and it's occurred to her lately that maybe their problems weren't necessarily all Peter's fault.

THAT PROFESSOR OF hers showed up late that afternoon for his espresso breve, his cookie, and to pull her into the bakery's back office and kiss her senseless.

"I can't stop thinking about you." Anthony buries his face in her neck. "God, you always smell like vanilla and butter. It's sexy as hell."

Natalie's breath catches. "Wow, you really do have a sweet tooth."

"What can I say? I know what turns me on."

His mouth is on hers again and Natalie draws him close, dizzy with desire. She feels like a teenager experiencing her first crush.

But then she remembers where they are. "I should get back out there. I still have a few cakes to finish." He has her up against the door and she hopes they aren't being too noisy. Luckily, it's late enough in the day that almost everybody's gone home.

"What's the rush? Stay back here and play grab-ass with me some more."

"Grab-ass?" She laughs. "That's so romantic. Gosh, you're like Romeo under the balcony."

"It's terrible," Anthony admits. "I'm usually smoother than this."

"So how come I'm not getting the smooth lines?"

"I don't know." He rakes a hand through his hair. "You make me nervous."

"That's the second time you've said that. But why would I make you nervous?"

He doesn't reply right away. "You just do, Miss Natalie."

Natalie considers him. He's about a thousand degrees out of her league. If anyone should be nervous, it's her. And he does make her nervous, nervous and excited. Everything feels brighter when she's around Anthony. Like after a whole life of sitting in a dark room, someone finally turned the lights on.

"It must be my skill at baking exceptional desserts. I mean, let's face it, I'm basically your dream woman."

A wicked gleam enters his eye. "You might have something there. We both know I'm a slave to your 'cookies.'" His eyes flicker down her body and Natalie blushes as the memory of the Ferris wheel comes back.

He seems to be thinking the same thing, because he asks her how she's been since that Ferris wheel ride.

"I'm fine. That whole panic thing really only happens at amusement parks."

"I hope you don't think I took . . . advantage of the situation."

Natalie is stunned. "Are you kidding? Anthony, you saved me. I was so scared," she shakes her head at the memory, "but you took care of me. You knew just what to do. And as far as the part where we played grab-ass," she smiles, "that was hot."

"Yeah?"

She nods.

"I thought it was hot, too." He catches her hand in his. "I wouldn't mind doing it again sometime."

They study each other and Natalie knows she's supposed to be keeping it mellow, isn't supposed to be letting her emotions get involved. But it's not easy. She's not sure if she knows how to do that. It's not like she's falling in love with Anthony, though he's hard to resist.

I'll bet women fall in love with him all the time.

But I won't be one of them.

"Anywhere but on a Ferris wheel," he says with a grin.

Knock! Knock!

Natalie jumps away from the door as she realizes there's someone on the other side.

Anthony reaches down for the handle and opens it. "Hi, Blair," he says.

Natalie peeks over Anthony's arm at her friend, co-owner, and fellow baker.

Blair's hazel eyes go from Natalie to Anthony and back to Natalie again. She raises an eyebrow. "What are you two doing in here?"

"Nothing!" Natalie says.

Blair smiles. "Well, I hope that's not true."

Natalie can hear Anthony chuckling.

The door opens wider as Anthony reaches over for his satchel sitting on the office chair.

"I should get going," he says. "I have a meeting in a short while and I know you guys are closing up soon." He turns to Natalie. "I wanted to let you know that if I'm still invited, I'll be at your house for dinner on Friday."

"Really? That's great. Are you bringing Serena?"

He shakes his head. "No, it turns out I won't be picking her up until Saturday."

"Oh, okay. Well, I'm glad you can make it."

He nods. "What kind of dish should I bring?"

She explains how it's a vegetarian potluck, so he can bring any dish as long as there's no meat.

His eyebrows raise. "Are you a vegetarian?"

"Chloe's the vegetarian in the house, but I don't eat much meat either."

"Serena's a vegetarian, too." He smiles and rolls his eyes a little. "It's a recent thing." Anthony throws the strap of his satchel over his head and positions it across his body. He's wearing his motorcycle jacket and looks mouth-wateringly hot. Natalie can barely believe she was playing grab-ass with him only a few minutes ago. "I'll see you guys later." And then he does something that completely stuns her.

He dips his head and kisses her on the mouth. "*Ciao,* Miss Natalie," he says softly.

When he's gone, Blair turns to her. "Tell me everything! And remember there's no detail too small!"

"I don't know where to start. We went to that star party and sort of connected."

"I can see that. Have you slept with him?"

"No, of course not! We've only gone out a couple of times."

"You mean no, not *yet.*"

Natalie sighs. "I don't know what I mean. This is all so new for me. Do you know how long it's been since I dated someone? I was married fourteen years. I'm trying to have fun, though."

Blair nods with approval. "Good, you deserve it. Seriously. And I hope you have *lots* of fun with Anthony."

Natalie shakes her head and laughs.

Blair gets a crafty expression. "I'll bet he gives us that space now for sure. Has he said anything about it?"

"No, come to think of it, he hasn't even mentioned it." Natalie frowns. "I'm sure he's still collecting data. He really is a serious geek. You should have seen him at that star party when he was totally in his element."

"He's a hot geek though. At least tell me this much—is he a good kisser?"

Natalie grins. "Yes, he is."

"I knew it—ha! Who's Serena, anyway? I take it she's not his girlfriend?"

"His daughter."

Blair's eyes grow wide. "Really? I wouldn't have pictured him as a dad."

"I was surprised, too. He sounds like a good father though." Natalie grabs her apron off the chair where Anthony put it when he untied it from her. "And now what's happening with you and Graham? Are you still bringing him on Friday?"

"He's coming, but we seem to be headed for the friend zone."

"I'm surprised. I thought you liked him."

"I do." Blair picks up some baking trays and takes them over to the sink. She stacks everything in a neat pile for their dishwasher. "Road set up a Facebook page."

"Oh?"

Leaning against the counter, Blair wipes her hands on her apron. "Tori told me about it."

Tori is Blair's sister-in-law and best friend. She's also a web designer who created and maintains La Dolce Vita's website. Natalie spoke to her recently about making some changes to their site.

"I know I shouldn't have done it. I mean, I don't care what Road does anymore, but I looked at it." Blair shakes her head. "I wish I hadn't."

"Is it bad?"

Blair nods. "He was in India for a while and then Budapest. He's living quite an adventurous life."

Without me. That's what Blair leaves unsaid.

Natalie puts her arm around Blair's shoulders and squeezes it. "Forget him. You're too good for him"

Blair smiles. "I know. After all these years, it was a shock to see even a photograph."

"That makes sense." Natalie tries to imagine what it would be like if Peter had run out on her four years ago and she hadn't heard from him since.

"Anyway, forget all that." Blair pushes away from the counter. "You're right—to heck with Road. I'm not going to think about him anymore. Maybe I'll finally file for divorce."

ANTHONY PULLS OUT his phone and tries to call Graham again. His voicemail says he's in Bellingham, but why isn't he returning any of his calls?

"I think this is the fifteenth message I've left for you. I'm starting to feel like a chick—call me."

He checks his own voicemail. There's one from his assistant, Maya, about his SWIFT proposal, another one from the *Seattle Times* asking to speak to him about the Smyth Medal, though he doesn't understand why they keep calling. It's not like he's won the damn thing. It's just a nomination, and there are four other people nominated in the same category. The last one is from his father.

"Anthony, I consulted my schedule and it appears I have an opening the weekend of the Smyth Science Awards Banquet. Your mother and I will both be attending. My secretary will be calling you to get the pertinent details."

And that's it. No hello or goodbye. No 'how are you?' Just his commanding baritone telling him how it's going to be. Why he should expect anything different from his father, he doesn't know.

Anthony shoves his phone back into his jacket.

I'm surprised he's bothering to come at all. Of course, he does have an opening in his schedule.

Passing a flower store, Anthony slows down, and then after a moment's deliberation, decides to go inside. He wanders around the shop examining the flower bouquets, wondering if he should send one to Natalie. Is it too much too soon? He's not sure. And the not knowing is what's making him uneasy. He's not used to courting women or being the instigator in relationships. Women have always come to him.

"Can I help you?" A pretty brunette salesgirl comes over.

"Yeah, I'm trying to decide if it's too soon to send flowers to a woman."

The brunette tilts her head and smiles. "It's never too soon to send flowers. Is this woman your girlfriend?"

"No," but then he pauses, "maybe, I'm not sure."

"Are you trying to send her a message? Or convey something? There's a language to flowers."

"There is?" Anthony considers this. He's given a lot of gifts to women over the years, but he can't remember ever giving flowers. It's usually candy or jewelry—there was a blonde flight attendant he met coming back from an observing run in Chile who wanted a belly chain.

"Something romantic," he tells her. "That's the kind of message I'm going for."

"Red roses are always good for romance, especially to say 'I love you.' The lavender roses can be used to convey love at first sight."

The phone by the cash register rings and the salesgirl excuses herself to go answer it.

Anthony studies the flowers, mildly panicked. He wonders which ones say, 'I really like you and I want to sleep with you.'

There's probably a good reason I haven't been giving flowers to women all these years.

Luckily, his phone alarm goes off, telling him he has ten minutes to make his class, so he doesn't have to decide anything right now.

It's drizzling outside again and he wishes he'd worn a different jacket as he heads up toward the campus to meet with a couple of his postgraduate students about their Ph.D. projects. Coming from L.A., he's not sure if he'll ever get used to the wet Seattle weather.

When Anthony gets there, his student, Navez, is already working on the whiteboard while his other student, Brad, looks on. They're both working with neutron stars and black holes, so their projects are closely tied to his own area of research.

After taking a seat, Anthony starts scanning the equations Navez has been writing. His eyes narrow as he searches for mistakes, but also creativity. Finally, he leans forward.

"You're looking at stellar initial mass function using N-body simulation, but is your IMF slope too shallow?"

Navez goes to check through some of his notes.

When he comes back to the board, they go through the equations step by step again, with Navez changing some of his variables. The three of them hash out more things on the board and the time goes by fast. It's the kind of work Anthony enjoys and can easily do for hours. As they're finishing up, he nods to himself, and decides that overall he's satisfied with both of his students' progress.

He's in good spirits as he heads toward his office, thinking about seeing Natalie again on Friday. Although he'd prefer if it were just the two of them. Unfortunately, when Anthony turns the corner to his office, he discovers there's a group of young female students waiting to ambush him.

Shit.

He tries to escape, but it's too late. They've already spotted him. Like a pack of hungry wolves.

"Professor Novello!"

Desperate, he searches around for his assistant, Maya, who usually helps wrangle all these women. And, of course, she's nowhere in sight.

"I have some questions about astrology!"

"Do you have a girlfriend, Professor Novello?"

"What's gravity?"

"Could you come to our sorority tomorrow night? There'll be dancing!"

They're all chattering at once and he's already getting a headache from their shrill voices.

"I'll be with you in a moment," Anthony says, rushing into his office and quickly closing the door.

He wishes he could teleport away. Glancing toward the window, he thinks about that scene from *Raiders* where Indy climbs out of one to get away from his female students.

The problem is, Anthony's office is on the third floor.

Pulling out his phone, he texts an SOS to Maya. He's tempted to leave, but knows they'll only follow him wherever he goes. A posse of determined young females is harder to lose than you'd think. Pretty soon, they're going to start knocking on the door, rattling the knob as they try to get inside. It's like keeping out a zombie attack.

Luckily, Maya shows up within a few minutes. Turns out she was only getting coffee and was already on her way back. *Thank God.* He can hear her through the door.

She sweeps through the group in her efficient way, telling them how they'll each need to make an appointment and how she handles most of Anthony's student questions herself. That typically gets rid of all of them, and this time is no exception.

"Thank you," Anthony says, peeking his head out.

Maya rolls her eyes. Her dark curls form a halo around her face. With a Cuban mother and an Ethiopian father, Maya is nobody's fool. She's also hot tempered and as smart as they come.

"You're like a reluctant rock star, you know that?"

"I don't want to be a rock star."

"I know. But that's partly what makes you so irresistible."

Maya hands him one of the lattes she bought and Anthony thanks her. She then reminds him about the SWIFT proposal.

"Oh, yeah, that's right." He gets his computer out and switches the keyboard over to Italian so he can email his colleague in Naples. They met when Anthony spent time in Italy working on a postdoctoral fellowship with the Italian Space Agency. Having produced some of the world's finest astronomers, Italians still have a strong presence in the world's astronomical community.

Maya is sifting through his mail. "Have you seen this?" she asks, holding a letter up. "There's an invitation here for you to speak at the European Astrophysics conference in Rome later this year. I assume you're going to that."

Anthony nods, still typing. "I submitted that paper I wrote on redshift measurements a while ago. What does it say?"

Maya reads it aloud and Anthony listens with half an ear. The conference is months away and he'll have plenty of time to pull together a short lecture. His mind wanders back to Natalie and all the kissing they've been up to lately, mostly because it's driving him nuts.

You were an idiot to agree to it in the first place.

He's not used to this kind of sexual frustration. His only hope is that it's wearing on her, too—and he suspects it is. Even his dreams are working against him. Last night he had the boxing one again. She was wearing the tight T-shirt and shorts that he likes to imagine her in. They were boxing at first, but that turned into wrestling, and it didn't take long before their clothes were gone and he was on top of her, buried deep. Her legs were wrapped around him and that sexy mouth was screaming his name.

He woke up sweating with a rock hard dick and he had to finish himself off.

It would have been far better if she'd actually been there.

Seeing Natalie in the morning after having spent the night rolling around in his bed—now that would be something. She'd look so pretty. All mussed and well-tumbled. He can think of a million things he'd like to do with her, each one dirtier than the last.

"Do you want to schedule extra time in Rome so you can visit your family?" Maya asks, bringing him back to reality.

"Uh, yeah, an extra week should do it."

"I'll go ahead and put the paperwork through then."

"Sure," Anthony says, but he's already back to thinking about how he can make his dream with Natalie come true.

Chapter Eighteen

Diet Plan: Humiliation followed by relief
for dessert. Throw in a glass of a nice
Italian red.

Exercise Plan: Freak out. It burns a
surprising number of calories.

THIS IS THEIR third potluck dinner and the first one where Natalie feels nervous.

"You look great," Lindsay says. "Stop freaking out."

"I'm not freaking out."

"Really? How many times are you going to change clothes?"

"I think ten times should do it."

Lindsay laughs. "You look fantastic. Trust me, I'd tell you if you didn't. You're my greatest project yet."

It's almost time for people to arrive so Natalie starts laying out dishes of food on the dining room table. Lindsay likes Mexican, so she puts out the makings for tacos using refried beans. Oliver will probably bring beer. Blair mentioned something about a bread pudding, though she's not sure about Graham or if he's bringing anything. Natalie decided to make a tiramisu.

I like tiramisu.

Though who is she kidding? She made the tiramisu for Anthony. In truth, it's a pleasure to make sweets for a man who appreciates them so much. Peter was often disdainful of some of the rich desserts she created. Of course, it didn't help matters that he was a dentist.

The doorbell rings.

"I'll get it," Lindsay calls out. "I think it's Oliver."

Natalie continues setting a stack of plates out for everyone. She doesn't see a sign of either Lindsay or Oliver for about five minutes. When they finally come into the dining room, Lindsay has a smug smile on her face, while

Oliver is in a daze and can't take his eyes off her sister.

Natalie feels a twinge of envy and wonders, not for the first time, how her sister does it. She seems to have a magical ability to enslave men.

"I'll take that from you," Natalie tells Oliver. She puts the beer he brought in the fridge, offering him one first, which he grabs eagerly.

"Do you need any help?" Lindsay asks.

"No, there's not much else to do."

In a short while, Blair shows up with Graham. The two of them look like they stepped out of the pages of a preppy college catalog. Blair is wearing a scarf in her ponytail, a cardigan sweater, beige capris, and black ballerina flats. Graham looks handsome in a white button-down shirt and dark khakis. He offers her a bottle of white wine, which she thanks him for and, after uncorking it, places next to the food.

"How are you?" she asks Blair.

"I'm fine." Blair waves her hand dismissively. "I'm over it. I blocked Road's Facebook page, so I won't even be tempted to look at it anymore."

A couple of Chloe's friends arrive and after loading their plates, Natalie helps the girls get settled in the family room with their sleeping bags. There's a stack of board games and Chloe has a few favorite movies picked out. Natalie figures she'll make popcorn and bring it in to the girls later. She's happy that Chloe wanted to have friends over tonight and has been encouraging her to do normal kid things since the divorce. Both Natalie and Lindsay also finally drove out to meet Cinnamon, Chloe's new horse. Natalie still isn't crazy about any of it, but there isn't much she can do.

The grown-ups are sitting in the living room, drinking and talking. Natalie is waiting for Anthony to arrive before she has everyone get food, but when the clock hits twenty after the hour, she decides to let people eat.

He's probably just running late, she tells herself as she checks her phone for a text again. Still nothing. No voicemail, either.

A small pitiful part of herself worries that she's being stood up.

"Isn't Anthony coming?" Blair asks.

"He's supposed to be here."

Graham adds salsa to his plate and dips a chip into it. "Don't worry, he'll show. That guy is late for everything, trust me."

Natalie nods, but there's a growing sense of dread in the pit of her stomach. She chastises herself for letting this mean so much. Men like Anthony are all the same and she should know better. He's probably juggling a dozen women at once and she's just another number in that perfect memory of his.

Grabbing a plate, Natalie helps herself to some food, though she's basically lost her appetite.

"If he stands you up, he's a dead man," Lindsay says, coming over to her. "I'm serious. I'll have Oliver kick his ass."

Natalie glances over at Oliver. He's wearing a hockey jersey from the Phoenix Scorpions. It's gray with an orange scorpion tail and hugs his muscular shoulders. "Whatever. I'm not going to let it bother me. We're just keeping it casual, anyway."

She pours herself a glass of the wine Graham brought and takes a large swallow. Natalie takes another swallow and just as she considers pouring a second glass, the front doorbell rings.

Thank God.

The clock says he's forty-five minutes late.

"I'll get it," she announces, trying not to let her annoyance show. Her pulse kicks into overdrive. The worst part is she's thrilled he showed up even if he is so late, but that doesn't mean she isn't pissed.

Natalie swings the door open, ready with a glare and a tongue-lashing.

She sees his handsome face. And then her eyes widen—standing right next to him is a little girl with long, dark, curly hair and the same set of perfect features as Anthony.

"SORRY WE'RE LATE," Anthony says. He can see Natalie is in a state when she opens the door, but also that she recovers quickly. "This is my daughter, Serena." He introduces the two of them.

"Hi, Serena, it's nice to meet you." Natalie invites them both inside.

Serena is carrying the dish of vermicelli they picked up at Whole Foods, while he's carrying a bottle of wine. Natalie leads them both into the dining room where coats are taken and more introductions are made. Anthony says a quick hello to everyone.

"The other girls are all playing board games in the family room," Natalie tells Serena. "Do you want to make a plate of food and then you can join them?"

"My dad said the food is all vegetarian?"

"That's right. My daughter, Chloe, is a vegetarian."

"Okay, that's cool."

Anthony gets a plate for Serena. He can tell he's still getting the cold shoulder from Natalie and some groveling will be required. After helping Serena get food, they both follow Natalie into the other room, where the girls are sitting on the floor gathered around a large square coffee table. They look up when the three of them enter the room.

"Chloe, this is Serena," Natalie says to a blonde girl. "Can you guys make room for her? I'm guessing she might like to join your game."

Chloe scoots over. "She can sit next to me."

He sees Chloe look back over at him. "Are you my mom's friend that pulled out Excalibur?"

"Yes, I am."

The girls all turn to stare at him and he smiles politely.

Serena takes her plate over and sits beside Chloe. Immediately, Serena asks her about being a vegetarian and the two are off on a discussion. Anthony also notices with relief that the girls are playing Settlers of Catan—one of Serena's favorite games.

"I'll just be in the other room," he tells her.

Serena turns to him and nods, but he can see that she's already preoccupied.

"That was easy," Anthony says to Natalie once they leave the room. "I wasn't sure what to expect."

Natalie doesn't respond

"Look, I'm sorry we're late, but as you can see, I had extenuating circumstances and I almost didn't come at all."

"I'm glad you brought your daughter and I'm glad you came, but why didn't you let me know you were going to be so late?"

Anthony stops walking and grabs her hand. They're alone in the hallway. "Is there somewhere we can go talk?"

Natalie hesitates, but then leads him toward another door and they go into a room with a large desk and big leather chair. The walls are bare with discolored patches where pictures once hung.

"My ex-husband's study. I haven't had time to get rid of the desk and chair yet."

"Maybe we could talk in your bedroom?"

Natalie snorts.

"How will I be able to climb through your window at night if I don't know which one it is?"

There's a smile playing on the corners of her mouth, but then she turns her head away.

Instead of explaining anything, Anthony decides to wait her out. It's not like he had much control over the situation here. Nicole called him at the last minute telling him to pick up Serena.

"This probably isn't going to work between us," Natalie finally says.

Now it's Anthony's turn to snort. "You're kidding, right?"

Natalie tosses her head. "No, I'm not. This is just some casual thing anyway, so what do you care?"

"I care." Anthony's jaw tightens.

He watches as Natalie's fingers trace over the smooth stone on the necklace she's wearing. She studies it. "Tell me what we're doing here. I don't think I'm clear on it anymore."

Anthony takes time with his response and in the end decides to keep it simple. "I like you. And I know you just got out of a marriage and I'm probably an idiot for wanting to get involved with you, but I still do."

She looks up. "Really?"

"Yeah."

"Is this still casual then?"

"Natalie, I think we left casual behind on that Ferris wheel, don't you?"

She bites her lip as she considers his words. Finally, she nods. "It feels different to me, too. That's why I was upset when you were so late."

"Look, I would have let you know, but I didn't have my phone. I left it on my desk at work." Anthony rolls his eyes. "It's been a comedy of errors all afternoon, plus I've been ambushed every single day this week."

"Ambushed? By who?"

"Never mind. It's a long story." He reaches out for her hand again. "And very boring."

"I want to hear all your stories, even the boring ones. I feel as if I hardly know anything about you."

"Come here," Anthony says, pulling her toward him. She rests her head against his chest. Anthony sticks his face in her hair. She smells good. Like vanilla, but also some kind of coconut shampoo.

"I'm on to you," she says into his chest. "All your clever deflections. They don't fool me."

He grins to himself. It figures nothing would get past Natalie.

Her body feels soft pressed into his and if circumstances were different and they weren't in a house full of people, he'd find that bedroom of hers and make damn good use of it.

When they head back out to join the others, Anthony immediately goes over to talk to Graham. They stand off to the side of the kitchen.

"Before you say anything, I was up in Bellingham on business all week and had to get a new phone," Graham tells him.

"You haven't mentioned anything to Blair about how I'm leasing that space, have you?"

"No, I got your messages before I saw her. You realize she and Natalie are going to figure it out, though."

"Look, I've been thinking. Can I cancel the lease with the new tenants?"

Graham balks. "What? No, you can't. It would take months and cost you a fortune. Plus, you'd need a reason and you don't have one. That's a terrible idea."

Shit.

"All that money has already been deposited in your account," Graham continues. "You signed a year's lease with them."

Anthony thinks it over. "What if I just gave them their money back?"

"Then they'd sue you for breach of contract and they'd win. You don't want to go there, trust me."

Anthony's gaze travels the room and touches on Natalie. She's joking with her sister and Blair about something. *I am so screwed.*

Graham shrugs. "Just tell Natalie the truth. She'll no doubt be pissed, but it's not like you didn't give them a chance."

Anthony knows this is true. It's been months and from all the numbers he's seen, the bakery can't afford to take over that second space. At this point, it would be a huge mistake for them. On the other hand, he doesn't want to ruin things with Natalie.

"All right, I need to explain it to her myself though."

Graham shrugs. "Whatever. I'm your lawyer, so I won't say anything."

"Okay, thanks. Did the new tenants say when they plan to start setting up shop?"

"No, it sounds like they're waiting for some private financing to go through."

"So not right away?"

"I can't say for sure, but it doesn't sound immediate."

Anthony nods. *So I have a little time to get this straightened out with Natalie.*

THEY SIT ON the loveseat together with Anthony's arm draped behind her and it feels like a statement that they're a couple. Natalie is surprised at how okay she is with it. She's never been the most trusting person, but she can feel her guard slipping with Anthony.

Looking around the room, it strikes her how much her life has changed since Peter left. *Suddenly, I'm hanging with the cool kids.* Lindsay always hung with the cool crowd—and still does—but even in high school, Natalie always felt more like everybody's mother. Peter's friends were mostly other dentists and their wives. She tried to fit in with them, but always felt out of place there, too. Most of the wives didn't work and her being a baker was only tolerated.

Now there's a photographer, a lawyer, and an astronomer at my house for dinner.

My life has become interesting.

Everyone is done eating and they're all relaxing together in the living room. Lindsay and Oliver are piled together on the recliner, while Blair and Graham seem comfortable on the couch, despite her friend zone comment.

Anthony's drinking some of the wine he brought—Italian, naturally— and Natalie doesn't bother pouring her own glass, but just takes sips from his. He seems happy to share.

Earlier, she noticed Anthony having an intense conversation with Graham in the kitchen and she can't help but speculate what they were talking about.

They both glanced over at her and Blair a few times. He hasn't mentioned anything and she doesn't want to get too excited, but keeps wondering if maybe he's finally going to lease them that space.

First thing is to knock out that back wall and expand the kitchen. She already has her eye on a new Doyon jet oven. *No more baking at home every morning!*

Natalie takes another sip from Anthony's glass and smiles to herself. "I think this wine is going to my head," she tells him.

He leans close so only she can hear. "I think you're going to my head, Miss Natalie."

They gaze at each other and she still can't believe this beautiful man is here with her. It's like being in the throes of her first crush, except unlike high school, where the guys she crushed on didn't know she was alive, this guy actually wants her.

"So, Anthony," Oliver says. "I understand you're an astronomer. What's your main area of study?"

Anthony turns toward Oliver. "My primary research centers on long gamma-ray bursts."

"I've heard of those. They come from black holes, right?"

Anthony nods. "In a manner of speaking. We think they can also come from high mass stars collapsing into neutron and quark stars." He continues to describe them in more detail and Natalie tries to follow what he's saying, but it's way over her head.

Graham asks a question about supermassive black holes and Natalie is surprised the men seem to know so much about astronomy. Is this some kind of 'cool' guy thing? She's pretty sure Peter didn't know a single thing about astronomy.

"Have you ever had time with the Hubble?" Oliver asks.

Anthony plays absentmindedly with Natalie's hair. "I've been fortunate enough to have a couple of observing runs with the Hubble."

"You guys are asking all the wrong questions," Lindsay says as she stretches her long legs out over Oliver's lap. "What I want to know is, have you ever seen a UFO? That would be fascinating."

Anthony chuckles. "No UFOs—sorry." He's still playing with her hair, and Natalie wants to curl up against him and purr. "At least none that were of alien origin."

"Do you think aliens exist?" Blair asks. "What about crop circles? Is any of that stuff real?"

Lindsay and Blair pepper him with questions, each one more absurd than the last, while Anthony patiently answers them all.

"You two sound like a couple of conspiracy nuts," Natalie finally says, feeling slightly embarrassed. She turns to Anthony. "Is it always like this?"

He shrugs. "I get asked about UFOs and aliens fairly often. You'd be surprised how many people believe in those things."

"See," Lindsay says. "It's not just us."

Blair takes a bite from her tiramisu. "And how often do we have an expert here to set things straight? Though I have to say, I think you're holding out on us, Anthony."

"He's probably sworn to secrecy," Lindsay tells her. "Not allowed to divulge any of the real juicy stuff."

"It's a government plot," Blair agrees.

Natalie laughs and rolls her eyes. She takes Anthony's wine glass and sips from it. "What about X-wing starfighters? Surely you've seen a few of those around."

His eyes twinkle. "Now that you mention it, I have seen a few. And I'm getting a little concerned with the number of battle cruisers I've noticed lately."

"We'll have to get that information to the new rebel base."

Anthony leans over and whispers in her ear. "Better stop, Miss Natalie, or I might have to kiss you senseless in front of all these people."

LATER, AS EVERYONE leaves to go home, Anthony hangs back. Serena has fallen asleep with all the other girls and he decides not to wake her just yet.

"So what are your plans next weekend?" he asks Natalie.

She hesitates before answering and he suspects she knows what he's really asking her.

"Why don't you come over to my place," he says. "I'll make you dinner."

"Can you cook?"

"Of course, I'm Italian."

Natalie gives him a skeptical look. "Talking to you, I get the impression that Italians are good at everything."

"We are." He lets his gaze catch hers.

"Is this . . . are you inviting me for a sleepover?"

He laughs at her description. "I'm not sure how much sleeping will be involved," he says, stepping closer to her and lowering his voice, "but yes."

They're standing in the hallway and Natalie leans against the wall. She fidgets with her necklace. "Chloe is going to her dad's on Friday and Lindsay will be at Oliver's all weekend."

"Does this mean you're available?"

"I suppose I can fit you in somewhere."

Anthony grins.

Natalie's eyes widen at her choice of words. "I . . . uh, that didn't come

out exactly right."

"Let's count on next Friday night, okay?"

TUESDAY MORNING NATALIE is in her van driving to the bakery when she gets a call on her cell phone. It's her one late morning, so it's already almost eight o'clock.

"Where are you?" Blair asks.

"I'm on my way in. I should be there in a few minutes. Why?"

"You know that empty space next door?"

"Yes."

"Well, it's not empty anymore."

"What do you mean?" Natalie wonders if she's misheard.

"I'm saying there's a group of contractors in there right now."

"Seriously!" Natalie's nearly swerves her van off the road with excitement. "Is Anthony finally giving us that space?" Her mind races through different scenarios. Maybe he wanted to surprise them? Give it to her as a gift?

"No, that's not it."

"It's not?"

She can hear Blair let out a deep sigh. "Just get in here."

Natalie parks in her usual space in the alley right behind La Dolce Vita. The air smells like diesel, and it's cold and damp outside. The back door to the space next to the bakery is open.

Blair comes out to meet her. "I went over and spoke to them. The contractors said they were hired by the people who are leasing the space."

"Somebody's leasing that space?"

"Apparently so."

"Who?"

Blair shrugs. "I don't know. From the way they're talking, it sounds like a clothing store."

Natalie is shaking her head. "That can't be right. Anthony would have told me—told us. I'm going to call him and find out what's going on."

She dials his number with Blair standing there. It goes directly to voicemail. Natalie leaves a message describing the situation. "Call me, Anthony, okay?"

"Maybe there's a mistake or something," Blair says, though it doesn't sound like she believes it.

Natalie leans back against the van trying to make sense of the situation. There's a knot in her stomach along with a growing sense of dread. She recognizes this feeling. The feeling of relying on someone, trusting them, and being let down.

I should have known.

"Are you okay?" Blair asks.

Natalie takes a deep breath. "I'm fine. Let's just unload all this stuff from the back."

They get Carlos to come out and the three of them carry in all the baking Natalie did that morning. Natalie goes out front to make herself a latte while Carlos unloads items for the pastry case. They have a new barista working the cash register and Natalie says a quick hello to her.

Finally, she sits down in their little office and tries calling Anthony again. There's still no answer.

"It looks like someone else just arrived next door," Blair tells her. "Let's go talk to them."

They head over and enter through the back. Natalie's only been inside this space once, ages ago. She steps over rolls of plastic and other tools.

Natalie sees a couple of people with Starbucks cups and gets a bad feeling. It's a woman and man, both talking to a couple of other contractors.

As Blair and Natalie approach, the group turns to look at them.

"Hi," Blair says. "We're the bakers from next door and just wanted to come over and find out what's happening.'"

"Oh, hello!" An Asian woman with black hair and short blunt bangs puts her hand out. "I'm Amy and this is my business partner, Daniel. We're going to be your new neighbors!"

Amy goes on to explain how they're opening a clothing store. "Tasteful, but for the younger set. That's why being near the university is such a perfect location."

"And you've spoken with our landlord, Anthony?" Natalie asks.

"We signed contracts, but we haven't met him yet. Just Graham, his lawyer."

"So Graham handled the whole thing?" Blair asks.

Amy nods. "Yes, I got the feeling that was typical though. Is there a problem?"

"No, no problem." Blair turns to look at Natalie.

"You'll have to come to our grand opening!" Amy tells them. "We'll hire you to help cater desserts!"

Natalie tries to smile, but feels queasy.

When they leave and walk back to La Dolce Vita, she stops Blair. "I have to go find him." She doesn't need to say who she's talking about.

Blair nods. "I'll cover for you. Do you want to drive Isadora? You'll need her today. Let me get you the keys."

Natalie is so furious she can't even enjoy driving Blair's amazing car. Her hands grip the steering wheel as if it were Anthony's neck. She finds a parking spot near the Astronomy-Physics building, remembers where his office is, but when she gets up there only finds Maya.

"Where is he?"

Maya looks at her with surprise. "Anthony? He's in class. What's wrong?"

"Where is this class?" Natalie asks, trying to control the anger in her voice.

Maya gives her instructions. "Do you want me to write it down for you?"

"No, that's okay. I've got it." Anthony's not the only one with a good memory. She remembers things too, very well, in fact. She remembers how he told her he'd lease them that space. He said they only had to prove to him they could afford it, but apparently, he forgot about that.

Natalie finds the room number that Maya gave her. It's another lecture hall, but when she pulls the door open to go inside she discovers it's empty. She hears voices though and down near the front she can see a few people. Some are sitting at a table while Anthony is standing in front of them writing on a whiteboard.

As she makes her way down, a couple of the people at the desk turn to glance at her. Anthony is still writing and doesn't seem to notice she's entered the room.

Taking a seat behind the group, Natalie stays quiet. Anthony is talking as he writes, something about the Schwarzchild radius—whatever that is, and his voice carries authoritatively. His blue shirtsleeves are rolled up and reveal the dark hair on his forearms. He's not wearing a watch or any other kind of jewelry, not that he should. It would only distract from his blinding appeal. Even now, she's still drawn to him. It angers her further. He should look like an ugly toad with warts all over, but he still looks like the handsome prince.

One of the students asks Anthony a question. He still doesn't seem to notice that she's sitting there.

Finally, after he answers the question and still doesn't notice her, she speaks up.

"I have a question, Professor Novello."

He turns to her, pushes his nerd glasses up on his head. His expression changes from confident to surprise. "Natalie?"

"Maybe you can explain the hypothesis of keeping a promise."

Anthony is confused. "Natalie, I'm in the middle of class. Could you wait and we'll talk afterward?"

"What I have to say won't take long." She leans forward. "This has to do with an empty space that now contains matter."

"What?"

"The matter is a group of contractors setting up a clothing store right next to a certain bakery."

Anthony grows still. She can see understanding wash over him. He opens his mouth. "Wait . . ."

She pushes herself up and wishes she could kick something, kick him, kick herself for being such an idiot. "Don't," she says, putting her hand out to him. "Just, *don't!*"

And then she leaves. She hears him excusing himself to his students, hears his footsteps running up behind her, but she doesn't slow down. Finally, his hand is on her arm.

She shakes him off. "Don't touch me."

"Stop, Natalie, let me talk to you. I need to explain this."

They're at the top of the stairs and she turns around. Up close, his expression is worried and she can see that he's rattled.

"How could you, Anthony?"

"I'm sorry. I meant to tell you sooner."

"Then why didn't you?"

"Things were just starting to get good between us. I didn't want to screw it up."

Natalie is incredulous. "Are you kidding me? You signed contracts! You couldn't have maybe mentioned that?"

"You're right. I should have. I was planning to tell you this week, actually."

"How could you rent that space out when you know how much we wanted it?"

He plows a hand through his hair in frustration. "Look, you and Blair don't have the income."

"Yes, we do. But you didn't even give us a chance. Your stupid program is wrong and so are you!"

"No, I'm not."

"You think you know everything, don't you? Poor Anthony, always the smartest person in the room."

"I don't have to be the smartest person in the room to be able to add and subtract!"

"Why couldn't you have waited just a little bit longer? Why?"

He's silent.

"That's all we needed to prove it to you."

"I just admitted it was a mistake not to tell you, but I doubt more time would have made any difference with your financial information. It wouldn't have changed anything. Your rent would have doubled. You and Blair can't afford that."

"You don't know that for sure. We would have extended our hours. That extra space would have been a deal changer for us."

Anthony shakes his head. "And I thought you said you never gambled?"

"That's not gambling!"

"Nothing you're saying changes the fact that you don't have the income and I have bills to pay and mouths to feed just like you do."

"You never should have told us you'd give us that chance, then." Natalie hugs herself in frustration. "How could you not tell me what was going on?"

Anthony lets out a deep breath. "You're right. I admit I made a mistake there. I should have told you sooner, but it doesn't change the facts."

"Well, it looks like I made a big mistake, too. I thought I could take you at your word, but I was wrong!"

Chapter Nineteen

> Diet Plan: Popcorn and comfort movies.
>
> Exercise Plan: Try not to wallow in self-pity.

ANTHONY DOESN'T COME into the bakery all week, doesn't call or text. Natalie doesn't hear a word from him, not that she expects to, but still. Apparently, there's a small part of her holding out hope that somehow he would come through for her and fix this mess.

Meanwhile, she and Blair have been getting to know their new neighbors, Amy and Daniel. They get coffee and pastries every day, along with some of the contractors who are building the fixtures for the clothing store.

"I wish they'd stop coming over," Blair says. "I know it isn't their fault, but it's like having our faces rubbed in it."

"I know," Natalie sighs.

"Maybe we should keep looking for a new space."

"Probably." Natalie sighs again.

Lindsay's eyes narrowed with anger when she heard. "Who knew geeks could be so sneaky?"

By the time Friday rolls around, it's hard for Natalie not to feel depressed, though she's doing her best to try and put it out of her mind. Especially since it was the night Anthony was supposed to cook dinner for her and they'd have had their first sleepover. She's bummed thinking about her little joke.

I was ready to go to bed with him.

She wanted to more than she cared to admit. And it wasn't just because he would have been the first man since Peter, or even because she felt so strongly attracted to him. Oddly, it wasn't his outer appearance at all. It was because of what happened on that Ferris wheel.

He took care of me.

She had to give him that. Anthony didn't get annoyed, or tell her she was being silly, or to get over it. Instead, he took care of her without hesitation. It was the first time in a long time she felt she could rely on a man.

And now what?

And now she's sitting here at home alone on what would have be their first night together. Chloe and Lindsay wanted to stay, but she told them to go ahead with their plans. Peter picked up Chloe with his usual phone call from the driveway, still avoiding her.

Watching from the front window, it occurred to Natalie that she hasn't actually seen Peter in ages. *He's never even seen me with blonde hair.*

"I can always invite Oliver over here," Lindsay tells her. "I think he'd be cool with it if I explained everything."

"No, I'm fine. Go on. It's been a while since I had time to myself. And you guys already have tickets." Lindsay and Oliver were going to see the Arctic Monkeys.

Lindsay studies her and then gives her a hug. "Okay, but remember I'm only a phone call away."

Once Natalie is alone, she starts a thorough search of the entire house. It takes her almost an hour to find what she's looking for, but in the end, she's victorious.

"Ah ha!" Natalie grins, holding up her brown *Lord of the Rings* hoodie. "I knew you were still around here somewhere!" It was well hidden, tucked away in the back of the linen closet behind an old bottle of fabric softener. She holds it up to her nose and gets a whiff of laundry soap. "Perfect."

Natalie showers and then puts on black sweat pants, a white camisole, and her comfortable hoodie, which used to be merely large on her when she was more overweight, but now fits her like a circus tent.

"That's okay. I'm not dressing to impress anyone tonight." The hoodie feels as good as a hug from an old friend.

Padding barefoot into the kitchen, she makes herself a big bowl of buttered popcorn and some fruit salad. She glances at the wine cabinet, but opts for ice water with lemon instead.

She studies her collection of movies. She considers *The Fellowship of the Ring,* but for some reason her eyes keep going to *The Empire Strikes Back.*

"Oh, what the heck." She isn't going to let any memory of Anthony ruin one of her all-time favorite movies.

ANTHONY STARES INTO his refrigerator.

There's a bottle of ketchup, a bottle of mustard, hot sauce and a jar of mayonnaise.

I really need to go grocery shopping.

No salami. No cheese. He sees a box of crackers on the counter and considers squirting ketchup on them for dinner, but that sounds pathetic. There isn't even peanut butter and jelly. Serena must have eaten the last of it. He usually keeps more food in the house, but he's been too busy. Plus, he didn't want to think about the grocery list because then he'd have to think about the dinner he was planning to make Natalie and the reason he's no longer making it.

Closing the fridge with a low sigh, he goes upstairs to take a shower. He's drenched with sweat from lifting weights in the garage, trying to take his mind off how pathetic he feels. He gets under the hot water and debates whether he should jerk off or not. That sounds pathetic, too. It depresses him to think of what he could have been doing tonight. Natalie, with her pin-up girl body and that x-rated mouth. *God.* Her charms are more than skin deep though. She's insightful and down to earth. Basically, the whole package. Her good opinion matters to him, and he wants to be the man she thought he was. A smile grows on his face when he thinks about the way she plays him. He likes it. Few people can shine him on like that.

And I fucking blew it.

He's wanted to call her all week. Keeps picking up his phone—staring at it, then putting it down, trying to figure out the right thing to say to fix this. Anthony soaps up and starts thinking about the night he should be having. Natalie, so soft and luscious, and then decides—what the hell—closes his eyes.

So I'm pathetic.

Later Anthony sits at the dining room table with his laptop and reads the latest research papers on the astro-ph website. He considers calling Maya, they've become pretty good friends, but she has a toddler and he doesn't want to bother her with his woman problems. He picks up another cracker and squirts it with ketchup. And just as he pops it into his mouth, the house phone rings. He doesn't bother checking the caller ID.

"Hello?"

"*Ciao, Antonio?*"

He recognizes his mother's voice. They haven't spoken in a few weeks.

"*Ciao, Mamma, come stai?*" he says, switching to Italian.

"Not so good. I'm glad I got hold of you. There's a problem with your father. He called me a few minutes ago from Seattle and—"

"Wait a minute, did you just say Dad's here in Seattle?"

"Yes." She goes on to explain that his father has been in Seattle for the past few days attending a medical conference and that the hotel shuttle he was in had some kind of accident. "It doesn't sound serious and I spoke to him on his cell a few minutes ago, but we were cut off and I can't get hold of him again."

"Where is he?" Anthony is already stuffing the crackers back into the box. He gets up and searches around for his phone and car keys.

"The ER at University Hospital. I called, but the switchboard has me on hold and I can't get through to anyone. I'm sorry to bother you with this, Antonio, but would you go make sure he's all right?"

"I'm leaving right now."

He takes the quickest route to Seattle. When he gets to the hospital ER, he parks and heads straight for the main reception. After waiting in line briefly, he explains who his father is. They tell him to take a seat, and Anthony finds a spot near the large fish tank.

It's been years since he's been in a hospital.

He watches the fish swim in the tank peacefully, a kaleidoscope of tropical colors. Everything comes back to him from when he was a kid and used to visit his dad at work. The acrid smell of antiseptic, the bland artwork, and the brisk sense of purpose hospital workers always have. Back then, he wanted nothing more than to be just like his father.

"Are you Dr. Novello's son?"

Anthony turns and finds a nurse in blue scrubs standing in front of him. "Yes."

"Come on back," she motions for him to follow. "Your dad just had stitches."

Anthony follows her through the double doors and into a long hallway with patient rooms lined up like honeycombs. Finally, she pulls the glass door open on one.

His father is sitting on a bed, fully dressed, speaking with another man, presumably another doctor.

He turns. "Anthony?" The inflection in his deep voice is the only thing that gives away his surprise. "What are you doing here?"

And a big hello to you, too.

"Mom called. Said you were in a car accident."

"I see." He turns to the doctor. "This is my son, Anthony."

"Dr. Weber," he says, putting out his hand.

Anthony shakes it and then turns his attention back to his dad. "Are you all right?" He notices the bandage on his father's left hand. "What happened?"

"It's been nice to meet you, Dr. Novello," Dr. Weber says. "I'll go ahead and let you speak with your son, and I'll see that the discharge papers are put through right away, so you don't have to worry about missing your flight."

"Thank you," Anthony's father tells him.

When the two of them are alone, Anthony asks him again what happened.

"I was taking a shuttle back to the hotel from the conference I was attending, and we were struck by a police car."

"And you cut your hand?"

"One of the other people in the van had an umbrella and the tip punctured my skin."

"Did they give you a tetanus shot?"

His father frowns and stands up. "Of course they gave me a tetanus shot. I don't know why your mother called you. She shouldn't have bothered."

Anthony feels the same old sense of disapproval emanating from his father. And it still brings out the worst in him. "Doesn't change the fact she did call. Are you all right otherwise?"

"I'm fine. They weren't driving fast, and I was wearing a seatbelt."

Anthony considers the situation. "So a police car hit your shuttle van? That's kind of weird."

"Yes, it is." His father gathers his coat and computer bag. "But weirder things have happened, haven't they?"

Like his son dropping out of medical school to become an astronomer.

Anthony recognizes his disparaging tone and tries not to roll his eyes. It's amazing how his father has the ability to turn everything into the same old problem.

"Since you're here, you can give me a ride to my hotel," his father tells him. "I have a flight back to Los Angeles tonight."

"Sure." He watches his dad slip into his coat, struggling a bit with the bandage. "Can I help? I could carry your bag for you."

"I'm fine."

"What time is your flight?"

"Ten."

Anthony glances at the clock on the wall. It's already almost seven-thirty. "You're cutting it close. I can give you a ride to the airport."

"That won't be necessary. I already have another shuttle lined up."

Anthony doesn't reply. His dad is still the same. Clearly, nothing has changed between them.

They head out toward the lobby, with his father stopping at one of the nurses' stations to thank everyone first. They all talk enthusiastically with his dad, occasionally glancing at Anthony, who just stands there with his hands in his coat pockets. His father doesn't bother to introduce him.

Finally, they head out to where Anthony is parked. They're almost to his car when someone calls out. "Dr. Novello?"

Both Anthony and his father turn at the same time. "Yes?" his dad says, but Anthony recognizes the guy. It's one of his graduate students from last year.

"I thought that was you," the guy says, walking up to Anthony. "How have you been?"

"I've been good—it's Chris, right?"

He nods. "I just heard recently that you were nominated for the Smyth

Medal. That's pretty sweet."

"Yeah." Anthony chuckles self-effacingly. "I heard that same rumor."

"Congratulations—that's really great, Dr. Novello, I hope you win it. Seriously."

"Thanks, I appreciate that."

Anthony explains that he's in a rush and they say their goodbyes. He can feel his father bristling next to him once they're in the car.

"*Doctor* Novello? Is that really what you call yourself?" his father asks.

In truth, Anthony rarely asks anyone to call him that. He prefers Professor or just plain Mister, but some people seem to prefer calling him by the Doctor title. Of course, he doesn't tell his dad this. Instead, he shrugs. "I did earn a Ph.D. after all."

His father scoffs. "In *astronomy*." He says astronomy with as much derision as if he were saying astrology.

"So, what hotel are you staying at?" Anthony asks as he starts up the car.

But, of course, his father won't let it go. "A hobby—that's all it should have been for you. People like us don't ignore our calling."

People like us.

If Anthony never heard that phrase again in his life, he'd die a happy man.

"We don't ignore our talents and let some silly hobby become our life's work."

"Apparently we do," Anthony murmurs as he pulls out of the parking lot, heading toward downtown Seattle.

"I know you made some mistakes when you were younger and that's how you got off-track. I probably should have intervened more like I did with your brother."

"What is your hotel?" Anthony asks. "I need to know where I'm going."

"It's not too late though," his father continues. "I've been thinking about this recently. It wouldn't take much to get you back on track, *Antonio.* We can still fix this."

"What do you mean?" Anthony looks over his shoulder and changes lanes so he can get on the Interstate. "Fix what?"

"You're still a young man. You could still practice medicine. Neurosurgery wouldn't be an option anymore, of course, but there are other routes you can take. I'd have to pull a few strings, but I'm certain I could get you in at UCLA's school of medicine, or even out here, if you prefer. I know you like to be close to Serena."

"*What?*" Anthony turns to stare at his father. "Is this a joke?"

"No, it isn't," his father snaps. "I'm trying to help you stop squandering your life."

"I'm not squandering anything. This is what I've chosen."

"But it's meaningless. People like us don't throw our lives away. We help others. It's our duty, and I thought I raised you better. I thought I raised you to understand your duty."

"Apparently, you raised me to be a selfish asshole," Anthony mutters.

"Goddammit! Do you have to make a joke out of everything?"

Anthony takes a breath and tries to rein in his temper. "I'm not going back to medical school, all right? You can forget it. After all these years? That's a crazy idea."

His father doesn't reply, but Anthony can feel the waves of disapproval and anger rolling off him.

"And maybe you haven't noticed, but I'm not doing too badly with my little hobby. I was just nominated for a Smyth Medal in Astrophysics."

"And what is that?" his father brushes him off. "Some award? Is that all you care about? You should be helping people and not just thinking about yourself."

"Jesus!" Anthony hits his palms against the steering wheel. "It's not like I'm a bank robber or a bum on the street!" They pass the exit for Mercer. "And I don't even know where I'm driving! Which hotel are you staying at?"

"The Hilton. It's on Sixth Avenue."

Anthony is fuming. He hates being pushed to the point where he loses his temper. Every time he talks to his father, it's like speaking into a vacuum—his words swallowed without being heard.

He takes the Union Street exit and turns left onto Fifth Avenue.

"Were you even planning to see me or Serena?" Anthony asks. "Mom said you've already been here a few days."

"I did see Serena," his father says. "I saw her yesterday evening. We had dinner together."

"You did?" Anthony tries to look at his dad, but can't because he's pulling up in front of the hotel.

"She played her violin for me and, I admit, I was impressed. I understand she's going to a private school for music."

"That's right." Anthony nods. "And if she wants to be a musician, you can be damn sure I won't stand in her way."

His father gives a deep sigh as he gathers his belongings. "I know you think I don't care about what you want, but I do. You forget I've known you all your life, *Antonio*. You would have made a gifted doctor—it's been killing me to watch you throw it all away."

"Is that why you don't call me to have dinner when you're in town?"

"What does it matter? I'll see you in a month anyway at that awards ceremony that means so much to you."

"You know what? Don't do me any favors."

"What are you saying?"

"I'm saying I don't want you there. Don't come."

His father studies him. "Aren't you getting a little old for temper tantrums?"

Anthony's shoulders tense. "You say you know me, but you don't know the first thing about me. I don't give a damn about that medal! You really think I care about awards? You think that's why I chose this over medicine?"

"I think you've made some poor decisions," his father says, reaching for the door handle. "That's what I think."

"Then you would be wrong. Maybe you don't agree what I do is important, but I *know* it is."

"As you wish," his father says, always having to get in the last word. "You won't have to suffer my presence at your ceremony."

He slams the car door behind him.

On the drive home, Anthony curses and hits the steering wheel again. Dammit!

Why do I let him get to me?

He'll never give me his approval, so why do I keep trying? It's like hoping to solve a mathematical impossibility.

Once he's home he goes inside only long enough to grab his motorcycle jacket, and then heads straight to the garage where his Ducati Diavel is waiting for him. A ready and eager mistress.

Anthony punches it and it feels good to ride his bike hard and fast, the world blurring past. It's a cold night, but the backcountry roads are empty, so he twists the throttle, trying to clear his head. *Why couldn't I have been born into a different family?* It's a selfish thought and he knows many people would be surprised to hear it. He's tired of their disapproval, though, their disappointment. He had a privileged childhood, but things aren't always how they appear. Few people would understand that.

It occurs to him there's one person who might get it.

And he wants to be with her right now. He turns his bike west, heading back toward Seattle.

Maybe there's one relationship I can still fix.

Chapter Twenty

Diet Plan: A taste of desire like you've never known.

Exercise Plan: Finally, an exercise plan you'd love to do every day and twice on Sundays.

ATALIE IS AT her favorite part in *Empire Strikes Back*—right after Luke goes to Dagobah and meets Yoda—when her front doorbell rings.

She glances at the clock. It's almost ten. Kind of late for visitors. Pausing the television, she goes over and peeks cautiously through the front window.

A bolt of lightning streaks through her.

Anthony is standing on her front porch. He's wearing his motorcycle jacket and holding his black helmet at his side. The big bad wolf at her door.

What's he doing here?

She glances at herself in the hall mirror. No makeup and her hair a mess. *Great.*

He rings the bell again and she marches over, ready to take the offensive. Ready to tell him to go away. But when Natalie yanks open the door and sees the expression on his face, she hesitates.

"What's wrong?" she asks finally.

He takes his time with his reply. "I needed to see you tonight."

"Did something happen?"

"It's a long story." He smiles, but there isn't much humor in it.

She's never seen Anthony like this before. He never looks anything less than perfect, but there's strain on his face and around his eyes, and she suspects this is the real man

He takes a step toward her, lowering his voice. "Let me in, Natalie."

Broad shouldered and solemn in her doorway, he's an imposing figure, but she isn't afraid. Despite the fiasco with the bakery, she realizes she still trusts him.

She steps out of the way to let him come inside.

The door closes and she walks back into the living room. There's a sound and she sees Anthony has dropped his motorcycle helmet on a chair.

"This is a bad idea," Natalie tells him. "I don't know why you came here. I shouldn't even be talking to you."

"I think you know *exactly* why I'm here." His voice is low as it vibrates through the room.

There's an erotic thrill at his words. "How can I be with you after what happened?"

"Because this isn't about any of that." For a moment, his eyes darken with regret, but then turn heated. "Whatever happens next is between you and me."

Natalie shakes her head, but Anthony moves closer until he's in right in front of her. She feels his hand on her cheek as the other cradles her head, gently holding her still. "*Don't,*" he says, his tone imploring. "Don't say no. Tell me to stay."

And then she understands what she didn't a moment ago—why he came tonight. The two of them are at the top of that Ferris wheel again, only this time, it's Anthony who's in trouble. Anthony is hurting.

She closes her eyes. A part of her is still angry. Furious at what he did. But there's another part of her that doesn't want to send him away. Because despite everything that's happened, she knows one thing with certainty.

I still want him.

She opens her eyes, looking right into his.

"What's it going to be?" he asks softly.

She licks her lips. Takes a deep breath and lets it out. "I want you to stay."

There's relief on Anthony's face before he dips his head and kisses her. His mouth tastes wild and sweet. She's surrounded by his windblown scent and the leather from his jacket—a heady and potent mixture.

Pulling back, he lets out a shaky breath. "Now, tell me you want me."

Natalie's arms slide around his neck and she draws him close, puts her lips to his ear. "I want you," she whispers.

Anthony groans and pulls her in roughly. His mouth captures hers again and this time his kiss is demanding, savage, and it's turning her inside out.

"*God.*" He sucks in a deep breath as he tries to gain control. Something snags his interest and he turns his head. "Were you watching *Empire?*"

"Yes. I was mad at you, but I wasn't going to let you ruin one of my favorite movies."

He turns back, a grin tugging at the corners of his mouth. "You really are my dream woman."

Natalie tries to draw him in for another kiss, but he glances down at her body and then up to meet her eyes. "Why don't you show me your bedroom?"

She swallows and then takes his warm hand. Her heart is hammering so loudly she's surprised he can't hear it. Or maybe he can.

He follows her upstairs and down the hall to the guest bedroom where she still sleeps. Natalie opens the door, and after peeking to make sure there's nothing embarrassing on display, turns the light back off.

Immediately, Anthony turns it on again.

"I want it off," she says.

His eyes search the room. "How about we use that light instead?" He points at her bedside lamp.

She bites her lip. Tries to figure out how to convince him to leave the room pitch black.

"I want to see you," he insists.

"But I'm shy."

"Let's just cover the lamp with something so it's dim."

Natalie hesitates. "I guess that might work." She goes over to the closet, pulls a blue cardigan sweater out and hands it to him.

He holds it up. It's big and dark and looks an awful lot like a blanket. "I was thinking more along the lines of a sheer scarf. Do you have something like that?"

Natalie stares at him, but doesn't make a move.

Anthony puts the sweater down. Rubs his jaw. "Why do I feel like I'm negotiating a hostage release?"

"I'm sorry." She smiles sheepishly. "I guess I'm kind of ruining the moment, huh?"

"No, it's all right."

Getting up, Natalie goes to her dresser and finds a dark red scarf she hasn't been bold enough to wear yet. He takes it from her and soon the room is draped in a sexy red glow.

Anthony glances around, nodding with approval. "I think this is going to work." He shrugs out of his leather jacket and tosses it on the chair. Kicks his shoes off. And then he's standing there in a T-shirt and Natalie smiles when she sees what it is.

"You're wearing my Hulk shirt."

"Yeah, I wear it all the time."

Natalie feels more pleased than she probably should. And as he's standing there, draped in a red glow, handsome as sin, something occurs to her, something she can't believe didn't occur to her before. Yes, if there's a light in the bedroom he'll be able to see her.

But I'll get to see him, too.

He's watching her from over by the bed and wordlessly puts his hand out.

She goes to him and slips easily into his arms. His mouth covers hers and they kiss while his hands roam down her body over her clothes.

Anthony suddenly breaks the kiss. "I just have to ask you something."

"Okay." She blinks.

He looks down at her. "What is this thing you're wearing?"

"It's my *Lord of the Rings* hoodie. Remember I told you how Chloe and Lindsay hid it from me? I searched the house tonight and found it. Check this out." Natalie flips the hood up to show him how it's long and pointy like Gandalf's wizard hat. "And the sleeves too." She holds them up. "Cool, huh?"

Anthony nods. "It is kind of cool."

"Do you really think so?" Natalie's eyes widen in surprise.

"It reminds me of Ben Kenobi's robe," he grins, "though I have to admit, I'd rather see you in Leia's gold bikini."

"I can't believe you like it. No one has ever liked my hoodie." Natalie is amazed.

"Yeah, it's the same with all my *Star Wars* T-shirts."

Their eyes meet and Natalie feels something inside her relax, a part she didn't even realize she'd been holding back.

His expression grows sly. "Though I'd like to see you out of it now." His eyes search the front. "How does it come off?"

"There's a hidden fastener." Natalie reaches up to show him how it unbuttons near her neck. She undoes the buttons and once it's unfastened, Anthony helps her pull the miles of fabric off, tossing it aside.

Underneath, she's wearing a tight white camisole and his hands immediately slide up her sides. "What a luscious treat you are, Miss Natalie."

Her mouth falls open. No man has ever spoken to her like this and she's speechless.

"You definitely have nothing to be shy about," Anthony murmurs and then dips his head, doing that sexy thing from the Ferris wheel again where he licks along her cleavage. "And you taste delicious, too." His voice is a low rumble.

A shudder of wanting runs through her at the sheer maleness of him.

She reaches down to tangle her hands in his soft hair. His breath feels warm against her skin and he smells like mint shampoo. Natalie worried that she'd feel uncomfortable being with another man for the first time after Peter, but instead, she's amazed how right it feels.

"Kiss me," she says, bringing his face up to meet hers.

His mouth lingers lightly, teasing her lips until she finally takes control and grabs him, deepening it. Anthony's fingers trace over her nipples—sending streams of pleasure through her.

He pulls back from their kiss and looks down at her breasts again, continuing to fondle and mold them. She watches the way he's mesmerized.

"You know they're attached to an actual woman, right?"

"Yes." He chuckles softly. "But a reminder doesn't hurt." He continues to play with her. "This top looks so hot on you. It's almost a shame to take it off."

"I can keep it on."

"No," he says quickly. "No, I don't want that. Let's take it off."

He swallows and she can hear him breathing unsteadily as his fingers slide up and hook under the straps, gently pulling them from her shoulders. She helps by keeping her arms down and then finally lifting them through, so the camisole slips lower.

Once it's all the way to her waist, he stops and takes her in.

"So pretty."

Natalie closes her eyes with pleasure at his words, trying to let herself believe them. *Anthony would know.* She opens them and watches his tan fingers against her pale skin, still molding and stroking her. Venturing upward, she expects to find him still captivated by her breasts, but is surprised to see he's looking at her face. Their gazes lock on each other.

He dips his mouth to hers and one kiss turns into another, deep and thorough. Long, drugging kisses until she feels achy and hot all over.

Where have kisses like this been all my life?

His hand slides lower to her ass, pulling her close—tight, so she can feel his erection pressing into her. She starts tugging on his T-shirt.

"Can you take this off?" she whispers.

He nods, reaches behind and quickly pulls the shirt over his head and tosses it aside. Natalie nearly groans aloud when she sees the planes and ridges of his muscular body. *Anthony doesn't have anything to be shy about, either.* There's dark hair on his chest that travels downward and into the top of his jeans.

The room is dimly lit, draped in ruby colors, and ironically, Natalie now wishes she hadn't fought so hard to turn the lights off. She wants to see him, too.

Her fingers trail over his collarbone and down to his pectoral muscles, grazing over his nipples and then back to squeeze and pluck them the way he was playing with her.

There's a hitch in his breath and his hand comes up to her face, holding her cheek. His thumb rubs along her lips—tracing the upper first and then the lower one—and then he does something unexpected and slips it inside her mouth. Natalie stills at first, but then goes with it. Looks at him as she sucks and licks his thumb, bites it.

Anthony's eyes go dark and glassy. His mouth opens. His breathing sounds choppy.

"Your mouth . . ." he says in a ragged voice. "I've had some dirty thoughts about this mouth of yours." He pulls his thumb out and smudges it over her bottom lip again.

"Really?" She's so aroused she can barely think or talk, but she wants to hear more. "You've thought about me like that?"

He seems incredulous for a second and then nods slowly. "Yes, Natalie. A lot."

She's stunned, but the thought also warms her, warms her all over. Makes her feel sexy and desirable. God knows she's fantasized about him plenty.

"I like the way you say my name," she tells him. And she does. There's something about the sound of it on his lips, the idea he's tasting a bit of her. "I even like that pet name you've given me—Miss Natalie."

He grins a little at that, but he's mostly contemplative. Who knew Anthony would be so serious in bed? So absorbed. She likes it, though—it's sexy. Natalie imagines his beautiful mind a step removed from all the day-to-day living, the mind he uses to solve mysteries of the universe, and she wonders if that's who she's seeing now.

And then she wants to kiss him again, so she does, eagerly.

When their lips part, he draws back and sits down on the edge of the bed. "Come here," he says, and reaches out to pull her between his parted legs.

Stepping close, she rests her hands on his shoulders, sensing the strength beneath them. His hands are on her hips and they move upward, and soon they're fondling her breasts again as he presses his face into her naked skin. "God, I can't resist you," he breathes. It sounds like an apology, but Natalie isn't complaining. He takes one of her nipples in his mouth, licking and swirling his tongue around, and then the other, before finally suckling her. Hard.

She gasps aloud at the pleasure, sharp and angled—the way it slides through her. She starts to throb between her legs and even wonders if she's going to come. He continues the ministration with his tongue, but Natalie finally pushes him away.

Anthony regards her questioningly and she reaches down, lays her palm against his jaw.

"Not yet," she whispers, hoping he'll understand.

He nods slowly. "Let's take these off you," he says in a husky voice, glancing down at her pants. His fingers slip into the waistband of her sweats and he slides them to the floor so she can step out of them. Next comes the camisole, but not her white cotton panties, she notices. He leaves them in place.

And then he remains still, taking her in. He doesn't say anything for a long moment. "Damn." He lets out a slow breath. "You're gorgeous, Natalie."

She closes her eyes and thinks about all the dieting, and the time on the treadmill, and the weight lifting, and realizes that for this moment, it was all worth it all. To have Anthony look at her with this much desire, she'd do it again.

"I still need to lose more weight," she tells him. And it's true, she's hardly thin—far from it. Not to mention, she's had a baby so her stomach will never be flat.

"No," he says emphatically. "Don't do that."

She isn't sure how to respond, but he's already moved on, his head tilted to the side as he contemplates her panties.

"Now, what have we here?" he murmurs.

Natalie doesn't say anything. Peter usually preferred that she be the sexual aggressor, but it was a role she never felt entirely comfortable with. Anthony seems to be the exact opposite and it's erotic to let him take the reins.

"More pretty things for me to uncover?" he asks.

His hand slides down her thigh, caressing the sensitive skin there first, before sliding between her legs. He strokes her, but only on the outside of the cotton. Gentle at first, but then harder, applying just the right pressure as he moves his fingers back and forth, and then slow tight circles. Her eyes fall shut. It's good. Oh, so good.

She can't stop her hips from arching into him, her hands grabbing his shoulders. He's watching her, too, she can feel it. Studying her reactions, solving her like a puzzle. Then he stops stroking and his fingers snake under the elastic in front.

She sucks her breath in.

He doesn't touch her yet though, just slides along the elastic band, barely brushing against her.

It feels like she's holding her breath, waiting for him. And then finally, his fingers are there, sliding through where she's hot and slick. A whimper escapes her throat as he plays with her.

"Let's take these off, too," he says with a note of urgency. He reaches up to pull her panties down. When she finally steps out of them, he looks at them in his hand for a second, before putting them aside.

And then his hand slides up her leg and thigh, where he gently continues his exploration. When he reaches her center and discovers how wet she is, there's a groan of approval from him.

"You feel nice, Miss Natalie."

She can hear his labored breathing and her own, too, the way it fills the small space of her bedroom as his fingers continue to tease and play with her. He slides one inside her and then another and Natalie gasps. Her eyes fall shut and she clutches his head, pulling his hair. She's going to come, but decides she doesn't care anymore. Doesn't want to fight it.

He's watching her again. And maybe she should feel shy, but the pleasure is overwhelming. His thumb keeps rolling over her clit and it's so close, a slow build at first as she looks down at Anthony, meeting his eyes. They're sensual and dark, absorbing every detail of her.

He's nodding. "That's right," he whispers. "Let it happen."

And then she gasps as the full force of it hits, rocking her to the core. Her eyes close again and she moans and grabs him, everything blown apart and then slowly, slowly coming together again.

They linger as she tries to catch her breath. And then Anthony slips his arms around her, hugging her tightly. She wraps her arms around him, too—his skin and the muscles of his back are hot and tense. Anthony's heart is pounding. He's breathing hard. She realizes that while she's calmed down, he's aroused.

$$\ast \; \reflectbox{$\ast$} \; \ast$$

"LET ME MAKE you feel good, too," Natalie tells him.

Anthony doesn't respond right away. He can't. Watching Natalie climax had almost set him off and he had to start reciting the Periodic Table to try to gain some control. He was just starting on the Noble Gases.

He takes a deep breath. His cock is rock hard and his balls ache, and there's this beautiful sexy woman standing naked in front of him, telling him she wants to make him feel good.

Thank God, I jerked off in the shower earlier.

He usually has better control, but there's something about Natalie with her lush body and her stubborn ways that really has his number. Who knew she'd be so responsive too?

Finally, he draws back and looks at her. So pretty all over. Those incredible breasts are making him nuts. His hand automatically reaches out for her again, and he wishes the red light wasn't so dim. Wishes he could see what color her nipples are—pink maybe, or light brown?

He meets Natalie's gaze and something in his chest tightens. He's relieved all over again that she let him in tonight, that she didn't turn him away.

"Tell me what you like," she says.

Anthony doesn't reply, but kisses her for a little while instead, enjoying the taste of her. Finally, he pulls away and stands up, his erection pressing uncomfortably against the front of his jeans. When he reaches down to take them off, he sees her eyes drop lower. She reaches her hand out, molding her palm against him.

He undoes the top button and she wants to help, so he lets her. She undoes the rest of them and together they push his pants and boxer briefs off, then his socks. His cock is jutting out and Natalie puts a hand on him, grasping him, while the other one cups his balls.

He breathes out a low sigh.

Her fingers are cool and inviting and his eyes close for a moment as he gives in to the sensation. She strokes him lightly and he reaches out for her breasts again, can't help himself, her skin so soft that he doubts he could ever get tired of touching her.

Bending his head, he kisses her mouth, exploring her. She's sweet and eager. Their tongues slide over each other.

But then Natalie changes tactics and grips him harder. He's leaking and she rubs the liquid over the head of his dick and under the rim and it feels good. Her other hand is gently massaging his balls and it's all feeling a little too over-the-top good.

Anthony opens his eyes. He doesn't want to have to start reciting the Periodic Table again.

"Do you like that?" she asks softly.

"Yeah." He lets outs a breath. "I like it too much."

He takes her hands and tucks them safely behind his back. Then he reaches for her, drawing her close. Her soft body, the cushion of her breasts, it all fits so well into his. She tilts her head up to kiss him again and when he reaches down with both hands to knead her plump ass, a hard jolt of lust hits him.

"Natalie," he says, his voice husky. "I need you. Now."

He looks into her face and is relieved to see she's nodding with understanding. "I want that, too." And then she hesitates. "Do you have a condom?"

"In my wallet."

She smiles. "So guys really do carry those in their wallets."

He grins back a little, but is too aroused to joke around much. Besides, it's true. Ever since he got Nicole pregnant all those years ago, he never goes without a condom, no matter what. Even if the woman he's with is using birth control.

"Is it in your pants?" She looks down on the floor.

He motions toward the chair. "It's in my jacket." He makes a move to get it, but she's already headed there and he lets her go, wanting to watch her walk naked. The sway of her breasts and that bit of ass jiggle is enticing. Once again, he wishes the room wasn't so dim. *Next time the lights are staying on.*

"Which pocket?" she asks, holding up his motorcycle jacket.

"Left," he tells her, his eyes wandering down her body. Even her legs are curvaceous and pretty. "I mean, right. The right pocket."

I sound like an idiot.

"Is it okay if I get it out myself?"

"Sure."

She finds the condom and then stuffs his wallet away again. He watches her walk back toward him, her breasts bouncing with every step, the sight sending more jolts of lust through him. By the time she's in front of him, holding up the condom packet, he's already reaching out for her. Now that it's close—and he's finally going to have her—excitement is pounding through him. His cock feels thick and hard and all he wants is to grab Natalie and sink into her.

Get a grip.

He swallows and even closes his eyes. Anthony can't remember the last time he wanted a woman this badly, but he knows he needs to keep a clear head.

He pulls her onto the bed and has her lie on top of him, thinking maybe it will help him calm down. But he's wrong. She smells so good, like a woman, but also like vanilla and cream. Her skin is silky all over and even her soft hair falling around him is turning him on.

Without a thought, he wraps his arms around her and rolls them both over, so he's on top. He puts his face in her neck, kissing and licking her skin. But he wants to be closer. She's breathing hard, grabbing his shoulders, and he reaches downward between her thighs. His fingers slip through her folds, into all that slick heat.

And then he can't wait any longer. Sitting up partway, he asks Natalie where the condom went.

"I still have it," she says, holding it up.

He takes it from her and sits up more.

"Should I put it on for you?" she asks.

"No . . . it's best if I do it myself."

"Okay." She lets out her breath. "I wouldn't know what to do, anyway."

"What do you mean?" He looks over at her.

"We never used them. I'm on the pill. And I've never been with anyone else, so . . ."

"Anyone else—ever?"

Natalie seems embarrassed and doesn't say anything for a moment before finally nodding.

Anthony stills, trying to take in the enormity of what she's telling him. "You've never been with another man besides your ex-husband?"

"That's right," she says softly.

He sits up and stares at her. Something like this had never even occurred to him. And if he's honest, he's not sure how he feels about it.

"It's not like I'm a virgin, so you can stop looking at me like that."

Anthony doesn't know what to say. He's quiet, thinking it over, and then finally, he knows what to do. "Come here, Natalie. I'm going to show you how to put on a condom."

Her eyes light up. "Really?" She sits up and Anthony smiles to himself.

"First off, this is the only condom we have, so try not to break it, okay?"

She nods solemnly. "Yes, Professor."

Tearing the wrapper with his teeth, he pulls it out. Holding it up for her, he explains how it slides down over his cock. "But you need to leave the gap at the top."

"Why?"

"So there's room for when . . . I come."

Her eyes go dark and she licks her lips. "I see," she says in a low voice. *Which hopefully won't be any time in the next five minutes.*

"Here," he says, handing it to her.

She considers the condom, then looks at him. "Why don't you lie down and I'll put it on you."

Anthony lies back on the bed, but stays propped up on his elbows, while Natalie positions herself at his waist.

She takes her time and doesn't put the condom on right away, instead running her hand over his cock, fondling him. His pulse jumps. It feels so good that it's hard not to let go and enjoy it. Not to mention the view of those magnificent breasts as she leans over. Between the red light and watching the way Natalie is touching him, there's something almost surreal about the experience.

His hips are moving with the motion of her hand and his breath is getting more unsteady. "Anytime would be good now," he tells her.

"So I slide it over your cock," she imitates the motion with her hand on his shaft, "and then I leave the space on top," she rubs her thumb over the head, "for when you come."

"Yeah," he breathes, "that's right." He's getting even stiffer the more it sounds like she's talking dirty.

He watches as she finally takes the condom and carefully rolls it down over him, following instructions perfectly.

"How did I do, Professor?" She comes over to lie beside him, her face close, eyelashes fluttering.

And then he understands. He shakes his head. A grin pulls at his mouth. "You're shining me on again, aren't you?"

She bites her lip. "A little bit."

"What part?"

Her face grows serious. "Everything I told you is true. I've only been with one other man. But come on, Anthony," she gives him a teasing smile, "any dumb-ass knows how a condom works!"

He chuckles in a low voice. It surprises him to hear it. He seldom laughs during sex.

Natalie is laughing, too. "I couldn't resist. I hope you aren't mad."

"No, but you're forcing me to bring out the big guns now."

"What do you mean?"

"You'll see." He pulls her close, and then quickly rolls on top of her, so she's beneath him and he's cradled between her hips. She grabs his shoulders with helpless laughter.

"Voglio fare l'amore con te adesso," he says in a low voice. *I want to make love to you now.*

Natalie's laughter dies away and her eyes go dark and smoky. "Uh oh," she whispers.

ANTHONY'S FACE IS pure male ego as he watches the effect his words have on her.

"*Dio*," he whispers in her ear. "*Sei così bella.*"

"What are you saying to me?" She hears the passion in his voice.

He pauses. "I said I think you're beautiful."

"Is that true?"

"*Sì, Natalie.*"

They're gazing at each other and her heart feels like it's in her throat at such an outrageous statement. She doesn't say it back, figuring he's heard it plenty over the years from far too many women. Besides, it isn't what she finds appealing about him.

"I think you're . . . good."

"Good?"

She nods. "Here," she says, touching his head. "And here." Natalie places her palm over his heart.

Anthony doesn't reply at first, taking in her words. He seems pleased by them. "Thank you."

It's an odd sort of compliment, but she realizes he is good. He's not perfect—the fiasco with the bakery has shown that, but she suspects that in his heart Anthony is a good man.

He shifts position on top of her and she feels him then—hard and ready—pressing at her center.

"*Fammi di mostrare quanto sono bravo,*" he says with a sly smile, his breathing unsteady.

Lust spirals and skitters. Natalie widens her legs and slips one ankle over his hairy calf, arching against him, sending a message. He's gazing down at her. For a moment, it's as if time is suspended, but then Anthony is pushing into her. He goes slowly at first, easing his entry, as if sensing it's been a while for her, but then somewhere along the way his control slips and he thrusts hard and deep.

Natalie gasps at the invasion, her eyes falling shut. The sensation is so intense. So bright and true. It's been a long time, so long she's nearly forgotten.

How have I lived without this?

Anthony groans, thrusting into her again, and when she looks at him his eyes are already half-lidded. Lost in pleasure. Wild even. As if he's been holding back this whole time.

She's still gazing at him and, even though she didn't say it earlier, she has to admit, he is a beautiful man.

Anthony says something more in Italian, his voice low and rough, but melodious, too. A language made for sensuality.

She pulls him even closer. His body is hard on top of hers, pressing downward, his muscular arms caging her in on each side as he takes her. It was never like this with Peter. And then she banishes all thoughts of Peter. It is only Anthony.

After a while, his movements begin to slow. They're both breathing erratically and he reaches for her arms and pulls them out from behind his neck and stretches them above her head. He holds both her wrists in place, the position making her back arch, thrusting her breasts high.

"Look at you," he breathes, his eyes roaming over her—feasting.

Then he does feast on her. Holding both her wrists in one hand, he bends over, lapping at her breast, capturing a beaded nipple in his mouth, working her over before moving on to the other.

Natalie moans and squirms, mindless, her back arching even more, pushing herself into his mouth. Sharp pleasure angles through her, but this time she wants it. *Oh, my God.* He's still holding her wrists tight over her head and then he starts to move inside her again. And it's so good. Just right. Everything.

"Don't . . . stop . . ." she manages to say, her voice hoarse.

Anthony isn't gentle, but she doesn't want it gentle. She wants his urgency, wants him to use her. The small of her back tingles. And then it's her whole body vibrating. He seems to sense how close she is, because he's murmuring things in a low voice. Naughty things, things no one has ever told her before. Telling her how good she feels. How hot and wet. How perfect.

She whimpers and moans, and then finally, it's a tidal wave, sweeping her under. Her wrists are trapped and it adds to the peak, pushing her higher.

Vaguely she's aware that Anthony is lost, too. He lets go of her wrists and reaches down to grab her ass. Hooks another hand under her knee as he drives into her, taking what he needs. And then Anthony groans, low and long, the sound torn from someplace deep. He's still moving and groaning and she feels a tingle of desire even though she just came.

Finally, he stops, his weight heavy on her. His face in her neck rains soft kisses.

Anthony lifts up, gazing into her eyes, not shying from the intimacy, and Natalie feels the strongest sense of peace she has known in a very long time.

Chapter Twenty-One

Diet Plan: A large helping of sexy man.
A side dish of Ohmigod.

Exercise Plan: Wild monkey love.

*J*OAN JETT'S "BAD Reputation" blares from Natalie's phone. She grabs it off her nightstand and declines the call from her sister, who programmed the song as her personal ring tone. Lindsay does it with everyone. Her recent ring tone for Natalie was "Brick House" and Natalie wasn't sure if she was complimented or annoyed.

"Who was that?"

Natalie turns. Anthony is lying on his stomach with his eyes closed.

She snuggles back under the covers. "My sister."

"Does she always call so early?"

"It's ten o'clock."

Anthony's eyes open. "Seriously?"

"I know. I was shocked when I saw it, too." Natalie can't remember the last time she slept so deeply.

He scoots closer and nuzzles her neck. "Good morning, Miss Natalie."

The room is on the cold side and Anthony's warm body feels toasty wrapped around her. His dark stubble is as rough as sandpaper, but she likes it.

"Good morning," she whispers, winding her arms around his neck.

His mouth slides up to hers, his beard abrading her skin, before closing in on her mouth. Their tongues stroke each other languidly. His hips move as his erection rubs against her thigh.

"We're out of condoms," he murmurs huskily. "But there are plenty of other things we can do with each other."

Natalie's mind immediately tries to figure out what "other things" he's

215

talking about. She thinks she knows, but . . .

"I can't believe I haven't tasted you yet," he continues. "That's a travesty we have to fix as soon as possible."

Her breath hitches. She swallows and her thighs spasm. *Yes, please. God.* It's been such a long time. For whatever reason, Peter stopped doing it years ago.

Anthony rises up on his elbow and gazes down at her, stroking her hair.

Even in the harsh morning light, he still looks incredible. His dark hair is rumpled, but instead of having dorky bed hair, it's mussed and curling onto his forehead in a way that actually adds to his appeal. His rich brown eyes are clear and his skin unmarred.

He's so far out of my league I might as well be living on Pluto.

The thought intimidates her. Anthony intimidates her. She never wakes up looking good. In fact, she's sure her hair is sticking out and her skin is blotchy and pink with a fresh zit or two thrown in for good measure.

"What's wrong?" he asks, his dark brows drawing together. He's astonishingly perceptive, too. When she thinks about the inner Anthony, she feels comfortable and at ease. But it's the outer Anthony who puts her nerves on edge.

"Nothing," she says. "I'm just feeling shy again."

"There's nothing for you to be shy about. That reminds me," he gets a boyish grin, "now that it's light outside, I finally get to see you naked." He starts pulling the sheets down, but Natalie clutches them tight.

"I don't think so."

"Come on, you're kidding, right?"

"You might be disappointed. I'm not as pretty as you are."

Anthony rolls his eyes. "How about you let me be the judge?"

She doesn't say anything.

"You're going to have to get out of this bed sometime," he reminds her. "I'll see you then."

Natalie figures she'll wrap herself in the sheet when she gets up. She glances at him. By his expression, he knows she's working on her escape strategy.

"I saw you naked last night," he says, changing tactics. "And trust me— you totally turn me on, so there's no reason to still be shy."

But it was dim last night, everything draped in a deep red glow. She knows she's probably going overboard with all this, but after being told for years by Peter that she's unattractive—a part of her believes it.

"How about we start slow," Anthony suggests. "You could maybe let me see your breasts?"

He sounds so hopeful, it's hard to say no. And she appreciates that he's being patient with her.

"Please," he adds for good measure.

"All right, I'll show you." She sits up, leaning back against the pillow. Her hands are still gripping the sheets. Then taking a deep breath, she slowly lowers them.

Anthony is watching her as if it's Christmas morning, and when the sheets are finally at her waist his expression doesn't change.

"See, I was right," he says, his voice huskier than before. "You're gorgeous, Natalie."

✦ ✹ ✦

HE WAS WRONG last night. Natalie's nipples aren't pink or brown, but a dusky rose color. And her skin is like milk. Pale and smooth. His tan fingers are a stark contrast against her.

"You're even prettier than I remember," he murmurs. Letting his hand stroke the underside of her breast, his thumb moves up, rolling over her nipple.

Her breath catches.

"Thank you for showing me," he says, meeting her gaze.

Natalie puts her hand on his jaw. "I'm sorry I'm being like this."

He swallows and shakes his head. "It's okay." His thinking is already getting muddled by her naked body. "We'll figure it out."

She nods and he bends over to kiss her left breast, when suddenly her phone starts blaring "Bad Reputation" again.

"Ignore it," he says. "I have a whole list of dirty things I plan to do to you this morning, so there's no time for you to be taking phone calls."

Their eyes meet and his cock stiffens even more when he sees the heat in hers. Apparently, she's on board with his dirty plans.

"Bad Reputation" finally stops as Anthony is running both his hands over her breasts, kneading and molding them while Natalie lies back like a goddess watching him. Her cheeks have a pretty pink flush and he can tell she's getting turned on.

"Does that feel nice?"

"Yes." Her eyes darken with desire. He bends over to take one of her nipples in his mouth when "Bad Reputation" starts blaring again.

Natalie sighs. "She's never going to stop calling. I should answer it."

"Can't it wait?"

Then suddenly his own phone starts, too, *Star Wars* music blasting from inside his motorcycle jacket.

"*Madonna mia!*" Anthony says in frustration, sitting up. The dueling phones go on for about twenty seconds. "This is ridiculous."

"I should call her back. She's probably worried. If I don't call her, she'll show up soon to check on me."

217

"Why would she be worried?" Anthony asks, getting up to go grab his phone, just in case it's Serena.

"Because of what happened between us over the bakery."

He feels a flash of guilt and then annoyance. "I apologized for that."

"Did you?"

"Yes, I did."

She sighs. "All right, whatever." She looks over at him. "Who called you?"

"My brother." Anthony is holding his phone, flipping through the recent calls. He sees the voicemail from Gio, but decides to listen to it later.

"You have a brother?" Natalie's eyes are wandering over his naked body as he walks back toward her. His cock is at half-mast. But with that expression on her face, he suspects it won't be long before it's flying at full-mast again.

He sits down on the bed.

"Does he look like you?" Her eyes are still absorbing him.

Anthony chuckles to himself. It's the first question all women ask when they find out he has a brother. "Yes and no."

"What does that mean?"

"It means we look alike somewhat."

"I see."

Not a satisfying answer, he realizes, but it's the truth. Most women want to know if his brother is good looking, but Anthony never knows how to answer that, either.

"What's his name?"

"Giovanni."

"Is he an astronomer, too?"

Anthony shakes his head. "No, he's a pediatric surgeon."

"Wow, really? That's impressive."

"It is. And he's very good at what he does."

"He must be kind of intense."

Anthony nods. It's an astute observation. "Yes, he is intense. Very."

"Are you guys close? Like Lindsay and me?"

"Not like you and your sister, but we're somewhat close. My brother travels even more than I do for work, so we don't see each other very often."

Natalie rolls over onto her side, unfortunately pulling the sheets back up with her, covering herself. "I've never heard you mention him before, but I guess I don't really know that much about you."

Anthony hears the mild reprimand in her words. He knows he's told her little about himself, but it's an old habit. He seldom shares many details about his personal life with his lovers. It just makes for fewer complications.

"My brother's kind of a character. In some ways he's a saint, but in other ways he's the biggest asshole you'll ever meet."

"Really? He must be great with kids, though."

"He is. Serena adores him."

"So how is he an asshole?"

Anthony doesn't answer. Instead, he moves closer to her on the bed and pushes her long blonde hair aside, lets his hand glide down over the smooth skin on her back. "Your skin is so soft. I could sit here all day and touch you."

She turns her head to study him. "Maybe I'll let you touch me all day."

"Will you?"

"Yes, but let me call my sister first."

"What are you going to tell her?" He's curious to hear her answer. He doesn't want to be on the bad side of all these people who are important to her, but at the same time, what's done is done.

"I'm not sure." Natalie thinks about it. "But I'd like to talk to her alone, if you don't mind."

"I don't mind at all. Go right ahead." He motions toward the door. "I'll just wait here in bed for you."

Anthony knows she's not going to get up naked after all the fuss she made about it earlier, but he can't resist teasing her. Challenging her, even.

The room is quiet. Natalie remains still, but her eyes narrow on him. There's a stubborn set to that sexy mouth.

And then to Anthony's utter astonishment, she throws the sheets aside and sits up.

"Fine." A little smile plays around the edges of her lips, though her eyes are hot with emotion. "I'll just go talk to her in the hall."

Natalie slides out of bed, grabs her phone, and then leans down to kiss him. "I'll be right back."

Stunned, Anthony watches her walk across the room, his eyes glued to her body, taking in every luscious curve. Every bounce and jiggle. His mouth goes dry.

Damn.

Natalie is hot. She's not skinny, and she's built like a real woman, which is exactly the way he likes it. Plump ass and round hips, narrow waist, and then of course there are those magnificent breasts. She's far sexier than any fantasy image of her he's tried to come up with.

When she gets to the dresser, she unfortunately picks up that blue cardigan sweater from last night and covers herself with it. As she reaches the door, she turns and looks at him over her shoulder.

Their eyes meet and he can see this was a big deal for her.

"Hurry," he tells her. His list of dirty things can't wait, and when she gets back he's starting at the very top.

NATALIE IS IN the hallway leaning on the wall to catch her breath.

I did it!

It's all Anthony's doing, though. No man has ever looked at her the way he does. With such blatant desire.

The phone in her hand starts playing "Bad Reputation" again.

"Hey, Lindsay," Natalie says, answering it immediately.

"Where have you been? I've been calling nonstop!"

"I know, I turned my phone off and forgot to turn it back on." Natalie cringes at the lie. She hates to lie to anyone, especially Lindsay, but she isn't ready to explain the situation with Anthony. Truth is, she isn't even sure what the situation is yet. Plus she suspects Lindsay isn't going to support this, not after what happened with the bakery. Both Lindsay and Blair are going to think she's lost her mind.

And maybe I have.

But then she thinks back to last night, to the best sex of her life. To the way Anthony keeps looking at her as if she's eye candy. And she doesn't care if she's lost her mind.

I need this. It's as simple as that.

It doesn't mean she wants to tell anyone about it yet.

Lindsay asks what she's been doing and Natalie tells her about watching movies and eating popcorn. *At least that part is true.*

"Are you okay?" she asks. "You sound funny."

"I don't know what you mean. I'm fine."

"Hmm." Lindsay considers things. Natalie hopes she sounds convincing. She's actually a pretty good liar, a skill she unfortunately honed during childhood, but Lindsay is better. Plus, her sister is like a bloodhound if she gets even the slightest whiff that someone isn't telling her the truth. "I could come home. Oliver and I don't have any special plans today."

Natalie yawns, pretending to be bored. "Honestly, it's not necessary. I was thinking of vacuuming and then cleaning the bathrooms. Though you could come help with that if you want." Natalie finds housework relaxing, while Lindsay hates it so much it's practically a phobia.

"Oh, I'll leave you to it then," her sister says quickly. "I just don't want you sitting around feeling sorry for yourself because of that asshole, Anthony."

"No, I'm fine." *More than fine.* "Don't worry."

They hang up and Natalie ventures back into the bedroom. That "asshole" is lying sprawled on her bed like a Roman god waiting to be serviced.

"Finally," he says, with an expression that indicates he's been thinking about her naked this whole time. "That took long enough."

A frisson of heat runs down Natalie's spine.

She comes over and stands by the edge of the bed.

"You can get rid of that sweater," he tells her firmly. "I've seen the goods and I'm not letting you hold out on me anymore."

Natalie smiles, but doesn't take off the sweater.

He's watching her. "You enjoyed that little show didn't you? Admit it."

"I enjoyed your surprise. It was worth forcing myself to walk naked." She can't help her laughter. "You should have seen your face."

"I'll bet."

"I don't know why, but it's really fun to play you like that. I can't resist doing it for some reason."

"You're good at it, that's for sure," he mutters. Anthony is quiet for a moment, thinking about something. "Let's take a shower together," he says, reaching out for her. "I want to soap you up and do wicked things to you. What do you say, Miss Natalie?"

Her smile grows shy. "I say . . . okay."

Anthony follows her into the main bathroom at the end of the hall, the one Natalie uses to shower these days. He hasn't said anything about going home and she wonders if they really are going to spend the whole day together.

I hope so.

A little sliver of fear runs through her at the thought. She doesn't want to let herself get too attached, but then she pushes the worry aside, determined to enjoy herself. Be more like Lindsay for a change.

"What's with the sweater anyway?" Anthony asks, after turning on the shower. "I thought you were over your shyness."

"I guess I'm still a work in progress." She does feel a little better, but knows she'll never be as comfortable naked as he is.

"Let me help you with that progress," he says, coming over. Anthony kisses her and then his hands reach down to untie the belt at her waist, sliding the sweater off completely.

He looks down at her again and shakes his head. "Damn, you have no idea how good you look to me."

Natalie feels the compliment all the way to her toes.

They get in the hot shower. Anthony stands behind her with the soap in his hands, sliding it everywhere, as she leans back into his hard chest. He's gentle and thorough, even remembering to clean the area behind her ears. He lingers in a few spots where he can't seem to help himself—her breasts and ass are clearly two favorites, and between her legs.

"Have to make sure you're clean," he murmurs, soaping her breasts again, playing with her nipples. He's kissing and biting her shoulders from behind, sucking on her skin, making her crazy.

The whole time he has a huge hard-on. She can feel it prodding her from the back and then see it when she turns toward him. Occasionally, she puts her hand on his cock, stroking, but he doesn't let her keep it there for long.

"I want to take care of you first," he says.

He has her tilt her head back, getting her hair wet and then shampooing it. His hands feel so good. She's amazed. No man has ever done anything like this for her before. He's strong, but gentle, working the shampoo and then the conditioner through her hair, rinsing it away.

"When is it my turn?" she wants to know, sliding her hands over the muscles of his chest down to his tightly ripped abdomen. "When do I get to clean you?"

"Not yet," he breathes.

They're both breathing heavily. The whole bathroom is in a cloud of moist steam and they're only adding to it. After rinsing the soap off, Anthony has her lean against the cool shower wall, where he kisses her some more— his tongue slick and wet, plundering her mouth. And then he slides lower, and lower, until finally, he's on his knees and Natalie knows what he's planning. Her stomach is already tense with anticipation.

"Just want to make sure you're clean everywhere," he tells her in a husky voice.

He takes one of her legs and lifts it so her foot is balanced on the edge of the tub, spreading her open.

Tenderly, he kisses her thighs, nibbling, working toward the goal. He slides his fingers gently between her legs, still playing with her. She arches against him, wanting to feel his kisses *there*.

"So eager," he murmurs.

And then—finally—he leans forward and puts his mouth on her.

Natalie starts to moan. She can't help it. She even wonders if she should be embarrassed that she's reacting so strongly. He's licking her gently, flicking his tongue around and then side to side, then licking some more.

God. He really knows what he's doing.

What's worse is she feels like she's already going to come, but she doesn't want to. Not yet.

I can't. It isn't fair!

She takes deep steadying breaths, trying to control herself. Her hips are rolling and lifting toward him and Anthony grasps them, holding her still.

Natalie's fingers play in his wet hair as she tries to distract herself. It's so good. Too good, this delicious pleasure. She has to make it last, has to keep herself on the edge of bliss without going over.

And she succeeds for a little while.

But then she opens her eyes and looks down at Anthony. His head is moving back and forth, and then bobbing slightly as he licks her. And the whole thing—him, the shower, what he's doing—is just all too much, too hot.

She starts to tremble, her hands grabbing his head. The dam bursts and sensation floods through her.

"Oh, God," she breathes. "*Anthony.*"

Clutching his head, she thrusts her hips forward like a wanton, but she can't control herself. He's still working her over and it's lasting forever, and what's more, she doesn't want it to end.

When she finally slows down, Anthony is up on his feet, grabbing her—kissing her wildly. His hands clutch her ass as he grinds into her.

"God, I want you so bad," he says hotly.

She reaches down for his cock and this time he doesn't try to push her hand away. Instead, he's saying, "*Yes,* grab me. *Hard.*"

Natalie puts both hands on him, squeezing her fingers tight, while he's kissing her violently, groaning into her mouth.

She slips one hand lower and takes hold of his balls, gripping those too, and then he jerks back, breaking the kiss as he lets out a low groan, almost a growl, and she can feel his cock pulsating in her hand as he comes on her stomach.

Afterward he kisses her neck again softly, chuckling.

"What's so funny," she asks.

"We have *got* to buy more condoms."

NATALIE EVENTUALLY KICKS him out of the bathroom to do "girl stuff," though he wants to stay and see exactly what that is.

"I can help," Anthony offers.

But she's not going for it. Instead, he goes back in the bedroom and finds his clothes from last night. Getting dressed, he decides they'll have to go out soon. They need condoms. And coffee.

He thinks back to the shower after Natalie came. God, he wanted her. She was so beautiful and earthy in her passion. And what's crazy is a small part of him considered it, considered taking her, drowning in her heat.

Damn.

Yeah, they definitely need to go to the drugstore.

After he's dressed, he runs a hand over his jaw and figures he'll ask Natalie if he can borrow a razor. He gets his phone out and listens to his messages. The final one from Gio is a surprise. Apparently, his brother is coming to town next month for the Science Awards.

"You better win that damn medal," Gio says. "I'm flying all the way from Africa. Plus, it'll piss the old bastard off."

No doubt, Anthony thinks in agreement. He reflects back to the conversation he had with his father yesterday. The craziness of trying to convince him to go back to medical school after all this time. It's like he's never going to let it go.

Hell, I could win the Nobel and it wouldn't mean a thing.

Anthony puts his phone back into his jacket and finds himself glancing around Natalie's bedroom. He doesn't want to invade her privacy, but at the same time he's curious about her.

He looks at her nightstand. There are a few novels and some kind of baking encyclopedia. Some earrings and a tube of lip balm. Everything tidy and organized.

Looking down on the floor, something catches his eye. It's Natalie's cotton underpants from last night. He picks them up and can't help himself—puts them straight to his nose.

He goes hard in an instant. That slight tangy scent. They smell just like her. Just how she was in the shower, when he had his mouth on her, so hot and eager. He's going to be reliving that moment for a while.

He glances at his jacket. He's tempted to take them home, but figures that's crossing the line into being a perv.

Still.

Dude, you are not stealing Natalie's underpants.

Anthony is still holding them when Natalie breezes through the door—wrapped in a white towel, hair blow-dried straight.

She glances at him, smiles, and then turns back when she sees what he's holding. "What are you doing?"

"I'm sitting here contemplating whether I should steal your panties or not."

Natalie comes over and stands by him. "I doubt they'll fit you."

He snorts with laughter. "I wasn't planning to wear them."

"What were you planning to do with them?"

"I, uh . . ." To his surprise, Anthony feels his face grow warm. He's never shared this particular proclivity with a woman before. "I was going to use them for something else."

She tilts her head and then her eyes widen with understanding. *"Oh."* And then, "Really?" Natalie breaks out in a smile. "That's so sweet!"

"It is?"

Natalie nods.

"You don't think it's kind of pervy?"

"Actually, I do. But it's sweet, too. It's both."

Anthony doesn't say anything, processing her response.

"You can have them, if you want. I don't mind."

"Yeah?" He looks down at the underpants still in his hand and tries to decide if he wants to take them. He doesn't want Natalie thinking he's a pervert, though. "I better not." He forces himself to put them down. "Listen, do you have a razor I can borrow?"

She sits next to him on the bed. "Don't shave. I like you like this." Her hand goes up to stroke his stubble.

"Thanks, but you won't be saying that tonight when I turn into Chewbacca."

"It can't be that bad."

"I typically have to shave twice a day, occasionally three times in the summer—how's that for bad?"

"Wow." Her fingers are still gliding over his jaw. Instead of being repelled by his hairiness, though, she seems thrilled.

He has to admit he likes the enamored expression on her face. For some reason he wants to please her. "All right, I won't shave. But you'll only have yourself to blame when my face is covered in fur."

They're studying each other. He notices that she put some makeup on, but only a little. He's dated women who wore a lot, but Natalie doesn't seem that into makeup. Her blue eyes are pulling at him. Making his chest feel tight again. Oddly, he's still a little nervous around her, but it's a good kind of nervous. Like it matters.

"So we're doing this, right?" he finds himself asking.

"Doing what?"

"This—you and me."

She seems a little surprised, but then nods. "We are."

Anthony nods too, smiling to himself. "Good."

He reaches out for her. He's still hard from the panties and now from staring at her wrapped in nothing but a towel. Her skin looks dewy and pink. He wants to kiss her, but holds back, not wanting to get himself all worked up again. Instead, he trails his fingers over her shoulder and down her arm.

"Are you going home now?" she wants to know.

He's taken aback. "Not unless you're kicking me out. Why do you ask that?"

"Because you're dressed."

"I figured we'd go do a condom and coffee run."

Natalie raises an eyebrow. "Condoms and coffee?"

"Life's little necessities."

"You can stay the night again—if you want," she tells him. "Neither Lindsay or Chloe will be home until tomorrow."

He takes her hand and plays with her fingers. "That sounds good."

They eye each other, though neither of them speaks.

"I should get dressed then." She pulls away from him and stands up.

Anthony kicks back on the bed, figuring he'll get to enjoy the show, but Natalie is still standing there, not making a move toward her closet. "What's wrong?"

"I'll need you to leave . . . the bedroom."

"Seriously?"

"I'm still feeling shy. I'm sorry."

He studies her. It's hard to believe she'd still feel this way, especially after taking a shower together. "Why are you so shy, exactly?"

Natalie bites her lip, and looks to the side. "In my marriage—Peter, my ex—he didn't think I was very attractive."

Anthony frowns. And then gets angry. Jesus, what kind of dickhead was she married to?

"You know that isn't true though, right?"

She sighs. "I guess, but it's hard to accept. I still feel like hiding."

He sits up. "Natalie, you are hot. Seriously. God, I was ready to steal your panties, just so I can jerk off some more thinking about you."

Natalie is smiling at him. "That's so nice."

Anthony laughs. "I'm not doing it to be nice, trust me!"

"If it's any consolation, you're helping a lot. I just need to take it slow."

"All right," he says, getting up. "I'll wait in the hall, but we are definitely going to work on this."

"Thanks, I'm sorry."

Anthony goes over to her. "Don't apologize." He puts his hands on her cheeks, holding her for a soft kiss. "I don't want you to feel bad about yourself when you're with me—ever."

"Okay," she whispers.

He grabs his phone and goes to wait out in the hallway.

At first Anthony leans against the doorframe, answering emails, but after noticing some of the photos on the wall, decides to check them out instead.

They're mostly family shots with plenty of Chloe as a baby and small child. He notices the same blond guy in many of them and figures it must be Peter.

So this is what that testa di cazzo *looks like.*

Near the end of the hall there's a photo of Natalie when she was much younger. She has long brown hair and is wearing some kind of peasant dress. Standing next to her is a guy who looks kind of like George Clooney, along with a young Lindsay.

And this must be the womanizing father.

He keeps browsing and stops when he comes to a more recent photo showing Natalie the way she looked when he first met her.

The photo is taken in the back kitchen of La Dolce Vita. She's noticeably more overweight than now, but he's still struck by how pretty she is. There's a mischievous grin on her face that makes him smile. He can't believe he didn't take more notice of her initially. Studying the photo of Natalie, it's hard to imagine how any man could fall out of love with her.

That's a strange thought.

The door opens and Natalie steps out into the hall wearing jeans and a purple T-shirt.

She comes over to where he's standing and sees the picture he's been studying. "That was taken on my birthday. It's kind of a running joke that I'm so picky I always make my own cake every year."

"Yeah? I hope you'll make my birthday cake this year. There has to be some fringe benefit to dating a pastry chef."

She laughs. "Of course I'll make your cake. When is your birthday?"

"Not until June, but it's one of those milestone birthdays."

"What do you mean?"

"I'm turning thirty."

"What?" Natalie stares at him with alarm. "You're only *twenty-nine?*"

He's startled by her strong reaction. "Yeah, how old are you?"

She doesn't answer him though, just keeps gawking. "My God, you're younger than Lindsay! I thought you were in your thirties!"

"Why would you think that?"

"Because you *told* me! You told me Serena was born when you were in your senior year at UCLA."

"That's true. She was born right before I got my undergraduate degree."

"So?"

Anthony is trying to figure out her reasoning and then finally he gets it. "I think I understand your confusion. I was nineteen during my senior year at UCLA. I started college when I was sixteen."

Natalie blinks and then shakes her head. "Why?"

He shrugs. "Because that's how it worked out. I tested and got in early."

"No," she says, annoyed. "Why didn't you tell me you were so much younger than me?"

"I don't know. I've dated older women before. Besides," he says, getting annoyed himself, "you can't be that much older than I am."

She doesn't say anything.

"How old are you exactly?" Not that he really cares. He's mostly curious to see why she's stressing so bad.

Natalie sighs. "I'm thirty-five. I'll be thirty-six in May."

"See," he says. "Only six years."

She looks at him like he's a moron. "*Six years* is a lot."

Anthony rolls his eyes. "Whatever. Let's go. You can stress while we're getting caffeine."

Chapter Twenty-Two

Diet Plan: Non-fat latte. Bite of a cookie. Turns out coffee and chocolate aren't the only things you're addicted to.

Exercise Plan: Play a fun game of Tease the Sexy Geek.

ON THE WAY to get coffee, they stop at the drugstore for condoms. Except Natalie doesn't want to go inside. She's too embarrassed. "I'll guard your motorcycle. You won't even have to pay me. Well," she reconsiders, "maybe only ten bucks."

"Very funny. This neighborhood looks perfectly safe. Come on," he takes her hand, "I'm not letting you wiggle your way out of this. It'll be good for you to face down some of these fears."

Once they're standing in front of the condom section, Anthony puts on a show, trying to decide which ones to buy.

"Should we get the ultra-smooth, or how about the contoured ones for the *ladies?*" Anthony deepens his voice on the word ladies. "Fire pack, maybe? That sounds kind of dangerous. I'm worried they might sting. What do you think, Miss Natalie?"

Natalie is peeking around the corner, praying to God no one she knows sees her. "Let's just grab some jumbos and go!"

Anthony chuckles and then finally reaches for a box without even looking at it. She suspects it's the same brand he's used for years. "You need to get over your embarrassment. So we're having sex, who cares? It's nobody's business but ours."

They head down one more aisle, where Anthony picks up a razor and shaving cream. He holds his hand up. "I know what you're going to say, but at some point, I will *need* to shave. Trust me on this."

Eventually, they make their way to the front.

The cashier is a young woman who almost swallows her tongue when she gets a look at Anthony and then smiles when she sees what he's buying. She looks at Natalie too, but in a more confused—she's with *him?*—kind of way, or at least that's how Natalie interprets it.

"Thank God, that's finally over," Natalie says once they're outside again. Anthony tucks the bag in a small storage compartment on the back of his bike.

They climb aboard and Natalie is already looking forward to the ride. *Maybe I should buy a motorcycle.* She imagines herself as one of those badass motorcycle mamas you see cruising around town. *I could even get a tattoo.* She already feels tough wearing the aviators Anthony bought her.

The sky is gray overhead with the occasional sunbreak as they ride and there's the scent of diesel and wet pavement in the air.

The Ducati is purring loudly as they pull up to a Starbucks. People are sitting at tables out front, a few of them turning to watch as Anthony parks his bike. The notion of going inside Starbucks both repels and fascinates Natalie.

"It feels like I'm going behind enemy lines," she says as they walk up to the store.

Anthony puts his sunglasses on top of his head and holds the door open for her. "It's good to occasionally see what the enemy is up to."

The place is crowded. Lots of people talking and waiting for drink orders.

Natalie glances around with interest, surprised at the crowd. *Hmm, maybe we should keep La Dolce Vita open on the weekends.*

Anthony orders his usual espresso breve and gets Natalie a nonfat latte. She doesn't want any food yet, but he gets himself a chocolate chip cookie.

They stand close to each other as they wait for their coffee. Anthony holds her hand. At one point, he even bends down to kiss her, lingering longer than he should. Natalie's stomach goes quivery as she inhales his musky scent. He's like a drug she can't get enough of.

A small table near the window opens and they grab it, sitting with their knees, legs, and arms touching. In truth, she'd sit in his lap if she could and something tells her Anthony wouldn't object.

"And what's this I see?" Natalie points to his bag with disapproval. "You're already cheating on my cookies? That was fast."

He smirks. "Of course not. I'm only observing the enemy, like you are."

Anthony pulls the cookie out and takes a bite. She can't help watching his reaction as he eats it. "How does it taste?"

"Terrible. Nothing compares to *your* cookies, Miss Natalie."

"Hmph. That better be the truth."

"Do you want some?"

Natalie accepts a small piece and has to admit it's not bad, but it's not as good as hers, either. She glances around at some of the people. There's quite a mixed crowd of casual and dressed up. As usual, women are staring at

Anthony. Some of them discreetly, but others are not so discreet, though she has to say he ignores them all and focuses solely on her.

"So, how many lovers have you had?" she asks curiously.

Anthony nearly chokes on his coffee. He puts the cup down. "You want to discuss this *now?*"

"Nobody can hear us." Which is true. The place is busy and they're sitting close together, talking quietly.

Anthony takes a deep breath and lets it out. "To be honest, that's probably not a number you want to know."

"Is it that high?"

"When I was younger I got a lot of female attention."

Natalie can't stop her snort of laughter. "When you were younger? Are you blind, Anthony? You still get a lot of female attention."

"I know, but it's different now. My perception has changed."

"Why is that?"

He shrugs. "I was a young horny guy back then and women were constantly approaching me, so it was hard to resist."

"And now what? You're not horny anymore?"

He gives a low chuckle. "I'm definitely still horny, but like I said, it's different. All that attention has become noise, like static. I'm not interested in bedding a bunch of women I barely know."

"So you're like a serial monogamist now?"

Anthony glances around. He grins a little and seems embarrassed that she's called his number. "Something like that."

"Answer me this. Are you still in the double digits?"

"Yes."

"Barely, though, I'll bet."

He takes a sip of his coffee. "Hey, I'm just an innocent boy here. You're the cougar lady trying to sink her sharp claws into me."

"Don't say that!" Natalie laughs despite herself. She's been trying not to think about their age difference.

"Are you still stressing about that?"

She toys with her coffee cup. "Of course. Six years is a bigger age difference than I thought."

"What if it were reversed? And I was six years older than you—would it matter then?"

"No." She thinks about Peter and Lena. They don't seem to care. In fact, Lena is older than Peter by more than six years. "I've just never seen myself as the cougar type."

"Come on, Natalie. Those labels are nonsense. I hope you realize that." He takes her hand and entwines their fingers.

"Yeah, I know."

They're gazing at each other. She can't pull her eyes away, but at least it seems to be the same for him, too. He's so good looking it's ridiculous. But as she gets to know him she's finding she likes his personality even more than his looks.

"So how did the phone call with your sister go earlier?" he asks. "Did you tell her you invited the evil landlord into your bed?"

"No, not yet."

He takes a drink from his coffee, watching her.

"I told her I was spending the day vacuuming the house and cleaning the bathrooms."

His brows draw together. "Why?"

"Because she wanted to come home and it was the only thing that would keep her away."

"So you didn't tell her we're together at all?" It's clear Anthony doesn't like this. He sounds annoyed and pulls his hand away.

"I'll tell her eventually. And Blair, too, but it's going to be weird. Everybody is really angry about what you did."

Anthony releases a frustrated breath and looks out the window. "And what about you?" He meets her eyes. "Are you going to get past this?"

Natalie is still angry about what happened, but she wants Anthony. She wants him a lot. "Yes, I'll get past it. It's like you said when you came over last night. This relationship is about you and me."

"So you're going to tell people we're involved? You can't just start lying to everyone."

"I know. I'll tell them."

✶ ✹ ✶

ANTHONY FROWNS TO himself. He doesn't like lies and he doesn't want to be anybody's big secret. Ironically, the women he dates usually want to show him off. This is the first time someone has tried to hide him in the closet.

"They might not like it at first," he says, taking her hand again, rubbing his thumb over her baking scars. "But they'll come around. And even if they don't, it's your life to live, not theirs."

"I know. Just let me figure out how to handle this, okay?"

"All right, fair enough."

They finish their coffees. Anthony pulls his sunglasses off his head and puts them back on. "I'd say we accomplished our mission today. Are you ready to leave, Miss Natalie?"

"Ready when you are, Moondoggie."

He takes the shortest route back to her house. Usually he takes the scenic route if there's a choice, since he enjoys riding his bike, but he can't wait to get Natalie alone. He's been trying to hide it, but the anticipation of having her again has become unbearable. He's intensely aware of her. The way she looks, feels, and smells. It's been a struggle to keep his hands off her.

Once they're parked in her driveway, he locks his bike and practically pulls her to the front door, his jeans tight with the erection that's been plaguing him since Starbucks.

"I can't wait," he murmurs in her ear as she unlocks the door. "I'm already hard thinking about all the things we're going to do."

He can tell she likes hearing this as she fumbles with her keys. Once the door is open, and they're inside the house, Natalie turns to him.

"Do you want me, Anthony?"

"Yes, you know I do."

There's a wicked gleam in her eyes. "Then you're going to have to catch me first!"

To his surprise, she suddenly runs past him. He's so startled he doesn't even grab her and before he knows it she's already gone around the corner.

What the . . . Anthony stills for a moment and then grins. He likes this kind of game.

Thinking ahead, he opens the bag from the drugstore and pulls out a condom, slipping it into the front pocket of his jeans. Then he walks into the living area. Natalie is standing on the other side of the room, near the bottom of the stairs, watching—waiting.

Their eyes meet and lust slams through him.

"You're a naughty girl, Miss Natalie. Teasing me like this."

He knows she's expecting him to go around the furniture and make a run for her. That's the most obvious path.

"Somebody has to make you earn it for a change," she tells him.

So that's what this is about. He glances to the side, letting her think that's the route he plans to take.

And just when she starts to relax, he suddenly grabs the edge of the couch and leaps over it. He lands only a short distance away from her.

"Aaah!" Natalie shrieks with girlie laughter. She starts running up the stairs with him right behind her. His fingers graze her shirt, but she's surprisingly fast.

She makes it to the top and he can hear her laughing as she runs down the hall.

"I've almost got you!"

"Ha!" Then she runs into her bedroom and slams the door shut.

When he reaches for the door, he finds it locked. He rattles the knob. "Let me in, Natalie."

"I don't think so." He can hear her voice on the other side.

"The door is locked."

"So it is," she agrees. "Guess you'll have to figure out that one next,

Professor Smarty Pants."

Anthony grins. He bends down to examine the brass knob. It's just a simple interior lock. He figures there's a pushbutton on the other side, so all he needs is something pointy to fit in the center hole and release the mechanism.

He stands up, considering for a moment what he can use. A nail would work, or a paper clip. Anthony goes downstairs and finds a paper clip on a small desk down near the kitchen. Straightening it out, he heads back upstairs, chuckling to himself. He can't remember the last time he had this much sexy fun.

When he reaches her door, he tries the knob again to make sure it's still locked and then pushes the paper clip inside. He fiddles around a few seconds until he hears the mechanism pop.

"I hope you heard that," he tells her. "Because that's the sound of your doom."

He turns the knob and enters.

Natalie is standing on the opposite side of the bed. There's a smile tugging on her mouth, but her eyes are heated.

"And now you're mine." He moves toward her. "To do with as I please."

Her eyes flicker toward the door.

"I don't think so." He smirks.

She's breathing hard watching him. "You haven't caught me yet!" And then she makes a final run for it.

This time he's faster though, and grabs her around the waist. Natalie squeals with laughter. She tries to squirm away, but he holds her tightly as she grips his arms, pushing at him. Her breasts are smashed against him and the whole thing reminds him so much of his boxing fantasy his groin aches and he's getting even more aroused.

"Let me go!" she says.

"No way, I have plans for you."

She goes still in his arms. "Seriously, let me go, Anthony."

Immediately, he releases her. "What's wrong?"

She pushes him away. "Nothing's wrong!" And then she laughs and runs for the door.

"Dammit!" A few choice swear words stream from his mouth as he starts chasing her again. "The gloves are off now, Natalie." He sees her at the end of the hall. She's trying to lock herself in the bathroom, but he gets there in time to shove his foot in the door before she can close it. "This game only has one ending. And I think you know what it is."

She's still struggling with the door, grinning at him. "I said I'd make you earn it, didn't I?"

"We'll see who's earning what here."

He manages to shove his knee inside and then pushes the door wide enough so he can slip through. She backs away, but there isn't any place for her to go.

"I can't believe you faked me out like that."

"I know, I'm sorry." She smiles sheepishly and has the decency to look embarrassed. "Lindsay used to do that to me and, if it's any consolation, I always fell for it, too."

"No, that's not any consolation." He steps closer. "Don't do it again."

She blinks. Her hair is messy, eyes bright.

And then he reaches out and kisses her hard. Natalie moans. Her arms immediately wrap around his neck. He's holding her tight and their kiss turns into something else, something crazy. Mouths feeding on each other, tongues and teeth colliding.

He grasps her ass with both hands. "Wrap your legs around me," he breathes urgently.

She does and he lifts her, carrying her until her back is pushed against the wall. They're still kissing greedily, bodies rubbing in all the right places, setting each other on fire. Anthony feels like he's losing his mind.

He puts her down, grabbing the front of her jeans, trying to get them off her. His hands are shaking. Both of them frantic, fumbling.

"Now, *now* . . ." Natalie chants, and it's making him even crazier.

Somehow he tugs her jeans and panties off. He wants Natalie naked all over, wants to touch her and see all she has to offer, but at this point all he can think about is getting inside her.

Thank God I brought a condom.

He pulls it out of his pocket and holds it between his front teeth as he unbuttons himself and shoves his pants down, his erection finally free.

Natalie is watching him, her breath choppy, the blush high on her cheeks. She looks dazed and Anthony can't help thinking that she's beautiful. Her lips are parted, the color like wild berries.

He pulls the condom from his mouth and kisses her again. Just because he can.

Finally, he tears the packet open with his teeth and quickly slips the rubber over himself.

"Grab me again," he tells her and when she does, wrapping her legs around him—he lifts her up, and then situating himself, brings her down—impaling her.

God. His eyes fall shut.

They both groan. Her arms and legs tighten around him and it's so sweet—so hot.

Still holding her, he drives upward and the two of them begin moving together. Natalie moans and sobs with every thrust. It feels so right, Anthony never wants to leave this moment, wants to stay inside her like this forever.

Eventually, Natalie starts squirming against him and he knows what to do. He slips his hand between her legs in front to help, rubbing his fingers where she needs it. She immediately goes nuts. Clutching him, digging her nails into his shoulders as she cries out with her climax. And then it hits Anthony, too. His self-control crashes and ecstasy ricochets through him. It's already white-hot before the final explosion comes and he groans, holding her tight, blind to everything but his release.

Afterward, they both sink to the floor. Anthony almost forgets to pull out of her and take the condom off.

"Wow," Natalie breathes, trying to catch her breath. "Is it always like this for you?"

"No," he answers honestly, his voice hoarse. What he doesn't add is that he's not sure if it's ever been like this for him.

✳ ✳ ✳

"I'M STARVING," NATALIE says, still breathing hard.

"Me, too."

She thinks about what she has to eat in the kitchen downstairs. Some leftover enchiladas that Lindsay made a couple days ago. She's not sure what else. Fruit and cheese—bread for sure.

Anthony is watching her. They're both still sitting on the bathroom floor, trying to recover. He puts his hand out to touch her breasts through her shirt.

"What is it?" she asks.

"I was thinking about how I didn't even get to see these. I was too excited to take all of your clothes off."

She considers his words and can barely believe the next thing that comes out of her mouth. "Do you want to see them now?"

He nods, and then grins. The expression on his face is so male it does something funny to her insides.

"Okay," she tells him. And then sits up and lifts her T-shirt above her bra.

His eyes go down to her breasts and stay there. His fingers reach out, caressing her through the fabric, her nipples beading again from the attention.

"Would you take the bra off, too?"

Natalie meets his imploring gaze. Pushing her shyness aside, she reaches behind herself to unhook and pull her bra off.

Anthony leans his head against the wall. "Thank you," he says and starts caressing her again, this time on bare skin.

Natalie closes her eyes for a moment and sighs. His hands are gentle. It's wonderful to have someone so attentive toward her, even if he is admiring her breasts.

When their eyes meet, they gaze at each other for a long time. His are a rich brown and the heat of them warms her all over.

"It's weird," she says.

"What?"

"I'm so comfortable with you. I thought it would be awkward with another man, but I feel . . ." She stops herself, doesn't continue. She almost tells him how she feels more comfortable with him than she did with Peter, but that seems like too much, too soon. Plus, she doesn't fully trust this feeling with Anthony.

Anthony looks curious, though. "What were you going to say? Tell me."

"Just that I feel good with you. I'm at ease." She hopes he understands her meaning.

He nods and his expression is thoughtful, taking in her words. "It's the same for me," he agrees. "It feels natural between us."

Eventually, they make their way downstairs and start pulling things out of the fridge. They wind up on the living room couch with a smorgasbord of leftovers.

"Is this bread yours?" Anthony asks, loading up a piece with a hunk of cheese.

Natalie takes a bite of cold enchilada. She's too hungry to even bother heating it. "Yes, I make it for Santosa's—a bistro up the street."

"Really? I've eaten there." He takes another bite and chews for a bit. "It's fantastic. I didn't know you baked bread."

"That's because I only make a few small batches a week." She sighs dreamily. "If only I had a large stone deck oven with steam injection."

He continues to eat, listening.

"I've been steaming the loaves myself, but that's a huge hassle. I still love making bread, though."

"I always think of you as a pastry chef."

"I am, but I worked in a bread bakery as a teenager and it kind of stuck. If I had a larger space, I'd definitely expand and do both."

Anthony stops eating and gives her a look.

"Sorry. I wasn't trying to guilt trip you, honest."

He doesn't reply at first and then finally shrugs. "Forget it. I forgive you because this food is so good."

Natalie watches as he leans forward to help himself to more bread. "Can I ask you something?"

"Sure."

"What made you come here last night? You seemed upset."

Anthony is quiet. He studies his plate. "Do you remember how you told me that people think your childhood sounds more glamorous than it was?"

She nods.

"It's kind of the same for me." Anthony tells her how he grew up surrounded by doctors, that it was a privileged kind of life. "But there were all these expectations that went along with it," he says. "Everybody expected me to go into medicine, and when I chose not to, it caused a lot of problems. My father can't let it go."

"Is it because your brother became a doctor?"

Anthony shakes his head. "No, all my family are doctors. My father is a heart surgeon, my brother a pediatric surgeon, and my mom is a medical researcher. Plus they all practice medicine on my father's side."

Natalie raises her eyebrows. "Wow."

"Yeah."

"So you're like the misfit, huh?"

Anthony chuckles. "You could say that. I dropped out of medical school during my first year to pursue astronomy."

"What kind of doctor were you planning to become?"

"Neurosurgeon."

"What's that? Wait a minute, is that like a brain surgeon?"

"Basically." He picks up his food again and takes another bite, chews for a few seconds. "Brain and spinal cord, anything to do with the central and peripheral nervous system."

Natalie starts to laugh. "So you were planning to become a *brain* surgeon?" She tries to wrap her own brain around that.

"Laugh all you want, but I would have been a damned good surgeon."

She quiets and considers his words. Oddly, she knows they're true. Anthony is certainly intelligent enough. "To be honest, it's not that hard to imagine. You're super smart. Plus, you're compassionate and I suspect you're good under pressure."

He listens, but doesn't say anything.

"So why did you drop out?"

"Because I'm selfish." He smiles, but it doesn't reach his eyes.

"What do you mean?"

"For some reason, I've always been good with numbers. I can do a lot of abstract math in my head. Physics and astronomy were both hobbies when I was a kid, but it was understood that they were *only* hobbies." He puts his plate down on the end table. "Sometime during med school I started sitting in on astrophysics lectures when I was supposed to be studying for my biochem classes. It felt like a guilty pleasure, but it also felt natural. Way more natural than anything else I was doing. And then this professor I knew helped me publish a paper on quasars that was very well received." He looks over at her. "I'd figured something out, you know? I contributed something to understanding the universe." Anthony smiles again, this time for real. "It was amazing."

"So you dropped out of medical school?"

Anthony rests his feet on the coffee table and leans his head back. "Yeah."

"And then your family freaked out?" She thinks back to the comment he made when they were going on the Ferris wheel, about how he's not saving lives. It makes sense now.

He closes his eyes and nods. "Mostly my dad, but yeah, they all freaked out—except my brother, I guess."

"But you love what you do, right? They should be happy for you."

Anthony's eyes are still closed as he shakes his head. "I'm Italian, Natalie. You just don't go against your family. It's a big deal."

"I see."

"I'm the youngest kid. Not to mention I have a daughter from a girl who I got pregnant when I was a teenager. I'm basically a disappointment to my parents in every way."

"That's crazy though." She pauses, thinking this over. "That doesn't explain why you came here last night."

Anthony opens his eyes and turns to look at her. "I felt bad about what happened with the bakery and I didn't want to leave things like that between us." He reaches for her hand. "I didn't want to be a disappointment to you, too."

Chapter Twenty-Three

Diet Plan: Indulge a little. Food isn't what you're craving.

Exercise Plan: The Lust Workout.

"YOU'RE IN A good mood," Lindsay comments to Natalie during boxing class on Wednesday. "You've been in a good mood since the weekend, now that I think about it."

"It's true," Blair says in agreement as she tapes her hands. "You didn't even get upset when all those bags of bread flour were delivered by mistake yesterday, though it's the third time it's happened."

Natalie smiles and shrugs. "It must be this spring weather."

Anthony's been texting and calling every day. Sometimes he's witty or more often he's naughty—asking her what kind of panties she's wearing and telling her how much he misses her "cookies." Natalie carries her phone everywhere and is constantly hiding in the storeroom giggling into it like a teenager.

She still hasn't told anybody about what's going on between them though. *I just want to savor this.*

Natalie understands now that the romance was dead in her marriage and had been for a long time. Not to mention the sex.

And then there's the sex with Anthony.

Ohmigod.

All these years, she never knew what she was missing. During the early days of their marriage, Peter was a gentle and patient lover, and at the time she thought it was sweet, but looking back on it she realizes there was no zest—ever. In bed, Peter was as passionate as a bowl of oatmeal.

On the other hand, Anthony is like a spicy stew that lingers on your tongue so you can't stop craving it.

239

Later, after work the next day, Natalie is changing out of her flour en-crusted work clothes when Lindsay calls her into the bathroom.

"What is this?" Lindsay asks, holding up a can of men's shaving cream.

Natalie stares it with a straight face. It's the can Anthony bought at the drugstore over the weekend. He forgot to take it home. "Men's shaving cream."

Lindsay's nose tilts up, twitches like a hound dog catching the scent of a rabbit. "Was there a *man* here?"

"No," Natalie says with a laugh. "I bought that by mistake. I figured I'd just use it anyway."

Lindsay glances at the shaving cream and seems to accept this answer, but then suddenly her eyes go to the toilet and the bathroom floor. They nar-row.

Uh oh.

And that's when Natalie realizes her mistake. She told Lindsay she was vacuuming and cleaning the bathrooms on Saturday, but didn't actually do any of it.

She had planned to quickly clean them Sunday, but forgot. It's a classic amateur mistake.

No follow through.

Lindsay looks at Natalie again, making it clear where her eyes just were. "You want to tell me the truth now?"

Natalie opens her mouth ready to spin her tale some more, but figures—why bother? "All right, you got me. There was a man here last weekend."

Lindsay stares at her, on high alert. "Who?"

"Anthony."

Her eyebrows rise. She considers this for a few seconds and then there's a sly smile on her lips. "I should have known the professor wasn't going to give up that easy. It was pretty obvious he's into you."

"Really?" Natalie grins, wanting to hear more.

"Yeah, you could see it whenever you were around. He couldn't take his eyes off you."

Natalie wants to giggle, but somehow refrains.

Then Lindsay frowns. "I can't believe you, though."

"I know. I'm sorry, I lied."

She shakes her head. "I'm seriously disappointed, Natalie."

"I just wanted to keep this to myself for a little while. It's been amazing."

"I'm disappointed because you didn't clean any of the bathrooms or even bother vacuuming."

Natalie smiles and in that moment remembers why she loves her sister so much. She sighs. "You're right. It's pathetic."

"I mean, where's your *follow through?* Answer me that?"

They look at each other, but nothing further needs to be said.

Lindsay links her arm with Natalie's. "Okay, I get you're stoned on great sex, probably for the first time in your life—which is pitiful, by the way—but you're required to give me at least *some* juicy details."

Later that evening, Chloe comes home from her weeknight visit with Peter.

"Daddy and Lena had a fight!" Chloe says after coming through the door and throwing her stuff down.

"Oh?" Natalie follows her into the kitchen.

"Can I have an apple walnut muffin?" Chloe asks when she sees them on the counter under the cake dome. "I'm starved! They don't have any normal food at their house at all. It's just raw vegetables and these weird sprouted things Lena grows in jars."

"I didn't know that."

"It's okay." Chloe takes a bite of the muffin. "Daddy showed me some bread and peanut butter he keeps hidden in the coat closet."

Natalie opens her mouth, but then closes it. She isn't sure how to respond to this. "Let me make you some dinner. There's still leftover chili in the fridge." Natalie gets the cold chili out and dumps a good-sized helping into a pot. The cornbread she made is all gone, but she slices up a chunk of sourdough and spreads it with butter. "I'll call your dad tomorrow and tell him he needs to keep proper food at home for you."

"Daddy and Lena were arguing about money. I guess Lena wants to buy a big house that costs a lot and Daddy said no."

Natalie listens with curiosity. "Why does Lena want a big house if it's just the two of them?"

"That's the same thing Daddy said. But Lena didn't really give a reason. She just kept saying they can afford it, so why not do it?"

The chili starts to bubble and Natalie turns down the heat. "Do your dad and Lena fight a lot?"

"No, not really. But it seems like more lately. I think Lena likes to spend money, and you know how Daddy is."

Natalie nods. Peter wasn't a tightwad, but he was definitely a saver. She's the same way herself, so ironically they never argued about money. She still wonders how he's coping with the added cost of Cinnamon, but he hasn't brought it up on the phone and neither has she. At least he hasn't asked her to help pay for the horse. She takes Chloe out to the stables at least once a week, but has never seen Peter there.

"Daddy doesn't want to have a big engagement party either, but Lena says as a life coach, she has to celebrate important events." Chloe finishes off the last of her muffin. "I wonder if they're going to break up."

"I doubt it. They seem happy, don't they?"

Chloe's eyes light up. "If they break up, then Daddy could come home. Maybe you could forgive him. What do you think, Mom?"

Natalie pours the chili into a bowl and brings it along with the bread over to Chloe. She wonders whether she should mention dating Anthony to Chloe, but decides it's probably too soon for that.

Chloe picks at her bread. "Do you think you'd let him come home if he wanted to?"

"Your dad and I aren't married anymore."

"I know, but he and Lena are fighting. We could have our family again."

Oddly, there's a tiny part of Natalie that still finds the idea appealing, but it's only because Chloe wants it so much. "Chloe, I don't want to hurt you, but your dad isn't coming home. We're divorced now. He plans to marry Lena."

Chloe stirs her chili. "But what if he changes his mind? Will you forgive him?"

"Don't ask me that." Natalie takes a deep breath. She puts her hand out and fiddles with Chloe's ponytail. "It's hard for me, too, sweetheart, but we all have to move on."

AT LA DOLCE Vita the next morning, Natalie is stunned when she sees Anthony coming through the front door as she's putting fresh croissants in the pastry case. Instantly, there's a zing of pleasure, but then she glances around, hoping no one else sees him.

She intercepts him before he gets in line to order coffee. At least it's crowded with the usual morning rush.

"What are you doing here?"

Anthony smiles and Natalie can't resist that gorgeous grin. He's wearing a blue *Star Wars* T-shirt and jeans and she swears he gets hotter every time she sees him. A fresh wave of desire rushes through her and she wishes she could pull him into a corner and jump him.

God, I'm insatiable.

"I had to stop next door for something and I thought I'd come see you."

He bends his head to kiss her. She kisses back, but somewhat hesitantly.

"What's wrong?" He gives her a wicked grin. "I thought you'd be happy to see me."

"I am."

His eyes wander down her body. "Because I'm happy to see you. I can't wait to see more of you. Are you staying over this Saturday?"

Anthony's been asking her to stay over all week, but she wasn't sure if she could.

"I think so." It turns out Chloe was invited to a friend's slumber party on Saturday and Lindsay said she'd be home anyway.

"Yeah? Because I have a big screen television in my bedroom, and you're going to love it."

"I am?" Natalie tries to figure out where he's going with this. "We're going to watch something?"

His eyebrows wiggle up and down.

Natalie's not sure if she's quite up for this adventure. She laughs nervously. "What exactly do you want to watch?"

"*Star Wars.*"

"Oh, of course!" Natalie feels a rush of relief. "I knew that." Oddly, there's a twinge of disappointment.

He looks at her from the corner of his eye. "What did you think I was talking about?"

"Nothing."

A slow grin pulls at his mouth. "Miss Natalie, you have a dirty mind."

"No, I don't. Of course not!" Her face grows warm.

Anthony chuckles and seems to be enjoying how flustered she's become. He reaches out and tucks a stray hair behind her ear. Lowers his voice. "We can watch some dirty movies if you want."

"No! I didn't say I wanted to do that."

He meets her eyes, but doesn't say anything more.

Natalie watches him, feeling both embarrassed and titillated, but then something occurs to her. "Wait a minute, did you just say you're here because you had to stop next door? What were you doing there?"

He shrugs. "Paperwork."

Natalie's eye flicker to the brick wall between their bakery and the new clothing store. Resentment sinks its teeth into her. And she can't help it—her temper flares. She lets out a deep breath as she tries to rein it in.

Unfortunately Anthony notices it, too. "Look, I can't keep apologizing forever."

But his attitude only fans the flames. "You could at least seem more apologetic."

"Why? This is business for me, not personal."

Natalie rolls her eyes. "Listen to yourself. Is this an Italian thing? You sound like you're in the Mafia."

Anthony bristles. "I hate that stereotype. So you can drop it right now."

"It's hard not to take getting stabbed in the back personally." She cringes at the sharp tone in her voice, but he can't expect her to forget all this so quickly.

"I didn't stab you in the back. That's ridiculous. Is that what you really think?"

Natalie doesn't have time to respond because Blair has suddenly come over to them.

"Someone in the kitchen told me you were out here," she says to Anthony, "but I had to see it with my own eyes. You've got some nerve showing up."

Anthony considers Blair. "Maybe you've forgotten, but I do own this building. And besides, I'm here to see Natalie."

Blair shakes her head and laughs. "You can forget it, pal. Natalie isn't interested in you anymore. And she's right. You did stab us in the back."

"Seriously?" His eyes travel from Blair to Natalie. "You still haven't told her yet?"

"Told me what?" Blair asks.

"I haven't had a chance." There's a sinking feeling in Natalie's gut. What a mess. She should have told Blair days ago.

Blair is staring at her, so Natalie braces herself and finally admits the truth. "Anthony and I have started . . . dating."

"*What?*" Blair's hazel eyes flash with anger. "You're still going out with him after what he did?"

"It just . . . happened."

Blair glares at her and Natalie can see she's not only angry, but hurt, too. "Don't you have any self-respect? He totally screwed us over!"

Natalie winces.

"I did not screw you two over," Anthony says, obviously angry. "I saved you a ton of misery. The fact is you should both be grateful to me."

"Grateful!" Blair and Natalie both say at the same time.

"Yes." Anthony nods. "Grateful. If I'd leased you that space, it would have put your bakery out of business."

"You're delusional," Blair tells him, and then turns to Natalie. "I don't even know what to say to you. I'm going back to work."

After she leaves, Anthony's dark eyes glare at Natalie. "I thought you said you told her."

"I told Lindsay, but I haven't had a chance to talk to Blair yet."

"I see." His jaw is tight.

"So I'm the bad guy in all this now? That's rich, coming from you."

"I have to go. I have class in a short while." He's shaking his head. "And besides, I can't listen to this shit anymore."

Natalie doesn't try to stop him. Once he's gone, she lets out a shaky breath. And then she goes to find Blair in the back kitchen.

"Don't even speak to me," Blair says. She's aggressively rolling out lilac fondant. "I have two cakes to make and a bride who keeps changing her mind, so I really don't have time to deal with your betrayal."

"Blair . . ." Natalie stands there, trying to decide how to handle this.

"I hope he's worth it, because I think you're making a big mistake." Blair cuts the fondant, hitting the knife harder than necessary before putting it aside and starting on a fresh sheet. "I know he's hot. But really?"

"Believe it or not, he's a good guy," Natalie finds herself saying.

Blair stares over at her in disbelief. "Is that what you call it when somebody lies to you?"

And then suddenly a very strange thought occurs to Natalie. *What if Anthony is right?* She hasn't actually looked at Anthony's program. Is it possible they missed something in their own calculations? She pushes the thought away for now. "What do you think of keeping the bakery open on weekends?"

"Weekends?" Blair glances over at her. "You'd have to handle it. Obviously, I have wedding cakes to deliver."

"I'd take care of everything. I'm thinking we could focus on coffee and offer a limited bakery selection—mostly sweet breads and cookies."

Blair slices off more lilac fondant, but doesn't say anything.

"I went to Starbucks last weekend and it was packed."

"You went to a Starbucks?" Her expression grows incredulous. "I don't even know who you are anymore. What are you going to tell me next? That you're baking with a mix?"

"I'm serious, Blair. There was a line out the door. I don't see why we shouldn't be getting some of that business.

Natalie can see the wheels in Blair's head turning. She's nothing if not pragmatic. "I suppose we could try it and see how it goes."

SATURDAY MORNING ROLLS around and Natalie hasn't heard anything from Anthony about her going over there. He's obviously still angry. She wonders if she should do what he did and show up at his house unannounced. The problem is, she doesn't even know where he lives. All she knows is his house is somewhere out in Carnation—a small town on the outskirts of Seattle, where it's dark enough to avoid the city's light pollution.

Forget it. I'm not chasing him. Women have been chasing him his whole life. If he wants me he's going to have to make the first move.

By noon, Natalie still hasn't heard anything. It's like playing poker. Except who's going to call the other's bluff first? *It won't be me.* When three o'clock rolls around and there's still nothing, she figures he's not giving in.

To heck with Anthony. I was doing just fine before he came along. I don't need him. And I don't care if I ever see him again.

If only she meant it.

At exactly three-twenty, her cell phone chirps and she dives for it. Pulse racing.

Are you still coming over tonight?

Natalie smiles and stares at his text for a long time, and then she puts her phone down. Decides to let him stew. She putters around the kitchen. Helps Chloe pack for the slumber party she's going to at a friend's house. Texts

Lindsay, who's working in her studio. She even does a load of laundry. Then finally at five-thirty, she can't stand it any longer and texts him back.

Yes.

A few seconds later, he replies. *You made me wait over two hours for that?*

She responds. *I was busy.*

Doing what?

Laundry.

There's nothing for five minutes and she can practically feel the heat billowing through the phone lines. Then finally, he texts his address, followed by the words.

Get over here right now.

Natalie's eyes linger over his text. She should be annoyed, but instead, erotic sparks are dancing through her.

She takes her time packing an overnight bag, figuring Anthony can cool his heels some more. It's like proofing dough—you want to get it just right, though she's sure he wouldn't appreciate the comparison.

Sifting through her clothes, Natalie wishes she had some kind of sexy nightie to bring along. After losing weight, she had to buy new bras and panties, but even those are mostly just cotton. She usually sleeps in a T-shirt.

I might have to go shopping.

All her life she's hated clothes shopping, but it's starting to grow on her. It's kind of fun to try on new clothes, and instead of cringing at her appearance, there's a hesitant sense of pride.

When her bag is finally packed and she can't think of a single reason not to leave, she glances at the clock. It's almost seven. Anthony's not going to be happy. Once she's in her car she punches his address into her GPS and sees it's about thirty minutes to get there.

She imagines him pacing around, waiting for her, getting angrier by the second. Or maybe she's got it all wrong and he's geeking out on his computer, totally unaware of the time.

Eventually, she leaves the city behind and is driving down a country road, the sun low in the sky. Those erotic sparks are still dancing and they're growing stronger the closer she gets.

Her GPS guides her to turn off onto a private drive with tall trees in front that eventually clear away to reveal a two-story craftsman-style house sitting on a flat piece of land. It's modest, but well-cared for. Anthony's black SUV is parked in the driveway and she pulls up beside it, glad for the confirmation that she found the right place.

Walking up his driveway with her overnight bag, Natalie gets a jolt when she hears Anthony's voice.

"Where the hell have you been?" he growls.

He's standing at the front door leaning against the frame. Arms crossed. Face stern. All his usual good humor seems to have drained away.

Drawing closer, she sees he's wearing a fitted white *Star Wars* T-shirt and jeans, his feet bare. Even with the scowl on his face he's devastatingly handsome. It's an effort to not let his appearance intimidate her.

Anthony steps aside to let her enter his house. She tries to look around, but can't because he's now looming directly in front of her. He takes her bag and puts it down.

"Answer me."

Natalie doesn't reply and his intelligent eyes are taking her in.

"You did it on purpose, didn't you? Making me wait because you want to jerk my chain."

"No, it's not like that." Though it occurs to her it's a lot like that.

"I don't believe you. I think you're holding a grudge." He steps closer and lowers his voice. "But you're torn, aren't you, Miss Natalie? Because no one's ever made you feel like I do."

Part of her is astonished at Anthony's perceptiveness, but the other part is annoyed by it. "Considering you're only the second man I've ever slept with, it's not that impressive."

There's a smirk on his face. "It wouldn't matter how many men you'd slept with." He leans down and whispers in her ear. "We'd still be hot together."

Her breath hitches.

She's wearing a pearl blouse with a dark camisole underneath and his deft fingers make quick work of the buttons. Natalie doesn't stop him. When he sees the camisole beneath her blouse, he studies it—his smile turns wicked.

"I approve," Anthony says in low murmur, his hands traveling to her breasts.

Those erotic sparks are turning to a bonfire now. She's already shaking with lust—embarrassed at her strong reaction. Everything he said was true.

No one has ever made me feel like this.

He leans close, but instead of kissing her, runs his mouth along her neck where he takes little bites, then licks them, blowing on her skin to cool the sting.

Natalie's eyes fall shut as she gasps with pleasure.

I'm helpless. My desire has made me helpless. Her hands grip his shoulders and then travel up around his neck. He smells clean, like soap and mint, and when her hands run through his hair at the back of his neck she finds it damp. He must have just taken a shower.

Anthony draws back and the two of them gaze at each other. His eyes are feverish. She's glad to see she isn't the only one affected.

His warm hand envelops hers and he pulls her along toward the staircase.

Natalie watches the way his muscles move beneath his T-shirt.

"Aren't you going to show me your house?" she asks, just to annoy him.

"Later."

ANTHONY LEADS HER upstairs.

He's still pissed off by the way she's letting him swing in the wind. He didn't even know whether she was going to show up tonight and he doesn't like that kind of uncertainty.

She's got this grudge and it only seems to be getting worse, but he also knows she wants him just as much as he wants her.

So to hell with everything else.

He pulls her into his bedroom and can see her glancing around. His bed is big with an elaborate wood headboard he picked up years ago in Kenya when he worked with the ISA. The sheets and duvet are white because they're the easiest to wash. He'd made the bed hastily earlier, and now sits down on the edge.

"Get over here," he says, reaching out and pulling her between his open thighs.

Anthony grasps Natalie's hips through her jeans then slides his hands around to grip her ass. For a long moment he closes his eyes. There's a strange feeling in the pit of his stomach. He's glad she's here. Relieved, and it's the depth of his relief that worries him.

Her cool hands are on his shoulders. They move to his face where her fingers trail over the stubble he left for her. She notices and smiles, but Anthony doesn't smile back. He's past that.

"I want you to take your top off," he says.

Natalie pauses, her blue eyes studying him. She licks her lips nervously. He hasn't kissed that sultry mouth yet, but he will soon. He knows Natalie doesn't like his request. Can see it on her face. She doesn't want to undress in front of him because the room isn't dark enough to suit her. There's a lamp burning in the corner and he'll definitely be able to see everything, but maybe he doesn't care, maybe he wants to punish her a little.

It's my turn.

Natalie removes her hand from his cheek and he wonders if she's going to turn skittish, but instead, she takes her long hair and gathers it so it's falling at her back. The scent of vanilla drifts toward him. She slips her blouse off and hands it over. He tosses it onto the leather bench at the foot of his bed.

Her breasts look sexy in the camisole, but then he decides he wants it gone, along with the bra.

"All of it."

She hesitates, but then reaches for the thin material at the bottom and pulls it over her head, tossing it with her blouse. His erection stiffens as he anticipates seeing her bare breasts.

"Keep going." His voice is low with a note of urgency.

Natalie hears that note. "You do it," she says in defiance.

They study each other for a few beats and then he snorts softly, reaches around and unfastens the clasp on her bra, slips it off, and throws it with the rest of the pile.

His eyes are on her face, but then he can't help himself, looks down and takes in the sight of her—so luscious. Like whipped cream with two sweet cherries on top. He swallows and actually feels lightheaded before a wave of lust crashes over him.

Then he doesn't want to play games anymore, doesn't want to think, doesn't want anything but Natalie wrapped around him while he's buried inside her to the hilt.

Anthony grabs her wrists and pulls her down onto the sheets. She lets out a little shriek and he checks her face, but she's grinning. He's not surprised. Despite her overall stubbornness, he's noticed Natalie likes to be dominated in bed.

Good.

Because I'm in a dominating kind of mood.

He unfastens her jeans and strips them off her, flinging them aside, along with her panties.

"I only want you to come to me in dresses from now on," he says impatiently.

Then he pulls his shirt overhead and starts on his own jeans. He can see the way she's watching him, laying back on her elbows, eyes hot with wanting. It isn't the first time he's seen that look on a woman's face, but on Natalie he particularly likes it.

She tries to sit up, but he shakes his head.

"Don't move. I want you right there."

Once he's naked, he opens his bedside drawer and grabs a strip of condoms, pulls one off and tosses the rest onto his nightstand for later. He quickly slips it on.

The bed dips as he moves over her, caging her with his body. Natalie is squirming beneath him, grabbing his shoulders, then his face.

"Kiss me," she says. "You haven't kissed me."

His breathing is harsh to his own ears and he shuts his eyes, trying to pull it together. Natalie is so soft beneath him everywhere—breasts, hips, and thighs, such a luxurious woman.

"*Preghi,*" he says to her. "*Voglio che tu mi preghi.*" *Beg. I want you to beg me.*

He's speaking Italian, so she doesn't understand, but he says it anyway.

Christ. I don't even know why I'm saying these crazy things.

Opening his eyes, he gazes down, their faces so close. His body shifts between her thighs and he positions himself right where he needs to be, but he doesn't enter her.

"Please kiss me, Anthony."

And it's only because she's pleading that he finally lowers his mouth. He intends to give her a small nip, but their kiss turns into something else, something deep. Natalie tastes like every desire he's ever had. He swears he could kiss her forever, but he's not done punishing her yet, so he pulls away. She complains and tries to draw him back, but he doesn't let her. Instead, he thrusts his cock into her slick heat, but only briefly, before pulling out again.

Natalie gasps. Her eyes were closed, but they open when he withdraws. He likes to watch her like this. Hot and desperate.

He continues teasing her—pushing in, then pulling out—until she's grabbing his ass.

This time he pulls out and lavishes attention on her breasts. Stroking and fondling them, playing with her nipples, using his mouth to suckle her. When her breathing gets thready, he stops and goes back to teasing her with his cock.

Natalie thrashes around. "Stop this," she breathes. "Stop doing this!"

"Why?"

Her face is flushed and she looks at him like he's crazy. "What do you want?"

And that's the cosmic riddle, isn't it? The puzzle he's trying to solve. In a way he wants her acquiescence, but he knows he wouldn't be happy if she was easy.

So he doesn't answer and instead, continues the torment, sweat breaking out on his forehead and back, his hands gripping the mattress for control. It's killing him to tease her like this and in the corner of his mind he wonders who's really being punished here.

"*You,*" he whispers finally, the answer suddenly coming to him. "I want *you.*"

Natalie's eyes are glazed with desire, but he can see she understands. The moment between them is intensely intimate. She reaches up and holds the sides of his face with both hands. "You have me. Don't you know that? I'm yours."

And then his control crumbles, his body rebelling against all the prolonged tension. His balls ache like crazy and before he can stop himself, he thrusts fully into her.

Blood rushes in his ears and it's from a distance he hears her moan, feels her legs wrap around his waist.

It's a miracle he lasted.

And then everything is up close again as he kisses her, groaning into her mouth. Natalie's nails are digging into his back and then his ass and it's as if nothing can stop him. His muscles pull and stretch and finally his orgasm arrives—exploding like the core collapse of a supernova.

Chapter Twenty-Four

> Diet Plan: A large slice of happy. Kisses on top.
>
> Exercise Plan: Try something new. And maybe a little kinky.

"YOU'RE LIKE A different person in bed," Natalie tells Anthony, breaking the silence. They'd dozed for a short while after that intense bout of lovemaking. She glances at the bedside clock and sees it's after ten pm.

"How's that?"

"You're so serious." Natalie thinks about his recent possessiveness, but doesn't want to mention it, since she's still trying to decipher what it means. "I can't believe I'm the only woman who's ever commented on it."

Anthony shrugs. "I may have heard it before."

"So what's going on there?"

"I don't know."

"I think you do."

"First, I want to ask you something." He's lying on his side and props himself up on one elbow. "I'd like you to go to the Smyth Science Award Banquet with me. Will you?"

"Really?" A delighted thrill rushes through her. Nobody ever asked her to prom, but Anthony might have just made up for that. "I'd love to go with you."

"Good." He gives her one of his boyish grins. "And just so you know, Miss Natalie, I expect you put out afterward whether I win the medal or not."

"As if," she scoffs. "I'm not putting out for a loser."

"And what if I win?"

"Well, then I'll have to get out my bag of sex tricks, won't I?"

"Cougar lady sex tricks?" he asks with big eyes.

Natalie turns away, unable to hide her irritation. "You've *got* to stop calling me that."

Anthony laughs and then captures her hand, bringing it to his mouth. She tries to pull it back, but he won't let her. Instead, he holds her hand and kisses every baking scar. Her heart catches in her throat watching him—his lips so soft.

"Did you know," he says, kissing her wrist, "that Lucille Ball and Desi Arnaz were six years apart in age?"

Natalie digests this piece of information. "How do you know that? Were you googling famous cougars again, young man?"

"Maya told me." He moves from kissing her wrist to licking it and she can't believe how arousing it is. *Who knew my wrist was an erogenous zone?* "Apparently Lucy and Desi lied and told people it was only three years, but it was in fact six, so there you go."

"You told Maya about us?"

He nods in affirmation.

"What did she say? Though I guess she already figured out we're dating."

Anthony lets go of her hand to tuck a pillow under his head so he can lie down on his side facing her. When he's comfortable, he takes her hand again, intertwining their fingers. "Maya thinks I'm falling in love with you."

"What?" Natalie stops breathing. There's a range of emotions conflicting inside her. She studies him. "Do you think that's true?"

"It might be."

"That's not much of an answer."

Anthony chuckles softly in reply.

"Why does Maya think that?"

"Apparently, I talk about you a lot. Plus I'm constantly checking my phone. I guess she's never seen me act this way with anyone before."

Natalie doesn't know what to say.

He plays with her fingers. "How do you feel? Do you think we're falling in love?" His tone is light, but she suspects the question isn't. Especially when she thinks back to how he acted when they made love earlier.

She looks at Anthony's beautiful face and thinks about how the man behind it is even more beautiful. It would be so easy to fall in love with him. Too easy.

"I don't know." It's a cowardly answer and she hates it, but what is she supposed to say? "How many women have said they were in love with you? I'll bet it's another big number."

He shakes his head. "You're asking the wrong question this time."

"I am?"

"What you should be asking is how many women have I said it to?"

"How many have you?"

Anthony doesn't reply right away and then shrugs. "Some people fall in love easily."

"That's true." Natalie figures he must be one of them, though she doubts he's in love with her. "I can never decide if they're lucky or not."

"Were you ever in love with anyone besides your ex-husband?

The question causes a small ache in her heart. "No, he was the only one."

"That must have been difficult for you when it ended."

"It wasn't easy." She doesn't want to talk about Peter, though.

They're both quiet. Rain has started outside and Natalie can hear it tapping on the roof. Sitting up with the sheet tucked under her arms, she lets her eyes wander around Anthony's bedroom. It gives the impression of a space that was hastily cleaned and she smiles to herself. There's a big screen TV on the wall across from his bed. There's also a framed poster from the original *Star Wars* movie and another small poster with a picture of outer space.

"That's an ad for the first telescope I ever owned," he says, seeing where her eyes have landed.

"Do you still have it?"

"I gave it to Serena."

There's a hamper in the corner stuffed with dirty clothes. Natalie likes the idea of Anthony doing something as mundane as laundry. There's a bookcase with a small desk attached, crammed with books and papers. His familiar battered satchel is on the desk along with his notebook computer. Looking around, she decides it's just a guy's bedroom. No great secrets revealed

"You should give me a tour of your house, so I can learn more about the mysterious Anthony."

"There's nothing mysterious about me." His hand reaches up to stroke her back from where he's lying. "I'm an open book."

"Hardly," she snorts. "You only want to appear like an open book."

"That's silly. Go on, ask me anything. I'll answer it."

"You mean you'll cleverly deflect it."

Anthony chuckles. "What is it you want to know so badly?"

Natalie thinks it over. His hand is still caressing her back and she lets her eyes fall shut, giving in to the sensation. *What exactly do I want to know?*

"Just tell me something," she says softly. "Something intimate."

"You already know me intimately. I even shared my panty-sniffing perversion with you."

A smile tugs at Natalie's mouth.

"In fact, why don't *you* tell me something for a change?" he says. "Something nobody knows."

She wonders if she should. There's a lot he doesn't know and she's good at deflecting, too. "I grew up poor." Natalie's eyes open as she runs her fingers over the white sheets. She doesn't look at Anthony.

His hand stills on her back. "I thought your dad was some big time poker player?"

"He was, but he was also a compulsive gambler who spent everything as soon as he won it."

"What about your mom?"

"She was an artist who liked her wine too much and she thought the sun rose and set on my father. I basically raised Lindsay."

"I see." He lets out a deep breath. "Where are they now?"

"My mom lives in Arizona with her second husband, though I rarely see her, and my dad died."

Anthony's hand continues with the caressing. "So you've had to be tough." His voice is a low murmur, but she detects a note of admiration.

"I didn't have a choice. No one's ever fought for me. I've always had to fight for myself."

"What about Peter? Didn't he take care of you?"

Natalie shakes her head. "No, Lindsay always said he treated me like I was his mother, and it's basically true."

She pulls away from his hand and lies down beside him again, so they're facing each other. "I haven't cried since I was a little girl."

His expression grows incredulous. "Seriously?"

Natalie nods.

"That can't be right. Why?"

"I just stopped one day. I don't even remember why."

Anthony studies her, his dark eyes compassionate. There's a part of her that wishes she could let herself sink into them. Stay there forever.

"How about you? Do you ever cry?" she asks curiously.

"Of course I cry. I'm Italian—we're always crying about something."

Natalie smiles. "What's the last thing you cried about?"

"I cried when I saw I was out of cream for my espresso this morning."

She can't help her giggle. "Now that's something to cry about."

"How about when you cut onions, do you cry then?" he asks.

"My eyes will water, but that's it."

"So it's not a physical thing."

"No, it's emotional. I didn't even cry when Peter left me."

"Damn."

"I know." She swallows. "I wish I could. But then sometimes I'm glad I can't, you know?"

Anthony frowns, but doesn't say anything.

"So what's the last thing you cried about for real?" she asks.

He's silent, thinking it over. "When my grandfather died. He was a mathematician, so we had a lot in common. I admired him—he was a good man and always kind to me."

"When did he die?"

"A few years ago. He left me a little money. It's how I was able to afford the building where you're leasing the bakery. Plus, I bought the Ducati."

"He was Italian?"

Anthony nods. "My mom's dad. He was a professor at one of the universities in Rome."

"Wow, you do have a lot in common with him."

"He was definitely a role model, though I know I disappointed him."

"Not the doctor thing again."

"No." He tucks his hand under his head. "When I married Nicole, we didn't do it in the church and I got divorced, anyway. Though he loved Serena, he was very traditional and frowned on the whole thing."

"Do you think you'll ever marry again and have more kids?"

Anthony shrugs. "Maybe. I'd definitely do it differently next time. Nicole and I eloped, so we didn't have any family at our wedding, and it caused a lot of bad feelings. My parents never got over it."

"Would you marry in the church next time?"

"I don't know." He thinks it over. "I don't really care about that. I'm not particularly religious and being divorced, I doubt they'd let me, anyway. Mostly I just want my family there."

"Peter and I got married at the courthouse. He was in dental school and it was all we could afford at the time. When Chloe was born, he was just starting his practice."

"Why didn't you guys have more kids?"

Natalie lies on her back and stares at the ceiling. Old resentments come to her with a fresh clarity. "I wanted more, but Peter didn't. And now I'm too old."

"That's not true. You could have more if you wanted."

"I'd have to find another husband first."

Anthony gives a dry chuckle. "That would be helpful."

Something occurs to Natalie. "Is that why you're so obsessed with birth control? Because of Serena?"

"What do you mean? I'm not obsessed with birth control."

"Yes, you are. You still insist on condoms, even though I'm on the pill and we're both safe."

She's watching him and she can see the embarrassed expression creeping up Anthony's face.

"I'll bet that's why you're so serious in bed, too," she says.

He stares at her.

"You don't want to lose control."

"Whatever." He rolls his eyes. "Will you take a credit card for the psychoanalysis, or do you only accept cash?"

Anthony is so deft at making jokes, but she can see she's hit a bullseye. She thinks about how hard it must have been for him to become a teenage father. Especially someone with a moral compass as strong as she suspects Anthony's is.

"I'm sure we can work out a payment that involves neither cash nor credit," she says, going along with his joke, letting her eyes glance downward.

"Yeah? I like what I'm hearing."

Rolling onto her stomach, she moves closer to him on the bed. He watches as she leans over and kisses him softly, lingering so it's something slow and sensual. Anthony shifts so he's on his back and reaches beneath the covers to run his hands down her body.

"Lie on top of me," he tells her.

Natalie slides over so she's straddling him and then scoots down, his cock pressing into her stomach.

They kiss some more—long exploratory kisses, as she stays on top and slides her body slowly against his. The heat between them simmers. Her hair keeps falling around them like a curtain and he gathers it in his hands, drawing it back.

His eyes roam her face. "Look at you, Miss Natalie. So beautiful."

"You don't have to say that," she whispers.

"I'm saying it because it's true. You should believe me."

"Okay . . . I believe you."

She's balancing on her arms, hands pressed into Anthony's shoulders. He reaches up to caress her breasts.

"Move higher," he says. "Press them into my face."

Natalie does as he asks, putting her hands out on the headboard to balance herself. Anthony lets out low noises of approval as he grasps her, lapping at her nipples, then smothering himself. His stubble is abrasive, but it excites her, too. She starts to squirm on top of him.

"God," he murmurs after a while. "That's fantastic."

"You seem to be enjoying yourself."

"I am." He runs his hands down her backside. "But now I have other plans for you. Why don't you scoot up some more and sit on my face?"

Natalie watches him and bites her lip. "I have some plans of my own, actually."

Anthony looks at her questioningly.

"You've been so generous with me, but I haven't returned the favor." She watches the spark in his eyes and knows he understands her.

"Are you sure?"

She shifts down, kissing his chest, then stops to look up at him. "I would have done it sooner, but to be honest—I haven't done this in years, and you've probably had women who are amazingly good at it."

His brows draw together. "Don't compare yourself to anyone else. It's just you and me in this bed."

"I know."

Anthony caresses her shoulders. "Look, I only want this if you do."

Natalie smiles. "I want it."

THANK GOD. NOT that he didn't mean what he said to Natalie. He's never been one of those guys who likes a blow job no matter what. Over the years, he's found if the woman isn't into it, it just isn't as pleasurable for him.

All the same, just the thought of Natalie's mouth on his cock gets him hot.

She's still giving him a little smile and Anthony tries not to appear over-eager.

Dude, relax.

He takes a deep breath and closes his eyes for a few seconds. She kisses his chest some more and works her way down.

When he opens them, he can see her blonde head bent over his stomach and he's grateful for the bedroom lamp. It would be torture to have her mouth on him and not be able to see her.

Those full breasts are pillow soft, pressing right into him as she continues trailing light kisses. She kneels between his legs and takes hold of his erection.

His heart rate kicks up as she examines him this way and that. Her cool fingers handle him gently. He wonders if for once she's glad there's light, too.

"You have a good-looking penis," she declares. "It's as gorgeous as the rest of you."

Anthony chokes with laughter. "Thanks."

But then she lowers her head and puts her mouth on him and his laughter stops.

God.

He reaches down to lift her hair out of the way. "I have to see you do this," he tells her, his breathing unsteady.

She gives him a saucy look and helps by tossing her long hair over to one side.

At this point, nothing can pull his eyes away from the sight of Natalie swallowing him. That sexy mouth wraps around his cock, then pulls out to swirl her pink tongue. He's imagined this a hundred times, but the reality is far better than any fantasy.

What a sight.

He reaches down and slides his fingers into her hair, cradling her head.

Sweat breaks out all over his body. He continues to watch, eyes half-lidded with lust.

She was right about what she said. Fumbling a bit, she does seem less experienced than other women he's been with. It's turning him on even more, though. There's never any performance with Natalie. Her enthusiasm is so real. Her passion authentic.

The sensation is wet and good. The sounds she makes and his own harsh breathing fill the room. She strokes his balls—then tugs. Puts her mouth on them.

A low groan escapes him.

And then Natalie does something surprising.

She shifts her body up and presses his cock right between her luscious breasts and the sight nearly ends his control.

His hands fall to his side and he's gripping the sheets. Part of him wants to close his eyes to try and hold it together, to start reciting the Periodic Table, but the other part of him doesn't want to miss anything.

"Do you have any lotion?" she asks in a breathy voice. Her face is flushed, her mouth open. He recognizes she's aroused, too, and he likes seeing that. A lot.

"In the . . . nightstand," he manages to say.

She pulls away from him and opens the drawer, comes back with a bottle of the unscented lotion he keeps there. Squirting some in her hand, she rubs it between her breasts and then takes the excess and smears it all over the rest of herself, tugging on her own nipples.

Anthony is spellbound and can't take his eyes off the sight of Natalie touching herself.

He swallows. "I could watch you do that all day."

She gives him a slow, naughty smile. Then she positions herself over him again and slides his cock right between her breasts, holding them together for him.

Christ. He already knows he's not going to last much longer. His hands reach out and grip her shoulders to help steady himself.

He watches Natalie, her pretty face, and the way she's looking down at him. Then he watches the sight of what she's doing for him and lets himself go, enjoying the earthy experience. In truth, he's had this fantasy about Natalie many times, but he never knew it would come true, and when he finally climaxes, there's a sense of gratitude at her generosity.

NATALIE DISCOVERS ANTHONY owns a big claw-footed tub. "I'm so envious. I've always wanted one of these."

"Yeah? I had it put in after I bought the house. I mostly take showers, but every once in a while I like a long soak." Anthony fills it with water and they both get inside. There are no candles, but his bathroom light has a dimmer.

He helps guide her down so she's sitting with her back to him. The hot water feels like bliss and Natalie sighs as she leans into his chest. She decides being with Anthony is like dancing under a warm summer night sky when all the stars are out and you realize how lucky you are to be alive.

She thinks back to how it was between them in bed and how she's never done anything like that before. It was arousing. Plus, she felt sexy and bold.

"Have you ever dated a woman with small breasts?" Natalie asks, as Anthony takes a washcloth and runs it down her arm. His bathroom soap smells like sandalwood, a scent she's come to associate with him. She also notices some salon brand mint shampoo off to the side.

"Of course."

"Really? I'm surprised."

"Because I'm so into yours?"

"You do seem to like big ones."

His deep voice vibrates behind her. "I don't discriminate. I love all women's breasts—big or small."

"Listen to you . . . so diplomatic. What are you, the boob ambassador?"

Anthony laughs. "Now that's a job I wouldn't turn down. Though, I'll admit to a weakness for larger ones." He runs the washcloth across her chest. "Yours are particularly nice."

"Thank you." Natalie can't help her smile. For years she hated being so busty, and had even considered breast reduction, but not anymore.

He kisses her shoulder. "What about you, Miss Natalie? Do you have any favorite male body parts?"

Natalie thinks about his question. "I definitely like a nice butt. And chest, too. And, of course, you get an A plus in both those departments."

"I appreciate that," he murmurs.

He bends his knee to get more comfortable and Natalie can't help but notice it's masculine and perfect like the rest of him. "What's it like for you?" she asks.

"What's what like?"

"Being so good looking."

Anthony is silent and she wonders if he's going to deflect her question or pretend it isn't true.

He lets out a deep breath and then surprises her. "It has its good and bad points."

"What would be bad about it? It seems like it would open a lot of doors."

"It closes them, too. People don't always take you seriously if you look a certain way."

"Are you complaining about being beautiful?" She turns to glance at him over her shoulder.

"No, but you have to remember the kind of work I do has nothing to do with appearance and everything to do with intellect. I have to prove myself on paper and then when people meet me, I often have to prove myself again. It can be frustrating at times."

Natalie considers his words.

"And then I keep being asked to teach that damn survey course—Astronomy 101," he groans.

"What? I thought you enjoyed teaching."

"I do, but not that class. It's filled with girls who couldn't care less about astronomy and just want to flirt with me or worse."

"I see." Natalie remembers how the young women who sat behind her in class were talking about him, not to mention the way she was ogling him herself. "You don't feel complimented?"

Anthony snorts. "Are you joking? It's a nuisance. Not to mention all the inane questions they're always asking. They're screwing it up for the students who do want to learn. "

"Professor Novello," Natalie speaks in a dreamy voice, "is the moon really made out of cheese?"

"Exactly."

"I could see how that would be annoying. So, what are the good things about being beautiful?"

He chuckles behind her. "You make me sound like a supermodel."

"Come on, there must be some perks to being gorgeous. I can't believe it's all bad."

He nuzzles her neck. "Why don't you tell me? You're gorgeous."

"Not like you. Seriously, I'm curious."

He runs his hands down her arms. "All right. In the same way it closes doors, it opens them, too."

"How?"

"I get preferential treatment a lot. People, especially women, will go out of their way to do things for me, and I definitely get away with stuff I shouldn't. I can't even count the number of times I've been helped next, even when there are lots of people who have been waiting longer than me. It's weird. Also, people always assume I'm a nice person."

"But you are a nice person."

He sighs. "Trust me, I wasn't always nice. I'm ashamed to admit it, but when I was younger I took advantage." He's quiet for a few seconds. "Luckily, I was raised in a family where everyone has a strong sense of duty, so it never got too out of hand."

"What's it like to have practically any woman you want?"

"Fantastic."

"I'll bet."

She can hear him chuckle again and when she turns to look at him, he seems embarrassed.

"What is it?" Natalie asks.

"I don't know. I've never admitted these things to anyone before."

"I'm not judging."

He nods. But then his expression changes and he grows sober. "You're still holding a grudge against me though, aren't you?"

Natalie lifts up and turns around in the water, so she can face him. They study each other and finally she lets out a sigh. "Yes, but I'm trying not to."

He traces a finger over her collar bone. "How are we going to fix this?"

Natalie takes the washcloth. "I'm not sure, but we will." She squeezes the warm water onto his chest, watching it drizzle down over muscle and dark hair. She gets the soap and rubs it in her hands until it's foamy. Then she suds him all over—his chest, neck, under his arms—the woodsy scent of sandalwood filling the air. Anthony lays his head back on the tub and lets her wash him in a sleepy way, like a large cat, relaxing in the sun.

As she rinses the soap off him with the washcloth, something occurs to her. "Could you let me see that software program you created? The one with all our bakery's financial information on it?"

He raises his eyebrows. "Sure, I could send you the program and a copy of the file."

"Okay, thanks."

After their bath, they get dressed again. Natalie didn't bring a heavy coat, so Anthony loans her one of his, rolling up the sleeves for her. He continues to bundle her up with a scarf, gloves, and a ski hat.

"Are we going to the North Pole or your backyard?"

He tucks the scarf into her coat. "I just want you to be warm."

She watches as Anthony pulls on a black puffy ski jacket, but doesn't bother with the rest.

They head outside. Anthony's backyard is a big open field. Apparently, astronomers don't like too many trees hindering their skyline. It's the witching hour and the world is quiet and still. It's chilly enough that she's grateful for the hat and scarf.

Natalie glances up at the sky and is surprised to see it's mostly clear even though it rained earlier.

"It's just a little ways over there." He points to a small structure a short distance from the house.

They walk side by side over the wet grass, and Natalie thinks about how she should be exhausted. She worked that day, so she's been up a long time, but instead, she feels more awake than ever. More alive somehow, even.

Finally, they get to a medium-size shed where Anthony unlocks the door with a key and switches on a red light. Inside there's a large tubular object with metal arms that almost look alien, holding up a huge bucket on top. It's attached to a platform with a pivot.

"Wow, is this your other telescope?"

"This is it. It's a Dobsonian I built myself." She detects a note of pride in his voice and it occurs to her Anthony seldom boasts about anything, even when he could.

Using a handcart, he maneuvers the telescope out of the shed.

"Do you want help?"

"I got it. Actually, you could grab one of those flashlights on the wall inside and then shut the door."

Natalie does as he asks and then follows him as he carts the telescope a short way out to an area with lawn chairs and a table. She tries to be helpful as he sets up, but it's obvious he doesn't need any help, so she takes a seat in one of the chairs.

"It's so peaceful," she murmurs, leaning her head back to gaze up at the sky again.

"I know. It's fantastic out here at this hour."

He fiddles with things and it takes a while as he adjusts the pivot on the large telescope. Natalie remembers what a finderscope is from last time and watches Anthony as he keeps looking through it. Eventually she sees him peering through the main eyepiece.

"Come here." He motions to her, putting his hand out.

Natalie gets up and walks over. Anthony pulls her in for a quick kiss before stepping out of the way to let her view. She looks into the eyepiece and sees a field of small stars that all appear the same. "What am I looking at?"

"I tried to center it. Let your eyes adjust and then find what looks like a medium size star in the middle."

She does what he tells her and focuses on the bright point in the center. "I think I'm there. What am I seeing? It's not a star?"

"No, it isn't stellar. It's a quasar called 3C273. I know it's not impressive looking, but you have to see it with more than your eyes. This is deep space. That quasar is two-point-five billion light years away."

"Really? But why does it look like a star?"

"It's close to a supermassive black hole. The energy it emits outshines everything else in the galaxy."

Natalie continues to stare at the small bright object, thinking about what Anthony is telling her. "So I'm looking two-point-five billion years into the past?"

"That's right."

"Incredible . . ." she breathes. Then she pulls away from the eyepiece and smiles at him. "This is amazingly cool."

He grins, his expression pleased. "Would you like to see more deep space objects?"

"Definitely. But what about long gamma-ray bursts, the stuff you work on, can we look at those?"

Anthony shakes his head. "No, it's not something I can show you with a regular telescope." He explains how gamma-ray bursts are extreme bursts of energy—the most powerful in the universe. "It's a frequency we can't see with our eyes. They're narrow beams and some of our theories suggest they'll vaporize everything in their path within 200 light years. "

"Wow, I hope Earth isn't in danger!"

He chuckles. "No, luckily we're safe. There aren't any stars massive enough nearby to affect us. Often long gamma-ray bursts come from the most distant galaxies, so by studying them we're looking at explosions that happened close to the Big Bang—which is what most of my own work centers around."

Natalie nods, dazzled. *Whoa.*

She spends the next hour and a half with Anthony as he shows her various nebulae, open star clusters, and galaxies. He explains about each of them and she can't help but feel a sense of wonder at all that is out there.

"You're a good teacher. And I'm not just saying that, I mean it."

"Thanks. You're a good student, actually."

After they put the telescope away and before they go back inside, Anthony pulls her into his arms and kisses her. He smells woodsy and tastes like the night.

"I want you to come to Rome with me this summer."

Natalie's eyes widen. *Summer. So we're thinking that far ahead.* "I haven't traveled much."

"I know, but it's time to fix that. I'd love to show you Rome. It's my favorite city."

She sighs. "I'm sure it would be wonderful, especially with you. I don't know if I can leave for that long, though."

"It's only a couple of weeks. Promise me you'll think about it."

"I will."

When they finally go inside, neither of them falls asleep right away. Instead, they lay quietly in bed, gazing at each other as the early dawn filters through the window. Anthony strokes her hair. And Natalie knows something has shifted. She feels brand new. As if the world has changed from black and white to color, as if she were a princess awoken with a kiss. Part of her pulses out a warning, tells her to hold back, to be careful. The specter of being hurt lingers so near, hiding in the shadows, but she decides to forget the shadows.

She's going to enjoy every single moment she can with Anthony.

Chapter Twenty-Five

> Diet Plan: Revenge is a dish best served
> hot to cheating ex-husbands.
>
> Exercise Plan: Party all night. And I mean,
> all night.

"TURN AROUND," LINDSAY tells her as Natalie comes out from the dressing room with another fancy ball gown. Shopping for a dress to wear to the Science Awards Banquet is like buying her first prom dress. "Mmm." Lindsay considers her. "I think I like the last one better."

"This is exhausting. I'm starting to think I should just wear my *Lord of the Rings* hoodie."

Lindsay laughs. "Don't even joke about that."

"Hey, Anthony likes my hoodie."

"It figures, but I'm not letting you wear it to this banquet."

"I've never been much of a shopper."

Her sister rolls her eyes. "Cry me a river. You're going to the hottest party in Seattle with a guy who's brilliant and gorgeous. Do you know how hard it is to get tickets to this thing? It's like the Academy Awards or something."

"Anthony got extra tickets for the afterparty at the university. You and Oliver should come to that."

"I'll probably go alone." Lindsay pulls down another dress for Natalie to try on, "Oliver and I might be breaking up."

Natalie turns sharply. "Are you dumping him?"

Lindsay shrugs. "I haven't decided yet, but I'm thinking about it."

"Why? He's such a nice guy."

Lindsay pauses to study her. "You really have changed, do you know that? And in a good way."

"What do you mean?" Natalie pulls down the side zipper on her dress and steps out of it. She's wearing a full coverage bra, panties, and shapewear.

For trying on dresses even Lindsay agreed shapewear was a good idea.

"When you were still with Peter you would have dismissed Oliver based solely on his appearance. You wouldn't even have given him a chance."

"You make it sound like I was a snob."

"No, but you were way too conservative. You never wanted anyone to color outside the lines. And you acted like all the guys I dated were ex-convicts."

Natalie pauses. She does remember thinking that about Lindsay's boyfriends. It seems like a long time ago now. "I think I was too influenced by Peter and his attitudes."

"Like I said, you've changed for the better."

Natalie shrugs. "Who am I to judge? I'm dating a guy six years younger."

"That's so cool. You, of all people, as a cougar."

"Please don't use the 'C' word around me." Natalie wiggles into the next dress, an elegant sky-blue gown. She stands in front of Lindsay to be zipped up. "So, why are you dumping Oliver? You're going to break his heart. I'm pretty sure he's in love with you."

"Because I've got to ramble, baby."

Natalie goes over to study herself in front of the full length mirrors. "You're just like Dad. Never satisfied."

Lindsay comes over to stand beside her. "Wow, I like this one. That color is amazing on you. Plus it shows off your boobs without looking tacky."

Natalie examines herself in the mirror, turning this way and that. A frisson of excitement runs through her. Lindsay is right. The color is gorgeous. It's an elegant dress, and it does show off her cleavage without making her look like a hooker. "This might be the one!" She glances down at the price tag. *Yikes.* But she knew whatever dress she bought would be expensive.

Lindsay inspects her from every angle. "You look amazing. It totally gives you an hourglass figure. Plus, we'll have fun with your makeup. This color really makes your eyes pop."

"Do you think Anthony will like it?" And then wishes she hadn't asked that. *I'm not buying this dress for him, but for me.* At the same time, it's his big night and she doesn't want to let him down.

"Are you kidding? He'd have to be dead not to appreciate you in this dress."

"Thanks." Natalie smiles and then walks over to grab her phone and check the time. "I should probably get back to work. I've been gone longer than I intended."

"So how are things going with Blair?" Lindsay gathers all the rejected dresses into one pile. "Is she still pissed at you?"

Natalie fingers the band of material around her waist. It's silky soft, but has some kind of firm support beneath it, too. "I invited her to come dress shopping with us. It's her day off, but she said she was too busy."

"Don't worry, she'll come around. After all—I did."

Lindsay doesn't like how Anthony handled the situation with the bakery, but after seeing how happy Natalie is with him, she's agreed to give him a chance. Plus, Lindsay liked that he didn't give up easily—said Anthony might be enough man for her, but that the jury was still out.

The salesgirl who's been helping them knocks on the dressing room door, and Lindsay opens it to hand her the rejected dresses. "We're going to get the blue one," she tells her.

"Wonderful!"

When the door is closed again, Lindsay helps unzip Natalie.

"I hope she does come around," Natalie says, worried. She knows Blair feels betrayed. What sucks is, Natalie gets it. If the situation were reversed she'd feel the same way, because in Blair's eyes Natalie is putting a man first. But what Blair doesn't understand is, she isn't putting a man first. *I'm putting myself first.* And it's been a long time since she's done that. If she's honest, she can't remember ever doing it. It feels healthy, like finally having a scab heal over. *I need this.*

"WE STILL HAVEN'T watched all the *Star Wars* movies," Anthony complains. He calls to tell her he wants her in his bed again as soon as possible.

"We watched the two best ones." They watched the original *Star Wars* and *The Empire Strikes Back,* but the last time they tried to watch *Return of the Jedi,* they couldn't stop making out. She's been at his house a lot the past few weeks. They even had a barbecue-slash-star-party with Chloe and Serena. Both girls had a good time and Chloe thought it was cool how Anthony knew so many constellations.

He snorts. "That's not enough."

"Are you pouting?"

"Of course I'm pouting. I'm a selfish asshole and I demand satisfaction."

"I found a dress for the Science Award Banquet."

"Perfect. Why don't you put it on and come over here and show me, then I can have some fun taking it off you."

Natalie laughs and leans back on the couch. She's going to see a movie with Lindsay and Chloe tonight. And then the rest of the week after work she has salon appointments set up. "Very funny. I'll call you after the movie, but I'm not coming over."

He grumbles.

"I saw the article about you in the paper," Natalie says. The *Seattle Times* had been trying to interview Anthony for ages and Maya finally forced him to speak with them. "I liked it. I never knew you taught astronomy to kids in the

Central District. You're full of surprises."

"Yeah, whatever. Today's newspaper is tomorrow's cat-box liner."

Natalie can't believe she ever thought Anthony was full of himself. If anything, he seems to hate being under the spotlight. Not to mention the closer the award banquet gets the worse his mood seems to be.

"I liked that present you left me, Miss Natalie," he murmurs, changing the subject.

Her face grows warm and she glances around to make sure she's still alone. "I thought you might." She left her used panties on his pillow when she was at his house last time.

"You'll be pleased to know I've made good use of it."

"Did you?" Natalie's breath catches. "You might have to show me exactly what you did."

His voice takes on a husky tone. "Only if you show me, too."

She wonders if she could ever be that bold and thinks with Anthony it's possible. "Maybe," she whispers teasingly. "Maybe we'll show each other."

There's a pause. "You're killing me. I want to see you *now*."

"We'll be together this weekend after the banquet." Anthony booked a room for them at the Olympic Hotel.

He groans. "I don't know if I can wait that long."

By Saturday, Natalie has her hair freshly foiled, nails and toenails done, legs and eyebrows waxed, and she's been consuming nothing but salad and green smoothies all week, determined to look great in that dress.

"I'm tired of eating so healthy," Natalie complains to Lindsay and Chloe as they help her get ready for the banquet. "Next week I'm having a chocolate pastry every meal along with a bowl of whipped cream for dessert."

"Your first prom," Lindsay sighs, putting her hands together. Natalie told her how she keeps thinking of this whole thing like prom, and the notion stuck. "They grow up so fast."

"How come you never went to prom, Mom? Didn't you want to go?"

Lindsay just finished blow-drying Natalie's hair straight. It looks blonde and shiny thanks to the recent foil and the glossing serum she ran through it. Her tackle box of makeup is sitting on the dining room table.

"Nobody asked me. Though looking back on it now, I should have just gone with friends."

"Yes, you should have," Lindsay agrees.

"I think prom sounds fun. I hope I get to go when I'm older." Chloe looks through Lindsay's tackle box. "And I can't wait to start wearing makeup."

"All in good time," Natalie says. She glances over at the clock. There's more than an hour to kill before Anthony arrives to pick her up. "And speaking of fun, let's have some right now. I want to rock out."

"You do?" Both Lindsay and Chloe look at her with surprise.

Natalie nods. "You guys are always doing it and I'm tired of missing out."

And before you can say fun-kay, the three of them are dancing to a 70s playlist that Lindsay put together. There's "Rollercoaster" by the Ohio Players, "Play That Funky Music" by Wild Cherry, and "Sexy Thing" by Hot Chocolate.

Chloe is jumping up and down waving her hands in the air. Lindsay looks like she needs a stripper pole. And Natalie is bumping and grooving her hips to every song.

When the Commodores' "Brick House" comes on, Natalie starts to laugh. Instead of feeling ill at ease with herself as she has for years, she realizes she's come to embrace her curves. She decides that being a 'brick house' ain't half bad.

ANTHONY HEARS MUSIC through the front door when he arrives with the limo to pick up Natalie. "It sounds like the party has already started in here," he tells Lindsay and Chloe after they let him in.

Lindsay laughs. "Oh, it has, believe me."

He looks around for Natalie and when he sees her coming down the stairs his chest tightens. She looks beautiful and sexy, basically every man's dream. *But the lady's with me.* He'd been viewing this whole evening as a chore, but having Natalie at his side is going to make it far more bearable.

When she sees him a smile breaks out on her pretty face and Anthony can't stop himself from smiling, too. He relaxes. Everything about Natalie makes him happy. Maybe this night will be all right, after all.

Her dress is light blue and when she comes closer he sees it matches her eyes. She looks stunning. Not to mention the way it shows off every curve.

"I approve, Miss Natalie."

"Do you?" she smiles.

He leans closer. "You look dazzlingly beautiful."

She meets his eyes and he's glad to see she believes his compliments now. There's no hesitation on her part at all.

Natalie steps back and takes him in, too. He's wearing a black Armani tux, a crisp white shirt, and a black bow tie, his dark wavy hair tamed with gel. Her eyes roam from head to toe and then settle on his face.

"I guess you look okay." A teasing smile plays on her mouth.

"Now, don't hurt yourself with the compliments."

Natalie's expression softens and she steps close to cradle his face with those cool fingers. "I think you look beautiful, too."

"Thank you." Oddly, there's real pleasure at her words.

The two of them gaze at each other. It's only been a week, but it feels like a long time. Anthony wishes he could pull her into his arms and kiss her until they're breathless. It'll have to wait until later, though.

Before they leave, Natalie heads back upstairs to grab her wrap, and Anthony reaches into the front pocket of his jacket to give Lindsay a couple extra tickets for the afterparty. "I hope you and Oliver are coming. I know Natalie really wants you there."

"Take good care of my sister tonight," Lindsay says, closing up a tackle box. "Or you'll be answering to me."

"Of course." Anthony is surprised at her tone. "I plan to take excellent care of her."

Lindsay nods, her brown eyes studying him. "Actually, now that I see you two together I feel a whole lot better."

"Excuse me?"

"You've got it *bad,* don't you?"

He doesn't even bother pretending he's confused by her words. "Yes, I do." He sighs. "Very bad."

Lindsay breaks out into a smile and pats his arm. "Trust me, Anthony, she's worth it. You won't be sorry."

THEY ARRIVE AT the convention center and the place is packed with cars and people all over the streets. There are big white news vans with cameras attached. Reporters who look like paparazzi. It's basically a circus.

"There's literally a red carpet!" Natalie squeals. "Are you seeing this, Anthony?"

"Yeah, I see it."

They walk down the red carpet together, cameras clicking away. Natalie's forehead and underarms are sweating. She feels like a movie star. When they get to the door, somebody is alerted and they're escorted to a large ballroom. As a nominee, Anthony is given a special red pin to wear on his jacket.

"You're sitting at the governor's table, Dr. Novello," their escort tells them.

The governor's table? Natalie feels like she's going to faint.

"Did you know about this?" she asks.

Anthony nods. "We're VIPs tonight, Miss Natalie."

She studies his handsome face. He's smiling at her, but it isn't quite right. The smile looks forced and she suspects Anthony would rather be hanging out with a telescope in his backyard or writing equations on a whiteboard—any-where but here.

Reaching down, she takes his hand in hers and for a moment his face eases. "It's okay to be nervous. Anybody would be."

He squeezes her hand. "I'm glad you're here. It helps."

After that Natalie puts on her best public face as she finds herself introduced as "Dr. Novello's girlfriend" to the governor and her husband, the mayor and his wife, the dean of the university, and a dozen more people with important-sounding job titles. Rick—the friend of Anthony's whose house she went to for her first star party—is there. Turns out he's head of the Astronomy Department.

"I didn't even recognize you," Natalie tells him. "I only know what you look like in the dark."

He grins. "I get that a lot."

Anthony and Natalie are pulled into one conversation after another. There's plenty of small talk and as usual, most people are delighted when they find out she's a pastry chef, since almost everyone loves sweets. She manages to talk about La Dolce Vita a bit and people are enthusiastic about stopping by.

Of course, most of the women are gawking at Anthony, though they try to hide it. A few make comments to her about how lucky she is. Natalie just smiles politely in agreement. In truth, she's been ogling him herself every chance she gets.

What's strange is a lot of the men are staring too, but at *her.* Since her makeover, she's gotten far more male attention than she used to, but this is the most yet. She feels confident and sexy, and wonders if that has more to do with it than anything. Every time she glances at the mayor, his eyes are on her. She can't wait to tell Lindsay, who will for sure get a kick out of it.

The Mayor of Seattle was checking me out all night!

After a while, all the niceties start to wear on her. The sea of well-clad bodies, the air thick with perfume, sweat, and alcohol. Natalie's cheeks ache from all the smiling and to make matters worse, she's on her own. The nominees have all been pulled away into some special pre-ceremony meeting.

Natalie wanders around, admiring the opulence. The decorations have a baroque theme, which she enjoys, but seems surprising considering it's an award banquet for scientists. She would have expected something more modern. Eventually, she makes her way over to the bar and gets another glass of wine, since she misplaced her first one.

And that's when she sees him across the room.

Peter.

It's been ages since they've seen each other in person, not since the divorce. They talk on the phone about Chloe occasionally, but even that's become more infrequent.

Despite everything that's happened, Peter still looks endearingly familiar. The way his dark suit hangs on his lanky frame and the finicky set of his shoulders brings to mind all the years they shared. Maybe it's because he was her first love, or because he reminds her so much of Chloe, but she knows there will always be a tiny place in her heart for him.

Peter's blond head is tilted to the side as he talks to someone, and there's a bitter taste in her mouth when she sees it's Lena. Even from this distance, Natalie can't help but notice that Lena is striking. Deeply tan with long golden hair. She's wearing a strapless red dress that showcases her spectacular arms. Her shoulders are too muscular though—like a linebacker.

Natalie stands still, watching them both.

Then to her surprise, Peter and Lena are walking toward her. *Did they see me?* The convention center is large and crowded, but they seem to be headed directly her way.

Natalie braces herself. She ignores Lena and concentrates on Peter. When he's almost up to her, she swallows and then speaks.

"Hello," she says, trying to be pleasant.

Peter nods and smiles briefly, but he and Lena continue to walk past.

Huh?

Natalie whirls around. "Peter?"

This stops him. He turns. Searches.

"Right here, hello?" She gives a small wave.

He walks back toward her with a polite smile. "Hello, there!" He's using his enthusiastic dentist's voice.

"Peter, it's me."

"Yes?" He's still smiling politely and that's when she realizes the truth.

He doesn't know who I am.

"It's me, Natalie."

Peter's smile falters. He looks into her eyes, and she sees the moment when truth and recognition collide.

"*Natalie?*" his voice sounds as high-pitched as Mickey Mouse.

"Yes." She nods. "It's been a while."

His brows slam together and his mouth drops open. All the color drains from his face and he looks disturbingly pale.

"Peter, are you okay?" She puts her wine glass down.

His eyes are galloping all over her now, her body and face, back and forth.

"*What happened to you?*" he sputters, still sounding like Mickey. "I didn't even recognize you!"

"I'm not sure what you mean," she says coolly, though he's already talking over her.

"Your hair and your *body*. And your face. My God, you're wearing makeup!" He stares at her feet. "And high-heeled shoes!"

Natalie glances down at her gold peep-toe sling-backs. "So I am."

Peter is shaking his head. "What did you do to yourself? You look like a completely different person!"

"I wouldn't go that far. I lost some weight and lightened my hair. That's about it."

"I can't believe it." He's still staring at her. "You're . . . You're beautiful," he stammers.

Natalie's eyes widen. Fourteen years of marriage and those words never crossed his lips, not even once. "Thank you."

She glances over at Lena, who is standing beside Peter with a scowl, though he appears to have forgotten she's even there.

In contrast, Peter is now smiling. The color is back in his face. "Really, Nat, you look incredible. What a change!"

Natalie nods and knows she should be relishing this moment, and she is. He cheated on her. Dumped her for another woman. *But guess what, Peter? I didn't curl up and die.*

"Bravo," Lena says, suddenly wearing a fake smile. "I'm so happy to see you followed my advice and got back on track with your life."

Natalie bristles and decides the best thing is to ignore her.

Peter is talking animatedly. "Obviously it's been a while since we've seen each other. I had no idea all these changes were going on. Chloe never said a word! And here we are running into each other at this science banquet, of all places."

"What are you two doing here?" Natalie asks.

"I'm not even sure." Peter laughs and rolls his eyes. "Lena somehow managed to get tickets. She was so desperate to come to this thing, you wouldn't believe. It was downright comical." He turns to Lena. "Wouldn't you say?"

Lena doesn't seem to appreciate his humor though. "It's a major event," she says in a tight voice. "As a life coach, I need to be here for my clients."

"You have clients here?" Natalie asks.

"No, of course not," Peter answers for her. "Her brother's wife's decorator or somebody managed to get her some tickets. Though you wouldn't believe how much we had to shell out for them. Crazy."

Lena's eyes flicker with annoyance. "It's important that I be seen here, so I consider it a business expense."

Peter nods, but clearly isn't buying it.

"What are *you* doing here?" Lena asks her. "I have to admit I'm surprised."

"Oh, I'm here with my boyfriend."

"Ah, yes." Lena's smile turns condescending. "Good for you, Natalie. I was so happy when I heard you were dating someone. That you'd opened your heart to new possibilities. I understand he's an elderly gentleman? Some kind of professor? It's nice that you finally found someone on your *level*," she pauses to let the insult sink in, "and it's very nice that he was able to get you both tickets to such an important event."

"Where is this professor of yours, anyway?" Peter asks, looking around. "Chloe's mentioned him a little. I'd like to meet him."

Natalie glances around too. "He should be out soon. I'm not sure where—" Suddenly, she sees Anthony headed her way and waves to him. "He's right there."

Peter and Lena are both turned in Anthony's direction. "I don't see him," Peter says still searching.

Lena has stopped searching though and can't take her eyes off Anthony, who looks like a handsome billionaire playboy on his way back from winning at the poker tables.

"There you are!" Anthony comes up and slips his arm around Natalie's waist. "I've been looking for you."

"I ran into someone I know," she tells him. "This is Peter, my ex-husband, and his girlfriend, Lena."

"Oh?" Anthony stiffens beside her and there's a stunned expression on his face. Though, it's nowhere near as stunned as the expressions on Peter and Lena's faces.

"This is my boyfriend," she says casually. "Anthony Novello."

They're both silent.

If I go to hell for enjoying this so much, it's worth every year of my eternal damnation.

Anthony recovers first. "Nice to meet you." He puts his hand out to Peter.

"Same here," Peter mumbles as they shake hands, though it's clear he hasn't recovered.

Lena quickly puts her hand out to Anthony. "Fiancée," she says when they grasp hands.

"Sorry?"

"I'm Peter's fiancée, not his girlfriend. Natalie misspoke." Lena still has Anthony's hand in a death grip and eventually he manages to extricate himself.

"Well," Peter says, taking a deep breath. He tries to smile, though it looks more like a grimace. "Somehow we got the wrong impression. You're Natalie's boyfriend then? The professor?" His tone indicates he's still hoping there's some kind of misunderstanding.

Anthony nods. "Yes, that's right. I'm a professor of astrophysics."

Suddenly, Lena's eyes grow wide. She's staring at the red pin on Anthony's tuxedo jacket. "You're *that* Anthony Novello? You're one of the nominees!"

"That's true, I am."

"And you're here with *her?*"

They're all quiet.

Lena's face changes to horror as she realizes the mistake she just made. "I mean, I . . . We just assumed . . . you were much older, that's all."

Natalie watches Anthony. She expects him to get angry and defend her, but instead, he smiles at Lena. "Actually, I'm a few years *younger* than Natalie, but luckily," he turns to Natalie and brings her hand to his mouth, "she'll still have me anyway."

Anthony's brown eyes are warm and sincere and she sees he means it. She doesn't require any defense.

Natalie touches his cheek. "I'm the lucky one."

And then something weird happens. Peter starts defending her to Lena. "Natalie is fantastic. Of course she can have whoever she wants. You shouldn't be so surprised." Peter smiles over at Natalie as if he's on her side, as if they're a team again.

Lena takes a haughty stance. "I'm just glad she finally listened to me. This is what I *do,* remember? I'm a life coach."

"You know what?" Natalie says to Lena. "I did finally listen to you."

"You did?"

Natalie nods and leans in toward her. "I finally found someone who's . . . how did you phrase it? On my *level.*"

After Peter and Lena walk away, Anthony turns to study her. He's still holding her hand. "That was a nice moment for you, Miss Natalie."

"Yes, it was."

✴ ✴ ✴

ANTHONY FROWNS.

"What's wrong?" Natalie asks.

Peter keeps glancing back at Natalie, though Anthony seems to be the only one noticing it.

"Nothing, I meant what I said. I feel lucky to have you."

She smiles. "Me, too."

They head back toward the governor's table to find their seats, since the ceremony is starting soon. Unfortunately, Anthony can't shake the uneasy feeling he got from Peter. It was the way Peter kept checking out Natalie. He didn't like it.

That jerk wants her back.

And why wouldn't he? It's hard to imagine any man choosing that drill sergeant, life coach, or whatever it is she calls herself, over a class act like Natalie.

"Where's your brother?" Natalie asks after they take their seats. "I thought he was coming."

"His flight got delayed. Apparently, there's some kind of airline strike going on. I just got a text that his plane landed at Sea-Tac, so he's going to try and make the afterparty."

"And your parents?"

Anthony picks up his water glass. "No, they aren't coming." His mom called him a week ago. They'd talked, but nothing was even mentioned about the banquet. He shouldn't feel bad, since he was the one who told his father not to bother, but he'd said it in anger and a part of him still hoped his parents would be here.

Natalie studies him. Then she puts her hand on his leg. "It's their loss."

"Sure, whatever."

The ceremony begins. They had a meeting with all the nominees beforehand, so he knows what to expect for the most part, though they don't know the winners yet. Unlike the Nobel Prize, where the winners know in advance, Smyth Medal nominees find out whether they've won right along with everyone else.

Anthony shifts uncomfortably in his chair. Rubs his jaw. He hates stuff like this. He's happy to support his colleagues, and he's glad the nomination will give him tenure, but beyond that he'd rather be anywhere else. And not just because he knows he isn't going to win, but because he's already tired of all the attention and interviews, all the people who suddenly want to be his best friend.

Clapping politely as each science category winner is announced, he watches as they go up to receive the medal and give their speech. Anthony can't stop his mind from wandering. He didn't even bother preparing a speech. Instead, he keeps thinking about the way Peter was staring at Natalie. There's no way she'd go back to him, though. No way. Not after the way he treated her. That *testa di cazzo* left her for another woman.

But then he thinks about the way Natalie told him Peter was the only man she ever loved. It bothered him to hear that, even though it shouldn't have. She's not someone who gives her love easily.

But neither am I.

"Your category is up next!" Natalie says, reaching over to hold his hand.

Good. Then this thing is almost over.

He listens as the announcer lists off each of the nominees for astrophysics, stating the person's name and accomplishment. He hears his own name followed by a brief description of his work with gamma-ray bursts and the early universe. A few more of his colleagues are mentioned—most of whom he admires, though one of them is an ass. Then suddenly, he hears his name again. There's a weird pause and for a moment, he's confused. Everyone around him is staring his way.

"Anthony, you won!" Natalie tells him.

"I did?" he says and then feels foolish.

There's a rush of excitement. Their entire table is on their feet, clapping wildly.

Holy shit! I just won the fucking Smyth Medal!

Anthony stands up and tries to get his bearings. He makes his way to the front stage, smiling at everyone, but it feels stiff and formal. His heart pounds. At the podium, they give him the medal and shake his hand, and he's expected to make a speech. He's sweating all over and hasn't the foggiest idea what to say. He's still in shock. His stomach is churning and his palms are slick from nervousness.

Anthony leans toward the microphone and stares out at the crowd where everyone is still applauding. When it dies down, they're all watching him expectantly.

He tries to smile. "I, uh, don't have a speech prepared." He starts telling them how he wasn't expecting to win. There are a few snickers in the audience and he knows he's floundering.

Dude, what kind of idiot gets nominated for a Smyth Medal and doesn't prepare a speech?

For a moment, he wishes with all his heart his parents were here. At a time like this, you want your family. He wants them to accept him and be proud of him, but also to ground him. His eyes search the audience and then suddenly he sees Natalie. In a sea of unfamiliar faces, she's his anchor.

Immediately, he relaxes. Then he knows what to say.

"First of all, I didn't do this on my own. I've been working with a team of incredibly talented people." He takes a deep breath and starts thanking colleagues here in the U.S. and his team members from the Italian Space Agency. He goes on to briefly describe the work they've done and future plans. He keeps his speech short, but does his best to include what's most important.

In that moment, as his eyes drift back to Natalie sitting out in the audience, he knows without a doubt what's most important to him.

Chapter Twenty-Six

Diet Plan: Drink champagne. Nibble on a hot geek.

Exercise Plan: Show some meddling groupies exactly how it's done.

"THIS PLACE IS a zoo," Natalie says when they arrive at the afterparty.

It's being held in a large pavilion that's been turned into a ballroom.

Everywhere they go, Anthony is treated like a celebrity. People are constantly coming up, slapping him on the back, and congratulating him. Everybody's taking photos and video. Three news stations have interviewed him.

He's been on his cell phone nonstop. He called Serena first and then various other family members, though he can't get hold of his parents. Half of his conversations are in Italian as he talks to colleagues and family members in Italy.

Natalie called Chloe, who is staying at a friend's house, as they rode over in the limousine. "We saw you guys on TV," Chloe said. "That is so neat!"

At first, Anthony seemed to be taking it in stride, though after a few hours she notices it's wearing on him. He's already taken his medal off. Put it in his pocket and keeps telling her he doesn't deserve it.

"Of course you deserve it," she says when they finally have a moment alone together. "You just can't believe you were wrong about something."

"I'm never wrong."

"Give me a break." She rolls her eyes.

Anthony laughs. "I know how arrogant that sounds, but it's basically true."

"Well, you were wrong in a big way tonight, weren't you? You thought you wouldn't win."

He takes her hand. "There's one thing I'm not wrong about, and that's you."

She suddenly hears her cell chirping and pulls it out from her small gold purse to check. "Huh. That's weird."

"What?"

"Peter just sent me a text."

Anthony stiffens and lets go of her hand. Takes a sip from his glass of scotch. "What does it say?"

Natalie stares at it. Stunned.

It was great to see you tonight. You look beautiful.

Before she can stop him Anthony snatches the phone from her hand and reads it himself.

"Hey." She frowns. "Don't do that."

"Why?"

"Because it's rude."

Anthony is shaking his head, staring at the text. "That dickhead wants you back."

"No, he doesn't."

"Of course he does. Don't be naïve."

Natalie doesn't say anything. She knows this whole medal thing has really thrown Anthony for a loop. Even though it's great to win, she can see he's uncomfortable and under a lot of pressure. Plus, she suspects it really bothers him his parents aren't here. Italians are obviously big on family.

He starts typing into her phone.

"What are you doing?"

"I'm texting him back for you. Telling him to leave you alone."

"Stop it." She pulls the phone out of his hand and deletes the text he started. "What's gotten into you?"

He doesn't get a chance to respond because some big blond guy is suddenly shouting Anthony's name and before she knows it, the two of them are hugging.

"I knew you'd win! Congratulations!"

"Thanks," Anthony says with a grin after they stop hugging. "I have to admit I didn't see it coming."

"You definitely deserve it. It's fantastic. Have you heard from Mom and Dad yet?"

"Not a word."

The blond guy is shaking his head. "Dad just hates to admit the whiz kid's been right all along." It dawns on Natalie that this must be his brother. It's confirmed when Anthony finally turns and introduces her.

"Giovanni, this is Natalie." Anthony grins at her. "Natalie, this is my older brother, Giovanni."

Giovanni turns to look at her. He takes his time examining her. "Nice to meet you," he says finally.

Natalie nods and decides to check him out just as thoroughly. Why not? He's big and blond, which is the first surprise. He's taller than Anthony and his coloring is almost the exact opposite. Oddly though, they do have a passing resemblance. She has to admit he's handsome, but not really her type.

Giovanni's eyes flicker to her mouth. "So you're the one who's got my brother in such a tailspin."

"Am I?" She turns to Anthony, who looks embarrassed.

"Gio, shut the hell up," he says, though it's in a good-humored way. "Don't be a dick."

"You don't look Italian," Natalie tells Giovanni. If anything, he looks like a rangy Viking.

The Viking chuckles. "You'd be surprised how many blond Italians there are." He turns back to Anthony. "I'm glad you won that medal, even though you're probably already feeling guilty about it." He looks at Natalie. "Would you make sure he doesn't start in with the self-flagellation too soon? Encourage him to enjoy it for at least five minutes."

The three of them sit down to talk. People come by the table, congratulating Anthony. Natalie listens to the brothers. Apparently, Giovanni just flew in from Africa where he works with a doctor's organization that helps children. From what she can gather, he's a pediatric plastic surgeon who specializes in fixing cleft lips and other birth deformities. While his work is certainly admirable, Natalie has to admit he doesn't come across as very doctor-like, or even very likable. He seems like an arrogant womanizer. The whole time they're talking, Giovanni is checking out every female in sight.

Finally, Natalie excuses herself to go to the bathroom, cutting across the dance floor where everybody is getting down with some Lady Gaga.

On the way back, she happily runs into Lindsay and Blair.

"Hey!" Natalie is relieved to see them. She's having fun, but this evening has been an experience. "I'm so glad you came," Natalie tells Blair. She hopes seeing her here means she isn't mad anymore.

"I can be very persuasive," Lindsay says with a grin, tossing her wavy brown hair over her shoulders. Her chandelier earrings glimmer. She looks dazzling in a tight black dress that has a slit on the side, showing off her long tan legs.

"I can't believe she broke up with Oliver even though he would have saved her from the banditos," Blair tells Natalie. Blair looks gorgeous in a dark green dress that sets off her auburn hair.

"I know." Natalie shakes her head. "She's never satisfied. He was such a good guy."

"Hello?" Lindsay says. "I'm standing right here."

Lindsay and Blair decide to get some drinks, so Natalie points over to where she's sitting with Anthony. Natalie is glad the ice between her and Blair has thawed. Or at least she hopes it has.

Anthony and Giovanni are still sitting at the same table, except much her to annoyance there's a crowd of women surrounding them now.

Great. Anthony's groupies.

Natalie pushes through the crowd. Some college girl wearing too much pink lip gloss is sitting in her chair. "Excuse me," she says. "That's my spot."

Pink Lip Gloss gives her a smug look. "I don't think so."

Anthony is talking with Giovanni and doesn't notice her standing there.

Natalie moves closer and puts her hand on the back of the chair. "Get up," she tells her. "Now."

"I'm sorry," Pink Lip Gloss says, raking her eyes over Natalie. "I don't know who you are, but I'm sitting next to Professor Novello."

Unbelievable.

Natalie considers telling Anthony to get rid of her, but decides on a different strategy. She pushes her way over and then without a word, sits on his lap.

Anthony pulls back for a moment until he realizes it's her. His eyes drop from her face to her cleavage and then back to her face. "Why, hello, Miss Natalie."

"Hello."

His arms slide around her waist. Glancing around, she sees how all the fawning young women are frowning at her. Pink Lip Gloss's mouth is hanging open in surprise.

Natalie slips her arms around Anthony's neck. "Why don't you introduce me to all your groupies?"

"I have a better idea," he murmurs, then captures her mouth, kissing her slow and deep, and long enough to make a point.

When they pull apart, he gazes into her eyes. Anthony tastes like scotch and she suspects he might be a little drunk.

"I think that worked," he says. "I should have you come by during my office hours."

Natalie glances around. The crowd of girls has thinned considerably. Not all are gone, though. Pink Lip Gloss appears to have shifted allegiance and is now talking to Giovanni. He's leaning back in his chair with a drink in his hand, watching her with a bored expression.

Suddenly, something catches his eye in the crowd. He looks down at his glass and then slowly looks up again. He's still pretending to listen to Pink Lip Gloss, but Giovanni is definitely captivated by someone. Natalie leans forward out of curiosity, trying to see who it is. And then finally, she understands.

It's Lindsay.

Natalie groans. *It figures.*

And, of course, Lindsay's walking right toward them.

Giovanni is openly staring at her sister now, a smirk on his face. He obviously thinks she's coming for him.

"Congratulations, Anthony!" Lindsay says when she's finally up to them. "Thanks."

"Don't you two look cozy," she refers to Natalie, who is still sitting on Anthony's lap.

"Where's Blair?" Natalie asks.

"Oh, she ran into someone who used to be in her sorority."

Lindsay glances casually over at Giovanni. Her gaze lingers, but then she pointedly turns away. "I'm going to go dance. Can I leave my drink here?"

And then she's gone.

Giovanni studies her departure with raised eyebrows. He puts his drink down and gets up. Pink Lip Gloss is still talking to him, but he ignores her. "I'll see you two later," he tells them and then disappears into the crowd.

Natalie turns to Anthony. "I think he's going after my sister."

"You're probably right."

She's not sure which one of them to be more concerned about.

Anthony is studying her. "The mayor came up to me tonight after I won the medal. I thought he was going to congratulate me, but do you know what he said instead? He told me I have a smoking hot girlfriend."

Natalie laughs, embarrassed, though not entirely surprised. "Really? What did you say?"

"I said, I know." Anthony drains his scotch and sets the glass down. "I'm ready to get out of here." His lips brush her ear as he whispers, "I want to be alone with my smoking hot girlfriend."

SITTING IN THE back of the limo on the way to their hotel, Natalie texts Lindsay and Blair to let them know she's left. "Do you want to tell Giovanni we're leaving?" she asks Anthony.

"He'll figure it out."

Natalie checks messages and discovers another text from Peter.

She stares at it with surprise.

Thinking of you. Need to talk about something important.

"What is it?" Anthony says.

"Nothing."

"You got another text from that *testa di cazzo* didn't you?"

"What's a *testa di cazzo?*"

"Let me see your phone." The limo changes lanes to get onto the Interstate. "I want to see what he said."

Natalie hesitates, but then hands it over.

Anthony's jaw tightens as he reads it.

"I have no idea what he wants," Natalie says as the car picks up speed. "Why the sudden change?"

"I already told you. I know exactly what he wants," Anthony growls. "He wants you back."

"No, he doesn't. He has Lena."

Anthony shakes his head then thumbs something in, pushes send before she can stop him.

"What did you just do?" Natalie grabs her phone in annoyance. "You can't send messages without asking me."

"Someone needs to set him straight."

Natalie finds the text Anthony sent Peter from her. It says, *Fuck off, asshole.*

"Seriously? What are you thinking?" Natalie stares at him in frustration. "Now I'll to have to apologize."

"Don't apologize. Not after the way he's treated you."

Natalie is quiet. "He's still Chloe's dad and I have to deal with him on a regular basis. I'm trying to be civil."

Anthony leans forward to pour himself a drink from the limo's bar. "There are limits to civility."

She brings up the thread on her phone and starts typing in an apology to Peter, figuring she might as well get it over with. She spins a story about someone else getting hold of her phone, but doesn't mention who.

Anthony leans back and tenses when he sees what she's doing. "You better not be apologizing."

Natalie ignores him and continues her text. The next thing she knows, Anthony is opening his side window. Cold air rushes in. Suddenly, he grabs the phone from her hands. "Hey!" she says. And then without hesitation, he throws it outside.

"Oh, my God!" she shrieks. "What are you doing?!"

"I'm solving a problem." The glass slides shut and they're encapsulated once more.

"You're crazy!" She's practically standing in her seat now, trying to see where it landed. They're driving in the diamond lane on the freeway, headed toward downtown Seattle, and her phone is now lying somewhere on the side of the road in pieces.

"I can't believe you did that!"

"I'll buy you another phone."

"You better!" She stares at the drink in his hand. "Are you drunk? Is that it?"

He rolls his eyes. "No, I'm not drunk. I've had two fingers of scotch all night."

"You should stop drinking anyway."

Anthony sneers. "Guess what, Natalie? Unlike your *mammone* ex-husband, I don't take orders from you and I definitely don't want you to be my mother."

She glares at him. "I should throw your phone out the window."

They spend the rest of the limousine ride in silence. Natalie is furious. By the time they get to their hotel lobby, she decides she's had enough and tells him, "I'm calling Lindsay or Blair to come pick me up. I'm not staying the night with you."

"Why not just call Peter? I'll bet he'd love to come get you."

She lets out a shaky breath. "What on Earth has gotten into you? I don't want to call Peter."

Anthony is silent. Brooding. "Let's not have this conversation in the lobby."

Natalie goes with him up to the room, figuring she has to get her stuff anyway. Her overnight bag with a change of clothes is upstairs. Maya brought everything over and checked them in earlier.

The room is fantastic, a full suite done in tasteful pastel colors, soft lights, and elegant furnishings. Not a garish orange bedspread in sight. There's a big basket of fruit and cheese on a table. There's also a bottle of champagne with two glasses and gourmet chocolates from a local chocolatier Natalie admires.

If they weren't having a fight, this would be amazing.

Searching for her bag, she finally finds it in the bedroom.

Anthony comes in, but she pointedly ignores him as she takes off her gold-chained purse, shoves it inside the bag then searches for jeans and a T-shirt to change into. She's angry, but hurt, too. He's acting like a jerk.

Suddenly she feels the weight of his hands on her hips. "Don't go," he says.

"Leave me alone." She shoves his hands away.

"Please . . . don't go," he whispers.

Natalie stills. His tone is low and there's something so utterly wretched in his voice. "Are you really that jealous of Peter?"

"Yes."

She turns around to face him. "There's no reason to be."

"Maybe not. But you didn't see the way he was looking at you." He pauses. "And I know you once loved him."

"Even if what you're saying is true, I don't want him back." She puts her hands on his solid shoulders. He's still wearing his tux with a loosened bow tie. Despite her anger, he's so handsome it's painful. "This night is special for you. We should be celebrating right now. Not fighting."

"Don't go back to him. Tell me you won't."

"Anthony, I'm not going back to Peter."

His eyes are dark, imploring. For a moment, he looks completely vulnerable and Natalie's anger melts away. She's never seen him like this. But then something shifts and his eyes turn fierce. His hands grip her waist, pulling her in tight.

"I'm not giving you up!"

And then his mouth is on hers. Hot and demanding. Wanting things from her, things that go beyond their bodies. Electrifying the air.

She lets him ravage her mouth, her hands sliding through his thick hair, clutching those dark waves, always so surprising in their softness.

A moan escapes her when he dips his head and buries his face in her cleavage. Ribbons of desire unravel inside her and she can feel the last of her resistance slip away.

Anthony draws back. Their eyes meet and Natalie still sees a glimmer of vulnerability. But then he turns her around, so her back is to him. He pushes her hair aside, exposing her neck, and she assumes he's going to unzip her, but instead, his hands are grabbing and pulling up bunches of fabric from her dress, trying to get at what's beneath.

"What are you wearing?" he asks when he finally encounters her shapewear. "Take all this off."

Natalie suppresses an embarrassed laugh. She reaches under her dress and tries to wiggle and peel all that nylon down. Anthony starts tugging at it, too, cursing with impatience.

"Damn, this stuff is like armor."

When it's finally removed, he stands behind her again. His mouth at her ear. "Where were we?"

Then he's pulling up her dress, except this time, she's naked beneath.

Natalie feels his hands on her hips then his fingers brush lightly between her thighs. She gasps softly when they dip inside. Her stomach goes tight. He's pressing his body into her from behind and she can feel his erection, a hard column beneath his slacks.

"This is how I want you, Miss Natalie," he says, his breath choppy. "Just like this."

She wants him, too. Any way she can have him. Natalie feels his hand behind her working his zipper.

"Get on your knees on the bed," he breathes. She does as he asks and then his cock is pressing right at her center. His hand tightens around her waist. "This is going to be so good," he growls. And then without further preamble, he thrusts into her. She gasps from the pleasure. It's hard and perfect. Exquisite.

Her fingers reach out, grasping at the bed's duvet, trying to steady herself.

"You're mine," he says. "Tell me you're mine."

Natalie moans, her body overwhelmed with sensation. She shouldn't like this terrible side of Anthony. This possessiveness. But it speaks to something in her she didn't even know existed, something that wants him wild.

He slips his hand between her legs to where they're joined. Stroking just where she needs it, the tension builds quickly. But then his fingers stop and she squirms and moans in frustration.

"Say you belong to me."

Natalie is so aroused, it takes a moment to register his meaning. They're both panting, but Anthony has slowed his movements, waiting.

"Tell me what I want to hear," he demands softly.

"It's you," she says finally. "Only you I belong to."

He moves inside her again. "That's right," he says. "That's so right."

Then his fingers are between her legs again and she's giving in to it. Anthony starts speaking Italian as he increases the pace. She doesn't understand his words, but understands the passion in his voice. When he finally pulls her in tightly, groaning, so does she—the two of them meeting ecstasy together.

Afterward, they collapse on the bed, trying to catch their breath, recovering. Natalie notices something different this time, though—she feels wet between her thighs.

Understanding dawns on her. "You didn't use a condom?"

"I forgot."

She looks over at him. He's lying on his back, eyes closed, still breathing hard.

"You forgot?"

He nods. "You're on the pill, anyway."

"You never forget anything, Anthony. You have a photographic memory."

He doesn't reply at first, but then finally turns his head to look at her—his eyes the color of a rich ganache. He licks his lips. "You were right about what you said. I worry about losing control a lot, and it's time I stopped."

Natalie stares at him. A sense of unease settles over her.

"What is it?" he asks, frowning. "You're still on the pill, right?"

She takes a deep breath. "I am, but I've sort of missed one recently."

Anthony's eyes widen as he sits up abruptly on his elbows. "Are you kidding me?"

"I'm not. I've been busy and I've never taken the pill for birth control, anyway," she says in an even voice, trying to stay calm. "Peter had a vasectomy. I started taking the pill to manage PMS, so I don't get migraines."

He stares at her in disbelief.

"I didn't think it was any big deal."

"No big deal?"

"You're always so careful about condoms," she continues, starting to feel nervous. "How was I to know you changed your mind?"

Anthony continues to stare at her. Then to her surprise, instead of being angry, he starts to laugh. He sits up all the way, still laughing and shaking his head. "I don't believe this," he says. "Unbelievable."

She watches him get off the bed and kick his pants off. Remove his shirt. His body is so muscular and beautifully proportioned that it's hard to pull her eyes away. He's still chuckling.

"You're not angry?"

"Come here." He motions to her. "I'll unzip you."

She gets up and stands in front of him. "It doesn't mean I'll necessarily get pregnant or anything. The odds are very small."

"I know all about the odds." He helps her step out of the gown and takes her bra off, too.

Standing before him, she realizes she doesn't feel shy anymore being nude around him. He's freed her of that. Anthony always makes her feel beautiful.

Even now, she watches as his eyes roam over her with obvious approval.

"You're handling this really well," she tells him.

"Let's get in bed." There's a tender smile on his face.

They climb under the sheets together and settle under the hotel's puffy white duvet, surrounded by pillows, and it's like sinking into a cool cloud.

Natalie tries to understand what's happening. He threw her phone out the window for texting Peter, but is calm now, when he hears they just had sex without birth control?

"These sheets are incredible," Anthony says, relaxing on his back. "My ass approves."

She rolls onto her side so she can see his face. His whole demeanor is surprisingly mellow.

"I can't believe you're not more upset."

He shrugs. "What's done is done."

"I suppose you're right."

Anthony puts his hand up and strokes her hair in that way he does. "I realized something tonight when I was onstage, scared witless, giving that terrible speech."

"Your speech wasn't terrible."

"Give me a break." He rolls his eyes. "I should have prepared something in advance. That was ridiculous."

"You didn't know you were going to win the medal. And your speech was fine."

He chuckles. "Why are you defending me all of a sudden? You usually don't let me get away with anything."

Natalie puts her hand to his cheek, trails her fingers along the dark stubble on his jaw. "I know, but you're being so hard on yourself. You deserve to be happy tonight."

"Even though I threw your phone out the window?"

Her fingers still and her eyes flash to his.

"I'm really sorry," he says. "I shouldn't have done that."

"You're right. You shouldn't have. I still can't believe you did it."

"Can you forgive me?"

Natalie thinks about what a crazy night it's been and decides not to dwell on it. "Yes, but I want a new phone. And it better be fantastic."

"I promise it'll be kick-ass."

"I'm baking *your* phone in one of our ovens if it's not."

"I'll keep that in mind."

They're gazing at each other, smiling, but then Anthony's smile slips away. He sits up in bed, leaning back against the pillows.

"What is it?" she asks, looking up at him with growing concern.

"Do you remember when you asked me how many women I've been in love with?"

Natalie nods, wondering where he's going with this. "You said you fell in love easily."

"No, I didn't say that." He pauses. His eyes go to the window and he seems to be searching for a way to say something. "The truth is, I've never been in love."

Natalie raises her eyebrows. "Never?"

"No."

She considers his words. "I'm surprised, especially after all the women you've been with. And what about your marriage to Nicole?"

"It's why we got divorced. I could never tell her I loved her."

Natalie is quiet, considering this. She feels real sympathy for Nicole. It would be unbearable to stay married to a man who didn't love you.

"I've never said it to any woman," he continues. "I've just never felt it and I didn't want to lie."

She takes his hand. "It doesn't mean you won't feel it for someone eventually."

Anthony's eyes meet hers. "Until now."

"What?"

He lets out a deep breath. "I love you, Natalie."

NATALIE DOESN'T SAY it back. Anthony didn't expect her to, though he hoped she would.

"I can't believe it's finally happened to me," he says, plowing his hand through his hair. "Now I get why people act so crazy when they're in love."

There's a stunned expression on Natalie's face. "You're really in love with me?"

"Yes."

She bites her lip and smiles. "Why me? Of all the women you've dated, you have to admit, I'm a peculiar choice."

He could name a hundred reasons why he loves Natalie, but all of them amount to the same thing. She makes him happy. It feels natural being with her.

"Who knows?" he jokes. "I'll be damned if I can figure it out."

She gives him a playful shove. "What kind of response is that?"

"Hey, it's not like you're saying it back to me or anything."

Natalie grows quiet. She moves up closer to him on the bed, then kisses him softly. "Just give me a little more time, okay?"

Anthony nods, his heart in his throat. He's not used to feeling this vulnerable. "I'll do that." He pulls her leg over, so she's straddling him and they're face-to-face. His hands slide down her hips and ass, her skin like silk. He's already getting turned on again, but tries to push it aside for now. "Do you really think you could fall in love with me?" he asks.

Her blue eyes take him in. "Yes."

"When?"

She smiles.

"Soon?" he asks hopefully.

Her smiles changes. "I'll tell you a little secret. I've been trying very hard not to fall in love with you."

Anthony is taken aback. "Seriously?"

"I didn't want to be another one of your groupies. Plus, I'm older than you."

"Not this again." He groans and puts his head back on the pillow, but then meets her gaze. "You shouldn't hold back your feelings. I don't want you to."

"Oh, really? How many women have told you they loved you? How many hearts have you broken?"

Anthony studies her. And then realizes where Natalie is going with this. *She's right.*

"So, what, I don't deserve you? Is that what you're saying?"

"Not at all. But you have to understand why I've been cautious."

Anthony doesn't respond right away. Instead, he thinks about all the women over the years who have said they were in love with him. The letters he's gotten, the cards and gifts. Some of them he barely knew and were only drawn to his appearance, and others he knew intimately. He never tried to lead them on, or break any hearts, but still it happened. He has to admit he feels a sympathy for those women he never did before.

"All right, I get your point. But that doesn't mean I'm giving up." He grasps her hips. "In fact, now that I've bared my soul to you—and had you *reject* me—" she tries to protest, but he continues, "I'm going to spend the rest of the night using all my powers to prove exactly how much I love you."

Her eyes widen.

"What do you say to that, Miss Natalie?"

THEY FORGOT TO pull the heavy curtains shut, so sunlight streams through their hotel room window the next morning. Anthony is still asleep on his stomach. A dark angel. Despite all the coffee Anthony drinks, he's a hard sleeper.

Natalie studies him, thinking.

He loves me.

It should make her nervous, but it doesn't. Instead, she's amazed someone this wonderful has fallen in love with her.

Suddenly, there's a hard knock at their hotel room door. Natalie startles. The brisk knock happens again.

"Anthony," she whispers, shaking his shoulder. "Wake up."

He opens his eyes and when he sees her, gives a purely male grin. Memories of last night come rushing back and she feels her face warm. It was quite a night.

"Good morning, Miss Natalie," he says, his voice husky.

There's another knock.

He turns toward the sound. "What's that?"

"I don't know," she says, still whispering. "Do you think it's room service?"

"I didn't order room service." He frowns. "Let me go check." He gets up and grabs one of the hotel's terrycloth robes to cover himself.

Natalie waits in bed. There's silence and then a few seconds later she hears voices and laughter.

Curious, she gets up and slips into the other terrycloth robe. When she ventures into the living room, she's surprised to see a well-dressed man and woman there. The woman has her hand on Anthony's arm, smiling and speaking Italian to him.

Anthony sees Natalie and waves her over.

"Guess what? My parents are here!" he says, grinning.

"Oh?"

Anthony introduces her to them as his girlfriend. He doesn't seem fazed in the least bit that she's meeting his parents for the first time wearing a hotel bathrobe after a night of energetic sex. Natalie draws her robe close, smoothes down her hair, and wishes she could vanish out the window like Batman.

She smiles politely.

Judging by their clothes and demeanor, his parents are conservative and wealthy. Affluence hangs over them like a thundercloud.

They're both staring at her.

"It's nice to meet you," Natalie manages to say.

"They just arrived this morning," Anthony tells her. "Apparently, their flight was delayed."

"*Antonio* has mentioned you," his mother says with an Italian accent. Her brown eyes—the same rich shade as Anthony's—take in Natalie's robe, messy hair, and then for some reason, stare at her neck.

"We've been dating." Natalie puts her hand up to her neck self-consciously.

His mother, who is strikingly beautiful, is still contemplating Natalie.

She probably thinks I'm too old for him.

Or not pretty enough.

Or not well educated.

All of which are true.

Natalie sighs.

Anthony and his father are talking about the Smyth Medal ceremony, with Anthony telling him how crazy it was last night.

"I didn't know you guys were planning on attending," Anthony says.

"Of course we wanted to be there," his mother interjects. She shoots his father a quelling look. "We would have been there if not for this *stupido* strike." She shakes her head and says something in Italian, which judging by the tone is a criticism of the airline.

"Listen, I need to speak with you," his father says to Anthony. "I know I said some things the last time I saw you."

Natalie notices the way Anthony's mother is nodding with encouragement. His father takes a deep breath. He's big, like Giovanni, with sharp blue eyes and a jaw that could cut glass. One of those types of men who seem larger than life, and who Natalie always finds intimidating.

"Go on," his mother tells his father. "Do not stop!"

"It's been pointed out to me that I've been misguided about some things over the years." His father looks at Anthony, puts his hand on his shoulder. "I now agree with that assessment."

Is this how they always talk?

"Thank you," Anthony tells him. And she realizes that must have been an apology.

His mother claps her hands together. "And now we will have breakfast, *sì?*"

"Sounds great," Anthony says cheerfully.

Natalie is about to make up an excuse to leave when she feels his hand on her arm. "You're staying, right? I want my parents to get to know you."

All three of them are turned her way. "That sounds nice," Natalie hears herself say.

They order room service while Natalie escapes into the bedroom to change into some clothes. Seeing herself in the mirror, she's mortified. Hair a snarled mess, cheeks pink from beard burn, and there's a giant red hickey on her neck.

I look like I've been ravaged all night.

Which is about right.

No wonder his parents were staring.

Groaning with embarrassment, she puts on the only clothes she has—jeans and a T-shirt—and does what she can to tame her appearance. When she goes back out, the food has already arrived.

Anthony's parents are nice, but intimidating. Growing up with so little, she's never been comfortable around people who are very wealthy. They talk a lot about work and various charity events. Natalie mostly stays quiet. It's obvious they care about Anthony, but it's also clear they have high expectations. She can see how it must have been exhausting for him to grow up like this.

Eventually, she manages to politely extricate herself, explaining that she has to go home. Luckily, they still have the limo on call.

Anthony throws some clothes on and walks her down to the hotel lobby, where they wait out front for the car.

"I think they like you," he says.

She seriously doubts this. "I'm embarrassed that I met them wearing a hotel bathrobe."

"Don't worry about that. It's no big deal."

"I can't even imagine what they must think of me." She shakes her head, still horrified.

Anthony is holding her hand and pulls her in close. "I know they seem uptight, but they have a passionate marriage. They won't hold this against you."

Natalie doesn't believe this is true, but keeps her opinion to herself.

On the ride home, insecurities she hasn't had in years are suddenly resurfacing. About money and the stigma she always felt as a kid for not having any. *What have I really gotten myself into, here?* She loves being with Anthony, but after meeting his family it's clear he comes from a different world. Even winning that medal puts him in another class.

It's unsettling.

When the limo finally drops her off at her house, there's something else that's unsettling.

Peter's black Lexus is sitting in the driveway.

Chapter Twenty-Seven

PETER AND CHLOE are sitting at the kitchen island together, laughing.

The sight was such a familiar part of Natalie's landscape for years, it does something funny to her insides seeing it now.

"Hi, Mom!" Chloe says. "Daddy stopped by. He's eating all the day-old pastries!"

Natalie drops her overnight bag beside the doorway and walks over to them. There's a large plate in front of Peter, stacked with the pastries Natalie brought home from the bakery a couple of days ago. "Those aren't day-old," she informs Peter. "They're more like two-day old."

"I don't care," he says, talking around a mouth full of food. "They're incredible. I'd forgotten what an amazing baker you are."

Natalie watches as Peter takes another bite from a chocolate croissant and closes his eyes. "My God, you have no idea how good this tastes after eating nothing but raw vegetables and sprouts for so long."

"Dad's already eaten two muffins and a chocolate chip cookie," Chloe tells her, laughing. "I guess he's hungry."

"I'm just sick of being deprived," Peter mutters.

Natalie can't help but notice Peter is completely at ease here and why shouldn't he be? This was his home for years. She takes in his short blond hair and pale blue eyes. Such a contrast to Anthony. Peter is a handsome man, though. Not in Anthony's league, but few people are born with Anthony's kind of beauty.

"What are you doing here?" she asks him.

Peter grins. His familiar smile—white teeth with slightly crooked lateral incisors he never bothered correcting. He turns to Chloe, who is already grinning. Beaming would be a better description. "Let me talk to your mom alone," he tells her. "Okay?"

Chloe nods and then giggles. It's obvious the two of them are sharing a secret. "I'm going to go watch TV in my room."

Uh oh.

Natalie has a sinking feeling she isn't going to like this conversation.

Once Chloe's gone, Peter turns to her. His eyes sparkle and there's an expression on his face that reminds her of how he always looked right before he gave her a birthday present.

"I'm back," he says, letting out a contented sigh.

"Back?"

"I'm coming back home."

Natalie stares at him. "Are you joking?"

"No, I'm not. I want to be a family again." He's smiling at her, though the smile falters when he notices her neck.

"What makes you think I want that?"

Peter is still studying the hickey Anthony gave her. A ripple of irritation crosses his features, but then he pulls his eyes away from it and focuses on her face instead. "I had a feeling you might resist. Just think about it, though. We got married so young, Nat. We both had some wild oats to sow, and we've both grown from the experience. It's time to put it behind us. Especially for Chloe's sake."

Natalie is speechless. So stunned at his audacity she doesn't even know where to begin. Her heart hammers. "You put me through hell."

He lets out a deep breath and meets her eyes. "I know."

She's surprised at the admission. A tiny part of her has to acknowledge that maybe he has grown. "Peter, I've moved on. There's a new man in my life now. I don't want to hurt you," *or maybe I do a little,* "but I'm not interested in getting back together with you."

Anthony was right. Everything he said.

"About that new man." Peter leans back in his chair with a smug expression, fiddles with his napkin. "He's younger than you, right?"

"Yes."

"By how much?"

Natalie considers ending this conversation and throwing him out right now, but a part of her, the insecure part she wishes didn't exist, is compelled to continue. "Six years."

His raises his blond eyebrows. "Not as much as Lena and me, but still a big difference."

Natalie swallows. "It's not that big."

"Trust me, I've been there, remember?" He picks up his water glass. "I'm the younger man, so I speak from experience."

She watches him drink. "What are you saying?"

Peter sets the glass back down with satisfaction. "It doesn't work. The older woman-younger man dynamic? It's doomed to fail. Eventually, he's going to want a woman who's at least his own age."

Natalie doesn't say anything. She wants to rage at him. Tell him he broke her heart once and now he's trying to ruin her happiness again, but instead, she pulls out the chair Chloe vacated and sits down. Somehow the wind has been let out of her sails.

They're both quiet and then Natalie finally speaks.

"Look, Peter, I—"

"How about a glass of wine," he says suddenly.

"Wine? It's barely noon."

"So, what?" He shrugs and then laughs. And it takes her back to when they were first married. They used to laugh a lot.

He gets up and goes over to the wine cabinet. There's still a few bottles left behind from when he moved his stuff out months ago.

"Remember the Romanée-Conti we were saving for our fifteenth wedding anniversary?" he asks.

Natalie watches as he gets two wine glasses out. She should have rearranged everything in the kitchen. It would have been fun to watch him fumble.

"Our fifteenth anniversary is only a couple months away," he reminds her.

"Aren't you forgetting something? We're divorced and you're engaged to Lena."

"Lena and I are finished. I don't want to marry her. I never did."

"What about that big engagement ring?"

He gets out a corkscrew. "She pressured me into it. The truth is, we've been having problems for a while. When I saw you at that awards banquet, I realized how much I miss you." He sighs deeply. "I made a mistake, Natalie. A big one."

She doesn't say anything. *What I would have given to hear those words a year ago.*

He grins over at her. "Let's get remarried."

"What?" Natalie nearly falls off her chair.

Peter puts his hand up. "Hear me out. A lot of couples do it. You'd be surprised how common it is. People get divorced and then change their minds all the time."

"I don't want to get married again."

"We could do it on our fifteenth wedding anniversary. It would be like this whole past year never happened. A hiccup in our marriage."

A hiccup?

"You're not hearing me, Peter. I don't want to marry you again."

He reaches down and selects a bottle of wine from the wine cabinet. Natalie watches him as he uncorks it and pours them both a glass.

"I opened one of those bottles of merlot we bought from that little vineyard in Napa. Do you remember it? The one where we sat watching the sunset together."

Natalie does remember. They'd been touring vineyards all day and their final stop was a tiny winery off the beaten path. The owners opened a bottle for them and it was such a peaceful location. They sat holding hands watching the sun go down, the sky a kaleidoscope of colors, and the wine they drank tasted just like that vibrant sunset. It was remarkable. Peter bought a whole case and shipped it home. It was the last romantic memory she has of them together.

He brings her a glass and then sits down beside her with his own. His eyes are on her face as he takes a sip from his glass, letting it linger before swallowing. "It's just as good as I remember."

The wine in her own glass is glistening red. And even though it's only noon, Natalie finds herself picking it up, taking a slow sip. Peter smiles at this small triumph.

To Natalie, though, it's just a pleasant merlot. That's all.

I don't taste that vibrant sunset anymore.

She takes another sip and notices that Peter is studying her.

"I can't get over the change in your appearance. You really do look beautiful, Natalie."

"Thank you."

His eyes are traveling from her face slowly down her body. Natalie's wearing a fitted V-neck shirt and a pair of dark bootcut jeans. And she knows she looks good. She's at peace with her curves at long last. Eventually, his eyes make their way to her face again and it's the expression there that startles her.

He's looking at her as Anthony does.

With desire.

If only he'd looked at me like that when we were still married.

She puts her glass down.

"It's time you went home," she tells him.

"Do you really think your relationship with this guy is going to last forever?"

"I don't know." Natalie thinks about last night. It was wonderful. Anthony is wonderful in every way. They haven't discussed the future, but that doesn't mean they don't have one.

Peter stares into his glass, swirling the dark liquid. "It won't." He looks up at her. "After meeting him, I can tell you it's not just the age difference, either. You and I are the same kind of people. That's why it always worked between us. But he's different."

She stares at Peter.

He nods. "I can tell by the expression on your face you know exactly what I'm talking about." He reaches over to take her hand. "I made a big mistake, but let's not compound it. Let's not waste any more time."

Suddenly, Chloe bounces around the corner into the kitchen. "How's it going in here?" She's smiling and when she sees that Peter is holding Natalie's hand, her smile grows even wider. "Have you guys made up? Is Daddy moving back home?"

Natalie takes in the joy on her daughter's face. She can't remember the last time she's seen Chloe this happy, not even when she found out Peter was buying her a horse. It squeezes her heart. All she's ever wanted was the one thing she didn't have growing up—a happy and secure family. She wants that dream for Chloe, especially. But at what price?

She draws her hand away from Peter's. "I don't think—"

"We're working on it, sweetie," he tells Chloe. "We just have to give your mom a little more time."

"YOU ARE SO *not* getting back together with the ass clown!" Lindsay says with disgust after Natalie tells her what happened with Peter. "Have you lost your mind?"

Natalie sighs. "I probably have. But you didn't see the expression on Chloe's face."

This gives Lindsay pause. Chloe is the one weak link in the chain of Lindsay's eternal hatred of Peter.

The two of them are sitting in the living room, drinking the rest of the bottle Peter opened earlier. Chloe went over to a friend's house. Before she left, though, she was so excited, hugging Natalie and telling her how happy it made her to see Daddy home again. Natalie wishes Peter hadn't said anything at all to Chloe. It was inappropriate to get her involved, but Peter obviously didn't see it that way. Natalie's been thinking about his visit all day. It's hard to put it out of her mind.

"What about Anthony?" Lindsay asks. "You just told me he's in love with you. I'd take Anthony over Peter any day of the week."

"He's six years younger than me."

"So what? That's nothing."

Natalie picks up her glass. "Peter says the whole older-woman-younger-man relationship is doomed to fail."

"*Peter says?*" Lindsay is incredulous. "Who gives a damn what Peter says? He'll say anything to get you back."

"He has some insight because of Lena."

Lindsay punches a couch pillow, then picks it up and throws it across the room where it lands in the corner. "I don't think I can listen to any more of this without screaming!"

"It's not that I want to get back with him, but he made some good points."

"He wants you back because he misses his mommy. That's all."

Natalie shakes her head. Lindsay is not exactly the most objective person to talk to about this. Ironically, a weird part of her wishes she could talk to Anthony. He's become her best friend. Plus, he's so good at seeing all sides to a problem.

"So where were you last night?" Natalie asks, changing the subject. "I know you didn't sleep here."

Lindsay picks up her glass and brings it to her mouth. "I hooked up with Giovanni." She takes a sip of wine.

Natalie closes her eyes and lets out a deep breath. She opens them and glares at her sister. "Please tell me you're joking."

"Nope, I'm serious."

"Where did this happen?"

Lindsay licks her lips. "We went to a hotel."

"Are you going to see him again?"

"I doubt it."

"So you had a one night stand with Anthony's brother? I think it's my turn to scream now, of all the men at that party? How could you?"

Lindsay shrugs. "What's the big deal? So I slept with Giovanni. It was *nothing*. Trust me."

Natalie's eyes flash to her sister. There's a strange note in Lindsay's voice. One she hasn't heard before. "What exactly happened?"

"Do you really want all the details?"

"No, but something unusual happened, I can tell."

Lindsay finishes the rest of her wine, picks up the bottle, and pours more into her glass. "He disappeared—okay? I woke up alone in a hotel room this morning."

Natalie takes this in. She's never had a one night stand, but assumes that's how they work. "Isn't that normal for this kind of thing?"

There's a snobbish expression on Lindsay's face. "Not for me it isn't. Nobody *ever* leaves me. I *always* leave first."

"I see. How was the sex?"

Lindsay grows quiet. Leans back on the couch.

"Was it bad?" Natalie has to admit she's not surprised. Giovanni seemed like an arrogant asshole.

Lindsay runs her finger around the rim of her glass. "The sex was . . ."

She trails off. "I can't quite put it into words."

"Honestly, I thought he seemed like a jerk. Even though he is Anthony's brother."

Lindsay sighs with annoyance. "I can't believe I'm admitting this, but it was probably the best I've ever had."

"Really?" Natalie is astonished. She doesn't know exactly how many men Lindsay has slept with, but she knows it's more than a few.

"Yeah," she says softly.

"I'm really surprised. He seemed so arrogant."

"He is kind of arrogant, but he's also got this other quality. He's deep. Soulful." Lindsay thinks about it some more. "I thought we connected."

"Until he disappeared."

"Yeah." There's a hard expression on Lindsay's face. "Until that happened."

"Maybe it's best you just forget about him. Like you said, you'll probably never see him again."

"You're right." A slow smile pulls on her mouth. "Unless, of course, you marry Anthony."

Natalie chuckles. "And wouldn't that be awkward at family gatherings? You and Giovanni with your one night stand." She takes another sip of wine, thinking back to her conversation with Peter again. "I don't want to give up Anthony."

"Then don't."

"But we've had our problems, too. He isn't perfect."

Though who am I kidding? Anthony is as close to perfection as I'll ever get. Just the idea of giving up Anthony makes her feel ill.

"But there's Chloe to think of," Natalie says. "I want her to be happy, to have stability. That means more to me than anything."

NATALIE'S NOT SURE how it happens exactly, but Peter starts coming to dinner almost every night. Chloe invites him and is so excited, Natalie doesn't say no. How can she deprive Chloe of seeing her dad? And she loves seeing that smile on her daughter's face. To his credit, Peter is a perfect gentleman and doesn't try to pressure her about getting back together anymore. Instead, he brings her gifts. Flowers the first night, then chocolates, and then a pair of earrings shaped like cupcakes. She has to admit they're whimsical and charming. Though she doesn't wear them.

The most noticeable thing is that he eats.

A lot.

"It's like you're starved or something," she tells him one night, watching him dig into a large slice of caramel cake. He's already had two helpings of eggplant lasagna.

"I can't believe I was married to a woman who can cook and bake like you do and I didn't appreciate it more."

Natalie blinks with surprise.

Peter swallows a mouthful of cake and his expression grows serious. "I took a lot of things for granted. Things I shouldn't have."

Chloe is on cloud nine. "Is it okay if Daddy stays and we have family game night? Please? Pretty please?"

Peter and Chloe both love complicated board games. It was one of the things the three of them always did together as a family. Natalie finds herself going along with it, as it's difficult to say no.

Later, when Peter goes to the bathroom and she's alone with Chloe, her daughter smiles and bounces in her chair. "Thank you so much for letting Daddy come over. It feels just like home again!"

And this simple comment knocks the wind out of Natalie.

She hasn't mentioned Peter's visits to Anthony. They haven't been doing their usual texting because he hasn't replaced her phone yet. When they talked yesterday, he kept apologizing and telling her he'll do it soon. Anthony also asked if she got her period, and she told him no, but it wasn't due. He still sounded amazingly calm about the whole thing.

In truth, between meeting Anthony's parents, and Peter's reappearance, she's been keeping her distance a little. Anthony wanted her to come over tonight, but she told him she couldn't. Understandably since winning the medal, he's been busy and distracted with reporters and meetings. There's even talk of him flying to London soon. Peter couldn't have chosen a better time to infiltrate her life.

"You were right about the horse," Peter tells her after their game night and after Chloe has gone to bed. They're sitting on the couch together in the family room. "We should have waited until Chloe was older. I don't know what I was thinking."

Natalie nods in agreement. "There's not much to be done about it."

"I've moved out of Lena's." His voice is quiet.

Her brows go up as she takes this in. "Where are you living?"

"A hotel, for now. I'll start looking for a place soon."

"Was Lena very upset?"

He shrugs. "She wasn't happy, but I told her she could keep the ring and I think that helped. She knew things weren't good between us anymore."

"What happened? I thought you two were in love."

Peter lets out a low sigh. "I thought we were, too, but you were right all along." He gives her an embarrassed smile. "It was just a midlife crisis. There were all these things I thought I was missing out on—not realizing I already had the life most people dream of."

Natalie decides to be honest. "Our problems weren't all you. I was work-obsessed and didn't want to look at myself too closely. I was afraid of what I might find. And I know I can be stubborn sometimes," she admits.

Peter relaxes. "You've really changed. And I don't just mean on the outside. I could tell right away after I saw you again. You were always a diamond in the rough, but now you are a diamond."

Natalie doesn't know what to say to this.

Peter moves closer to her on the couch.

She looks at him, thinks about what Chloe said earlier, and in so many ways Peter does feel like home. "You broke my heart."

He's watching her and his expression softens. "I know. And you have to believe me when I say I'm sorry."

"How can I ever trust you again?"

His hand goes up and touches her hair. She stills. It's strange to let any man but Anthony touch her. He brushes her hair back and his fingers caress her neck. She doesn't stop him, though. A part of her is curious.

"It's a leap of faith," he says. "You have to choose to trust me again."

She turns to him. Peter's eyes meet hers and then he leans in and kisses her. It's nothing like Anthony's erotic kisses. But it's Peter. His familiar scent and tender lips. And it isn't fair to compare him to Anthony.

"I don't want to rush you," he says when he draws back. "But you should know I want you in every way."

There it is again. Natalie sees it, the desire in his eyes.

"Okay," she whispers. "Let me think about all this."

After he leaves, Natalie sits and tries to make sense of things. It feels as if her life has been moving in uncharted waters for so long. Maybe this is her chance to find her way again, get back on course.

Suddenly, there's a knock on the door. It's late enough she figures it must be Peter, but when she opens it there's a jolt of surprise.

Anthony is standing there.

Chapter Twenty-Eight

Diet Plan: Food has lost all flavor.
Flavor is for wimps.

Exercise Plan: Hit that punching bag as
hard as you can for as long as you can.
Pain is for wimps.

"WHAT THE HELL is going on?" Anthony growls.

He's wearing his motorcycle jacket, helmet at his side, looking just like he did when he came to her that first night. The big bad wolf at her door.

The sight of him makes her knees go weak and her heart flutter. She can't stop the stupid smile on her face.

But Anthony isn't smiling. He looks concerned and she should have known he'd guess something was wrong. He's too perceptive for anything less.

After he comes inside, she turns so he can follow her into the next room, but his hand reaches out for her arm.

"Hey, where are you going? Come here."

He pulls her into him and kisses her, surrounding her with his windblown scent. His mouth tastes so good. Like love and happiness, and the hottest sex she's ever had. Natalie gives in to it. Kisses him with passion, hungry for more. But then she pulls back, because she knows this is going to be hard enough already.

"Miss Natalie, I've missed you," he murmurs, his hand on her ass. "I was getting worried."

She moves away from him, walks toward the kitchen as he follows.

"Are you still pissed about your phone?" He puts his helmet down on one of the chairs near the island. "I know I've been preoccupied lately. I swear, I'll get you a new phone by next week."

"That's okay."

He frowns. "Why didn't you want to come over tonight?"

Natalie leans against the counter. "Do you want anything to drink?"

"No, I'm not thirsty." He studies her. "You've been so distant. I've been racking my brain. Was it meeting my parents?" He lets out a deep breath. "I know that was awkward for you. In hindsight, I should have handled it better."

"Peter's been here."

Anthony freezes.

"He's been coming over for dinner."

Anthony still doesn't move. The tension in the room grows palpable. She waits for him to speak, and when he doesn't, she continues.

"He wants me back."

Anthony curses. Then suddenly he's in front of her, hands on her sides. She gasps when he lifts her so she's sitting on the kitchen counter. He stands between her thighs and places a hand on each side of her.

She stares at the white strip of leather that runs across the zipper on his motorcycle jacket.

"So I was right," he says, an edge to his voice.

"You were," she admits.

"Should I be worried here? You said you were mine." She can feel him watching her. "Look at me, Natalie."

She lifts her head. He searches her eyes. Judging by the hard expression on his face, he doesn't like what he finds. But then his face grows thoughtful.

"What if you're pregnant?"

"I'm not."

"How do you know?"

"I got my period this morning."

He turns his head. She thought he'd be relieved by the news, but he doesn't look it. She wasn't relieved either.

"Don't do it," he says, turning to her again. "Don't go back to him."

Natalie puts her hand to his jaw, scratchy the way she likes it. If only she could touch him forever.

"It'll be a mistake," he tells her. "So just don't do it."

"I think I have to."

Anthony closes his eyes.

She watches his beautiful face and her heart hurts. The ache of it travels through her whole body. She tries to swallow, but it feels like there's something blocking her throat.

Her breath gets shaky. She wishes things were different, but they're not.

When Anthony opens his eyes, they are dark and intense. He shakes his head slowly. "No."

His hand comes up and touches her cheek, his thumb rubs over her lips and then his fingers slide through her hair, holding her still for him. He claims her mouth. Kisses her roughly, at first. But then it changes to something erotic and deep. Both his hands move down and her arms wind around his neck, her breasts pressing into his hard chest. She feels his hands on her back, then under her shirt until he's caressing bare skin.

Natalie knows what he's doing. Seducing her. Using all his weapons. And for a little while, she lets herself enjoy it.

Her eyes fall shut. Inhaling him. His smell and taste. Trying to remember everything.

His palm moves over her breast. "Let's go to your bedroom," he whispers.

She's tempted. The pull of her desire for Anthony is so strong. Chloe is home, but even if she wasn't, she knows it wouldn't be fair to him.

So she draws back and unwinds her arms from his neck. "I can't."

He doesn't give up though. Moving closer, he tries to kiss her again. "I want you."

"You can't keep me like this. It won't work."

"We'll see about that," he murmurs. His fingers slide down each side of her leg.

Natalie takes a deep breath. "I'm letting Peter move back in." She's only now just decided it. But realizes it's what has to be done.

Anthony flinches.

It hurts her deeply to see it, but she continues. "Chloe is so happy when he's around. I haven't seen her like this in a long time. I have to give her the one thing I never had. A stable home."

Natalie tries to take his hand in hers. This time Anthony pulls away, shakes her off. But she knows he understands because he has Serena and he'd do anything for her, too.

"A stable home has love in it," Anthony says. "Are you telling me you still love Peter?"

Natalie sees the calculated expression on his face. And then she knows what she has to do. The one thing that will set Anthony free. She has to lie. "Yes," she says. "Yes, I do."

To her surprise, he smirks, though it's humorless. "I don't believe you. You're going to have to be more convincing than that."

"It's true."

He shakes his head. "No, it isn't."

"I still love him. I really do."

His intelligent eyes meet hers. "Is this really how you want to play it?"

"It's the truth. I want Peter back."

He lets out a deep breath. "I love you, Natalie. But if you want me out of your life so bad that you'll lie right to my face, then I'll step aside and give you exactly what you want."

"You will?"

"Yes."

Natalie tries to speak again, but can't. Wants to tell him this isn't what she wants, but it has to be this way. Can't he see? It's like she's suffocating, though.

Anthony doesn't make a move at first. Just considers her for a long moment. Finally, he steps in close and kisses her on the cheek. "Be happy," he whispers.

Then he picks his helmet up off the chair and walks out of the kitchen, out the front door, and out of her life.

Just like he said he would.

Natalie doesn't leave her spot on the counter for a long time. She tries to catch her breath, but can't. Tries to swallow, but can't. Her chest is tight and it feels as if she's coming out of her skin. Her heart hurts. The pain slices through her like it's cutting her to ribbons. She starts to shake all over and then a loud gut-wrenching noise comes out of her mouth.

It's a sob.

Oh, my God, I'm crying.

PETER MOVES BACK in the very next week. Chloe is over the moon and Peter is in great spirits as well. Everyone in the house is happy, except Natalie.

But she does a good job hiding it. She puts on her best poker face. The one she hasn't had to wear since she was a kid. And she's damned good at it. It's not for nothing that her dad was a World Series Main Event winner. Nobody suspects a thing except Lindsay, who of course, sees through it all.

"This whole thing is a train wreck," Lindsay tells her. "And I can't bear to watch knowing that you're in it."

Lindsay moved all her stuff out. She's living in her studio temporarily until she finds a place of her own.

"We're going to make it work," Natalie says stubbornly. "We have to."

She hasn't told Lindsay about the crying, though. Hasn't told anyone. Natalie decides to keep it to herself. It's bizarre, too, because after years of not crying, she now cries at everything. Cereal commercials, flowery greeting cards, even homeless kittens. Not that she's seen any homeless kittens. But just the thought of a homeless kitten—so sad!—is enough to get her crying.

Peter and Chloe think she has allergies and that's why she's carrying around a large box of tissues everywhere. And how can she tell them the truth? How can she destroy their happiness?

And then, of course, she cries when she thinks about Anthony. Which is a lot. She can't stop thinking about Anthony. He even invades her dreams at night. The way he whispered "Miss Natalie" in her ear. The way his arms felt around her. The way he laughed when she teased him. The way he made her feel beautiful all the time.

Natalie keeps that to herself, too.

She hasn't had sex with Peter. He wants to, but she can't bring herself to do it, even though they're supposed to be a couple again. Natalie moves her stuff back into the master bedroom. After a few weeks, she even agrees to let him sleep in there with her, as long as he doesn't touch her.

"I can't believe you gave Lindsay our bedroom while I was gone," he says, one night, lying in bed together. "Why would you do that?"

"I just couldn't sleep in here alone after all those years."

Peter softens. "I guess I understand that." He pulls her close and tries to kiss her, but Natalie stiffens.

"I'm still not ready."

He lets out an annoyed sigh. "It's been almost a month now, Natalie. I'm trying to be patient, but how long is this going to go on?"

"I don't know."

Peter runs his hand down her back and lowers his voice. "I want to be with you. You're so sexy."

Natalie swallows and tries to smile. She feels like crying, but she's getting better at controlling it.

"Just give me a little more time. I have to get used to all this."

He sighs. "That's what you keep saying, but I'm here and I'm not going anywhere. Do you still not trust me? Is that it?"

"You broke my heart. I'm still recovering," she lies.

When he finally falls asleep, she sneaks out of bed, puts her robe on and heads downstairs. It's summer and the nights are warmer, but she still wears her coat when she goes out into the backyard.

This is her new thing. Sitting out here at night alone, gazing at the stars.

She can still be close to Anthony this way.

First, she finds all the constellations he showed her, remembering how he told her they change with the seasons. And then she tries to find the planets, though that's harder.

And then she cries. Quietly sobbing after holding it in all day.

She knows she's in love with Anthony. She isn't entirely stupid, and figured it out pretty fast once she had to give him up.

A part of her wishes now she'd known sooner, that she'd told him the night he said it to her, but a part of her is glad she didn't.

Because then he never would have let her go. She's stubborn, but Anthony can be stubborn in his own way, too.

The week after they split up, true to his word, she got a new phone. Maya came into the bakery and delivered it.

"How is he?" Natalie asked.

Maya shook her head. "Not good. He won't talk to me about it. What's going on with you two?"

"I went back to my ex-husband."

"Oh."

"I had my reasons," she said defensively. "I wish I wasn't hurting him, though."

Maya tilted her head of dark curls and studied Natalie. "To be honest, you don't look so good either."

"I'm not sleeping much. Tell Anthony I said thanks for the phone."

"You should call him," Maya said. "Tell him yourself."

But Natalie knew that was a bad idea. She needed to let Anthony go.

And so she sits outside alone every night, gazing up at the stars. She knows he went to Rome recently. Made the mistake of googling his name. It was excruciating to see pictures and read about him.

I won't be doing that again.

At least she and Blair are solid once more. Though Blair and Lindsay have been hanging out together a lot, and the two of them seem to be of the same mindset regarding Peter.

"You know I felt betrayed after you started dating Anthony," Blair says one day. They're taking a break together, sitting out in front of La Dolce Vita where they set up some tables and chairs on the sidewalk. "I thought you weren't thinking clearly, that you were throwing away everything we'd worked so hard for on a fling. But after watching your deterioration these past weeks, it's obvious it wasn't just a fling. Things between you and Anthony were serious, weren't they?"

"My *deterioration?*" Natalie is taken aback. "What are you talking about? I'm in the best shape of my life."

She exercises all the time now, driven to it like a maniac. It's one of the few ways she can stop thinking and feeling. She works out every morning, including Sundays, and she's even started boxing three times a week—sweat dripping from her body as she hits that punching bag as hard as she can. Natalie has developed a wicked right hook.

"You look fantastic," Blair agrees. "I'm not talking about your appearance though. I'm talking about how you act."

Natalie takes a sip from her latte. "I'm the same as always."

"No, you're not. You're sad a lot."

"Sad? I'm not sad." She laughs. Or tries to. She has to admit her laugh sounds a little scary these days.

"When you think no one's looking, the light goes out of your face. At first Lindsay and I thought it was Peter's fault you were struggling. But now we think it's because you miss Anthony."

Natalie turns away and watches some of the pedestrians streaming by. Ironically, the clothing shop next door has brought more business their way.

"I can't talk about this," she says. "I just can't."

Blair nods with sympathy. She picks up her iced coffee and stirs the straw around. "Our lease here is up soon. We should decide what we're going to do."

"I know. I've been thinking about it, too."

Blair leans forward in her chair. "I heard something interesting recently. Apparently, Santosa's is definitely moving to that new place on Roosevelt."

"Where did you hear that? Did Austin call?"

"Graham told me. He's the lawyer for the investment group who owns the building. We've been seeing each other again." Blair gives a small smile. "I hope that isn't weird for you."

"Not at all. That's great. I always thought you two seemed well matched." Natalie pauses. "So how much is the rent for Santosa's old location?"

Blair tells her a number.

Natalie raises her eyebrows. "That's only a little more than what we're paying now. We could totally swing that."

"That's what I thought. Should I give Graham a call?"

"Definitely! That would be an amazing space for us."

Blair grins. "It sure would be."

A FEW NIGHTS later, as she sits outside contemplating the stars, she's surprised when Chloe comes out to join her.

"Hi, Mom."

"It's late, sweetheart. What are you doing up?"

Chloe comes over, stepping tentatively over the grass with bare feet, and then sits down beside her in one of the lawn chairs.

Neither of them speaks for a while and they gaze up at the sky. It's a clear night and late enough that it's both quiet and peaceful.

"Why do you come out here so much?" Chloe asks.

"What do you mean?"

Chloe tucks her feet beneath herself. She's only wearing a nightgown, but Natalie is too, since the nights have grown balmy lately.

"I see you out here all the time from my bedroom window."

"I didn't know that. Am I keeping you awake? I thought I was being quiet."

"It's okay." Chloe plucks at a loose thread and then speaks softly. "Aunt Lindsay told me you only got back together with Daddy for my sake."

"What?" Natalie sits up straight. "She had no right to tell you that!"

I'm going to wring my sister's meddling neck.

"Is it true?" Chloe asks. "That you don't love Daddy anymore?"

Natalie closes her eyes. Tries to be honest. "A part of me will always love your dad because he gave me you."

"Good, because I'm glad Daddy's home."

"I know you are." Natalie has always wanted to be a strong example for her daughter, to show her what's possible. She thinks about Chloe, and imagines her years from now as an adult. Would she want her daughter to spend her life in a loveless marriage? *No, I wouldn't.* Natalie takes a deep breath and lets it out. *Then is it right that I spend my life in one?*

Chloe looks around the yard. "I kind of like it out here this late."

"Me, too."

"It reminds me of that night at Anthony's with Serena, looking through the telescope. That was fun."

"It was," Natalie agrees.

Chloe chews on her lower lip. "Are you going to make Daddy move out again?

Natalie doesn't reply right away, just leans back in her chair and ponders her daughter's question. As much as she cares about Anthony, in some ways her life would be so much easier if she'd never met him. *But I did meet him.* She reaches over and takes Chloe's hand, meets her worried gaze. "Whatever happens, remember this—I love you. And I need you to trust me to make the right decision for both of us."

NATALIE HAS THE next day off and she does something she's been meaning to do, but hasn't yet. She opens the email Anthony sent her ages ago that contains his financial program and file on the bakery.

After installing the program, she studies the file he created for La Dolce Vita. Natalie compares the numbers against the ones she and Blair have in the spreadsheet they use to track all their finances. And after studying it for half the day, she comes to an astonishing conclusion.

Anthony has been right this whole time.

They can't afford the space next door.

Doubling their rent along with the cost of remodeling would have eventually put them out of business.

Blair is wide-eyed after Natalie tells her this. "Are you sure?"

"Yes, I'm sure. We overestimated how much business we're turning away. Plus, there are things we forgot to include with the cost of remodeling."

"I feel terrible." Blair shakes her head. "I've given him such a hard time. It looks like we owe Anthony a big apology."

"Yes, we do."

They're in the bakery's tiny back office, with Blair sitting at the desk. "I have some more bad news to add to that," Blair tells her. "I just got off the phone with Graham about Santosa's. They want a year's rent paid upfront for that space."

"Why?"

"I guess that's standard for them. There's a lot of interest, so they want to be sure whoever leases it is serious."

"We can't afford that. Not with the remodeling we'll have to do."

They look at each other with disappointment.

Finally, Blair sighs. "We'll just have to keep searching."

Natalie goes back to work and tries to push her disappointment aside. Her mind keeps straying back to Anthony. It figures he was right all along about their finances. Finally, before she can stop herself, she picks up her phone and types in a text to him.

Could you stop by the bakery sometime? Blair and I owe you an apology.

And then she hits send. Natalie tells herself it's only to apologize, it's not because she wants to see him. She just doesn't want to leave any loose ends.

Late that afternoon, Natalie is in the back kitchen closing up when Carlos comes in and tells her there's someone here to see her.

"It's Anthony," he whispers.

Natalie doesn't move or speak. She glances down at the croissant dough she's prepared for tomorrow.

That was fast.

"Tell him I'll be out in a minute," she says, finding her voice.

After putting the dough in the fridge, she washes her hands and walks to the mirror by the back door.

She pulls the hairnet off her ponytail so it swings free, wondering why Anthony didn't just come into the kitchen. Her hand is shaking as she dabs on lip gloss.

Finally, she takes a deep breath and goes out front. Anthony is standing with his back to her by the front window, looking outside. She walks over to him and it's like she can barely breathe.

Sensing her, he turns. It's warm out and he's wearing faded jeans and a short-sleeved *Star Wars* T-shirt.

Natalie smiles, remembering how she'd once counted all his *Star Wars* T-shirts and discovered he owned twenty-two. "That's it," she'd declared. "I'm calling Star Wars Anonymous and we're staging an intervention!" He'd laughed quite a bit over that.

Anthony pulls away from the front window. "Hi, Miss Natalie."

His pet name does strange things to her insides. Makes her heart hurt and her stomach flutter. "Hi, Anthony."

Right away, she sees he's tan and his hair is longer. He's still blindingly handsome. With his long hair and the aviators perched on top of his head, he looks like a rock star. His teeth and the whites of his eyes almost glow against his dark skin. She realizes the tan must be from his trip to Rome.

This does strange things to her insides, too, but not in a good way.

I should have been there with him.

"I got your text," he says, and she can feel his eyes roaming over her, studying her too. "What's this about an apology?"

Natalie glances around. Unfortunately, most everybody, including Blair, has gone home for the day. "Blair's already left, but we both wanted to apologize to you." She explains how she finally downloaded the file he sent her and how they realize now he's been right all along.

"Thanks, I appreciate that."

Neither of them speaks. They just stand there gazing at each other.

Finally, Natalie comes to her senses. "I guess I should get back."

"Are you done closing?" Anthony asks suddenly. "Do you want to take a walk? I have something I want to talk to you about."

"Uh, okay."

Natalie goes in back and tells Carlos she's leaving, that he can lock up.

She and Anthony go outside and head down University Avenue together. It's a sunny day and there are a lot of people out. It's strange, walking next to Anthony without holding his hand. They were always so physical with each other. She wonders if he's thinking the same thing.

"Your lease on the bakery is up soon," he says. "Graham tells me you guys are considering moving to another location?"

Natalie sighs. "That's true, we wanted to, but we just found out it's not going to work out after all." She tells him a little about Santosa's, how it would have been a great fit for them. "The location is perfect, and close enough we wouldn't lose customers."

"Why isn't it going to work?"

"The investment group who owns the space insists on a year's rent in advance, and we can't afford that."

They slow down and are standing near a flower shop when Anthony turns to her. Up close and in broad daylight, she notices he looks tired. There's strain on his face.

"It's good to see you. I was surprised when I saw your text," he tells her.

She bites her lip and watches the way he lingers on her mouth. Butterflies dance in her stomach.

"It's good to see you, too." And she means it. It's all she can do to pull her eyes away instead of drinking him in.

"How have you been?" he asks quietly.

Natalie glances at the flower shop window and then, unable to stop herself, blurts out the truth. "I miss you."

Anthony takes this in. He doesn't reply for so long she wonders if he's going to. It only highlights her embarrassment.

"I miss you, too," he says finally.

Their eyes meet. His are rich and warm just as she remembers.

"I shouldn't have told you that," she admits. "Was it wrong of me?"

"No, I'm glad you told me."

"I've started crying," she says.

He raises his eyebrows. "Seriously?"

She nods, smiling. "I cry all the time now. You wouldn't believe how much. Over every dumb thing, too. I haven't told anybody about it, though."

"When did this start?"

"The night we broke up."

Anthony is watching her face in an intense way, a way she's never seen before, and then he reaches out and takes her hand. His is warm as always. For a few moments, she allows it, because it feels so good, but then pulls away.

"Natalie," he says.

"I should go," she tells him. And then she turns and leaves as fast as she can.

ANTHONY WATCHES NATALIE move up the street. He doesn't stop watching until she's completely out of sight.

He's still in love with her.

Not that he's surprised, having never been in love before he's discovered it's not an easy thing to fall out of love.

Seeing her again feels like being slammed with a brick.

Giovanni keeps telling him the cure is to go bang another babe, but Anthony isn't feeling it. He doesn't want another woman.

He only wants Natalie.

It killed him to let her go, but he did it because it was what she wanted. He couldn't let himself get in the way of her happiness, but now that's all changed. Because after seeing her today, he realizes something. She isn't happy.

She's miserable.

He stands there contemplating all that's happened and when he notices the shop he's next to, knows exactly what he has to do.

It's time I sent a woman flowers.

Chapter Twenty-Nine

Diet Plan: Favorite recipes from The Bandito Test Cookbook.

Exercise Plan: Stomp around in a pair of strappy high heels. Rant and rave. You're on the right path, finally.

THE FIRST DOZEN red roses arrive for Natalie at work the next day. There's a card from Anthony.

I miss you.

She brings them into the bakery's back office.

The second dozen red roses arrive the day after that. This time the card says:

I love you.

Natalie stares at it for a long time.

She removes the card and displays the flowers out front where everyone comments on how beautiful they are.

This time Natalie leaves work and goes to find Anthony on campus, borrowing Isadora from Blair. She's already called Maya and gotten his summer hours.

She finds him in his office typing on his computer, wearing his nerd glasses. He looks up when she comes inside and gives her that boyish grin, but she ignores it.

"What do you think you're doing?" Natalie says, putting her hands on her hips. "Why are you sending me all these flowers?"

"I'm not giving up on you, that's what I'm doing."

"What?"

Anthony gets up and comes over to her, taking his nerd glasses off. "I'm fighting for you."

Natalie stares at him with shock, then amazement. "You can't do that."

"Yes, I can. And I will. Watch me."

"But I've already told you I'm staying with Peter."

"I know. Martyring yourself. Has it ever occurred to you what you're doing might not be the best thing for Chloe?"

Natalie grows quiet. "I've made my decision."

"Stubborn as always," he mutters.

"I know what I have to do."

His jaw tenses. "And so do I."

"Listen to me, Anthony," she says softly. "Don't do it. You'll only be disappointed."

He nods in agreement. "And possibly humiliated, but I'm going to risk it anyway. I don't care. I'm not giving you up without a fight."

As the next two weeks progress, Anthony doesn't just send her flowers. He sends her baking books, a bottle of Italian wine, and two *Lord of the Rings* T-shirts. He also sends her emails and texts. Some of them are thoughtful while others are witty and make her laugh. He sends her a copy of a paper he recently published in an astronomy journal and even though she doesn't understand it, she reads it three times—lingering over his words, amazed at the way his mind works. Every day is something new. One day he sends her a selfie they took of themselves in the back of the limo on the way to the awards banquet. She stares at that picture for a long time, both of them laughing into the camera.

Natalie knows she should delete all this, shouldn't accept his gifts, but she does anyway. And worst of all, she hasn't told Peter about any of it. He's completely oblivious.

She does tell Lindsay and Blair about it after boxing class one night.

"No man's ever wanted me like this," Natalie admits. "I'm at a total loss of what to do. It's like he refuses to give up."

"Go, Anthony," Lindsay says with approval. "I like it."

Blair is quiet, considering things, and then she smiles. "You know what? This is the Bandito Test."

"It is?"

Lindsay nods in agreement. "It definitely is. Think about it, Anthony's the second man. He's not giving you up without a fight, even if he makes a fool of himself."

Natalie stares at the two of them. They both have huge grins on their faces.

THE NEXT TIME another dozen red roses arrives, Natalie brings them home and sets them in the center of the dining room table. The card says, *Come back to me.*

Peter, of course, wants to know who they're from.

"Anthony sent them."

Irritation flickers across his face. "Why is he sending you flowers?" But then an expression of astonishment comes over his features. "My God, are you still sleeping with him?"

"You're really asking me that?"

His eyes narrow. "Because it would explain a lot."

"Maybe you've forgotten, but you're the cheater, not me."

Peter rolls his eyes. "I was wondering when you were going to throw that in my face. So what is this now—payback?"

"No." Natalie glares at him. "It's not. And I'm not sleeping with Anthony."

He's studying her as if he doesn't believe her. "If you're not sleeping with him then what is going on between you two? And why is he sending you flowers?"

Natalie finally tells Peter how Anthony has been pursuing her. How he still wants her.

Peter shakes his head in disbelief. "The nerve of him! What the hell is his obsession with you, anyway? You'd think you were the last woman on earth or something."

Natalie grows quiet at this. "I guess Anthony thinks I'm worth fighting for."

Peter frowns. "I hope you aren't encouraging him. You need to be firm when you tell him to stop."

Natalie doesn't say anything as she considers her next words. "Would you fight for me, Peter?"

"What do you mean?"

"If I was captured by a group of banditos, would you fight for me even if it meant risking everything—including your life?"

"Captured by banditos?" He gives her a strange look. "Have you been drinking?"

Natalie shakes her head. "Never mind." She already knows the answer. In her heart, she's known it all along, but didn't want to admit it. "This isn't going to work between us, and I think we both know it."

Peter studies her defiantly for a long moment, but then sits on one of the dining room chairs. His shoulders slump. "You're going back to him, aren't you?"

She lets out a deep breath, but doesn't say anything.

"You might as well," he goes on. "You're obviously in love with him."

Natalie is startled. "How do you know that?"

"Are you kidding? I could tell the minute I saw you two together at that banquet."

"What?" Natalie suddenly feels queasy. She sits down too, facing him.

"Are you saying you knew all along I was in love with Anthony?"

"Yeah," he admits. "I knew."

Her stomach churns. "And you broke us up anyway?"

"I wanted you back," he confesses. "I wanted what I lost. Our family. What was I supposed to do? Just let you go?"

And that's when she realizes Peter doesn't care about her happiness. Not in any real way. He always puts himself first.

She thought she was moving in uncharted waters this last year, but now realizes she's been on the right course all along.

The next day while Natalie is still absorbing the situation with Peter, something even more astonishing happens. Graham comes into the bakery and tells them they're getting Santosa's space after all. The investment group has agreed to lease it to them.

"Really?" Natalie and Blair both rush over to him.

"It's true," Graham says with a grin. "I've got the paperwork right here."

"Oh, my God!" Natalie and Blair hug each other, jumping up and down. "This is amazing!"

"But how is this possible?" Natalie asks when they finally stop yelling with excitement. "Did they change their mind about the year's rent in advance?"

"No," Graham says. "Somebody paid it for you."

Natalie and Blair both go quiet, staring at Graham.

"Who?" Blair asks.

"Anthony."

Natalie is taken aback. "Where did Anthony get that kind of money?" She knows he would never go to his parents, but she can't figure out where it would come from. "I hope he didn't take out a loan. We can't accept it then."

"It's not a loan," Graham says. "He asked me not to tell you any more, though. He said you could just pay the normal rent to him."

Natalie sits down. It's too much to take in. As she thinks about it, she feels her chest go tight, because she knows exactly where he got the money.

LATER THAT NIGHT, there's a knock on Anthony's door. He turns toward the sound. It's so quiet where he lives, he usually hears a car approaching.

He opens the door and his eyebrows go up in surprise.

It's Natalie.

And damn, she looks good.

"Hey," he says, trying to play it cool. He had a feeling he'd be hearing from her, but didn't realize it would be this soon.

She's wearing a sleeveless red dress and he sees lots of skin—bare arms, legs, and a nice eyeful of cleavage. Her long blonde hair falls loose around her shoulders. There's a cold pack in her arms. "Can I come inside?" she asks, an edge to her voice.

He looks at her pretty face and realizes she's highly pissed about something. "Sure," he says, stepping back to let her in. "Can I take that from you?"

"No, I've got it." She makes her way to the kitchen and he follows. The sundress is clingy in all the right places. It goes to about mid-thigh, and he can't take his eyes off her gorgeous ass.

She looks really hot.

Anthony figures to hell with it. Natalie is the love of his life and if he wants to stare at her ass, he will.

"What's in the cold pack?"

She glares at him. "Tiramisu."

He perks up. "You made me a tiramisu?"

"Yes, but you don't get to eat it."

"I don't?"

"No."

"Why not?"

Natalie sighs and rolls her eyes as if he's asking the most ridiculous question in the world. "Because it's for later, dummy."

Anthony's mouth twitches and he tries not to smile. He can't remember the last time someone called him a dummy. In fact, he's pretty sure no one ever has.

"I brought it as an apology," she says.

He shakes his head. "I'm not tracking. An apology for what?"

"For all the things I'm going to say to you right now!"

"I see." He sits down on the back edge of the couch, rubs his jaw, and tries not to smile again as he gets ready for the fireworks.

"First of all . . . ," she points at him, "you're a bastard!"

He crosses his arms and studies her. "Is that right."

"Yes!"

"I can't decide if that's better or worse than being called an asshole or a dick."

She shoots him a dark look. "You think you can buy me, don't you? By putting all that money up for us. Well, let me tell you, I'm not for sale!"

He uncrosses his arms. "That's not what I was doing."

"And I know where you got the money. I figured it out pretty fast. You're not the only smart one around here." She stops talking and then takes a deep breath. "You sold your Ducati, didn't you?"

He meets her eyes and then looks away.

"I knew it," she says quietly. "You shouldn't have done that, Anthony. You loved that motorcycle."

His eyes flash back to her. "Yeah, well, I love you more. And I wasn't trying to buy you back."

"Then why did you do it?"

"Because I'm taking care of you."

She blinks. Clearly it wasn't the answer she was expecting. "I don't need anyone to take care of me. I can take care of myself."

"I know, but I'm doing it anyway."

"Well," she sputters. "I'm still mad!"

And then she continues her tirade, hands on hips, marching around his kitchen. He knows she's on the defensive now because she's scared. Scared to let someone else take part of her load. He can't take his eyes off her. She's so beautiful. And then he notices her shoes, some strappy high-heeled fuck-me kind of shoes. He imagines what he'd like to do to her with those shoes on. Damn. *Maybe she really did come here just to torture me.*

"I kicked Peter out. It's over."

This grabs his attention and a spark of hope blazes. "I'm very glad to hear that. I hope you're saying what I think you are."

She leans back with her hands against the counter, her tirade winding down. "I can't believe you fought for me," she says, her voice shaking. "No one's ever . . . fought for me."

"I know. But you have me in your corner now. I've got your back."

He sees her chewing on her lower lip and then her shoulders quiver.

Immediately, he goes to her. Wraps her in his arms. She hugs him tightly then pulls back to look up at him as tears run down her face.

"Miss Natalie, look at you, you're crying," he says in wonder. He gently wipes the tears from one cheek with his thumb.

"I told you, I cry all the time now over every dumb thing. It's ridiculous!"

"So you did."

"Turns out I'm in love with you after all." She sniffs, still meeting his gaze. "Guess I'm just another groupie. What do you say to that?"

His eyes roam her face. "You can be my top number one groupie."

She makes a sound between a laugh and a cry. "That's a big offer."

He draws in a deep breath and lets it out. "I'd like to hear the actual words now."

Her expression changes as she puts her cool hand to his face. She considers him and then finally says it. "I love you, Anthony."

"It's about time," he mutters.

Natalie laughs through her tears. Anthony kisses her and everything is right in his world again.

"YOU WORE THAT little red dress to torture me, didn't you?" Anthony says later when they're lying in bed, both of them recovering from a passionate round of lovemaking.

Natalie is still catching her breath. "Maybe just a little."

"I approve. You can torture me like that anytime you want."

She rolls onto her side and props herself up on one elbow, studying his handsome face. "Did you know I was going to come back?"

"No," he admits. "But I hoped. And now you're here, I have big plans for you."

"Like what?"

He only smiles mysteriously. "You'll find out when we fly to Rome in a couple of months."

"Rome?"

"Yeah, you told me you'd consider going, remember? I want to show you my favorite city."

Natalie opens her mouth, but then closes it. The truth is she'd love to go to Rome.

"You'll like it, I promise," he tells her.

They lie quietly for a little while. Anthony strokes her hair and she closes her eyes. *How I missed this.*

"Remember that morning at the hotel when I met your parents?" she asks him.

"Uh oh."

"What?"

"Just that. Uh oh."

Natalie laughs. "I never told you how glad I was for you when your dad finally apologized. That seemed like a big deal."

"Oh, that was nothing." Anthony rolls his eyes. "He's always apologizing."

"What do you mean?"

"That's like the third time he's apologized for the same thing. My mom keeps putting him up to it."

"You're kidding!" Natalie is surprised. It's not what she imagined. His father seemed so intense.

Anthony lets out a deep sigh. "He's never going to get over the fact I didn't go into medicine, but you know what? It doesn't matter anymore, because I'm over it. I love my parents, but there are some things we'll never see eye to eye on, and that's okay."

She strokes his jaw. "That sounds healthy."

"It does, doesn't it?" Anthony suddenly shifts position and turns toward her. "And now I want to ask you a very important question, Miss Natalie."

Her fingers still. "What's that?"

Anthony picks up her hand, then kisses her palm. He meets her gaze.

"When can I have my tiramisu?"

Epilogue

> Diet Plan: Let there be cake!
> Wedding cake.
>
> Exercise Plan: The Princess Leia
> Bikini Workout.

I HOPE HE *doesn't kill himself.* Natalie listens as Anthony bangs the ladder around outside her bedroom window, or guest bedroom window, since she hasn't slept here since they got married. They decided to keep both of their houses for now, since they didn't want to move Chloe to a new school.

Anthony proposed to her on the Ponte Milvio in Rome half a year ago. It was a warm summer evening, and he brought a metal padlock, attaching it to one of the steel posts by the bridge as Natalie watched. There were hundreds of padlocks there already—the bridge famous for lovers.

"This means I love you forever, Miss Natalie," he said with a grin. He kissed her and then tossed the key into the Tiber.

Her heart melted at such a romantic gesture. Anthony took her hand and asked her if she'd marry him, which was the most romantic gesture of all.

"Yes," she'd said and promptly burst into tears. She still cries a lot, but now the tears are all happy ones.

Anthony gave her a princess-cut diamond engagement ring, which Lindsay helped pick out, and Natalie had to hand it to them both because it's a beautiful ring. In truth, she'd marry Anthony even if he gave her a ring from a gumball machine.

They had the wedding in Seattle. It took some doing, but they made it a family event. Friends and relatives flew in from Italy and others came up from California and Arizona. She could tell Anthony was pleased. It also endeared her to his parents, who were thrilled he was marrying "for real" this time.

And now here she is, two months later, in her former bedroom listening to her husband as he attempts to climb in through the window. The idea sounded sexy when he used to tease her about it, but the reality is proving to be more unnerving than erotic, since her bedroom is on the second floor.

Clang! Thump!

Natalie jumps as the ladder outside shifts again. She rushes over to the open window and looks down. She can see the top of Anthony's dark hair as he makes his way up. He's closer than she thought.

Quickly she runs over to the bed and positions herself. She's wearing Princess Leia's gold bikini, which she ordered off the Internet. It's skimpy and daring and she knows Anthony is going to love it. She even pulled her hair up into a braided ponytail, letting it fall over her shoulder. Before their wedding, she considered coloring her hair back to her natural color again. Anthony told her he didn't care either way, but in the end she decided to keep it blonde. Oddly, she feels more like herself this way. For years she thought of herself as a plain Jane, but turns out she's really more the blonde pin-up girl type. Who knew?

There's a commotion at the window and Natalie's pulse quickens when she sees Anthony's handsome face appear over the edge. He grabs the sides of the window, hoisting himself into the room with his usual grace, though she can hear the ladder bumping into the side of the house. *I'm not letting him leave that way, no matter what he says.*

He strolls over to her and then stops at the foot of the bed. Anthony's eyes roam her body from head to toe, lingering on all the important parts. He's wearing a long brown cape with a belted tunic beneath it. A sword is sheathed at his side. Natalie likes what she sees, but changes her expression to one of anguish.

"I've been captured and taken prisoner! Can you help me escape, Aragorn?"

Anthony strokes his stubbled jaw thoughtfully, his dark eyes still lingering on her nearly nude body. "It's possible, Princess," he says in a low growl. "For the right price."

"My family is wealthy. If you rescue me, I can assure you'll be handsomely rewarded."

"Money?" he scoffs. "I have no use for your money."

She studies him boldly. "What other reward interests a man like yourself, then?"

Anthony's expression goes hot as he steps closer. His hand drops to her ankle, fingers gliding slowly up her bare leg. His touch is electric.

Natalie sucks in her breath as excitement skitters through her. "Perhaps there is something else I can offer," she says in a husky voice, meeting his gaze. "Perhaps you'd enjoy a taste of my charms?"

He nods with approval. "A taste of your charms will do nicely."

And then he grins.

The End

Thank you so much for reading *Year of Living Blonde*. I hope you enjoyed the story and meeting all these characters who are close to my heart. The next book in the series *Return of the Jerk* (Blair and Road's story) will be available for pre-order this spring 2015. To get updates on all new releases please join my mailing list at *www.andreasimonne.com*.

If you enjoyed the story, and have time, a review or rating is always appreciated. I love hearing from my readers. You can also contact me at *authorsimonne@gmail.com*.

Again thank you for spending time with Natalie and Anthony!

~ Andrea

Acknowledgements

I AM EXTREMELY lucky to have had so many people help me on my journey to getting *Year of Living Blonde* published. Thank you to my first reader and sister-friend, Erika Preston, who always has my back and was both kind and brutal (ha!) with her edits. Erika, as usual your advice was invaluable, especially with Chloe and the travails of Natalie as a divorced mom. (And sorry I didn't call the book "Year of Living Chloe"! Ha ha . . .) I'm also immensely thankful to Hot Tree Editing, especially Olivia Ventura and Becky Johnson, who did a fantastic job editing and were instrumental in turning *Year of Living Blonde* into such a silky smooth read. I'm so grateful to my amazing friend Susan Gideon who both beta read and proofread the final manuscript. Susan, you have an incredible eye for detail! I'm beyond thankful for all your help and the time you spent. Writing is a solitary endeavor, but I'm lucky to have the Plot Princesses, a group of very talented writers to keep me company and keep me on track. Thank you Amy Rench, Haley Burke, and Tami Raymen, for all your encouragement and for always making me laugh. I want to thank my wonderful husband, John, for his never ending support and for his thoughtful help with some of the technical aspects of this book. (The liquid nitrogen on the axe was his fantastic idea.) John, you're my favorite geek, my biggest fan, and I wouldn't be here doing this without you. Thank you also to my boys, the geeklings, for thinking it's pretty cool their mom is a writer, even though she writes books where people kiss. (I know, *yuck.*)

About the Author

ANDREA SIMONNE GREW up as an army brat and discovered she had a talent for creating personas at each new school. The most memorable was a surfer chick named "Ace" who never touched a surf board in her life, but had an impressive collection of puka shell necklaces. Eventually she turned her imagination towards writing. Andrea still enjoys creating personas, though these days they occupy her books. She's an Amazon bestseller in romantic comedy and the author of the series Sweet Life in Seattle. She currently makes her home in the Pacific Northwest with her husband and two sons.

Some of the places you can find her are:
Website: *www.andreasimonne.com*
Email: *authorsimonne@gmail.com*
Twitter
Facebook
Goodreads
Amazon

13390794R00204

Made in the USA
Lexington, KY
30 October 2018